THE BLUES
AND
BALLET

Previously Published Samuel Locke Novel:

A Crimson Grace

THE BLUES
AND
BALLET

JOHN RIHERD

DUSTIVUS

MEDIA

All Rights Reserved
Copyright 2017 by John Robert Riherd
www.johnriherd.com
ISBN: 978-0990701910 (Trade Paperback)

Cover Photo: The Blues and Ballet
Copyright 2015 John Robert Riherd
www.johnriherdphotography.com

DUSTIVUS

MEDIA

C02

Published by:
Dustivus Media
P.O. Box 1432
Genoa, NV 89411
www.dustivusmedia.com

Dedicated to my granddaughters:

Amelia Jane
and
Ginevra Sharon

You redeem the past and promise the future.
Your sense of wonder illuminates the miracle of
existence.

ACKNOWLEDGEMENTS

First, as always, thanks to Jan, my lovely bride of more than four decades, for her sacrifices in giving me time to write.

Thanks to those who make the process easier: My editor, Dr. Susan Blassingame. My first-reader and editor, Vicki Beavers. Sheri Stephens for logistical support. Jim and Cathy Simpson for their support.

For being available to consult in their areas of expertise, thanks to: Mitch McFarland for legal things. Jerry Clayton for aeronautical things. Roy Osborne for law enforcement things. They all stand ready to offer great advice and information, some of which I ignore. Any deviations from reality are mine.

For providing assistance and services, thanks to: Anicia Beckwith, proprietor of The Beckwith Gallery and Studio Inspire, who provided the studio space to create the cover photo. Karla Coffman, ballerina, who provided the ballet shoes for the cover image.

Most of all, thanks to my readers who inspire me. For this book, they are represented by Debbie Tibbs Battle who inspired in the best possible way by mailing a check to purchase the book weeks before it went on sale.

John Riherd

She sings a song from yesterday
And angels quietly cry ...

From *A Song From Yesterday*
By William "Thumper" Lee

CHAPTER ONE

I LISTENED TO THE BLUES and watched ballet the night they fed the dead guy to the alligators.

The Jackson Ballroom was in Houston's Fifth Ward on the banks of the Buffalo Bayou. The big windows to the left of the Ballroom's stage framed the skyline of the city. When I arrived that night, the internal glow of Houston's downtown towers had started to outshine the glow of the sun setting behind them. The windows were open to capture any breeze in the humid night, but the air in the room moved mostly because of ceiling fans. The musty scent of the Bayou complemented the century-old patina of the ballroom.

A hot Friday night in June was perfect for slowly sipping a whiskey while listening to the blues, but I was there to see a client. As I walked in, I caught the eye of the bartender, Jake, and pointed at the coffee pot. He nodded. A few minutes later he brought me a mug of strong coffee laced with chicory. I wrapped my hands around the mug and breathed deep. The dark and rich scent of the coffee gave me goosebumps of anticipation. I sat back to enjoy the music.

My client William "Thumper" Lee, an eighty-something-year-old African American, did not look my way. But I knew he'd seen me. Soon after I sat down, he traded his electric guitar for his battered acoustic six-string and started singing his composition "My Wife Called a Lawyer." I know the song. The lyrics include a line, *I called up my lawyer, he set a court date.* That night, Thumper sang, "I called up my lawyer, he showed up late."

Thumper finished the song and made his way to my table. I said, "Cute, but I wasn't late."

He smiled as he sat down. "Hey, Samuel, the lawyer man. Good to see you. You drinking coffee? Here? At this time of night?"

"You said you had some legal stuff to talk about. I thought I'd stick to coffee."

"You're coming up to the river with me, right? Hope so. I need a ride home. You came ready to spend the night like I said, right?"

"Yep, I'm ready."

"Good. We'll talk about the legal stuff up there. Have a drink."

Thumper's invitation to spend a couple of nights at his place on the Trinity River intrigued me. When I measured clients by the size of collected legal fees, Thumper was by far my best client, but we rarely socialized outside various blues bars in and around Houston.

Although invited, he'd never been to my place on Galveston Island. I'd never even been invited to his place on the Trinity River. I looked forward to the visit. The summer had a melancholy slowness, and visiting his place would be a welcome diversion. Besides, I enjoyed doing legal work for him. His legal stuff was different from my other work. Some time ago I gave up trying to convince him to find a lawyer who knew recording and performance contracts when he told me, "You did me pretty good taking on the company. I reckon you got me enough money to die with. I'm happy. I don't much like lawyers, but you're better than most. It ain't about perfection, you yon zanmi, man. Yon zanmi."

I had to look up yon zanmi. It means "a friend" in

Creole. I've since heard it in the lyrics of a Zydeco song. It pleased me that Thumper called me a friend.

That night at the Jackson Ballroom, I said, "Let me get this straight. You had me come up here because you need a ride home? How'd you get here?"

"I had a ride. I need lawyer help. Right now, though, you're about to see something special. You just wait and see. It has to do with what I need you for."

He got up from the table and walked through the room, greeting a few people on his way to the door that led backstage. I admired the beer in frosty glasses sitting in front of the couple next to me. It was a hot night. I went to the bar and got one for me. After Jake handed me my beer, he came out from behind the bar with a push broom and started sweeping the dance floor in front of the stage.

The drummer, a white kid who looked about sixteen years old, started playing around on his drums, brushes shuffling on his snare with a rim-shot on the backbeat. The bass player, a skinny black guy known as Lefty Tom, got up from a table, picked up his upright bass, and started playing in time with the drummer, slowly walking the notes up and down. The percussive beat caused most everybody in the place to start keeping time with feet tapping on the floor or fingers on tabletops. Thumper returned to the stage, plugged in his electric guitar, and joined the percussive rhythms with chords, soft and slow and gentle.

Thumper said, "Now, you dancers out there, do me a favor. Sit this one out and just watch. You are about to see something special."

He kept playing the unformed song and looked with irritation toward the corner behind me. There, at three tables shoved together, eight people were having a good time enjoying their drinks but not paying attention to the music. They tried to talk over each other, and noise from their table got louder and louder.

"Hey," Thumper said. "Hey, y'all back there in the corner. Listen up."

Several of us turned to look at them. One or two of their crowd poked the others and let them know they were being spoken to from the stage.

"Hey," Thumper repeated. "I know y'all are having a good time. That's a good thing. But do something for me. We're about to have something special up here. Something you ain't never seen here in the Hall. Keep it down, will you?"

The noise lessened. The crowd's attention returned to the front of the house. The song took shape. I listened to a lot of Thumper's music. I recognized the repeating chords of his song "She Walks On Water."

Jake turned off most of the lights, leaving on those over the racks of bottles behind the bar, several small spots shining up against the wall behind the band, and a couple of spots making the dance floor the center of attention. Thumper started to sing.

> *She walks in the morning,*
> *But you can't see her cry ...*

A ballerina appeared from the backroom to a collective murmur of surprise in the room. She glided to the front of the stage balanced on her toes in that magical, ballerina way. She wore a cornflower blue bandeau top and brief shorts. Shimmering drapes of pale rose-red and white floated and flowed around her. Her skin glistened under the spotlights like silk. She was gorgeous. Not a sound came from the audience. She mesmerized us with her dance.

> *She walks in the morning,*
> *But you can't see her cry ...*

Thumper and the band played a little softer than usual. Everybody in the place watched the dancer. Even Jake. Jake was usually in constant motion. If nothing else, he polished glasses or wiped down the bar top. For this performance, he leaned with both hands on the bar and did nothing but watch the dance.

She walks in the morning most every day,
She walks all alone and nobody sees her cry,
She walks in the summer, the winter too,
She walks all alone and nobody,
No, nobody,
Sees the tears in her eyes.

I recognized the dancer. I enjoyed ballet. My Uncle Harlan, a benefactor of almost all performing art associations in Houston, shared his tickets to the performances. Plus, I occasionally went out with Carol Smithers, a vice-president at Texas Commerce Bank. Carol danced ballet from the age of two until she was seventeen. On our first date to a ballet, Carol told me, "When I was a junior in high school, my boobs grew too big to dance ballet. I was the only girl at my high school crying because her boobs grew."

Harlan had a box where the performances were enjoyed from a distance. Carol's tickets were up close. With her, I couldn't see the entire stage at once and tended to focus on individual dancers. I heard more of the effort. I saw past the stage expressions and noticed the intense concentration on the faces of dancers. I saw the sweat. I appreciated the strain and focus. I noticed the dancers as individuals.

I recognized Angelique Cambray dancing to the blues of Thumper Lee that night. She was a soloist with the Houston Ballet.

Thumper's trio made the song a little longer than usual

by sticking a harmonica solo by Thumper in the middle. The soulful wail of the harmonica perfectly accompanied Angelique's sensual movement. The music sped up during a guitar solo and Angelique's body carved fast, graceful curves in space. Suddenly, the song slowed with the final lyrics.

Take pity on the girl,
I say,
Take pity on the girl.
She walked on the water in the morning,
She walked on the water,
And the river,
The river washed her tears away.

With the last two lines, Angelique sank to the floor, the multicolored drapes pooling around her. A tear coursed down her cheek. I'd seen ballet done to blues and jazz in the magnificence of Houston's Wortham Theater accompanied by the orchestra. But on that hot summer night, in a century-old blues hall on the banks of the bayou with music provided by Thumper's music, Angelique danced the most moving ballet I'd ever seen.

That was about the time they were cutting the dead guy into pieces for the alligators.

Angelique did a simple curtsy to enthusiastic applause and ran off into the back room. Thumper walked over to my table, wiping his face with a handkerchief.

"Thumper, that was one of the best things I've ever seen."

He smiled. "Yeah, she's something, isn't she? She's the reason you're here."

"Why? What's up?"

"I done told you, we'll talk about it later, up at the river. First, I want you to meet her."

He went backstage. Thumper takes his own time to do

things. Curious about what kind of legal help Angelique Cambray needed, I knew I'd have to wait until Thumper decided to tell me. He's my richest client. I could be as patient as necessary.

I'D MET THUMPER LEE at the Ballroom a few years before. I'd seen one small ad in the *Houston Press* announcing a performance he would give on a Thursday night. I'd heard of him. He was a famous Texas blues musician. Up to the day I noticed that small ad, I thought he was dead. I'd seen a story or two that mentioned him being murdered in some mysterious way years before I was born. Out of curiosity, I went to the show expecting some kind of tribute performance, but it was the real deal. Before his last set, Thumper came out from backstage and talked to Jake who nodded in my direction. Thumper walked over to my table.

"Jake tells me you're a lawyer man."

"I am."

"Stick around after the show. I want to talk to you about something."

I stuck around. Thumper became my client, my first really good client since I'd left the law firm where I went to work right out of law school. Meeting him resulted in a lucrative relationship.

Like me, a record company thought he was dead. The company even won a Grammy Award for a collection of what they promoted as the lost recordings of Thumper Lee. Turned out they weren't lost to Thumper. The record company owed him money, not just for that record, but for years of recordings.

It was a lot of money. We stirred up some trouble, and the publicity made his recordings even more popular. I helped him get what they owed him plus some damages. My fee paid for my boat, *The Lonely Star*, with a lot left over. I easily put up with his idiosyncrasies.

THUMPER AND ANGELIQUE CAMBRAY came out of the backroom. She'd put on a pair of black parachute pants and a light blue jacket. He carried his two guitar cases. I stood when they reached my table.

Thumper introduced her, "Angelique, this is our lawyer, Samuel Locke. Sam, Angelique."

She extended a hand. A thin sheen of perspiration on her face reflected the lights in the room. Her eyes were large and dark and beautiful. She smiled, but there was something off about her demeanor. Her shoulders slumped a bit, and her smile seemed forced. She looked directly at me when introduced. After that, she looked around nervously, not looking at one thing with focus. Despite the heat of the night and the effort of her dance, she crossed her arms, hugging herself as if cold. I got the impression meeting me was a command performance, and she'd rather be somewhere else. Once, when I met her and spoke to her at a meet and greet hosted by the Houston Ballet, she'd been much more relaxed and animated.

"A pleasure to meet you," she said.

"Likewise. That was an incredible surprise. It was amazing."

Her restrained smile grew a millimeter, and she quit looking at Thumper to look directly at me. "Thank you."

"I've enjoyed your dancing before, but I've never seen anything like that."

She nodded and Thumper said, "She has to go, but I wanted you to meet her." Turning to her, he put an arm on her shoulder. They were the same height and eye to eye. "Are you going to be okay?"

"Yes."

"You go where you told me you were going, and you stay right there until we call you. Understand?"

"Yes. Straight there."

They hugged. She took a deep breath and looked like she was about to say something. She glanced at me and back at Thumper.

He said, "Go. It will be okay. Sam and I will get things fixed up. Don't you worry. Sam, I'll be right back. I'm going to walk her to her car."

Something needed fixing. I'd thought Thumper called me about something related to his music, another recording or concert contract. But the wordless communication between Angelique and Thumper suggested something more complex and emotional than a business deal, something darker. I'd worked on a lot of business deals with Thumper without him ever inviting me to his place for the weekend. That, plus the fact that Thumper knew and had a relationship of some kind with a soloist with the Houston Ballet, was unusual. I knew something interesting was happening.

He returned and said, "What did you think?"

"That was impressive. Beautiful."

"Yes. She is amazing." He looked at Jake behind the bar and raised a finger. Jake nodded and raised a bottle of Wild Turkey.

"How did you meet Angelique?" I asked. "How did this thing get started?"

"Now, there's a story. I need to fill you in about that."

Jake delivered him a shot of whiskey and he downed it. "Come on," he said. "I'm not going to do anything else here tonight. We'll talk on the way up to the river." He picked up his guitars and headed for the door.

Another group of musicians worked on stage, making tuning noises and doing sound checks. Thumper greeted a few people on the way out and signed two autographs.

He slid his two guitar cases into the back seat of my Range Rover, opened one, and took out a letter-sized envelope. He got into the passenger seat.

"Where am I going?" I asked.

"Head up toward Liberty. My place is on the river north of there. Up pass Moss Hill."

I left the dirt parking lot of the Hall and drove through the Fifth Ward toward the highway.

"So," I said. "You know Angelique Cambray."

"Yeah, ain't she something?" He was quiet for a moment, looking out the window and nodding his head at thoughts he finally shared. "When I was ten years old, I used to sit outside the Ballroom listening to the music. At twelve I earned a quarter a night on weekends clearing tables and mopping up spilled beer and whiskey."

"Tell me more. How in the world do you know Angelique? What kind of legal work do you need?"

"I know her through family. You know, I used to walk along here to get home about this time of night. I'd walk into Houston, play on corners for tips, and walk home. It wasn't really dangerous when I started doing that, but it got that way. It got so dangerous I went to New Orleans to be safe." He laughed. "Can you imagine that? Moving to New Orleans to be safe."

"I know it was really bad down here."

"New Orleans had its problems, but at least its lawlessness had rules. For a while, there weren't no rules in the Nickle."

We left the Fifth Ward, nicknamed the Nickle, and got on the highway. Thumper seemed determined not to talk about whatever legal work needed doing. I didn't mind. Instead, he talked about growing up in the Nickle, about the musicians he'd enjoyed, and about playing in blues clubs in Europe in the forties and fifties.

At the time of our lawsuit against the record company, I learned he'd spent time in Europe, disappearing from the States for years. But I'd never heard him reminisce in such detail about his history. I did that night as we traveled the dark highway leaving Houston. I treasured the moment and wished I could tape the oral history he shared. He got quiet as we entered Interstate Ten.

We weren't on the interstate long before I exited to State Highway Ninety. We continued riding quietly without talking much until we crossed the San Jacinto River. Thumper finally decided to let me know a little more about what we were doing.

"You liked that dancing, huh?"

"Yes. It was a great idea to have a ballet done with your blues."

"That was actually Angelique's idea. She thinks we ought to take it downtown to the Wortham."

"Good idea."

"Yeah. It's time for Thumperly to get into ballet."

Thumperly Efforts L.L.C. is the name of the company we set up as Thumper's production company.

"I'll start studying up on what we need to do."

He nodded. He had a look on his face, and he was holding that envelope, tapping its edge against his knee. I knew him. Something was coming about whatever was in the envelope, something about the tension between him and Angelique. I had to wait him out. We had time. He'd said his place was north of Moss Hill. The small town of Moss Hill was at least an hour away. I passed a sign advertising a service station just ahead.

"I'm going to pull off for gas. Want some coffee?"

"Sure. Coffee would be good."

"Anything you want in it?"

"Nothing they'll put in it."

I filled up the Range Rover, took my travel mug from the console, and went inside. I filled my mug with the questionably named house blend and bought a large cup of the same for Thumper. I settled behind the wheel and handed Thumper his coffee. He opened his door and dumped out some of his coffee. Taking a flask out of his jacket he put a healthy dollop of whiskey in his cup. My truck smelled like hot coffee and whiskey.

"Want some?" He offered me the flask.

"Nope. I can just breathe it in. I hope I don't get stopped."

"Me, too."

Back on the highway, there were fewer and fewer lights. We drove into the darkness, the air conditioner holding off the humid heat of summer. After the lawsuit with his record company, *Texas Monthly Magazine* did an article profiling him. They called him a Texas legend. Thumper frustrated the writer who wanted to do a feature-length article about his history, his disappearance, and his re-emergence. Thumper would not cooperate with any discussion of his past. The deadline loomed, and the article ended up being a one-page profile accompanied by a really nice photograph. His record sales in Texas bumped up a bit after the article appeared.

It felt good driving in the dark of East Texas with a certified Texas legend. I felt lucky to have the moment. The scent of whiskey and coffee fit the moment perfectly.

"You know what," I said, "give me a little. Very little."

I held my cup out, and he topped off my coffee with a splash of Wild Turkey from his flask.

"Hey, what if I want to give Angelique some of Thumperly? I can do that, right?"

"Yes, you can do that. What exactly is it you want to do?"

"Take care of her."

Was he falling prey to some crazy attraction to her? Was she after his money? Things were starting to sound strange. Something was up.

Before I could formulate a way to probe his motives, he said, "I need you to represent her about something."

"What would that be?"

"Here, take this." He held the envelope my way.

"What's that?" I kept both hands on the steering wheel. I did not want to touch the envelope until I knew what was going on.

"It's a check for ten thousand dollars and a letter from her asking you to be her lawyer."

Ten thousand dollars. Uh oh.

"Thumper, I cannot agree to be her lawyer without knowing what's going on."

"That's what I'm going to do up at the river. Fill you in on what's going on. But we need that lawyer secret thing in place."

That lawyer secret thing. Uh oh.

"If I'm supposed to represent her, I have to talk to her. Not you."

"You will, but everything I do from now until the day I die will be to take care of her. In fact, I need you to change my will up so she gets everything."

Uh oh.

"We'll talk about it. Thumper, who is she to you?

What's going on?"

"She is my granddaughter. Take the check. It's mine, not hers."

I took the check. Thumper was the grandfather of Angelique Cambray. That surprised me as much as any one thing could. The weekend promised to be very interesting.

"We'll talk about it tomorrow," he said. "I'm tired. Wake me up when you get to Moss Hill." He leaned the seat back.

We drove silently into the dark.

By that time, they'd fed the dead guy to the alligators.

CHAPTER TWO

I GOT ON THE HIGHWAY toward the city of Liberty. Liberty was forty miles northeast of Houston and Moss Hill fifteen miles north of Liberty. It looked like Thumper was sleeping, but the fingers on his right hand kept up a steady beat against his knee. Fine. If he wanted to pretend to sleep, he'd bought my silence with a ten-thousand-dollar check. I relaxed and waited for him to pretend to wake up.

I wondered how he was playing me with the things he'd said and the things he'd not said. I feared he thought telling me everything too soon would make me turn around and head for home.

It didn't take long to get through Liberty. It was a small town with a population of around eight thousand. I tried a few cases in Liberty, mostly in the criminal courts and did okay. It's kind of far from my home on Galveston Island, but an interesting case was an interesting case. Plus, if I ended a case in Liberty on Thursday or Friday, over the weekend, I could go after catfish or bass on the Trinity River or drive on up to Lake Livingston. I liked being able to write off most of the mileage for a fishing trip.

As ENJOYABLE AS IT was to fish up there from time to time, Liberty County was insular and outsiders were not always welcome. The worst home-court shellacking I ever experienced took place in a Liberty County courtroom.

I tried a custody case there for two weeks. I represented

the mom. Custody battles usually had good points and bad points about both sides of the case. We were fighting the step-mom more than dad. The step-mom wanted to receive the child support instead of having her husband pay it. Plus, she wanted the ex-wife to lose as badly as possible. As it turned out, my client should have hired somebody local.

All courts had their own personality, and it was important for a lawyer to learn the unique rules in a particular court and the unique quirks of that court. My custody case got transferred to a new judge three days before trial and not one before whom I'd ever appeared. I'd done what research I could. I talked to a couple of lawyers who practiced in Liberty. I'd read what news articles there were on-line about cases in that court and chatted up the court clerk just before we started. But, during the hearing, something was out of kilter. Many procedural arguments took too long to argue and settle. The judge allowed redundant testimony, and it took hours to get it all in. I got hammered beyond the circumstances of my client and her case, but, at the time, I had no idea why.

After two weeks of testimony and legal wrangling, as soon as both sides finished, the judge took one breath and ruled for my opponent. He ruled from the bench that the other side got the kids, and my client got supervised visitation along with the obligation to pay child support. The speed with which he ruled embarrassed me. The judge could have at least gone back to his chambers, drunk a cup of coffee, and pretended to give it some thought.

Opposing counsel looked at me, smiled sweetly, and said, "I'll fax a proposed order to you this afternoon." I'd bet she wrote it before we started.

After the awkward conversation with my client and her husband outside the courtroom, I stood alone on the steps of the courthouse thinking about what had happened. A man came up to me and said, "You were in Judge Halifax's court, weren't you?"

"Yes."

The man was thin, and his suit hung on him loosely. He carried a battered briefcase. His shoulder slumped as if the briefcase weighed a hundred pounds and he'd carried it for decades. He was obviously a lawyer.

"How'd you do?"

"Not good."

"You're not from Liberty are you?"

"No. I came up from Galveston."

"I guess you didn't know the judge is sleeping with the lawyer on the other side."

"Are you kidding me?"

The guy smiled grimly, nodded, and walked off slowly, lugging his briefcase through the doors to the courthouse.

That explained a lot. It explained the transfer of the case from one judge to another three days before the trial. It explained why the judge had an unusual patience with my opponent. All those extended legal arguments we'd tangled over had been foreplay between the lawyer and the judge. I'd just been the unknowing member of some courtroom ménages à trois.

It explained the fast decision. It explained why I preferred my side business of building custom barbecue smokers and grills to that of practicing law. It's an example of how East Texas had its own rules, and parts of it existed behind a wall hard for an outsider to penetrate.

I continued fishing on the Trinity River, but I tried to avoid the courthouse except for criminal clients who did something interesting.

THUMPER AND I TRAVELED north through the thick forest of pine and oak. In the past, I' driven this road many times at night, my car the only vehicle for miles. Traffic had increased, mostly due to a boom in oil and gas drilling. In addition to the occasional truck loaded with freshly cut timber, there were trucks laden with the machinery of the oil industry. They all drove too fast.

Folks living in that part of Texas benefited from the ongoing drilling boom. More people were up late driving to or from work in big, new pickup trucks. All in a hurry. I drove vigilantly, knowing many of those driving home from work would have stopped at one or more of the bars dotting the sides of the road.

Moss Hill was little more than a crossroad. As we passed through the intersection, I said, "You can wake up now. We just passed Moss Hill." Thumper's eyes popped open.

"Okay then, a few miles and we'll turn toward the river."

"We're going to your place first thing, right?"

"Yeah. Got something to show you in the morning, but we'll just go to my place for the night. I'm tired."

The Trinity River twisted like a snake a couple of miles to the west of the state highway we were on. Roads, some paved and some graveled or unimproved in any way, headed down toward the river. There were nice properties back in there, large homes with acreage, horse farms, and hunting lodges. There were also places along the river where dwellings dot the forest in haphazard communities for which the word rustic would be misleading and romantic. There were dwellings of patchwork lumber and aluminum siding. There were mobile homes running the gamut of age and quality. There were places where people live in pickup campers sitting on cinder blocks.

Those isolated communities were even more insular than the rest of the county, their residents extremely wary of strangers. That stretch of the river is the type of place people go to live when they want to avoid the complexities of a broader world.

"Okay. Slow down. Up here's where we turn."

He directed me to a road in good shape, graveled and with ditches for drainage. A worn-out sign of faded paint advertised lots and acreage in River Beach Estates.

River Beach Estates was rustic.

There were a few places fenced and normal looking on the road we turned on. After a mile or so, at a point where we were close to the river, the road made a right angle turn to the north. On that corner was a place walled off, in part, by an old school bus. The rest of the wall was a ten-feet tall hodgepodge of old road signs and corrugated aluminum.

"How far?" I asked.

"Just follow the gravel road all the way to where it ends."

My headlights tunneled through the darkness, lighting the road and the trees on both sides. Scrubby pines and the large trunks of red oaks rose eerily into the darkness. A couple of raccoons stood on the side of the road, their eyes glowing brightly in my headlights. I passed a property where a chain link fence ran parallel to the road. A barking pit bull kept pace with us as we passed his length of fence. Farther back on that lot, a travel trailer sat on cinder blocks. A propane camping lantern glowed brightly in its window. A few other places had lights or the blue flicker of television visible, but I saw no people.

"How did you end up here?" I asked.

"My daddy owned property up here. He thought he'd create a farm, but this ain't farmland. He paid for it with moonshine. It's not crowded much now, but there was nobody around back then. He made shine, sold it here and there. He could disappear into the woods easy enough if he had to. He paid the sheriff and stayed out of trouble. By the time he passed, he owned his land free and clear. I made sure the taxes got paid every year. When you got me that money, it seemed like a good place to build me a retirement house."

"Probably still some moonshine made up here."

"Oh, for sure. We'll get some you can take home if you want. Old man named James makes good stuff. He actually ages it a while. It's as smooth as anything you can buy in a store somewhere."

"Yeah, maybe. We'll see. When are you going to tell me why we came all the way up here? It obviously has something to do with Angelique."

He was quiet for a moment. His hand made a raspy sound as he dragged it over his whiskered face.

"Yeah. Soon as you tell me you'll protect her and keep her secrets, I'll tell you what's up."

"I won't commit to representing her until I know what's going on. I might not be able to do anything. I'm obligated to keep her confidences even if she doesn't become my client unless she's planning on committing a crime."

"No. She's done nothing wrong. Not everybody will see it that way, though. I probably broke the law, but not her."

"Thumper, it's time you tell me. Sounds like I'll have a conflict of interest between you and her."

"No. You won't. I told you, from here on out, it's all about her. Whatever it takes. We're almost at the house. We'll talk there."

Some clients said only what they thought you wanted to hear. Most said only the things that were in their favor.

Some talked too much. Some said nothing at all. It was exasperating. I had a mantra I often repeated to myself while talking to clients—the client is not your child, the client is not your child, the client is not your child.

We drove down the dusty, graveled road, Thumper quietly whistling a tune, me saying to myself he's not your child.

I did not have a good feeling about whatever we were doing. I felt like a traveler to a foreign country, caught at night off the beaten path in a place I should not be.

"It's right up here," Thumper said. "Just follow the gravel."

To our right was a well-built fence. The graveled part of the road made a sharp turn into a driveway that led to a gate offset in the fence. The gravel road went into the property beyond the gate. The main road continued into the darkness as a much less improved dirt road.

I said, "You must have paid for the road to be graveled."

"Sure did. You know how much gravel costs? A bunch."

As I made the turn into the drive leading to his place, he pulled a remote control out of his pocket and pressed the button to open the gate.

"Hold on," he said. "Damn."

"What?"

"That's not good."

He leaned forward, looking past me down the road we'd left. Up the road a fire burned, the flames a hole of light in the darkness. Its flickering orange light reflected on trees and some kind of metal building. A person moved in front of the fire and stood there, silhouetted against the flames, legs spread and hands on hips. I got the distinct impression he was looking our way.

"Damn. Let's get into the house. I need to fill you in

on some things."

I drove forward, and he pressed the remote closing the gate behind us. Thumper's lips pursed and his eyes squinted. In the air-conditioned cool of my car, his forehead glistened with a fresh sheen of perspiration. He stroked his face with his hand. My sense of unease did not improve.

"Follow the drive around back."

Built on tall pilings, his house rose above the flood level of the river. I parked next to his old, beat up pickup behind the house. I turned to ask him what was going on, but he was already out of the car and shutting the door

I followed him up the stairs. To his back, I said, "Thumper, what is going on?"

"Come on, let's get inside. I'll fill you in. It's what Angelique hired you for."

"I haven't agreed to be hired yet. And I'm starting to think I should just say no."

"Come on. You don't even know what's going on."

"Not my fault."

He opened the door to his place and ushered me in, locking the door behind us. I watched him. The silhouette of the man in front of the fire had sparked something in him.

"Listen," he said, "I may not have much time. Here's the deal. Angelique came home from rehearsal yesterday and found a dead man in her apartment. That's why she's hired you."

After a stunned silence during which my mind spun without direction, I said, "What?" I really wanted to have misunderstood.

"Yeah. I moved him up here to get him out of her apartment."

There was a noise outside. He turned toward the sound.

"You should have told me before we got here. You should have called me yesterday."

"Yes." There was the sound of someone coming up the stairs to his house fast and loud. "No doubt. But I thought we'd have time. He wasn't supposed to be ... "

Someone pounded on the door and shouted, "Thumper, you stupid son of a bitch. You better open this door, or I swear to God I will pull it off its hinges."

A surge of adrenaline hit me. I got light-headed. I became conscious of my breathing. The anger at the door did not sound good.

"I guess I better answer that," he said.

He went to open the door. I looked around to see if I could quickly get out another door if necessary.

The man came through the door carrying a scent of wood smoke with him. Compact and muscular, he had black hair with dark eyes, his face flush with anger. The most striking thing about him was the holstered gun on his hip, a large chrome revolver, the kind you always think about when you imagine a cowboy in the Old West. He was livid and focused on Thumper, pushing forward, thrusting his face within inches of Thumper's. Thumper stood there, not taking one step backward.

"What the hell were you thinking Thumper? Putting a dead Bobby Andrus in my ice house? You fool. What happened? Why did you do that? Why did you involve my brother in whatever the hell you did?"

"Bobby Andrus?"

"Yes, Bobby Andrus. Landry's little brother, you old fool."

The man swung around and pointed a finger right at me and said, "Who the hell is that?"

I'd been hoping he wouldn't notice me at all.

"That's my lawyer, Samuel Locke. He came up to tell me what to do."

"Your lawyer? You brought a damn lawyer up here? How much longer till the cops show up?"

"Ain't going to happen. Nobody else knows. Nobody."

The man visibly took three deep breaths and turned back toward me. He scared me for a moment by resting a hand on his gun, but it was just a natural move, like resting his hands on his hips. He just casually fit the handle of the revolver between his thumb and forefinger. It was a natural pose for him, but it didn't make me feel less wary.

He said, "So, counselor, what's the big plan?"

I had no idea, but tried to look calm and wise when I said, "We're working on it."

He snorted. I appreciated the sentiment. My only coherent thought was that somebody should have called the police the night before. I needed to find out what was going on before I said another word.

The man took one more deep breath as he turned back toward Thumper and said, "You work on your plan. You come up and tell me what's going on. I don't want no lawyer there. Whatever you do you better plan on leaving me out of it and leaving my brother out of it. The man is gone. I want this whole damn thing gone."

Thumper said, "Andrus is gone? What do you mean by that?"

The man just shook his head. He might have started to say something, but he just waved his hand in exasperation and turned toward the door. As he left, he said, "You come tell me what's going on in the morning. I've got things to do. If cops show up, I swear to God I'll ... "

He left without finishing his thought. Thumper stared at the door.

"Thumper, what's going on? You've got to tell me everything. Now."

"Yeah, I know." He walked over to lock his door, waved his hand around the room and said, "Welcome. I should of had you up here before now. Let's sit."

I glanced around the room. Most of Thumper's house was that room. It included a completely open kitchen area at one end and a large screen television on one wall in front of a couple of leather recliners. A sofa and chairs gathered around a low table. Several guitars hung in what looked like an atmosphere controlled, glass-fronted cabinet. In one corner, an old reel to reel tape recorder sat on a table along with a couple of old microphones. Framed album covers and photographs decorated the walls in that corner.

Now I knew where Thumper spent a sizable chunk of the money we got out of the record company. Briefly, I wondered why I hadn't been involved in any of the legal details when he built his place.

He waved me to the chairs around the table.

"Want something to drink?"

"No. Let's get down to the story. Tell me what's going on."

"I guess you've heard some of it. Like I said, Angelique came back to her apartment yesterday. There was a man dead on the floor. She didn't know him. She had no idea how he got there. She called me. I met her outside of her place."

"Thumper, why didn't you call the cops?"

"Because I didn't know what was going on. What if they said she did it?"

I thought what if she did do it, but chances were good she was a client, so I didn't say it out loud. "Go on. What did you do?"

"I went up and looked at him. I didn't know him." He paused. "It's not good that he's Landry Andrus's brother. That's not good at all." He shook his head.

I had no idea who Landry Andrus was, but I wanted to hear the story sequentially, so I didn't ask.

"Anyway," Thumper said, "I checked the guy out. He was dead all right. I think somebody bashed in his head. There was some blood but nothing I couldn't clean up. I put his head in a trash bag. I called a friend from up here, Mark Cole. That's his little brother Grant you just met.

"Grant was supposed to be out of town. He sells fresh fish and has a huge cold room and freezer on his property. Up there where we saw the fire. Anyway, Mark is a good friend. I can trust him. And he has a little crush on Angelique. He won't cause no trouble.

"I went through the guy's pockets, but there was nothing there. Mark came down and brought a big canvas. We rolled the guy up and walked him right out of there and put him in the back of my pickup. I tell you, I had the nervous jitters until we got out of there. I figured whoever left the guy wanted to get Angelique in some serious trouble for some reason. I expected the cops at any moment."

I made a mental note to discretely look around Angelique's apartment complex for surveillance cameras.

Thumper continued. "We drove him up here and put him in Grant's ice-house. I figured we could talk about it when you came up here. Try to figure out who he is, and what might have happened. I didn't expect Grant to be around until we figured out what to do. So, what do we need to do?"

"Are you kidding? I have no idea."

"You're the lawyer. You need to figure something out."

"Well, to start with you should have already called the

cops. It was against the law not to."

"Can't do that. You can't tell anybody, right? You have to keep my secrets. And Angelique's?"

I shook my head. "Yeah. But wow, Thumper. This thing is going to end up really messy." That's the moment I accepted Angelique as a client. She was an exquisite dancer. I didn't see how she could be a killer. I hoped I was right.

I asked, "What do you think Grant meant when he said the body was gone?"

"I don't know. We'll let him cool down and go see what's up with that in the morning. Maybe the problem is solved."

"There was a dead guy. Even if the dead guy is gone to who knows where, there's no way the problem is solved."

"Not much we can do about it tonight. Want to get some sleep?"

"No. I want to know who Landry Andrus is and why you think it is particularly not good that the dead guy is his brother."

"I need a drink. You want some really good shine?"

He got up and went to a cabinet where he took a bottle of something and poured it into a glass.

"Oh, why not. I'll have some."

The drink he gave me was the color of caramel. It was a smooth, obviously well made, homemade whiskey. A smokey, whiskey flavor presented itself before dissolving into the heat of the moonshine. I had to take a deep breath before I could speak.

"Now, Thumper, who is Landry Andrus?"

Thumper set his glass down on the table between us, rubbed his hands over his face and said, "Landry Andrus is well-known between here and New Orleans."

"I don't know that I've heard of him. What is he?"

Thumper was thinking. He wasn't looking at me. He stared at the wall. I didn't know if he was trying to decide just what to tell me or just how he should tell me.

"Landry is a businessman. He's got a construction firm in New Orleans and some other stuff. I don't know what exactly. I know he owns a nightclub in Louisiana somewhere and a couple of titty bars in Beaumont. Word is you don't want to get in his way. They say some of his competitors have gone missing."

"Great. So he's a gangster. And his dead brother showed up in your granddaughter's apartment."

"Guess so. I didn't know it was Bobby Andrus. That's bad. We do not want to get crosswise with any of the Andrus clan. I'd rather swim naked in a swamp of snakes. What are we going to do, Sam?"

I shook my head. Like a lot of clients, he'd kept me in the dark and let me be surprised by something. But it wasn't my job to worry about being kept in the dark. It was my job to respond to his plea for help.

"I don't know, Thumper. We have to talk to Cole and find out what he did and what he plans to do next. I need to talk to Angelique. We need to know what Mark Cole plans to do. I need to gather info, quietly, and quickly try to figure out what's going on."

It was a fact of lawyering that I needed to gather a lot of info, but be careful not to gather too much. I hoped I had time to learn a few more things before I had to arrange bail for somebody.

"So," Thumper said, "what do we need to do now?"

"Go home and go fishing. But, unless there's something else you haven't told me, I guess we go to bed. Get some sleep. We'll go see the Cole in the morning and figure out if there's anything else to do up here, and then go talk to Angelique. You can call her, right?"

"Yeah, no problem."

I SLEPT IN A SPACIOUS guest bedroom on a good mattress and woke the next morning to the scent of breakfast. Thumper had bacon cooking and eggs standing by. Strong coffee was ready.

"Well, counselor, what's the plan?"

"Same as last night. We need more info before we can formulate a plan. I guess we need to go see your friend Mr. Cole and then I want to talk to Angelique. I assume she's back in Houston."

"Yep. How do you want your eggs?"

"I don't care. On a plate. We need to get moving."

He turned to the stove and, over his shoulder, said, "Thanks, Sam. I'm glad you're up here."

While he cooked, I wandered around and looked at his place. I paused to look at the photographs on the wall by the old reel to reel recorder he had. There were photographs of him with Muddy Waters, John Lee Hooker, and other famous bluesmen. There were photographs of Thumper as a young man on various stages. I recognized only one of the venues, the Jackson Ballroom. A few of the photographs showed a very young Thumper on a stage that must have been in France. The signs on the wall in the background were all in French.

He had framed a photocopy of the seven-figure check he received for damages when we settled with his recording label for years of unpaid royalties and copyright violations. There was one color photograph on the wall. It was Angelique, on stage and en pointe, beautiful and serene.

I had Thumper go over everything again over breakfast, but there was nothing new. Angelique came home to find a dead guy on the floor. She called Thumper. He sent her away. Thumper found nothing in the pockets of the dead guy. He called his friend Mark Cole. They rolled up the dead guy. Thumper hauled him up to the river in the back of his pickup. They put the corpse in Grant Cole's walk-in freezer.

I didn't look forward to another encounter with Grant Cole.

"Tell me about Grant Cole."

"Grant grew up around here. Probably did some poaching and illegal fishing back in the day. Now, he's a straight commercial fisherman and seafood supplier. He buys and sells fish legitimately. Makes a good living, selling mostly to restaurants. Mark, his big brother, don't have his brains. He works for Grant and lives in a trailer on his property up there.

"Grant's kind of the top dog up here. He's the unofficial mayor, sheriff, and problem solver. Regular cops don't patrol in here and a lot of the people who live in here don't talk to cops. If you live up here and you have a problem with a neighbor, you go to Grant. He keeps everybody in line. If anybody does something really bad, usually somebody will snitch to Grant and he'll either fix the problem or call the sheriff. The sheriff knows what he is and listens to him. Probably appreciates not having to send his deputies up here all the time."

If Grant Cole had burned the body in that bonfire we saw, there would be a lot of evidence for somebody to find.

It was already hot and humid. There was a scent of wood smoke. We took Thumper's old truck up the road to find out just what Grant Cole had done.

CHAPTER THREE

THUMPER'S TRUCK RATTLED over a cattle guard turning into Cole's property. To the right sat Cole's house, built out of cinder block painted a reddish-brown with a low-pitched roof. It looked as if it belonged there, surrounded by the towering trunks of red oaks. Obviously well-maintained, the Grant house had to be one of the nicest houses in the neighborhood, second only to Thumper's.

A building in front of us did not blend in. It stood half again as tall as the house. Constructed of aluminum siding with only two small windows to one side, it had one regular sized door next to a large sliding door big enough to drive a truck through. Next to the building, a platform built of steel held refrigeration equipment and two gasoline-fired generators. A huge tank above them obviously held the fuel. A pipe ran down from that tank to a nozzle available to fuel his trucks or car.

From where we parked, a rutted track continued around the left of the aluminum building and down a steep slope to the river, visible through a gap in the trees. Neither the house nor the warehouse would be above flood waters, but the refrigeration equipment would be. I guessed that in a rising flood, Cole would try to get his supply of fish trucked to safety in the two trucks parked to the side. Each had "Cole's Fresh Fish and Seafood" painted on the side.

The sound of us driving over his cattle guard broughto

Cole from behind his house. Thumper parked and got out as
Cole came striding up. I checked. He had his handgun on
his hip. I got out and he frowned.

"Thumper, I told you to come up here alone."

"Sam's my lawyer, I tell him everything anyway. You
can trust him."

I almost laughed out loud at that. Thumper never told
me everything, not all at once, and Cole had to be smart
enough to never trust a lawyer.

Cole looked from me to Thumper and back again, his
lips pressed tightly together, his chest moving with each
short, angry breath.

"Fine. Come on, let's talk." He turned and walked
toward the back of his house.

Thumper looked at me, smiled, and with a nod of his
head invited me to follow. The backyard of Cole's house
sloped gently down toward the river. Forty or so yards from
the back of his house the property ended at a bulkhead made
of steel plates. Beyond the bulkhead, a slough of green water
sat still. Moss, so thick it looked as if you could walk on it,
covered the water. The slough disappeared into the brush
between the river and us. Its thick, swampy scent permeated
the air, competing with the smell of a still smoldering fire.

Cole led us past the smoldering fire pit to a picnic
table. I looked closely at the smoking coals in the fire pit,
wondering if the dead guy's ashes were there. I saw no sign
of bones, and it smelled only of wood.

Thumper and I sat on one side of the picnic table across
from Cole, who said, "So, Thumper, what's going on?"

"What did you mean last night when you said the dead
guy was gone?"

Cole looked at me. "You showed up with a lawyer.
Maybe there are some things I shouldn't talk about."

"Sam's been my lawyer for a long time. He knows all my secrets. He has that lawyer code thing. He can't talk to anybody about anything we say. That's right Sam, isn't it?"

"I have to keep your confidences, yes, because you're my client. Even if you tell me about crimes you've committed in the past. Like illegally moving a dead body from where you found it. Just to be clear. I am not bound to keep confidential any plans you might have to commit crimes in the future. In fact, I'm supposed to tell somebody if I find out you're planning to commit a crime."

Cole looked from me back to Thumper. "Yeah, he talks like a damn lawyer for sure. Saying one thing, maybe meaning another."

"Sam will help us, Grant. He's the one that got me all that money. He's a good lawyer."

"For you maybe, but a good lawyer will sell me out if he has to in order to protect you. I know how they work."

He was right, but I didn't say so. Instead, I said, "Look, my client, Thumper, has advised me of something that raises some legal issues. My job is to protect him. Right now I'm gathering the facts about what's going on so I can do that. Things that happened in the past remain subject to my obligation of confidentiality to him."

"More lawyer gobbledygook. I know how lawyers work."

He stood up abruptly, and his right hand went toward his hip. I seriously thought he might be about to pull his gun and shoot me, but just as that thought registered, his hand slipped into his pocket. He pulled out a thick roll of money. He peeled a couple of bills off and thrust them my way. They were hundred-dollar bills.

"Here. Take these. I'm paying you to represent me and my brother. That makes you my lawyer and Mark's lawyer.

Now you have to keep my secrets. If I owe you more, collect it from Thumper."

I thought it likely there were conflicts of interest to consider before accepting the Cole brothers as clients. Maybe if I'd been safe in an office, surrounded by law books and the other trappings of being a lawyer, I would have declined. But, there, in the woods by the Trinity River, sitting alone with Thumper and the gun-packing Grant Cole pocketing his cash seemed like the right thing to do, and I did.

"Now, where were we?" Cole said. "Thumper, how the hell did Bobby Andrus end up in my cold locker?"

"I did not know that's who it was. My granddaughter came home and found him on her living room floor. She called me. She didn't know who he was. She had no idea how he got there. All I wanted to do was protect her, get him out of there until I could figure out what to do. Mark helped me."

"Yeah, well Mark has gone down to my place in Mexico. If anybody asks, he's been there for several days. My wife and kids have gone to Tennessee to visit her parents. How sure are you that nobody saw you haul him out of her house?"

"Real sure. She lives in an apartment complex, but her front door is real close to where we put him in the truck. Nobody was around. If they were, they saw a couple of working guys hauling away some trash."

Cole snorted and said, "You've got the trash part right." He turned my direction. "So, Mr. Lawyer—what is your name anyway? I forgot. Guess I need the name of my own damn lawyer."

"Samuel Locke." I pulled out a business card and handed it to him. He tucked it into a pocket.

"So, Mr. Samuel Locke, what do we need to do?"

"I'm still trying to figure out exactly what's going on. What did you do with the body?"

He smiled. It was a grim smile, but not without pleasure behind it.

"Come on, I'll show you."

He stood and walked toward the bulkhead between the swampy water and us. We followed. The steel plates of the bulkhead extended two feet above the level of the ground. It was four or five feet down to the murky water.

Cole made a clucking sound with his tongue.

The water swirled below us. Slowly a hump appeared in the green water. Two reptilian eyes rose above the surface six feet out from the bulkhead. The head of the alligator was huge. An alligator hunter once told me you estimated the length of an alligator at one foot for every inch between its eyes and its nostrils. If true, that meant the alligator before us was thirteen or fourteen feet long. Rising from that murky water thick with moss, it was a primordial beast. My body reached into its genetic history and reacted appropriately by pumping adrenaline into my veins. I wanted to turn and run.

There were other swirls in the water behind the alligator. Another pair of eyes broke the surface just to the side of the first.

"That big guy is Sampson. I toss him some food every once in a while. But, I doubt if he's really hungry this morning. I fed Bobby Andrus to him and his friends last night. If Andrus is not gone yet, the leftovers are rolled up and tucked away somewhere in the swamp."

I really wanted to forget Thumper's trouble and go fishing. But, not on that river. I might never fish the Trinity again.

As we walked back toward the picnic table, Thumper said, "What was with the fire? I thought you'd cremated him."

"No. That would have left too much of him around. I had to burn up an almost new fish cleaning table. I couldn't just throw him in one piece to the gators. I burned the table along with what was left of all his clothes after I ripped the buttons off. He had nothing on him but a house key. Mark tossed it and his buttons one at a time between here and the airport. I'm going to invite some folks over every night for a while, and we're gonna burn a lot of wood in the pit grilling our dinner.

"So, what do you think Mr. Lawyer, did I cover our tracks?"

I shrugged. The whole thing was way out of hand. "I hear what you did. I doubt if anybody is going to find out. If somebody comes to talk to you, call me immediately, and don't say a word about anything to anybody until I can get here. I live in Galveston, so it might take a while."

"What if I get tossed into jail?"

"Same thing. Say nothing. Act like you have no idea what's going on, but you're too nervous to say anything at all until you speak to your lawyer. I'll get you out."

"What are you doing next?"

"Try to very quietly find out what's going on. Thumper and I are going to Houston, and he's going to get me with his granddaughter so I can start unraveling this thing. I don't want to attract anybody's attention, but we have to find out what's going on."

"Just don't drag me or my brother into her mess. Whatever is going on, it has absolutely nothing to do with us."

I nodded. The three of us walked toward Thumper's

truck.

Cole continued, "You keep me posted if there's really something I need to know. I'd just as soon not hear another thing about this. Let me know when we're all in the clear and I can bring my family back. I don't really care about anything else. I just want to know that me and my brother are not involved in any way whatsoever and that it's safe here for my wife and kids. I am not curious about who killed Bobby Andrus or why. Right now, I need to take a nap."

I started to come out of the daze caused by the things happening so quickly. I started to think better. "When you stripped him down, were there any wounds of any kind? Thumper said it looked like he'd been hit in the head, but was there anything else?"

"No. That hole in his head probably killed him. I almost barfed when I grabbed his head. It felt like my fingers were going into his skull. I'm no expert, but it didn't look to me like he'd been strangled and there were no other holes in him."

"Okay. We'll stay in touch."

"Only if you have to. Let me know if we need to talk and it's not an emergency. I buy fish in Galveston. Without Mark here, I'll be making the trip myself two or three times a week. We can meet there." He handed me a business card with his phone number.

I looked around his place. It looked innocent enough, but I imagined DNA and blood and other forensic evidence all over the place.

Thumper and I got in his truck and he said, "Well, maybe everything is okay. Nobody will be finding that body. I guess we can relax and get to work."

"Yes. I need to talk to Angelique, find out what connection she has with Bobby Andrus."

"No, man. Not that. We need to talk about changing my will and giving her a share of Thumperly."

I looked at him for several seconds.

"Thumper. Listen to me. Right now, the dead man you took out of Angelique's apartment, the man who has been fed to some alligators, is the most important problem you have. If that little problem doesn't get resolved, there won't be anything left of Thumperly to give her. You will be in prison. Maybe her, too."

He smiled. "Nah, man. You ain't gonna let that happen. I'll call Angelique and set her up with you, but we need to do them other things, too."

Thumper wanted to control things that were out of control. He needed to stop. I needed to get control but didn't know enough to do so. I needed to start learning something or run the risk of my clients being caught in an avalanche of trouble. I needed to find out the chances of someone having seen Thumper and Mark Cole moving a body out of Angelique's apartment. If someone did, I needed to be prepared for when somebody showed up to arrest somebody. I could at least get started on that.

"What's the name of Angelique's apartment complex?"

"Crester Ridge Apartments. It's west of the Loop on Post Oak, right off San Felipe. Over there where all those apartments are."

"What's her apartment number?"

"Fourteen-oh-five. Why?"

"Because I'm going to have somebody go scope it out. Look for surveillance cameras."

"I didn't see any. That would be bad, huh?"

"Yes. I'll get my investigator to check it out. See what he can find out discretely."

"You going to tell him what's going on?"

"Not yet, but if it becomes necessary, yes."

Thumper turned into his place and I followed him up the stairs to his deck and into his living room. I looked at my cell phone. One good thing about the oil boom, they must have put up some cell phone towers. I had a good signal, better than I used to have on the river. I called Wallace Rockwell, the private investigator I use.

"Investigations."

"Rocky, Sam Locke."

"What's up Sam?"

"You busy? I need something done kind of quickly and very quietly."

"I'm free until the wayward husband I'm going to follow gets off an airplane landing at seven tonight. I need to get to Houston Intercontinental by about six. What's up?"

"Crester Ridge Apartment complex, up in Houston. I want to find out if they have video surveillance that might have caught anyone coming or going from apartment fourteen-oh-five."

"How sure do you want to be? Do you want me to try to review or get a copy of any video they might have?"

"Actually, I'm hoping there is none. And if there is, as much as I'd like to see what's on it from Thursday through today, in no way do I want to draw attention to it."

"So, you're not hoping there's something to find. You want something to not be there."

"Exactly. The things I don't want to see far out-weigh the things I'd like to see."

"Okay. I'll go up there this morning. Hey, how about this? I'll have Jenny go in like she wants to rent an apartment. She can ask them about security. I'll be her older, wiser uncle, but let her do the talking."

Jenny is Genevieve Mills, Rocky's orphaned niece. She lives with and works for him. She's smart and capable. She would do a good job. She's in her twenties, but when she dresses to look old, she looks all of eighteen.

"Good idea. Be careful if you get there and see a police presence. Don't let any cop who knows you get suspicious about why you're there."

"We'll take care. If I see a friendly cop, do you want me to pretend I'm there with Jenny and see what I can find out? As the uncle worried about his niece's safety I might learn something."

I thought about that. His question illuminated the way this thing could get complex and out of hand quickly. But, if there were cops at Angelique's apartment, things would be out of hand anyway.

"Sure. Might as well. Just let me know as fast as you can whatever you find out."

"Okay. Understand. We'll be up there in an hour or so."

I hung up and stared out the window, thinking what else could be done. Nothing until I talked to Angelique.

"Can you get hold of Angelique now? I need to talk to her face to face as soon as possible."

"I don't know. It's important for her to act normal, isn't it?"

"Sure."

"Well, we don't want to upset her. I'm not even sure I can find her for a while. She performs tonight and tomorrow afternoon. I'd hate for her to get so upset she has to cancel a performance. That would not be normal. We just don't have time today. How about tomorrow night. After she's done."

"Well, the cops showing up and arresting her might be more upsetting. Besides, what could be more upsetting than finding a dead guy in her room? Thumper, we've got to move on this."

"We are. You got your man checking out the security cameras. I've told you all I know. We learned who he was and that he's gone. Not much more we can do today. You can talk to her tomorrow, reassure her."

Stubborn old coot. I knew him well enough to know I would get no further with him. Living a hard life and climbing out of his circumstances to his success made him leery and tough and guarded. He needed to have control. I needed to ding his complacency.

"You know, Thumper, maybe whoever left that guy there came after her and didn't find her. Are you sure she is safe?"

He thought, his eyes narrowing, his lips compressing into a tight line.

"She's going to spend all of today at the theater. She'll be safe there. She's told a friend her apartment complex is spraying for bugs, and she's spending the night with that friend. She'll get back to the theater as soon as possible in the morning. She's as safe as can be."

I hoped so. I'd once done my best to keep a client safe, and she got killed. Perhaps it colored my concern, but Thumper wasn't going to cooperate to get me to Angelique that day. It looked like the best thing I could do was discuss changing his will and transferring an interest in Thumperly to her. Then we could move on to mundane things like dead guys, crime lords, and alligators.

"Okay, then. Let's talk about your will and Thumperly."

We talked. Changing his will would be straight forward. She got everything. He wanted to give her half of Thumperly, but he wanted the fees that Thumperly paid me to be all out of his half.

"You sure? My fifteen percent out of just your half will be a pretty big bite."

"No problem. Do it that way. This is all for her. She'll get mine when I'm dead anyway. Get that done and my new will that says so. In fact, with dead people popping up, do the will before you do anything."

Thumper and I talked about things until Rocky called me.

"Sam. Here's the scoop. We didn't see anything that looked like official attention being paid to your apartment of interest or anywhere else in the complex. There are some video cameras, but I did not see any that would catch the door to your apartment. There are some windows in other apartments with a view of the door, but no way to know if anybody saw anything unless I go knock on some doors. There are video cameras on the gates you have to enter to get to the resident's parking area. There is a camera outside the office that catches the parking lot in front of the office and anyone walking up to the office door.

"In the office there is a desk with a pretty young thing sitting there with two monitors on a credenza behind her rotating through four cameras, but I doubt she pays attention. Perhaps they record, but, again, I'd have to ask somebody questions to find out for sure. I don't think they are monitored by anybody off-premises. There are little signs for AceMark Security Service. AceMark is an alarm service and runs on-site and mobile security. They're kind of second or third tier as a security service. But they're cheap. I called them pretending to need security for my convenience store. They do not actively monitor video feeds.

"Jenny went in to inquire about renting ... "

Jenny shouted, "Hi Sam."

"Tell her hi."

He did not relay my message to her. "She asked the leasing agent about security, and the discussion was limited to residents having the phone number of AceMark and the gates requiring a key code to open. I'm sure every pizza place in a five-mile radius has a key code posted on the wall by the phone for their delivery drivers. How much more do you want me to do?"

"Not much you can do at this point. There will probably be some other stuff. It's a difficult and unusual situation. We'll get together, and I'll explain what's going on, see if you have any ideas."

"Okay, let me know."

"Well?" Thumper asked.

"Angelique's apartment complex does not seem to have many helpful security cameras. There's no crime scene tape up. Not yet, anyway."

He smiled. "So, what do we do now?"

"Get me with Angelique. Avoid being anywhere alone. I don't know what else to suggest."

"So, nothing else we can do today?"

"Guess not."

"Okay, then. Sounds good. I've got a gig tonight at the Big Easy. Want to come?"

"Not tonight. I've got some work to do."

"I'll be going to watch Angelique dance tomorrow afternoon, and then I'll bring her back up here with me. Can you be here? We can talk, then."

"I've got a new office downtown a couple of blocks from the theater. Why don't you come there after her performance?"

"Okay. We can do that. She's spending the night with me up here on the river. I'd like to get here by eight."

A dead body appearing in Angelique's apartment, its disposition as dinner for some alligators, and Thumper's seemingly lack of concern about those things loomed large. What I wanted to do was get back to my house on Galveston Island and go fishing, but he had tossed the problem into my lap. I had to plot a course even if he would not be helpful.

AMONG OTHER THINGS, my Uncle Harlan develops real estate. I manage several of his rental properties on the coast. He owns a great old office building in Houston where he maintains an office and apartment. He'd recently bought an interest in another building in downtown Houston. He'd called me and told me he was making me a deal on an office there. That way, when necessary, I could be his eyes if any issues arose with the building. I didn't like being tied to things like office space, but Harlan's done much for me, like making me a deal on the rent I pay for my house on Galveston.

The deal on the office was great for downtown Houston, and I could use the office. In fact, I'd started thinking about hiring somebody part-time to work in that office assisting me, somebody to answer calls and do some bookkeeping for the various things I do. The smoker and grill business had grown to a point where tracking orders and the paperwork cut into the fun of building the products and into my fishing time.

The office is two rooms on the second floor of an older building on a street corner in downtown Houston. The office, in the corner of the building, is a great place to sit and watch people on the street.

I gave Thumper the address and directions on how to walk there from the theater where the Houston Ballet performs. He agreed to bring Angelique over as soon as possible after her performance.

"In fact," I said. "Why don't you come to the office before the ballet begins? I want to talk to you more about the body. We can go over every thing again before we meet with Angelique."

"I've told you all about that."

"Yeah, but sometimes it helps to go over it again."

"I don't know why you think it will help, but you're the lawyer. I'll get there about noon. You can buy me lunch."

"It's a deal."

In the short distance from Thumper's front door to my car, my shirt became sweat-damp, sticking to me with an itch. No breeze moved the trees lining the road away from his place. A fine white dust, raised from the gravel, coated the brush on both sides of the road. I'd planned to spend the night in Houston, but, as I drove away from Thumper's house, fatigue rolled across my shoulders and down my back.

I wanted to go home.

Home was two hours south and west. I headed that way. I wanted to sleep in my bed. I longed for a cooling breeze off the gulf, salt-scented by the sea.

I did not want to get caught in any more of Houston's massive traffic than necessary, so I skipped the route through Houston by taking State Highway One Forty-Six, crossing the water on the Lynchburg Ferry, making my way through La Porte and Seabrook down to where I got on the Interstate just before the causeway to Galveston Island.

It was almost peak high tide as I approached the causeway. Folks with cast nets worked the tidal pools and flats at the side of the highway, catching bait fish. Just before sunset would be an excellent time to do some fishing.

A hot summer Saturday meant Seawall Boulevard, which separates the beaches on the Gulf from everything else on the island, would be crowded. I usually enjoy making the drive down the length of Galveston and seeing the pageantry of people, but I had too much on my mind. I took the slightly less congested Stewart Road past most of the crowd. Once back on Seawall, I skipped my usual practice of driving down the beach and stayed on the pavement.

I used the remote control to open the gate to my place. My two goats, Briggs and Stratton, were munching on the weeds inside some temporary fencing there at the front of the property. They get moved around the property as needed to cut grass and control weeds. That meant Joshua Bell was there. He is the young man who works for me making barbecue equipment. He had to have moved the goats.

Joshua was working on a row of grills lined up under the covered work area outside the workshop. He was shirtless and bolting a logo plate to each grill. His girlfriend, Darla, pushed the utility cart along behind him.

I'd never seen Joshua interested in anything other than welding and fishing. I worried when he brought Darla around and introduced her as a friend from school. I expected her to be a distraction who might limit his interest in working or going fishing with me. It hadn't happened. He might not have been in the shop every afternoon as soon as he used to be, but he always made up the time. Darla seemed content to hang out at the shop, even helping him sweep up at the end of a work day. Occasionally, she joined us and held her own on fishing outings. I liked her. I liked seeing them holding hands. It was cute.

I parked by the shop. There were a couple of cars I did not recognize parked by Joshua's pick-up.

I looked at the unknown cars and raised my eyebrows. Joshua pointed with his thumb back toward where my property extends to the edge of the bay. I nodded. The marine biology department at Texas A&M University restores and studies the grass flats on the edge of my property. The cars meant there were summer students working in the flats.

"I've got things to do inside. Don't work too long in this heat. I'll be grilling something later if y'all are around."

Darla stepped up next to Joshua. "Thanks Mr. Locke, but Josh is taking me out to dinner tonight."

Joshua nodded. And blushed.

"Okay, then. Have a good time."

I was relieved. I needed some alone time to think about the dead Bobby Andrus.

I spent some time on the internet looking for anything on Bobby or Robert Andrus. There was not much there. I found several news articles about the older brother Landry. The Andrus business interests occasionally made the news. An undercurrent ran through most of the news articles, nothing explicit, but I sensed some journalists considered Andrus to be more unsavory than portrayed in the articles.

In a few stories out of Beaumont and Lake Charles, Bobby earned mention as the manager of a couple of bars where dancers got in trouble for lewd dancing or solicitation, common hazards of running topless bars. One article quoted Bobby as saying such things were absolutely forbidden, and any dancer discovered doing them would be immediately fired.

There were stories of complaints made against an Andrus-owned towing company by people who felt ripped off at towing and impounding fees.

I made copies of all the articles I found. I discerned no

clue explaining Bobby's demise.

I didn't know what else to look for on-line. I needed a path to follow. I hoped speaking with Angelique the next day would give me some direction. I looked it up and learned that by failing to disclose the existence and location of a corpse to law enforcement, Thumper and Angelique had committed a Class A misdemeanor. By moving the corpse, Thumper had committed another Class A misdemeanor. Class A misdemeanors could earn them four thousand dollar fines and a year in jail.

Angelique was going to get a share of Thumperly Efforts, but, frankly, I did not have the brain power that night to think about how best to do that. I would have to involve a tax consultant. That tended to dampen my enthusiasm. I left it for another day.

I was at loose ends. There was so much to do, but I didn't know what. I microwaved something for dinner. I tried to watch television, but couldn't get interested. I thought about sitting on the pier and fishing, but didn't want to go to the trouble. I finally went to bed and lay there a long time, my mind trying to fill in blanks about the man who got fed to the alligators.

I went to sleep thinking about dismembered limbs sinking into green water thick with algae amid violent swirls as reptilian predators dragged them deep, hopefully never to be seen again.

I dreamed of a ballerina on an empty stage in an empty theater, dancing to music I could not hear. In the wings behind her, things moved in the dark.

CHAPTER FOUR

I WOKE UP ON SUNDAY before dawn and checked the news. There was nothing about anything unusual happening at the ballet the night before. That meant Angelique must still be alive.

I stood on my porch, drank one cup of coffee, and thought about not running that morning, but I knew I would. While working on the case where my client ended up murdered, I'd encountered a couple of guys who beat me bad and eventually tried to kill me. I did not fight back effectively at all. I started working out. I started a martial arts class. I practiced with my handgun at the range. I ran every day I could.

On that predawn Sunday morning, a breeze blew in straight from the Gulf carrying the sea scent. It encouraged me to make my run.

I did the stretching and ran the length of my drive, across the highway, and down the sandy access road to the beach. Turning left, I ran on sand packed hard at the edge of the surf, concentrating on breathing deep and full. I nodded to those lucky enough to be standing by long rods fishing the surf.

There was a half-buried, salt bleached log buried about a mile and a half down the beach from where I started my run. I usually stopped there for a rest, did a couple of push-ups against it, and either continued running down the beach or, if I didn't have the time or energy, I turned around for home.

I sat there that morning and watched the glow on the horizon focus into the bright point of the sun. There were only wisps of clouds. It would be a hot day. The sun warmed my back as I ran back toward home.

After a shower, I still had more than three hours before I needed to meet Thumper in Houston. Having so much to do and no clue exactly what needed doing left me unsettled. I decided to go to church.

Twenty minutes later I'd crossed over to Follett's Island and pulled off the Blue Water Highway to park on the cracked cement apron surrounding what used to be an abandoned convenience store. It still had weathered plywood instead of glass in its windows, but the plywood now sported some well-done murals. I couldn't park close to the building because a rag-tag group of about twenty people gathered in a circle, banging on a variety of things—drums, metal pots, and plastic buckets. There was order to the chaos, hard beats, and a syncopated rhythm. Some of the drummers chanted sounds. Much laughter accompanied the noise.

Presiding over whatever was going on was my friend Preacher, dressed loud in worn jeans, sandals, and a bright yellow Hawaiian shirt patterned with bold, red flowers. He was a sight, tall and beefy and dancing to the beating of the drums. He danced my way, clapping his hands with the communal rhythm.

Preacher took possession of the abandoned convenience store some time ago. I was not sure of his legal standing there or how he got the power hooked up. But he led the church that met there, his congregation an ever-changing conglomeration of transient beach dwellers and a few full-time residents who preferred his non-demanding form of worship. I'd heard a few of his sermons. He drew from a variety of scripture and included a healthy dose of more secular sources of enlightenment such as Shakespeare, Babe Ruth, Kahlil Gibran, the Cookie Monster, and others. He consistently preached a doctrine that boiled down to a philosophy of be nice, don't hurt anybody, and help each other.

He danced over to my car. I rolled down my window.

"Hey, Sam. Join our drum circle?"

"No. Sorry. I have to be in Houston shortly. Thought I'd stop by and see if you wanted breakfast, but you look busy."

"No. This is just practice. We're going to drum in the sunrise on the Summer Solstice. Gretchen can take charge. Breakfast sounds good."

He pointed at a young woman with a tambourine. She nodded, stood up, and started dancing around the circle, taking charge. Preacher did not believe it necessary to dedicate Sunday to church activities. He climbed into the passenger side of my Range Rover.

"You have to practice that?"

"Funny. Practicing keeps a few of them with us longer. Gives me more of a chance to get them sorted out."

I drove the few miles to Clara's Bar and Grill where we both had Cajun shrimp omelets and lots of good coffee. I offered to drive him back to his church, but he said he preferred a stroll down the beach. I headed to Houston.

The most valuable thing about my new office was the reserved space in its parking lot within blocks of the courthouses. I parked and took the stairs to my office. Somebody had added my name to the door and pushed a bill for doing so through the mail slot. The bill was made out to Harlan Enterprises. I took a stamped envelope out of my briefcase, wrote a short note to Gladys, the go-to person at Harlan Enterprises, and dropped the envelope in the mail slot by the elevators.

Once again, I made a mental note to stock the office with some office supplies. The only thing in the office besides some really cheap furniture was a coffee pot. I made a pot of coffee, turned on my laptop, and settled down to wait for Thumper.

Next to the reserved parking slot, the best thing about that office was the window jutting out from the building over the sidewalk. It faced diagonally across the intersection but had angled sides such that I can look down the length of both streets that cross at that corner.

I propped my feet up on the window sill. I could see one guy in an office across the street, his feet on his desk while he talked on his cell phone. My office, with those windows, was a box seat to the theater of the street. I usually enjoyed it. That day it made me feel alone. The lonely feeling went with the melancholy that started early in the spring and promised to linger into summer. I sipped my coffee and thought about people I'd lost and people I'd let slip away and how, lately, even a day fishing felt like a transient moment.

Eventually, I snapped back to the problem of the day. Perhaps the caffeine kicked in.

I'd have loved for all the problems raised by the dead Bobby Andrus to have disappeared into the murky depths of the alligator infested slough up on the river. But even if his disappearance solved some issues, it did not address the fact that somebody had been in Angelique's apartment and left him there. Why? Was it an unexpected killing, a falling out between random burglars, and did his killer just leave town hastily? That would be nice. Maybe the killer was on the run, getting far away from Houston. But the situation felt like unfinished business. My big worry was that somebody intended to finish business with Angelique.

I needed to start focusing on little things, weave the details together. Maybe I could drag more details out of Thumper. I'd try again, but my best bet would be the conversation with Angelique.

Looking north, up the street toward the theater district, I saw Thumper walking down the sidewalk. I locked up the office, grabbed my briefcase, and took the elevator down to meet him in the lobby.

He walked in the door as I crossed the lobby.

"Hello, Thumper."

"Hey, counselor."

"Ready to eat?"

"Yep. Where are we going?"

"The Cafe."

The Cafe has been in downtown Houston since the forties. It's in the corner of a building that's avoided being torn down or having its soul renovated out of it. The Cafe had a more complete name sometime in the past, but in the fifties a new owner scraped the old owner's name off the window leaving only the word "Cafe." That owner and subsequent owners never got around to painting a new name on the window. So, its name became the Cafe. It was crowded during the week, but not so much on Sundays.

As we walked toward the Cafe, Thumper reiterated there was nothing more he could tell me about the body.

"Nothing, man. He didn't have a wallet. I didn't really even look at him closely. I knew he was a white guy. I knew he was dead, and I knew we had to get him out of there. I never met Andrus. I couldn't have told you who he was even if I'd looked at him."

He convinced me. He knew nothing else about the

dead man. We talked a bit about Angelique. He was going to her matinee performance and promised to bring her by my office as soon as possible afterward. He asked if I'd changed his will. I told him I'd have it ready in the week ahead.

We got to the Cafe and ordered burgers and fries.

"So, Thumper, tell me about Angelique and you. I never knew you had a granddaughter. I didn't even know you had a child."

"I didn't either until not too long ago."

I waited. Thumper was lost in himself. He looked up and looked around. Leaning toward me, he said, "Did you know I once played with Billie Holiday?"

"No. I didn't know that."

"She was a great lady."

He sipped his soft drink and continued, "It was in Paris in 1954. Yeah, man, Paris was another world. I'd been with Angelique's grandmother for almost a year when I backed up Ms. Holiday."

"You met her in Paris?"

"Yeah."

I was about to get a story. I kept my mouth shut. He looked at memories somewhere over my right shoulder.

"I got out of Houston and went to New Orleans in nineteen fifty-one. I was eighteen years old. I earned some money on the street and picked up a few gigs. There were places I could go where the stage was open to anybody. Me, a bass player named Cliff Medford, a drummer by the name of Paul Whitfield, and another guitar and mouth-harp player name of Marlowe Williams started playing together. We'd play blues in a club one night and do some jazz with other guys on the next in a different club. I was making enough money to live."

"Must have been something back in those days."

"Sure. Every group of days has their somethings. I was young. I was playing. I'd left a lot of crap behind in Houston. All the crap in New Orleans was at least different and felt more exotic or something."

"How did you get all the way to Paris?" The waitress brought us our food and asked if she could get us anything else. We declined.

"Jazz was a big thing in France back then. Lots of guys from Chicago started going over there. Word was a black jazz musician got lots more respect over there. I'd heard some of the stories. Like Miles Davis openly having a white girlfriend. About how in the jazz clubs there wasn't no black and white."

He took a moment to chew on his burger.

"A man came down to New Orleans from Chicago. Started hanging out in the clubs, making himself known. We called him Fat Leo Schuman. Leo fancied himself a promoter. He was full of words as big as his belly. He wanted to cash in on Paris."

Thumper laughed. "I'm pretty sure Leo wanted to get as far away from Chicago as possible for some reason, and Paris would put him that much farther away. Most of the guys thought he was full of crap. They'd talk to him as long as he was buying drinks, but they weren't buying into his plan to make them big in Paris. To most of them, Paris was harder to imagine than heaven.

"But, I was young. Real young. I had no ties. No woman holding me. Leo finally got around to pitching Paris to me and the guys I was playing with. At three in the morning, after a lot of whiskey, we told him we'd go to Paris with him if he showed up with a way to get us there and if he promised to feed us when we got there.

"He called our bluff. I don't know where Leo got his

cash or how much he had, but in a couple of days he found us and told us he had tickets. Tickets on a train and tickets on a ship. Leo really wanted to be something, and he'd picked us as his ticket to the big time. He talked a lot about how we'd make lots of money and come back famous. He knew what he was doing. I don't know how, but it took him very little time to arrange everything, including passports for us. I held that passport in my hand and looked at my picture and all that fancy language." He laughed. "The picture looked like the mugshot of a punk."

He paused to chew on his burger and sip on his drink.

"Whitfield was married and decided he couldn't go. Cliff was married, too. I think that was why he wanted to go. Me and Marlowe had no ties. We were the youngest. We were more than ready to see something new."

He paused. I watched him think, his face reflecting memories. Finally, I prompted him, "So, how was Paris?"

He smiled. "Paris was truly a whole other world. We caught a train to the coast. We had to sit in the colored car. I have to hand it to Leo. He stuck by us. Brought us food from the dining car and everything. It was a little better on the ship. There were places we clearly weren't supposed to go, but I'd hitchhiked and hopped a train to New Orleans. That ship and being out on that ocean was something. It took us to a whole new world.

"Being in Paris was something out of a dream. Leo didn't speak French. I don't know what he was thinking when he decided to go there. There on the dock, it took a while, but even while we just sat with our luggage, I could tell things were different. We were right there with everybody. There was no separate water fountain. A white lady and her little girl sat right down next to me without a second glance. The little girl smiled and said something to me I could not understand. But I smiled back and her mother said something to her like mothers do, and she smiled at me, too. A white lady acting like that was as new to me as that boat ride."

The waitress took our plates. We ordered pie.

"How come I never heard this story?"

"I don't usually talk about this stuff. That was a different world, and I was a different person. Everything was different. But you wanted to hear about me and Angelique. You'll still be her lawyer after I pass. I guess you need to know this stuff."

He paused when the waitress brought our pie.

He smiled again at memories. "Leo had the heart of a crook, but he was pretty smart. He showed up with a cab driver who'd learned to speak English during the war. René was his name. Wiry little guy. Had an aunt who rented us a room. Me, Cliff, and Marlowe ended up in one room smaller than my laundry room is now. The bathroom was one flight up, and we shared it with the folks renting three other rooms. We had a bed with two mattresses. We'd toss one on the floor at night and take turns sleeping with somebody on that tiny bed or alone on the floor."

"You keep smiling, though. I'm thinking you have pretty good memories of that."

He nodded. "Yes. Yes, I do. Paris in the fifties, Sam."

"If you're going to the ballet, we'd better start walking that way, but keep telling me about Paris. It's fascinating."

I paid, and we walked toward the theater.

"We were in that room only to sleep. That was usually during the morning, maybe till just after noon. We were busy at night. At first we were just going around listening to music in basements all over what we called the triangle, the part of Paris where jazz was king. We were soaking up the newness and freedom of that scene. People in Paris hungered for music. And they weren't concerned about who was playing it or who they rubbed shoulders with while listening.

"We got to know some of the other musicians from the states. We started getting invitations to sit in. We started to make our bones. We showed them we could play. There were lots of open stage opportunities. Eventually, Leo got us some bookings. Even then we mostly earned only tips, but the tips were enough for a while.

"The blues wasn't as classy as jazz. Jazz was bigger there than in the States, but there were some places I could play the blues. There was a place, a basement, on a street named Rue Cheval. We called it Rude Shovel.

"It was called L' Étalon Noir, The Black Stallion." He laughed. "We liked that. One of its owners was a black guy from Chicago who was in the war, married a girl from Algiers, and decided to stay in France after the war. It was noisy. It had brick walls and a seven-foot tall ceiling."

Thumper was talking while we walked, and every time somebody got close he'd get quiet. Eventually, we sat down on a bench across the street from the theater. I'd given up hearing about Angelique, but the stuff he talked about fascinated me. I'd never heard about his time in Paris, even when we were pursuing his copyright infringement claim against the record company. I knew he'd spent time there but nothing about the details.

He stretched his legs out from the bench. His eyes followed people walking up the steps to the theater, but he was remembering his time in Paris over sixty years ago, back in time before my parents had been born.

Finally, he said, "We'll talk some more, but I guess I better go get my seat."

"Okay, when she gets free, you and Angelique come back to my office. Give me a call when you head that way. If I'm out, I'll get back."

He nodded.

"And," I said, "I want to hear about the rest of your time in Paris."

"Yes, you do. It was there, in L' Étalon Noir, that I met Angelique's grandmother. I'll tell you about that later if you want. Right now I've got to go."

I walked back to my office.

I BIDED MY TIME in my office waiting for Thumper and Angelique. I used the internet to read a few articles about the Paris music clubs in the fifties. I found no reference to Thumper. There were a couple of mentions of the club L' Étalon Noir. I doubted if anything I learned about Thumper and how he met Angelique's grandmother could have any bearing at all on the dead Bobby Andrus, and, even though dead and digested, Andrus had priority.

I didn't have any other pressing legal matters to attend to. I looked at a new order for a barbecue grill that came in over the internet, reviewed the customized features requested, and forwarded the information, with some instructions, to Joshua.

About twenty minutes before the ballet should end, I took a walk around the inside of the building. I went to each of its eight floors and the basement. Uncle Harlan gave me a deal on the office space so I could be his presence in the building. Although to some degree I resented Harlan tying me to another obligation, I did like the space. Closer to the courthouses than his other downtown office building, it would come in handy. Plus, I knew how much I owed Harlan for all the opportunities he'd sent my way. I could have declined the space, but I didn't. I wasn't any kind of official building manager. In fact, as far as the actual building manager knew, I was just another tenant. If Harlan wanted me as his eyes on the property, I wanted to get to know that which I was keeping an eye on. After my careful and thorough walk through, I concluded it looked like an office building, mostly hallways and doors.

Finally, with nothing productive to do, I did what I preferred. I looked up the tide tables for the bays, checked the weather forecast, and the rise and set time of the sun and the moon. I thought about where I might park my fishing boat on the bays to best encounter a school of speckled trout in the next few days.

Thumper interrupted my day dream when he opened the door to usher in Angelique.

"Lawyer man," he said in greeting, nodding at me.

"Thumper. Hi, Angelique. How was the performance?"

She had her hair in a bun tight behind her head. She wore loose cargo pants, tennis shoes, and a Houston Ballet t-shirt. She looked lithely healthy in the way of serious dancers.

"Mr. Locke, good to see you again." She held her hand out to shake mine. "The performance was good."

"Call me Sam," I said. "Now that I know you personally, I'll be watching for when you're performing so I can come see you." She smiled. "Y'all have a seat and let's talk about some things." I turned to Angelique. "I hear Thumper met your grandmother in France."

She nodded. "I had no idea who my grandparents were until not long ago. My mom died, and in her stuff was a letter addressed to me. That's how I found out."

"Your daughter?" I asked Thumper.

He shook his head as she said, "I was adopted. My

biological mom never married my dad and died when I was two. I don't remember her. I got the stuff when my adopted mom passed away."

I wanted to hear the story, but talking to them about Bobby Andrus had priority. "I want to hear all about that, but we really need to focus on the body you found in your apartment."

She nodded.

"Tell me again exactly what you saw when you walked in and exactly what you did."

"I opened the door to my apartment, and there he was. Scared the hell out of me. At first, I thought some man was sleeping on my floor. He was kind of rolled up against the wall. I freaked. I probably screamed. I slammed the door behind me and ran. I didn't know he was dead. I didn't know who he was. I didn't know what to do. I called Thumper and went down the street to a Starbucks. Thumper came. We drove back to my complex. I gave him my keys and stayed on the phone with him, ready to call nine-eleven if needed."

"You know the rest," Thumper said. "I told you. I went in, figured out he was dead, and made her leave."

She continued the story. "I called a friend. Told her they had to do some work in my apartment and went to stay with her. We'd been roommates once. I've been there ever since."

"And you saw nothing else in your apartment? Nothing about him you recognized."

Thumper interrupted, "I told you there wasn't nothing there."

I held a hand up to stop him and looked to Angelique.

"No," she said. "All I remember is seeing him laying there. There could have been a clown sitting on my sofa, and I would not have noticed. I was so freaked. I didn't see his face and have no idea who it could have been."

"We know who it was."

She sat back, looking at me expectantly.

"You know a Bobby Andrus?"

She slumped. "Oh my God. That was Bobby. How? What? I mean ... "

"I guess that's a yes."

She nodded. Tears welled up in her eyes. She took a deep breath.

"Yes. I know Bobby Andrus." She looked at Thumper. and back at me. "I used to dance in his club."

CHAPTER FIVE

THERE WAS A MASSIVE CONNECTION between Angelique and the murdered Bobby Andrus. She used to dance at a strip club he managed. And by all accounts, the Andrus brothers were not the best of people. Thumper and I were speechless for a moment.

"In Beaumont?" I asked. Dumb question.

She nodded. "I guess you know what kind of place the Andrus brothers own."

My turn to nod.

A tear rolled down her cheek. "Oh my God. I don't know why he would be in my apartment. He shouldn't have known where I lived. I haven't seen him in years. Not since the day I left the club."

"Years?" I asked. "You had to have been at least eighteen to dance."

She made a noise and shook her head. "Don't kid yourself. When I turned eighteen, I retired from topless dancing. I started when I was barely sixteen. I haven't seen him for six years. I put all that way behind me."

Complexities were developing.

Thumper reached out and put a hand on her shoulder. "I never knew that, sweetheart."

"It's nothing I wanted anybody to know about. Especially you."

"It's okay."

"Thumper, I have got to talk to her about this. There are legal reasons I need to do that in private. You go downstairs and have a cup of coffee. I'll call you in a bit, and you can bring us up a couple of cups."

He started to say something, but I looked at him and shook my head no.

He took her by her shoulders and said, "Angel, it's okay. I'm going to take care of you. Sam is going to take care of you. You tell him everything, so he can do his job."

She looked at him and nodded.

I gave him a twenty-dollar bill out of my pocket and said, "I'll call you."

He hugged her one more time and left. She turned toward me with a grim smile.

"I grew up in Lake Charles. We were really poor. My adopted dad got killed in a bar fight when I was eight. There were three other kids. My mom worked as a maid. She did laundry. She waited tables. She did all she could do. Somebody had to watch over us. The YMCA had a program we could go to after school. That's where I started dance lessons."

"They must have had an excellent program."

She smiled. "One of the volunteers at the Y was Mrs. Canderly. She is the best ballet instructor in Lake Charles. She saw something in me for which I am eternally grateful. I'm not sure of the arrangement she made with my mom, but she started teaching me at her studio. I know at least twice a week my mom spent hours cleaning the studio. I guess that's how she paid. I'd sit on the floor and do homework until I fell asleep. Maybe that's all she made mom pay. I don't know."

"I'm glad Mrs. Canderly found you."

"Me, too. She did more for me than just teach me ballet. She was all about ballet, but she made it clear to me that there would come a day when I needed more. She made sure I did well in school. She made me study. She told me I might need a scholarship someday to advance as a dancer, and I better have the grades.

"Ballet took me to another world, a world away from what I knew. After a while, there was nothing I would not do for Madame Canderly."

"I can't imagine she liked you dancing topless."

Angelique laughed. "Oh, hell no. She'd kill me today if she found out."

"Tell me about that."

She took another deep breath.

"Money was just so very hard. And I could see my mom slowly being worn to death."

She was about to cry. I handed her a tissue out of the package I carry in my briefcase. I was always prepared to take care of my clients.

"There were opportunities out there for which I had to have some money. There were classes and summer workshops. Mrs. Canderly did her best to find ways for me to go, but sometimes there was just no way. By the time I was fifteen, I knew I'd never achieve what I wanted unless I found a way to make some money. I needed money for dancing and to help my mom. She had other kids she needed to feed. My older brothers never finished high school. They went to work. It wasn't fair that I was living in this dream world. I know they wondered why I got all those special privileges."

"I hope they understand now."

"I'm not sure they do. One's dead. The other is in prison."

"I'm sorry."

She laughed and sobbed at the same time.

"That's the life I knew. It's the life I thought I'd put

behind me. Maybe not."

"We're working on figuring that out. Keep talking before Thumper loses his patience."

"I'd just turned sixteen and felt the pressure of time. I needed training. My family needed support. I couldn't work a regular job and get the ballet lessons I needed. I did some babysitting, but people in my neighborhood couldn't pay much if anything. I had a close friend at the ballet academy named Carol. She was two or three years older than me, but I considered her my closest friend. I used to catch rides from her occasionally. She knew about my money troubles. She suggested a solution.

"At first, I didn't think there was any way I could do that, but she explained how it could work in the club where she danced. She'd danced there underage. I wouldn't have to dance out in the open. Being young I could earn a lot of money just doing private dances. She told me that Bobby, the owner of the club, would make sure nothing went wrong."

She gave a short laugh and shifted in her chair.

"Turned out I could work three afternoons a week and make four or five hundred-dollars, tax-free. I could do it on days my mom was somewhere working. They were really careful with me. I looked young. If Bobby wasn't there for some reason, I couldn't work. There were days when he wouldn't let me come to work. Somehow, he knew when police would be coming."

She sat thinking for a while and then shook her head as if shedding water.

"It worked out okay. I quickly learned which customers I didn't want to dance for. The bouncers wouldn't let anything happen. I know Carol probably let a lot more go on during her private dances than I did. She certainly made a lot more money. Other, older dancers could get in trouble for refusing somebody a private dance. Not me. I got to pick and choose. They really did take care of me.

"The money helped. It helped a lot. I could pretend I was dancing in a sensual ballet and temporarily forget what I was doing. Carol made me promise every time we drove to Beaumont that I would not be seduced by the money. She constantly talked about how ballet was my calling. Sometime later, I realized she never said that about herself."

She sighed and continued, "It worked out okay until I turned eighteen. I became more valuable at eighteen."

"What happened?"

"Bobby was still nice and all. In fact, I think he kind of liked me, but when I turned eighteen, he made it clear that he wanted me dancing at night. He wanted me on the main stages. He offered to pay for me to get a boob job and pay him back over time. I told him I was a ballet dancer, and my body was perfect for a ballet dancer. He told me I was a titty dancer, not a ballet dancer. I quit right then and there. I sat in Carol's car until she got off work, and I never went back."

"That doesn't make him sound like a nice guy."

"Oh, he was nice enough about it. Just a little drunk that night. But, I knew it was time to quit. Thanks to Mrs. Canderly I had auditions for the Houston Ballet coming up. I didn't want anything to interfere with that. I never saw Bobby Andrus again."

"Never talked to him?"

"No. Nothing. I worked there, and then I didn't. I didn't even go back and pick up money they owed me. That part of my life was over and gone, and so was he. I have not even thought about him. Nothing."

She was crying quietly. "You know," she said, "maybe it

was wrong to dance like that, but if I had not made that money I would not be where I am today. There was nothing else. I tried, but I was sixteen years old and desperate. Any other job would not have given me enough time to do the ballet. I don't feel like I did anything wrong. Some guys got to look at me, or rather they got to look at Tiger. That was my dancer name. I made some survival money, and I made some money that let me work at ballet. I got out when it was time. I auditioned for the company here in Houston. I left the topless dancing off my resume, and I made it. I've never looked back with regret. I don't want people to find out because it is none of their business, and people can be judgmental and mean, but I can't regret what I did. It made things possible for me."

She'd wadded the tissue she held into a tiny ball. I took it and gave her another.

"Have you stayed in touch with anybody from the club, anybody who worked there or anybody you met there?"

"No. Nobody."

"How about Carol?"

"You know how they sell flowers in the lobby for you to send back to dancers?"

"Sure."

"Three years ago I received a bouquet. In addition to my name, the envelope was addressed to Tiger. I freaked for a moment. I thought maybe some guy recognized me from the club. But on the inside, it said 'you go girl, you made it.' Carol sent it.

"I looked for her after the show but didn't see her anywhere. By then, the phone number I had for her was no longer hers. We had not been in touch for the longest, and I've never heard from her since then. I've been back to Lake Charles and visited Mrs. Canderly's studio several times. I've done workshops there to repay some of what I owe her, but I've never seen Carol. She quit ballet at the studio about the time I left. I wasn't a very good friend. I didn't really look for her. I think she was too much a part of the topless dancing. I'm still scared people will find out. I left it as far behind as possible. I left her behind, too.

"Carol could still be dancing at the club in Beaumont or at another place. I have no idea. She supported me quitting. On the drive back home the night I quit, she told me I was special, and she knew it was time for me to quit. I told her she should quit and come with me to Houston and audition, but we both knew she would not have made it. She had a plan to teach ballet. She was good enough to teach beginners. I hope she is doing that somewhere. It's sad, but when I left, I left everything and everybody."

"So, the only connection you have with Bobby Andrus is that club?"

"Yes."

"He had at least two places. Where did you work?"

"I only know the one where I worked, Fantasy Kings."

"I need you to write down the names of everybody you can remember from the club. Employees, dancers, and patrons. Anybody you can remember related to the club."

"I'll do what I can, but dancers come and go. I was only friendly with Carol."

"Do what you can."

"Okay. I'll try."

"Along with descriptions of what they looked like. Any details you can remember."

"I don't think I'll remember anything about any of the customers, but I'll do what I can."

"Anything you can think of, especially if any of the customers seemed particularly enamored with Tiger."

She nodded.

My phone rang. It was Thumper.

"Sam, ask her if she wants juice or water. I'm about to come back up."

I shook my head. Thumper was Thumper and hadn't waited for my call. I held the phone aside, asked her, and told him to bring her a bottle of water.

I said, "Thumper couldn't wait any longer, and he's coming up. You need to know, I am your lawyer. If there's ever anything you want to tell me that you'd rather keep confidential from Thumper, you call me. I won't disclose your confidences to anybody, including him."

"Okay. Thanks. It's fine. I'm not proud of my Beaumont dancing days, but not really ashamed either, you know. He has only my best interests at heart. I don't have anything to keep secret from him."

"Okay. We'll wait for him."

It didn't take long until Thumper was kicking my door. I let him in while he juggled a couple of cups of coffee and a bottle of water.

"How'd it go?" he asked.

"Fine."

"Learn anything?"

"Thumper," she said, "I am so sorry you have to hear about what I did."

"That's okay, baby. I know all about doing what you have to do. Trust me, I've done worse. I wish I'd known you then, I'd have taken care of you."

She reached out and touched his arm. He put his hand over hers and squeezed it. He turned to me.

He said, "So, did it help? What did you learn?"

"Mostly about how strong your granddaughter is."

"That she is. Are we getting anywhere?"

"I don't know. At least we have a connection to Bobby Andrus to follow. She was just about to tell me how y'all found each other."

"I still don't understand what's so important about all that stuff."

"It's important that we figure out what's going on. Somebody in her apartment killed Andrus for some reason. It has something to do with her. You should have called the cops, probably still should." He shook his head. "But since that's not happening, yet, we have to make sure she is safe."

He nodded.

I turned to her. "Don't go back alone to your place. We have to keep you out of there and, as much as possible, out of any public place until we have some kind of resolution. We have no idea about the danger you're in, but it's obvious something is going on. Understand?"

She nodded.

"So how did y'all get together?"

Thumper said, "Why do you need to hear all about the past? She's my granddaughter. We found each other recently. Let's move on."

"Thumper, listen to me. I have no idea. I have no idea about anything that's going on. A dead man was found in her living room. That obviously involves something in her past. She's going to give me some names, so I can look for other ties. Until we have more of a path to follow, I want to know as much as possible about her, and you are a part of her. Something or somebody might come up that I wouldn't realize is important unless you talk to me about the past. Just like what happened with Bobby Andrus. We found out she knew him.

"Speaking of Andrus, Angelique, do you know his brother Landry?"

"I know who he is. He didn't come to the club much and just like the cops, Bobby didn't want me there when Landry was around. I guess they owned it together or something. I don't think Landry wanted underage dancers at the club." She paused and shook her head. "It is just so weird. I haven't seen Bobby for years. There wasn't a reason for him to know where I lived. I have no idea what he was doing there."

"We'll work on figuring that out. Meanwhile, tell me about finding Thumper."

"My biological mom died shortly after I was born, so I was adopted as a baby. My adopted parents are both black and look at me, I'm obviously mixed-race. Kids in my neighborhood made fun of me for that, and my mom explained as soon as I asked that she had not given birth to me but that she'd chosen me to be her daughter. I eventually learned that my birth dad was white."

"Like your grandmother," Thumper said.

"So," she said, "I'm pretty watered down. After my mom died about a year ago, I was the only kid still around. I had to take care of things. I found an envelope in her things addressed to me. It was a letter." Angelique took a deep, emotional breath before she could continue. "It said lots of stuff about how much she loved me and told me my biological mom's name, Rose. There wasn't anything else about my biological family."

She was talking tighter and tighter, fighting back tears. Thumper put his hand on her shoulder. She smiled at him.

"Anyway," she said, "I asked my aunt, my mom's sister, about my biological mom. She told me I should let it go, but I persisted. Turns out my aunt had an envelope, too. She had my original adoption papers. She had a photograph of my biological mom. And a picture of her parents." She smiled at Thumper. His eyes were watery.

Thumper said quietly, "I didn't even know I had a daughter until Angelique sent me a letter and a copy of that photograph."

"You found him through the photograph?" I asked.

"Yes. It had been cut from a book and then copied. The caption said that the photograph was taken at a nightclub in Paris in the fifties. It was a picture of musicians sitting on the edge of the stage. On the left was a skinny guy holding a guitar. A woman stood to his right with her hand on his shoulder. It didn't name her, but it listed the musicians' names and his was given as William Lee." She smiled at Thumper. "My aunt thumped her finger on the photo and told me, 'There, those are your grandparents and enjoy them on paper because they're dead. Nothing good came from them except for you.'

"I did some research. Turns out, not only was William Lee not dead, he is alive, known as Thumper, and he and his lawyer got some press when they went after the record company for screwing him out of royalties for a couple of decades. I sent him a fan letter. He thought I was bogus and after his cash."

"Now baby," he said, "you know that ain't true."

"You thought that might be it."

"Aw, baby … "

"How come you never told me about this?" I asked him. He'd bruised my lawyerly ego by keeping secrets.

"Wasn't nothing you needed to know. We figured it out. It was family, not legal. I called you when we needed you."

All the family history was interesting, but I could not conceive that it had anything to do with the dead Bobby

Andrus. The link to him was her underage dance career at the Andrus strip club. Maybe blackmail? And a bad falling out among those looking to blackmail her? There were too many unknowns, but we had to start somewhere, and our only clue was the Andrus connection. I didn't have a great idea, but I had some idea about how to start looking into Andrus. I was anxious to get started on that.

I made Angelique promise not to go back to her place and to stay out of public until we got a better handle on things. I assured Thumper I'd have changes to his will done in a couple of days.

To Thumper, Angelique said, "I told you, you do not have to put me in your will. That's never been what this was about."

"Ain't nobody else, baby. Better you than the Blues Society."

I declined an invitation to join them for the evening at Thumper's place. I wanted time alone to flesh out my idea about looking into Andrus. I wanted to get home.

I wish I'd been a little smarter a little sooner. Maybe we'd have made better moves. Maybe more tragedy would fhave been avoided. Maybe there would've been fewer deaths.

CHAPTER SIX

THUMPER AND ANGELIQUE left to spend the night at Thumper's house on the river. I left for my place on Galveston Island. I thought about the details of my plan to start looking into Bobby Andrus. About thirty minutes down the interstate, my phone rang. I didn't recognize the number. I answered.

"Hello, counselor, this is your client Grant Cole, have you learned anything?"

"Not enough to talk about."

"I don't really need to know unless you learn something that might come back to bite my family or me."

"I will let you know."

"Good. And, in that vein, I think somebody was watching Thumper's house just now."

"What?"

"Yeah, I went down to the grocery store a bit ago. As I was on the way out, I noticed somebody off in the brush on a motorcycle. No big deal. People ride in the woods all the time. It was too far off to see if it was somebody I know. And, frankly, I didn't have a second thought about him. Then, when I was coming back about forty-five minutes later, just past Thumper's place I noticed the motorcycle still out there. It was just a flash of chrome, but I guess I'm sensitive right now."

"Did you get a better look?"

"I tried. There's a dirt road that cuts through there,

and I did a U-turn to go back past Thumper's so I could get up that road. Just pass the back side of Thumper's place I heard the motorcycle start and take off away from me. Never got a good look. I didn't try to chase him. I'd have never caught somebody on a bike. Anyway, might be something, might not be. I wouldn't have even thought about it if Thumper hadn't brought that package to my house."

"Who knows. But better safe than sorry. Frankly, I have no clue what's going on, but given who is involved, I better get Thumper on the phone. He's headed up that way. I'll give him a call."

"Good luck. I tried calling, but he didn't answer his phone."

"I have his granddaughter's number. I'll try it."

"Let me know what's going on. Don't let me and mine get splattered by his shit."

"Talk to you later."

One of the many things I didn't know was whether the bad guys knew about Angelique's connection to Thumper and whether they might be watching Thumper's house, but I couldn't take any risks. I called Thumper's number, and it went straight to voicemail. I left a message and called Angelique.

"Hi, Mr. Locke, what's up?"

"Angelique, tell Thumper to pull off the road. I need to talk to him."

"I'm driving. I'll give him the phone."

"Hey, lawyer man."

"Thumper, y'all need to turn around and avoid your place. Somebody may be watching it."

"What?"

I told him about my call from Grant and how we

couldn't take any chances. For once he did not argue. After all, it was Angelique.

"Where do we go?"

"Do either of you have to be somewhere tomorrow?"

"No."

"Then come to my place on Galveston."

"Hold on."

I heard him tell Angelique to take an upcoming exit and turn around. She asked why but didn't argue. He told her that for safety's sake, I suggested they come to my place.

"Okay, Sam, we're on the way. Tell me how to get there."

"Get to Galveston on the interstate. Take Sixty-First Street over Offatts Bayou and turn right at the Seawall. Drive just about twenty-one point four miles toward the end of the island. You'll see my gate. It has the silhouette of fish on either side of it and a sign with my name. If you somehow get to the toll booth at the San Luis Pass, you've gone too far. I'll leave the gate open."

"Okay. What are we going to do?"

"I'm thinking on it. Let's talk about it when you get there. Meanwhile, if you see a motorcycle following along behind you, or a car for that matter, you call me, and we'll get you to the nearest police station."

"Do you really think ... "

"I don't know Thumper, but we're not taking any chances with her."

"Yeah, you're right. Hope you have a spare toothbrush I can use."

"I'll stop and get you one. Do you need anything else?"

"Nah. She's got a bag. We'll be fine."

I called Grant Cole and told him Thumper would not be returning home that night and asked him to keep an eye open for someone watching his place. He gruffly agreed.

Unknown threats by unknown persons. There weren't enough of me. I called Rocky.

"Investigations."

"Rocky, Sam. You busy?"

"Nope. Watching television, what's up?"

"It's about the case for which I had you check the security at that apartment complex. Can you come to my place in a couple of hours? I'll cook you dinner, and you can meet some folks."

"Sure. Do you want me to bring Jenny?"

"I have no clue what I'm doing, so you might as well. We might need her. I'll feed you both if you won't charge me by the hour until we start talking about what you need to do."

"Not a problem. My wife has a church deal, so we're on our own tonight."

Jenny wouldn't be a bad person to have hanging out with Angelique, backstage at the ballet if possible. Jenny was very competent. I wasn't sure what we were doing, but we were at least doing something. I called my uncle.

"Yes."

"Harlan, Sam."

"What can I do for you, Sam?"

"I'm working on a case and need to do some investigation. I need an excuse to make some inquiries."

"What do you need me to do?"

"I want to talk to some folks and make them think I'm trying to sell some property. I thought you probably have some I could pretend to be brokering."

"Pretend all you want. As long as nothing comes back on me or any of the people I do business with."

"It won't come back on you. I just need to know if you

have some property around Houston I could say I'm brokering."

"I'll leave a message with Rosalind to give you a list of everything I have for sale. If you have any questions, she'll get you an answer. You don't have to pretend. Sell something, and I'll give you a commission."

"Okay, thanks. I'll talk to Rosalind tomorrow."

"Okay." He hung up. I like that. No questions. No curiosity. Just a complete trust I would never abuse.

I made the drive home down the highway to Galveston. I travelled against the heaviest traffic flow. That meant on the other side of the highway there were stretches of bumper to bumper traffic dead stopped while, on my side, the bumper to bumper traffic moved mostly at highway speeds. The collective consciousness of Houston did not believe in driving the speed limit or slower unless mandated by the laws of physics.

On the Island, I stopped at a grocery store to buy some fresh vegetables for the grill and a toothbrush for Thumper. At my house, I left the gate open for everybody making their way there.

I felt disconnected that summer, alone without any closeness to other people. You would never have guessed that from the crowd hanging out at my place as I drove up.

Preacher and Joshua were playing a loose game of one-on-one basketball, the bulky looking Preacher holding his own against the teenager. Preacher moved his beefy self with surprising grace and vigor.

Darla and Gretchen, Preacher's friend or assistant or congregant or whatever she was, were sitting cross-legged on the porch, leaning toward each other talking about something. Behind me, Rocky's car turned off the highway and followed me up the drive. He had Jenny with him.

The flatbed trailer held a dozen barbecue grills, wrapped in plastic and ready for delivery to a couple of my retailers. Over to the side, three custom ordered barbecue grills were crated, waiting for pick-up by a shipping company. Joshua would deliver the grills off the flatbed when I handed over the keys to my truck. All those grills represented a lot of work, more and more of it done by Joshua, and a lot of revenue.

It was getting harder for me to find the time to make deliveries to retailers. And it was more and more an inconvenience to give up my Range Rover to Joshua to do so. My fishing truck worked but didn't project the best image for the business. It mostly traveled up and down the beach, and it looked like a beach tramp. I needed to buy a truck for the business. I should probably get a custom paint job on it to advertise the grills.

The market considered the grills and smokers we built to be high-end products. I sold as many as we made. With a truck, Joshua could drive to more distant markets, and I could expand my market. All the barbecue cook-off shows on television increased orders for custom built and very nicely priced grills and smokers. Business was booming.

I had not spent a day fishing in a while.

My lover Cecilia called the week before, and I'd been too busy to spend time with her.

Life was getting way too complicated. I had to either back-off somewhere and slow down, or I needed to expand in a serious way. I needed to hire somebody to sit in the office downtown and take on some of the paperwork. I needed to consider hiring another welder. I needed to obligate myself to file more government forms. The pressure was tremendous to get tied down even more.

Everyone stopped what they were doing and looked at

me sitting in my car pondering life. Thumper and Angelique would arrive soon. I needed more food.

"Hey everybody," I said, getting out of my truck. "A couple of more people are coming for dinner. Are you all staying?"

"Yes, we are," Preacher said.

Joshua shrugged and said, "Sure, if it's okay."

"Then we'll need more food."

Preacher said, "Gretchen is a vegetarian."

I looked her way. "I'll be grilling vegetables. Is that okay?" She nodded.

"I have enough fish and shrimp. Somebody needs to go buy more veggies."

"I'll go," Joshua said.

"No. Gretchen and I will go." That was from Darla as she got up from the porch, dusting off her butt and coming down the stairs. Gretchen nodded and followed her.

I gave Darla money and told her to get some vegetables to grill. "Get some portobello mushrooms. You'll have to go all the way into Galveston for those. You can take my car."

She turned to Gretchen and asked, "Do you know what those are?" Gretchen nodded, and Darla said, "Got it."

"Hey, Rocky, we need to have a meeting. Let's go down to the pier."

He nodded. He glanced toward Jenny and raised his eyebrows. I shook my head no. We'd fill her in after we had a chance to talk.

As we walked down toward the pier, he said, "I have the feeling this is one of those meetings where I shouldn't be making any written notes."

"Yes. There are things we have to keep very confidential to protect the interests of our clients."

"I assume our client is Ms. Chambray and it has

something to do about something that happened at her apartment."

"Yes."

We settled on a couple of deck chairs, and I told him about Angelique finding Bobby Andrus dead on her floor, how our other client, Thumper and our new client Marcus Cole put him on ice, and how our other new client Grant Cole chopped him up to share with the alligators in his backyard. And, "Oh, by the way, Angelique used to dance topless at an Andrus club, and Thumper is Angelique's grandfather."

Rocky looked at me without saying a word for some time. Finally, he said, "Are you kidding me?"

I smiled.

He said, "I assume you know who Andrus is, or rather, who his brother is."

"Somewhat. I'm learning."

"You've got a big mess. This could be worse than the last big mess you dragged me into."

The heron that hangs out close to the pier glided in from the east, landing to make its nightly dinner stroll. Rocky watched it intently.

He took a deep breath, turned his head toward me, smiled without meaning it, and said, "Okay. I'll keep this conversation very confidential, but before I agree to do more, what's the plan?"

"Keep all our clients safe. In order to do that, I think we'll have to figure out something about what's going on."

He nodded and watched the heron. "My rates just went up. If Jenny is going to be involved, she has to know everything."

"I agree. When we get up there, take her into the house and fill her in. I want to keep it as quiet as possible until we know what's going on. So far, on our side, you, me, Thumper, Angelique, and the Cole brothers are the only ones who know what's happened."

He smiled a real smile. "And Sampson the alligator."

"Well, yeah, there's Sampson. I'm trusting Grant Cole when he says nobody is going to find out what happened to the body."

"This thing is going to rapidly become a cluster-fuck."

"That's why I need to get out in front of it."

"One of these days you need to limit your practice to simple divorces between nice people."

"No fun in that."

We talked for a while without coming up with any great idea. Citronella torches and burning charcoal scented the breeze.

"Let's go back up and enjoy some food," I said.

"I'm going to tell Jenny first thing so she'll know what's going on."

"Just impress on her the need to be quiet."

"You don't have to worry about her. I'd probably break under torture before her."

Joshua and Darla stood side by side at the table by the grill. He was slicing vegetables under her watchful eye. She stuffed flounder fillets with crab and wrapped each filet in foil under his watchful eye.

I smiled at Joshua's domestication. "Darla, you're doing a good job of taming that boy."

"Yes, yes I am."

"Hey, now," he said, "just who is teaching who how to stuff flounder for the grill?"

She smiled, blew him a kiss, and bumped her hip against his. He blushed. They were so darn cute.

"Don't you take him away from me," I said.

"Nope. We have a plan. He's going to teach me to weld, and I'm going to go to work for you."

Preacher stood over the fire. Gretchen sat on the porch steps, strumming a guitar. The shape of the evening was forming nicely. Everybody but me had a special friend or family member there. I thought of some I wished were there with me and felt that lonely pang, but it was a very good gathering of people I cared for a lot. Thumper and Angelique arrived. I introduced them to everybody.

Rocky called out to Jenny and gestured toward the house.

"Put me on the clock," I said.

"Dinner will cover tonight."

"Hey Thumper, I bought you a toothbrush. Let's get the rest of your stuff, and I'll show you where you and Angelique are sleeping."

A few minutes after we'd dropped their bags in my two guest rooms, Jenny came out to get Angelique. When nobody was watching, Jenny looked at me, made a face, silently mouthed an exaggerated "wow" and grinned big as she gave me a thumbs up. The two of them went back into the house.

I poured myself a glass of whiskey, stood on the porch and looked out over the yard. Darla and Joshua took on all the cooking chores. He spread the coals while Darla stayed close. There were a lot of hip bumps and laughter between them. Preacher chaperoned them. Thumper brought out his guitar, and he and Gretchen were talking and playing. Unformed melodies and mutual chords could be heard as they got to know each other. I wondered if Gretchen had any idea about the man with whom she was making music.

Rocky joined me on the porch.

"Well," he said, "they're talking about what to do.

Angelique is on a month to month lease where she is now, and she's going to find a new place. I think we need to make sure the new place doesn't go into her name until we figure out what's happening."

"True. We'll do something about that. She'll also need to keep the apartment she has until we find out what's going on. I don't know if a good forensic search of her place would help, but I'm reluctant to destroy that crime scene any more than we have to in order to protect her."

"I could do some things. Look for fingerprints and stuff like that. You need to think about finding a way to get the police safely involved. We are, once again, going way out on a limb here."

"I know. And believe me, I really appreciate what you are doing."

"She'll need to get her clothes and stuff. I'll go and make sure we disturb things as little as possible and take a look around her place."

"Good."

"Jenny will be hanging out with her. I'm going to charge you a daily rate for her to do that. Angelique says she can get her backstage at the theater during rehearsals and performances. Jenny will do a good job watching out for her."

I nodded.

He continued. "Looks like they are hitting it off. From the way they're talking, Jenny might become her permanent roommate. If she does, I won't charge you for weekends." He shook his head.

"It's funny, Rocky."

"What?"

"You have no problem with Jenny being exposed to the danger of being a bodyguard, but you have issues with her moving out on her own."

"Yeah, well, I know she's very competent and can take care of herself, but she's mostly like my kid."

He was quiet for a moment, sipping his beer and looking out over my yard. He laughed at how the goats on the property next door gathered at the fence to watch the things going on.

"And," he said, "I know one of the reasons she wants to move out is to make it easier to get laid."

I'd just taken a sip of whiskey. When I laughed, it went up my nose and burned. I waved toward Darla and Joshua working at the grill, standing close enough to touch each other. "Ah, Rocky, the children, they're all growing up, aren't they."

He made a noise.

Dinner was good. Good food. Good laughter. It was a good thing so many people showed up unexpectedly. It kept us from worrying and talking about things we did not know enough about to do anything but worry.

After dinner, Joshua and Darla wanted to do the clean-up. The rest of us walked out on the pier to watch the sunset. The sun back-lit the clouds and fringed them with gold. The sun and breeze made the grass on the flats a dancing wave of greens and yellows. It was an hour before low tide, and predators feeding on prey washed from the flats rippled the surface of the bay, causing it to shimmer with the colors of the sky.

Later, Thumper, accompanied by Gretchen, entertained us with a few songs. On one, making allowances for the rough wood of my porch and the tennis shoes she wore, Angelique danced. It was the best evening of the summer. Those who were leaving departed with hugs and laughter.

The three of us sleeping at my place relaxed for a while in my living room.

Thumper said, "This was good Sam. Thanks for having us down. I should have come before. I feel like things are changing for the good and are just going to get better."

"Hope so," I said.

I didn't know just how that night, but things were certainly about to change.

CHAPTER SEVEN

O N MONDAY MORNING, Angelique left early to meet up with Rocky and Jenny to find a place to live. Thumper and I would go in later and, if needed, I'd drive him all the way to his place. I spent some office time changing Thumper's will to leave everything to Angelique. I printed it out and put it in a folder, so we could take it with us and get Rocky and Jenny to witness his signature. I started making notes about what needed to be done for his business interests because of his new heir.

At nine I received a call from Rosalind, the legal assistant to Harlan's lawyer.

"Mr. Locke, I have a list of all property available for sale by Harlan. Do you want me to email it to you?"

"Yes, please. Thanks."

"Is there anything else?"

"Are there any promotional materials available for the properties?"

"Yes. I have copies, but if you want any, we'd need to get them from the real estate agent. He's in our building."

"Okay. Thanks."

"Yes, sir. Let me know if I can do anything to assist you in your mysterious legal practice."

"Thank you, Rosalind. What would any of us do without you?"

"Much more poorly, I'm sure. Have a nice day."

I printed out the list of property, found a map of

Houston, and started highlighting properties that would serve my purpose. A Houston ordinance governed where a sexually oriented business, like a topless bar, could locate. It had to be at least fifteen hundred feet from property used for certain other uses, such as schools, parks, and churches. I didn't have to do the type of due diligence I'd do if I was actually finding property for a real client. I just needed enough to look real.

I marked a few of the property descriptions as suitable. Printed in the corner of the property lists was the logo of a real estate firm, Tillson Commercial Property, and the name of an agent, James Smith. I recognized the name. It was on a discreet sign in the lobby of the building in which I had my new office as the person to call to rent space in the building.

I called Rosalind again and asked her to call the agent and get whatever detailed descriptions and photos were available for three of the available tracts. She agreed to have them in her office sometime that afternoon.

She said, "What are you up to now, Mr. Locke?"

"You really don't want to know."

Joshua and Darla showed up about ten. I wanted to hang on to my Range Rover, so we hooked up the trailer of grills to my pick-up. He would stick around and wait for the freight company coming to pick-up the custom orders. Thumper and I headed for Houston.

Just as we drove onto the mainland, Rocky called.

"Sam, we came by Angelique's apartment so she could pick up some things. Somebody broke in. Her door's been jimmied."

"Did you go in?"

"I went in and looked around quickly, but we got out of there so I could call and see what you want to do."

My mind raced. Was this related to the dead guy? Chances were. I briefly wondered what they thought when their friend was not there. It also raised a question I felt terribly stupid about not thinking about before. How had the dead guy got into her apartment without breaking in? Was that the house key Grant found?

It was an opportunity to get a police investigation started. It wouldn't be much, but not much was more than we had going, and it might be handy if things heated up. Or really bad, if it became known there was a missing body.

"Take her back. Have her look around to see if anything is missing. Ask her if anybody else had keys. It wasn't broken into the first time. Do you think you can learn anything about the break-in?"

"Doubtful. The door-jam is broken. The door was held shut with a piece of duct tape."

"You didn't leave your prints on it did you?" There was silence until my brain caught up with my mouth. "Of course you didn't. Sorry."

"I'll look closer, but I don't expect to find anything. Cops won't do much unless we tell them about the body."

"We're not going to do that, but we'll call them. At least they can preserve the tape as evidence. And, she can go on record as having a problem."

"Do you want me there when the cops arrive?"

"No. Stay with the girls to look around and then get out of there. Have Angelique call the police. When the police show up, Jenny can stay with her as her new room-mate. You might be a distraction. I assume the police will take the tape as evidence. If they don't, you will."

"Okay. I'll look around outside while the police are here."

"Good. It's going to take us a while to get there in

traffic. I'll call you when we get close."

"I bet we don't even get a cop here for an hour. Maybe longer this time of day. Want her to give them your name?"

I had to think on that and decided it might save time to have my name on record if something happened.

"Yeah. If it comes up naturally. Can't see how it would hurt. Might as well. She should just make it sound like I represent her in everything and have for a while."

"Got it."

I wondered if Angelique could reliably play the part we were asking for, but things had to move at a speed that precluded rehearsal. I had no choice but to trust her to talk to the cops and not let on about the demise of Bobby Andrus.

It did no good to assume the second break-in was nothing more than a coincidence. Did the bad guys wait to find out what would happen after the discovery of the dead guy? If so, it must have driven them nuts to hear nothing. Perhaps they broke in to check if he was still there. I kind of hoped so. Surprise.

Maybe they broke in looking for something they didn't find the first time. Maybe they didn't find it because Andrus getting killed was not a part of the plan and they left before they found what they came after. Maybe they broke in looking for Angelique and came back because they missed her the first time.

I knew only one thing for sure, I had no idea what was going on. Maybe the latest break-in would lead to new threads to tug on. Maybe it was a coincidence, and I needed to be careful not to let it be a distraction. I felt this thing, whatever it was, growing more out of hand every moment. We had to get ahead of it before we couldn't catch up.

"Sam? What's going on?" Thumper asked.

I told him what had happened.

"What do you think? Was it whoever left Andrus there? Are they after Angelique? What do you think is going on?"

"Thumper, I have no idea."

He slumped back against the seat. "Well, it's a good thing we got her out of there."

"Yes. That's one thing I am sure about."

He was quiet a few moments. "I'll get you some more money, Sam."

"I appreciate the thought, but I'll bill you when necessary. More money cannot make me work any harder."

"You let me know, Sam. You have to protect her."

I heard the fear in his voice. Never before did he sound like he depended on me. His life was about self-reliance. This thing shook him. I looked at him and realized he'd lost all the cockiness. Suddenly, he looked real old.

For a while, I drove Houston style. I changed lanes aggressively to gain a few feet. I squeezed out anybody trying to get in front of me. I drove too fast and too close for the crowded highway. I clenched the steering wheel, driving with one foot on the gas pedal and one foot on the brake. It didn't really help me move any faster. I have a fear that when the time comes for my heart attack, I will be in an ambulance caught in Houston rush-hour traffic. It will be a frustratingly crappy way to die.

Eventually, I was able to get into the commuter lane. It was crowded, but faster. Plus, it was one lane and lined with concrete barriers. As long as I could drive straight, I didn't have to worry about being hit from the side.

It took us a little over an hour after the phone call to get close to Angelique's apartment in west Houston. I called Rocky's phone. He said the police had come and gone. He was walking around the apartment complex. The girls were at the apartment. I called Jenny.

"Hi Sam. Rocky is busy being a detective."

"Yep, I talked to him. What's going on?"

"It took the cops forever to get here. They took a report. They told Angelique she could come down to the police station and get a copy for insurance purposes if she finds anything missing. They left."

"Did they take the tape off the door?"

"Yeah, but only because I insisted. They did put it in an evidence bag. They were polite about it and all, but they are not going to investigate. I doubt if they even process it for prints. They told Angelique, who is really cool by the way, to let them know if she discovers anything missing because that's how they usually catch any of the burglars they do catch. They get caught at the pawn shop or trying to sell something online."

"Okay, I'm at the gate. Buzz us in."

"Okay, hold on a second."

The gate rattled open. Thumper directed me to Angelique's apartment. We parked in the closest guest parking spot and walked to her place.

Jenny stood outside the apartment talking to a man. The splintered door frame had an inch wide gouge marks where somebody forced it open.

Jenny greeted us, stepped inside with us, and said, "Some neighbors are really friendly now that something's happened. Can you believe that guy out there is hitting on me, and he doesn't even know my name? I'm talking to anybody I see, but so far nobody saw a thing. Rocky is out there somewhere. They don't record the video from their security cameras, and what's that about? What good are they? Okay, let me get back outside in case somebody comes along who has something to contribute."

Angelique walked in from another room. Thumper went to her and hugged her.

"Angelique," I said, "did you find anything missing?"

Her voice shook. "Maybe a little cash. Not much. I can tell that drawers have been gone through. Paper is all over the floor. Nothing important, bills and stuff like that from the desk. I don't know if they took anything. I didn't have anything important. That's the worse thing they did." She pointed at her flat-screen television.

I hadn't noticed before, but there was a large kitchen knife in the middle of the screen. The knife had been pushed all the way through and into the wall. There was a large kitchen spoon jammed into her DVD player.

I shook my head at the senseless destruction and said, "That's just mean."

"That's what the cop said. He shook his head and told me to come down to the police station to get a copy of the police report for my insurance company."

"This is weird. It doesn't make any sense."

"Like a dead guy in my living room makes sense. What is going on?" Her voice broke.

Thumper put his arm around her. "Don't you worry baby. Sam and I are gonna figure this thing out and take care of you."

She turned her face into him. Her shoulders shook as she sobbed through deep breaths.

Rocky came in and stood by me, looking at the speared television.

"Look at that, Sam. That knife goes clear into the wall."

Rocky gestured with his head toward the door.

"I'll be back. Rocky and I are going to go talk to the front office."

Outside, the guy was still talking to Jenny. That earned him a scowl from Rocky, which earned Rocky a grin from Jenny.

Rocky said, "No real reason to go talk to the front office. They're useless. But, let me show you something."

We walked through the parking lot toward the perimeter of the property.

"I talked to her," he said. "She had her purse stolen in a grocery store a few months ago. She didn't replace her locks. She just started using her spare key. If that was them, they've been planning this a while."

"That was probably the key in the dead guy's pocket."

"The security at this complex sucks. Not recording their security cameras is being cheap. They don't even monitor the feeds. They're there to impress potential tenants and that's all. Worse than that is their dumpster." He gestured at a trash dumpster we were walking toward.

"When you put your dumpster right next to your fence, you might as well call it a ladder. It's not hard to climb over one of these fences anyway, but they make it as easy as possible."

"Did you find something?"

"Yeah. I bet this is how they came over the fence just in case somebody was actually looking at the video feed. Which they weren't. Let me show you."

An eight-foot-tall wrought iron fence separated Angelique's apartment complex from the adjacent one. Spikes topped the fence. The spikes might have discouraged a person from trying to climb the fence if they had been sharp instead of topped with balls to assure no one could be hurt by one and sue. Instead, the tops of the spikes made terrific handholds.

The fence was right next to the curb of the parking lot

where we stood. The dumpster was pushed up to the curb. On the other side, a bed of dense vines bordered the fence separating it from parking spaces. Rocky gestured at the bed on the other side of the fence.

"Look," he said, "you can see where somebody drove a vehicle over the curb right here." Tire tracks could be seen in the crushed vines. "He drove up here and stood on his vehicle to get over the fence. The dumpster makes it easy on this side."

"I wonder if they have security cameras in that complex?"

"Sure, as useful as the ones over here and their gate stays open."

"I guess you can't tell much from the tracks."

"No. I can't get a tire impression off the vines, and there aren't any marks on the curb. I measured the width, but it won't tell us anything. It's wider than most small cars and more narrow than the really huge SUVs. About all I can really do is rule out a motorcycle."

I looked up at the apartments lining the parking lot. Those on the lower floors had small fenced areas enclosing a patio. The two upper floors had balconies. On one of the balconies stood a woman wearing surgical scrubs. She motioned us closer.

"Are y'all the police?"

"Wallace Rockwell, ma'am. I'm a detective."

"Hang on," she said, "I'll come down."

"What if she asks for your badge number?" I asked. Rocky shrugged.

In a moment she exited the walkway leading from the parking lot to the other side of the buildings. She wore purple surgical scrubs from head to toe and bright white tennis shoes. A Houston Medical Center name badge labeled her as Page.

She walked up to us and said, "Hi. Are y'all investigating something? I saw a couple of guys jump the fence at the dumpster last night."

Rocky, sounding like a cop, responded, "Yes, ma'am. We are. There was a break-in last night. May I have your name?"

"Betty Anne Page. Yes, I know. I can't believe my parents named me Betty Page, but they did."

Rocky had a notepad out making notes. "Ms. Page, what exactly did you see and when?"

"I worked a double shift and had to stay late, so I got off a little after midnight. I stopped and got a coffee on the way home, so it was probably about one when I pulled into the parking lot. When I turned down this way to park, my headlights lit up a couple of guys climbing over the fence."

"Into your lot or leaving?"

"They were leaving. Otherwise, I'd have stopped right there, turned around and left myself. One guy, the big one, was already over the fence and standing in the back of the pick-up that was backed up to the fence. The other guy, the smaller one, was just climbing over the fence. He stopped and looked my way. He looked Hispanic, Mexican or something. He didn't hesitate long. He jumped over the fence. They got in the pickup and sped off away from me without turning on their lights. I tried, but with the fence and it being dark, I couldn't see the license plate."

"You're a big help. Can you describe them at all?"

"Like I said, one looked big to me. You know, bigger than the average guy. Not fat, but kind of like a big football player or something. I didn't see him very good because as soon as my lights hit them he was climbing out of the back of the pickup going away from me. I think maybe he had light-colored hair. It wasn't long. My memory is just that his hair was light-colored like the clothes he wore. Khaki from head to toe. Long sleeved shirt.

"The other guy was skinny and kind of small. Hispanic, I'm sure. He was wearing jeans and a dark t-shirt. He looked at me once, but I can't give you any better description, and I don't think I'd recognize him again. He was over the fence like a rabbit and jumping in the pickup on my side as it started to drive away. That's really all I can tell you about them."

"That's great Ms. Page. It's a lot more than we had before. There have been a couple of break-ins. We're looking for any information."

"A couple? I hate this place. But the price is right. Am I safe? Is my stuff safe?"

"The break-ins are directed at one person, most likely a domestic situation where she's the target. She's moving out today."

"An ex, huh? I know about those. You tell her to come find me if she wants me to help kick his ass."

"What about their truck? What can you tell me about their truck?"

"Not much. It was dark, the truck I mean. Maybe a dark brown? I don't know enough about pickup trucks to tell you anything about it. Maybe if I'd seen the back of it where they put Ford or Chevrolet on the tailgate. But when they zoomed off, they didn't stop to raise the tailgate. It had some kind of sticker in the back window. I saw it flash in the light, but I couldn't tell you what kind. And there was something in the back of the truck. Something bulky. I could just see a dim outline of something. I was afraid it would fall out when they bounced over the speed bumps."

"Was the sticker to the side or in the middle?"

"In the middle. That I can tell you."

"You've been a big help, the only witness we've found so far. Thanks. Can I get your phone number just in case? I doubt if I'll need to call, but you never know."

She gave him her phone number, and he wrote it down.

"And," he said, "here's my card with my phone number."

He gave her a card. She looked at it and said, "You're not a policeman?"

"No ma'am. I am a private detective assisting the young lady targeted by this break-in. I know she appreciates you helping me out. If you see anything or if any of your neighbors mention seeing something, please give me a call."

"I guess that's okay. I thought you were a cop. But okay. I don't know any of my neighbors, but I'll ask anybody I happen to see if they saw anything."

She made her way back into the interior of the complex.

"Well," I said, "that was better than nothing."

"You bet it was. We have a whole lot more than we did before. Maybe there are others. I'm going to put up some notes somewhere, probably in their laundry room and by their mailboxes, asking for anybody who saw something strange to call. I'll give Jenny a burner phone to take the calls. Now that we know a little about what happened, I'll say there was a break-in and somebody saw these two guys climbing the fence and ask if anybody else saw anything."

"Sounds good."

Angelique and Jenny had filled a couple of suitcases with clothes and a smaller bag with all the paper that had been scattered about.

"Anything missing?" I asked Angelique.

"I don't think so. Not other than the forty or so dollars I had loose in my nightstand. What were they doing?"

"I don't know. Maybe they think you have something they want. Where do you keep important papers?"

"Some in a safe-deposit box, some in my locker at the studio, and some in a locked box in the trunk of my car. I've never trusted the security of any apartment I've lived in."

"That's probably smart. Think about it. See if you can come up with any ideas about why somebody might think you have something worth stealing. Especially ideas related to your job in Beaumont. I'm going there tomorrow. Get me that list of people you worked with there. If you don't remember their names, write a description."

She nodded. "I'll do that tonight." Her shoulders slumped. A look of weariness came over her. "I don't even know where I'm supposed to sleep tonight. I'm not staying here. At your place Thumper?"

I answered before he could. "No. We're putting you and Jenny up in a hotel until you have time to find a new place. We're going to make sure your name does not appear on the hotel registry or the lease of a new place when you find it. In fact, now that I think about it, we better put Thumper up somewhere, too, until we have a better idea about what's going on."

I called a suites hotel and arranged for a two bedroom suite for a week. I mentioned I was a lawyer needing a place for some witnesses in town for a trial. I made it in my name, gave the place my credit card information, and let them know Jenny would be picking up the keys.

"Take care not to be followed," I said, as they moved Jenny's and Thumper's small bags to Angelique's car.

Jenny smiled, patted her bag, winked at me, and said, "I got this, boss. We'll be good and safe."

A maintenance man showed up with a new door to put on the apartment. Rocky said he'd stay until the place was secure. Before I left, he asked me, "What is your plan exactly? When you go to Beaumont?"

I explained to him how I intended to carefully ask about Bobby Andrus.

"That was my only plan originally," I said, "but now I'll be looking for a big khaki guy, a small Hispanic guy, and a dark-colored pickup with a sticker in the window and ivy caught in its bumper."

"You be careful. This thing is heating up in ways we don't understand. I should go with you."

"I thought about that. It is heating up. That makes it all the more important for us to not show up at the same place together. I'm going to make myself known. It might be to our benefit for you to remain incognito."

We discussed it and made a plan.

For the longest, Preacher did not have a phone. Finally, I'd given him one and added it to my cell phone plan. Getting him on it is a random thing. Often, one of his flock answers. I consider it a minor miracle the phone has not yet disappeared. This time, while driving toward my place, I called Preacher, and he actually answered. I asked if he was free the next day because I wanted to hire him to accompany me to Beaumont for the day. I told him I'd fill him in on the drive. He agreed, said he might as well sleep at my place, and he'd see me there. I told him to bring his dress-up clothes, including socks and shoes.

The next day Rocky would stop at the club a couple of hours before we intended to show up, have a beer, and look around. He'd meet us somewhere and brief us. Preacher would go in before me and sit by himself. I'd go in and do what I intended to do. If things got out of hand somehow,

Preacher would leave, call Rocky, who would be nearby, and the cops if necessary.

Things were getting complicated. We were investigating things we knew little about and preparing for the unknown. Hopefully, better than the unknown forces were preparing for us.

CHAPTER EIGHT

As I APPROACHED THE GATE to my property, Rocky texted me the number of the cell phone he'd given to Jenny. His text message said he was putting up notices in laundry rooms at the apartment complex, soliciting calls for information about the guys who climbed the fence or the pick-up truck they were in. I stored Jenny's new number in my cell phone.

Joshua and Darla were not back from delivering the grills. It surprised me to feel a little let down to be met only by my goats, even if it was a noisy, enthusiastic greeting. The gathering of friends the night before had been special, but, usually, I enjoy my alone time.

That night, a restlessness distracted me. I couldn't think of a thing I needed to do right then other than paperwork, and I was not in the mood for that. I checked the tide tables and confirmed that low tide would be a little after ten that night. That meant there would be a good outgoing tidal flow a little before sunset making it a good time to fish off my pier. Fishing would be a good thing, an organized calm removed from the chaotic unknown of Angelique's situation.

I hit the switch to start water circulating in the fish and bait wells down on the pier, grabbed a bait bucket, and drove back toward Galveston to buy some shrimp. The closest bait camp to my place flew white flags meaning it had live shrimp.

Back at the house, I changed into a t-shirt, soft jeans, and an old pair of boat shoes. I walked out with a couple of fishing rods and a small tackle box just as Joshua and Darla drove up in the pickup pulling the empty trailer. He swung the truck around to park, and on the back of the trailer, feet dangling, sat Preacher. He wore a Hawaiian shirt with huge red blossoms over a bright yellow background. The bag slung over his shoulder looked like a cheap Indian blanket. He waved and jumped off the trailer.

Holding up his bag, he said, "I caught a ride at the gate. I brought my undercover clothes. About to go fishing?"

"Yep, grab a rod if you want. And whatever you want to drink. I'm going to help Joshua park the trailer."

Joshua didn't need help. He was backing the trailer into its spot while Darla stood behind him signaling directions. He got it parked and jumped out of the cab.

"How did it go?" I asked.

"No problems. We got it done. The guy at Hardesty Hardware over in Lake Jackson wants more. He was our first delivery. He asked if there was any way I could give him a couple extra. He'd sold all he had. He said he'd give you a call."

"Good. You should start taking those orders. We'll talk about it and set some guidelines for how many new orders we can handle."

By the time he and I walked back to where we could unhook the trailer Darla almost had it done.

"Hi, Mr. Locke. That was fun. Thanks for letting me go."

"No problem. I'm sure Joshua enjoyed the company."

She smiled, and Joshua bent to help her. She bumped her hip against him. He bumped her back. I shook my head at the teenage mating dance. She glanced back at me ando whispered something to Joshua. He shook his head. I read her lips when she whispered to him again, "Ask him."

He stood up, blushing. "Sam, uh, I've been wondering. You don't really use the office in the shop very much, right?"

"True."

When I'd built the shop, I thought I'd be building barbecue grills full-time. I'd added a spacious office across the back wall of the shop. It was insulated with a window on the shop side and a couple on the back wall that look outside. It had air-conditioning. It had its own shower, fridge, and stove. There was a door that gave access to the shop's restroom where there was another shower. A desk and an old sofa were in there, but they were not much used. I'd thought I'd be working in there, meeting suppliers or customers, but I used the office in my house, and I held meetings on the porch. I used the shower on particularly dirty days and occasionally used the stove. I had an idea what was coming and realized maybe Joshua and Darla used the sofa for other things.

"Well, uh, it's like this, Darla and I ... we're ... uh ... we're going to find us a place together, and I thought maybe we could fix that office up into kind of an apartment."

"Y'all are going to move in together?"

They both nodded. Even Darla was blushing now.

I thought about things. They weren't my kids. They were good together. They were not going to stop anything they were doing with each other.

"Have you informed your folks about your plans?"

"I have," Joshua said, "I got a little of what you would expect, but my folks understand. You pay me enough to pay rent and I've saved a bunch. So they kind of think it is okay."

"My mom won't care," Darla said.

I didn't know much about Darla's life, but that sounded more complicated than I cared to know about.

"Darla, how old are you?"

"Eighteen."

"Promise?"

"I swear. I'll show you my driver's license."

"No. That's okay."

Joshua was nineteen. They were both legally entitled to make some adult decisions.

There was something to be said for having Joshua living on my property. I certainly seemed to be spending more and more time other places. I thought the office could legally be converted to rentable space. They were both signed up to take college classes in the fall. That was something Darla got Joshua to do. Maybe they would study together, maybe even something more than biology.

"Okay, we'll get it fixed up. Darla, you tell your mom. Y'all will sign a rental agreement for lots of reasons, and you'll pay me some kind of rent. Not much, but some." Enough, I thought, to pay the increase in the cost of my insurance and utilities.

Darla smiled huge. Joshua grinned. They bumped hips.

"Thanks, Mr. Locke," she said. Joshua nodded. They bumped hips again.

They turned and headed for the shop, anxious to look at their space. "Wait," I said. "I've been thinking. Darla, you've been a big help to us around here. Do you want to go to work for me, doing what you've been doing, maybe helping out with the record keeping? Keep learning, and eventually, you can help with the welding."

"Are you kidding? Yes. Yes. Yes. That would be great."

"Okay, we'll set it up. Part-time at first until we figure out what you're going to do and how long it will take for you to do it."

"Thanks, Mr. Locke. Thank you so much. One more thing."

"What's that?"

"Can I bring my cat? She won't be any trouble."

"Sure. Bring your cat."

She hugged me. She hugged Joshua. He actually picked her up and swung her around. They danced into the shop with arms around each other. I felt happy for them. And sad. Watching them made me realize how long it had been since I'd had a relationship with a woman like that, ignorant of the things life will do to you.

I shook that feeling off as much as I could and headed to the pier. Preacher joined me on the walk.

"So," he asked, "what are we doing in Beaumont?"

"Well, I hope it doesn't offend you or cause you problems, but I need you to sit in a topless bar for an hour or so and watch my back."

"I'm supposed to go to a topless bar and watch your back? Sounds wacky."

"I don't want to tell you everything, yet, but I have a client ... "

"That dancer. Angelique."

"Yes. She's had some unusual trouble and we don't know why. We've traced one of the guys giving her trouble to the bar we're going to, and I'm going to try to ask some questions about him without causing too much trouble. I need you to go in a little before me. Just sit there, order a beer, pretend you're a regular person. If you see me getting dragged out into the alley, you call Rocky, who will be close by, and then you call the cops. That's all. In the bar, you won't know me. I'm going to pay you to make you officially one of my investigators."

"Sounds easy enough. You don't have to pay me."

"Well, if things go really bad, you working for me covers you with the attorney-client privilege, so I'll pay you. You can use the money for some of your good works."

He nodded.

"And, Preacher, when we're there, don't attract attention to yourself. Be like a normal guy."

He smiled. "Hey. I am normal. I'm not sure about the guys who spend time in those places, but I'll be good. I won't try to preach or baptize anybody who doesn't ask for it."

"Okay. Seriously. I want to get in and out without attracting attention. There are some bad people involved."

"I hope it goes better than last time you had me working with you."

"Hey, you brought that case to me. And, yes, I don't want that kind of trouble. That's why you need to just sit there and watch out for me. Do not get involved, no matter what."

"Sure. Let's fish."

I put the bait shrimp into the live well gently. Shrimp have a tendency to die if you so much as look at them crossly. I pulled three dead shrimp out and put them on the cleaning table. Preacher and I hooked shrimp under popping corks and threw them out beyond the grass, out to where predators would be dining on shrimp and other tasty morsels washed there by the tide.

There were speckled trout there. We each caught one in short order. They were undersized and we turned them loose. We quickly caught a couple of more undersized specs. Schools of speckled trout held fish of similar size, and I didn't have much hope of catching a keeper. But the process was relaxing. Throw the cork out. Snap it in the water while reeling it in. Get to the edge of the grass and reel it fast to avoid a snag, and cast it out again. It was meditative. I could let my mind work on other things. It was a lot more fun than yoga. Plus, you never knew when you might catch that lone ranger, the big spec, patrolling just beyond his frantic brethren.

We fished. Preacher began to whistle softly. We watched the setting sun. There were slaps of water as fish took delight in their dining and birds skimmed the surface for leftovers. I turned on the low lights, the ones that light the deck of the pier, so we could see what we were doing, but left the brighter over-head lights off. I enjoyed the envelope of the night.

Joshua and Darla joined us, each carrying a fishing rod. They thanked me again. Darla told Preacher they were moving in together. He said, "Good. Bless you. You need to talk to me about your spiritual life together."

Darla said, "We will. Thank you."

Joshua seemed to stand a little taller and said, "And, maybe, someday, we'll ask you to marry us."

Preacher nodded. Darla dropped her fishing rod and leaped on Joshua, wrapping her legs around his waist. He dropped his fishing rod to grab her.

"Be careful with my fishing stuff," I said.

"You're supposed to ask me first, you dumb boy," she said.

"I haven't asked you yet. You'll know when I do."

"Dumb boy." She kissed him.

"Don't scare the fish," I said.

They unclenched but didn't pick up their fishing gear.

Joshua watched me pull in an undersized speck. I said, "They're small, but they're biting. You're welcome to some shrimp."

He nodded and rigged their rods. He didn't use popping corks, but put a slip weight behind a leader with a hook. I knew he was doing a smart thing. They baited their lines with the dead shrimp. She knew what she was doing. He asked Darla if she wanted him to cast for her. She gave him a look, hit him on the shoulder, took her rod, and made a great cast. Hip bump. He threw his line out just a little farther and gave her a look. She ignored him.

We fished. The earth made its turn and slowly moved us away from the sun. There were no clouds that night. The breeze was from the sea. An egret glided to the flats and made its quiet way into the grasses, alert. Its darting beak assured that a few mud minnows did not have to worry about being eaten by the speckled trout. Preacher and I talked about things. Joshua and Darla sat on the edge of the pier, feet dangling, pulling their baited hooks slowly across the sand beyond the flats and ignored everything but their awareness of each other. I could not imagine how that moment could have been better.

I liked that Darla caught the first fish between them. I knew how Joshua competed when fishing. She scrambled to her feet, keeping the tip of her rod high. The rest of us quickly reeled our lines in to get out of her way. Her fish took off on a solid run. Joshua looked at me once. He smiled and made one nod of his head, his pride in her evident.

It took a minute or two, but she landed a good redfish. It went into the fish box. In the time it took Preacher and me to catch another couple of undersized speckled trout, Joshua and Darla each boxed nice-sized redfish.

Preacher said, "Maybe we should re-rig and catch something decent."

"Nah, then we'd just have to clean it, besides I'm

getting hungry. Hey, Joshua, those look nice. You going to cook us dinner?"

"You bet."

She said, "Joshua, teach me to make blackened redfish." I didn't know if she was being sensitive to Joshua's fishing ego and the fact that she'd caught two to his one, but, if so, his relationship was off to a good start.

She was not, however, going to let us think she couldn't clean a fish. They stood across from each other at the fish cleaning table and quickly had their redfish cleaned and turned into fillets.

"Hey Sam," Joshua said, "We'll make some blackened redfish."

"Sounds good. We'll gather stuff up and be right behind you. I'll make some rice and biscuits."

Preacher and I fished for a few more minutes while talking about Joshua and Darla but ended up with no fish to clean. I dumped the surviving bait shrimp into the water and wished them luck. Up at the house. Darla was lighting the citronella torches. Joshua had hauled out the cast-iron flat-top grill and was hooking up a bottle of propane. Preacher made the rice while I made the biscuits. The biscuits were almost done by the time the grill got as hot as possible.

Steam erupted from the grill when Joshua put the seasoned fillets on it. The fish were on the table minutes later. We ate on the porch. The evening was good.

Eventually, Joshua said, "I've got to get her home. The grill will be hot for a while. I'll put it up in the morning. See you then."

"I'll probably be gone most of the day. Preacher and I have to tend to some business in Beaumont."

"Okay. Thanks again Sam. About the apartment."

"Yep. I'm going to be charging you rent, so you can start cleaning it out while you're on the clock if you've got everything else done, but I don't want it to cause any overtime pay. Just stack stuff in a corner of the shop. We'll discuss just what we need to do to fix it up when I get back."

They left. Preacher said, "Good kids. I have hope for them."

"Yes."

We washed the dishes and got ready for bed. Preacher bedded down on the porch and snoring by the time I'd checked my email, turned on the alarm system, and turned off the lights. It took me a while to get to sleep thinking about things.

I woke before dawn. Preacher came into the kitchen while I made coffee.

"When are we leaving?"

"Not for a while. I have to pick something up in Houston before we go. I just couldn't sleep any longer. I'm going for a run. Join me?"

"Sure."

We trotted down to the beach. Preacher kept up with me for about half a mile. At that point, he said, "I'll see you in a bit. I'm going to swim back."

I turned at the mile and a half point. By the time I ran back down the beach he was there, sitting cross-legged on the beach just out of range of the waves lapping the beach. He faced the rising sun, eyes closed. I sat next to him.

Without opening his eyes, he said, "I sense that we are, once again, entering a battle, Sam. Let's enjoy the rightness and goodness of the universe before we try to deal with its darkness."

I sat quietly with him and thought mostly about the darkness. He made me think, though. He was willing to go with me into the darkness not knowing exactly what was going on. What a humbling friend. He deserved to know more and, at some point, I would tell him more, but for now, I did not want to tell him about the dead Bobby Andrus in Angelique's living room. The fewer people who knew about that for as long as possible the better.

"I know you don't know everything that's going on Preacher, but I appreciate you coming along."

"No problem Sam. Sounds like an easy enough job. Drive to Beaumont, drink a beer, call for the cavalry if necessary. Drive home. Or hitchhike, I guess, if they kill you before I can save you."

"Yep. That's about it. Let's go get some breakfast."

We ate at Clara's in Surfside. Preacher wore khakis, lace up tennis shoes, and a blue Polo shirt. Clara whistled at him when he walked in. We made the drive to Houston in commuter hell.

I parked in the loading zone outside of Harlan's building, left Preacher in charge of the car, and went up to the floor housing the law firm of Sherwood, Thomas, and Cain. The receptionist knows me and waved me toward Clancy Sherwood's office as she picked up the phone to let his secretary know I was there.

I made my way to the corner office space where Rosalind Meyers rules. She greeted me and handed me an envelope. "Here's the stuff you asked for. You sure have Mr. Smith curious about what you're doing. I think he is afraid you're going to beat him out of a commission. I assured him that was not the case."

"Thanks. I'm not really trying to sell any of these. I just need them for cover."

"Hmm." She looked at me over her glasses. "Well, glad we could help. Hope you're getting paid this time."

"Yes. I am. Thanks for the concern."

"Have a nice day, Mr. Locke."

"You, too."

When I got to the street, there was a parking enforcement police officer leaning over the driver's side talking to Preacher. Great, I thought, why didn't he just drive around the block instead of getting a ticket. A ticket I'd have to pay. But, as I opened the passenger door, the police officer looked up and nodded at me. She leaned over and said to Preacher, "Well, it was nice talking to you. Have a nice day."

"What was that about?" I asked.

"Just chatting with the officer. Nice lady."

He turned the corner. He stopped at the red light at the next intersection. He opened his door and said, "Trade with me. I don't want to drive."

I jumped out and scurried over to get in the driver's side. Back on the road, I called Angelique.

"Hey, how are things? I have you on the speakerphone. Preacher is with me."

"Hi, Preacher."

"Good morning Angelique."

"We're doing great. This is a nice hotel. Thank you, Sam, for what you're doing."

"No problem. Glad to help. Besides, I'm getting paid. We're about to head to Beaumont. Do you have that list I asked you to make?"

"Yes, but I couldn't remember very many people. I'll keep thinking. Maybe I can add some more."

"If it's not a long list, can you just email it to me?"

"Sure. Give me a few minutes." We said goodbye.

There werre two good ways to get to Beaumont from Houston. One was to take Interstate Ten. The other was on

U.S. Highway Ninety through Liberty. It was about eighty-five miles each way, quicker on the interstate but more interesting on the smaller road to the north. We weren't in a big hurry. I headed toward Liberty and called Rocky.

"Investigations."

"Rocky, Sam. I talked to Angelique. They're fine. Thanks for letting Jenny stay with her."

"Not a problem. Jenny will do good. She'll be going with her everywhere. In fact, it sounds to me for sure they'll be renting a place together."

"Cool. Preacher and I are on our way to Beaumont."

"Me, too, but you know it's a little early to be going to a bar."

"Yep, but I'm going to scope it out. Then, I'll go to the library up there and do some research on things. See if they have something about the Andrus boys I couldn't find on the internet. I don't plan to go to the bar until about four. I figure you should go earlier in the afternoon and look around. Then we'll meet somewhere and you can brief us. I'll drop Preacher off to get settled about three-thirty or so. How come you're going up so early?"

"I picked up some papers I can serve there. You won't have to pay me mileage up there and back."

"Great. I'll call you in a bit."

PREACHER AND I DROVE through Dayton and Liberty and on east through the smaller towns, places with service stations, small grocery stores, and lots of empty building slabs.

We talked about things. Preacher told me he wanted to go see Angelique in a ballet. Maybe take Gretchen.

"Who is Gretchen?"

"You've met her. She's helping out at my church."

"Yes, but what is she? Just a helper? Girlfriend?"

"No, she's not a girlfriend. She's someone who needs the stability of my church right now."

I wondered about the stability of a church that meets in a mostly boarded up convenience store, a church with members who come and go, a church where the minister puts together drum circles and often cancels services if he wants to go surfing.

Preacher elaborated on Gretchen. "She married into a very wealthy Houston family to a boy she met at college. Her family is somewhere in the middle part of Texas. She doesn't see them much. Her husband felt the need to break away from his family and joined the military. He was killed over there. His family burdened her with his absence, taking her in too close, making her a substitute for what they'd lost, coupled with laying some guilt on her for seducing him away from his family.

"They probably blame her for him enlisting even if they don't say it. They gave her no room to grieve properly and no exit to get on with life. Right now she likes what my church offers her. Gretchen is recovering her own strength. Someday she'll be able to put his family in its proper place and move on. I just think she would enjoy the beauty of the ballet. That's all."

Gretchen was typical of members of his congregation, lost souls who gather at the edge of the sea for a short while before moving on to something better, something the same or something not quite so good. I believed Preacher to be much the same. There were things in his past he did not share and from which he distanced himself.

He seemed to have found a more permanent place here than most who attend his church or who gather with him on a beach at sunrise, making noise with drums beat in rhythm. Perhaps the drums are a way to amplify their heartbeats, to be heard in the world. Preacher is a friend I would miss greatly if he decided to move on.

I wondered if I'd done the same thing, stuck myself somewhere, somewhere directionless and lonely. I'd moved to Galveston after the destruction of my legal career and my marriage. Did I need to be moving on from my past, do something different? That thought was too complicated. I started a conversation about fishing and about Joshua and Darla and about other things.

We reached the outskirts of Beaumont. I knew we'd pass Chuck's, one of the Andrus topless bars, and I watched for it. Housed in an all-metal building, it looked more like a barn than anything else. That early, the oil-stained parking lot was empty except for one dirt-brown Lincoln parked near an emergency exit. Preacher noticed me look at it as we passed.

"Dreary places," he said.

"Yes. It's owned by the guy we're interested in. We may have to come back to it."

"Is that where Angelique danced?"

I looked at him. "I don't ever remember saying that Angelique danced in such a place."

"Oh, come on. I'm not dumb."

"No, she didn't dance there. Way before she could legally, she danced at another place owned by the same guy. A little nicer than that one, I hope. The fact that she danced is one of those things we're not talking about to anybody."

"Of course."

My phone rang. It was Rocky.

"Hey, Sam. Did you know that joint doesn't open until four?"

"Damn. No. I should have checked."

"Yeah, we're not in Houston where they open for lunch. It will take me a while to serve these papers, so it's no big deal to me, but I thought you should know."

"Okay. How about we meet for lunch somewhere?"

"Sure. Where?"

"I know a place. Where are you?"

"I'm headed for the courthouse."

"Okay, we'll pick you up there."

We picked up Rocky, and I drove out of town on the state highway toward Port Author. After a short distance, I exited the highway and turned onto a badly maintained, two-lane road. Off that small, pot-holed road a dirt track took us to a white clapboard house. The living room, two bedrooms, and the porch of that house have been turned into dining areas. The name of the place, Belle's, was written at the top of the chalkboard that served as a menu hanging by the front door. There was no other sign. That day, like most days, there were several cars and trucks parked on the lot surrounding the house. Most of those vehicles had boats attached.

Belle's did not look like much, but its menu included a mix of incomparable seafood. I have never had a better gumbo anywhere. I'd heard a story I hoped was true. One day the county health inspector showed up with some official complaints and an attitude. Belle never responded to correspondence about some silly health code violations. The inspector was ready to shut the place down, but doing so would have interfered with the dinner being shared by the governors of Texas and Louisiana who were dining with two state senators. The politicians announced clemency of dubious legal standing. The political entourage purchased the health inspector and the law enforcement officers accompanying him gumbo and beer.

The three of us ate gumbo over rice and drank beer while we made plans.

CARRYING OUT THE PLANS we made over lunch, Rocky went off to try to serve some papers. Preacher and I went to the public library.

First, I pulled up the list Angelique texted me of people she remembered from Fantasy Kings. Her text noted that she had not kept up with any of the people on the list, and she could not give me any of their current whereabouts. Her note said she'd thought long and hard, but could remember no specific names of customers, even the ones she thought came just to see her. She had no desire to get to know them back then and didn't really pay attention to their names. She remarked that a lot of people in the business, no matter what their jobs, and a lot of the customers did not use their real names.

First on the list was her friend, Carol Taylor, dancer name Cee Cee, age twenty-six or seven. Angelique described Carol as having a "dancer's body" when she knew her but noted she really had to work at not being chubby. Carol had red hair, probably enhanced, but believed to be naturally red to some degree.

Another underage dancer, Pamela, danced with the name Stardust. She started a few months after Angelique. She thought Pamela must be no more than a year younger than herself. That made her around twenty-three. When Angelique danced there, Pamela had short brown hair and dark brown eyes. Angelique described her as skinny, but with breasts developing quicker than most sixteen-year-old girls.

There were other dancer names listed, described as being a few years older and mostly bleached blonde, with a scattering of brunettes. Names, none of which were believed to be real, ranged from the common, such as Kathryn, Martina, and Cleo, to more informal like Kitty and Queen and to cliched dancer names like Skye Dancer, Baby Doll, and Mata Hari. It impressed me that a dancer would take the name of one of history's most famous exotic dancers. I wondered if the Mata Hari who danced at Fantasy Kings knew they executed her namesake by firing squad.

Angelique remembered a bartender named Rich. Her note called him the boss bartender. She said he spoke with a Cajun accent. She thought he'd be in his fifties, overweight but strong, bearded with "tons of tattoos." Her note said he was a biker type.

The DJ she remembered was Carl. She thought he would be in his late twenties or early thirties, but put a question mark after her guess at his age. She noted that DJs came and went. Carl was there when she started, and she thought he was there when she left. There were others who didn't stay that long and she could not remember their names.

Last on the list was a bouncer called Big D. She didn't know his real name, but she described him as being tall, big overall, and muscular. She noted that he'd hit on her when she first started but that Bobby Andrus had set him straight. After that, he stared at her, making her uncomfortable, but never really bothered her again. You would expect a bouncer to have muscle. "Big overall" fit in with Betty Page's impression of one of the men going over the fence at the apartment complex. It would be interesting to see if he still worked at the club.

After going over Angelique's list, I spent my time reading every news article I could find in the local newspapers about the Andrus brothers and their business ventures. I didn't learn a lot new. I did see more stories out of small Louisiana newspapers I had not read before. All the news confirmed my impression that the Andrus brothers existed on the border between legal and not so legal. Once again, things unsaid, but implied, made it clear some of the writers believed there were things about the Andrus businesses that couldn't quite be proved to a level passing journalistic standards for publication.

The Andrus family made some high-profile donations for the public good. There were stories noting financial donations to a school playground and a river-side park reclamation project. Although unreported, I'd bet there were some not so public donations to election committees and the like.

There were several whiffs of a darker side. There were a couple of accounts of violence by individuals employed at a salvage yard owned by Landry Andrus. There were stories of public officials making mysterious zoning decisions benefiting an Andrus owned business transporting unbranded gasoline. There were the occasional raids on the bars, which were, according to Angelique, anticipated by management. It looked to me that the Andrus family wanted to move out of the shadows and become legitimate and honest businessmen as much as possible. They wouldn't be the only entrepreneurs to have financed legitimacy with questionable resources. I made copies of the articles I hadn't already copied off the internet.

When time to go, I found Preacher reading the Wall Street Journal. We left to meet up with Rocky at a Denny's Restaurant a few blocks from Fantasy King's. He'd beat us there. He carried his coffee from the counter to join us at a table.

The waitress followed, and we all ordered burgers.

"Fantasy Kings was kind of dead when I was there," Rocky said. "Three girls sitting at the bar. I sat at the bar and had a beer and detected nothing other than confirming what I already knew. Those places are depressing, and their drinks are overpriced."

"Not a boisterous crowd in attendance," I said.

"Three guys in dirty work clothes at one table, nursing their beers slowly and waiting patiently for love. The DJ had to make one of the girls get up and dance. Nobody tipped her so he didn't push anybody else to dance."

"Anybody there who looked like management?"

"Not that I saw. There's a room behind the bar. Maybe management was busy back there."

"Tell me about the bartender."

"Looks like an aging biker. Could be from New Orleans with his accent. Served me quick and easy, didn't hang around to engage in conversation. I didn't think you'd want me to attract attention by asking if he knew where to find his boss."

I nodded. "His name is Rich."

"Yeah, probably so. That works. I heard one of the girls say something to him. I thought she called him Itch. It must have been Rich. Is he a clue?"

I shrugged. "Angelique knew his name."

"I don't think he looks like the guy described by Betty Page. I really have nothing else to report. Doesn't look dangerous, unless you are dangerously allergic to boredom. You might have to stick around a while or come back on a busier weekend night to find anybody in the upper echelons of management."

"Well, I'm here. I'll go in and ask. You stay here and Preacher will call if there's a problem. Doesn't sound likely, though."

"Looks to me like you'll be safe. Need any dollar bills?"

"I'm there only for business. I've already given Preacher some in case he needs them for cover."

I dropped Preacher off a block from the bar in case there were surveillance cameras. I didn't want us to be seen together. I went down the road and waited thirty minutes in the parking lot of an auto parts store, thinking. The thinking didn't help.

Several cars were in the parking lot of the bar when I returned. Guys were getting off work. The married ones probably called their wives and told them they were going to have a couple of beers with the guys. I could hear music pulsing before I walked through the door. A sign just inside the door of the club let me know I'd beat the six dollar cover charge by fifteen minutes. Whew.

Fantasy King's staged a routine atmosphere of erotic promise. The music was loud and overseen by a DJ in a booth over to the side. The main stage, lined with racing lights, had the requisite pole in its middle. A smaller stage jutted from the wall stage right of the main stage, dark and unused at the moment, saved for bigger crowds. The bar ran along the wall opposite the main stage, to the right of the entrance. The bar was book-ended by a hallway to the restrooms to its right and an unmarked door to its left. A door to the right of the main stage led to the dancer's dressing room.

A dancer on stage danced to what must have been the first song of her set. She was as fully dressed as she was going to get while working. She had that dancer gaze, looking out over the heads of everybody, not making eye contact with anyone unless they approached the stage with a dollar in hand. That wouldn't happen until she removed her top.

A few guys sat around the stage, waiting for the second

song and sipping beer. A few guys at tables had girls sitting with them or girls circling, testing the market. Back in a dark corner, somebody was getting a lap dance.

A dancer client once told me how the girls where she worked classified all patrons as fish. The minnows were the ones who could nurse a beer for an hour. They never paid for a dancer's drink, and they never purchased a dance at the table. They only rarely approached the stage to slip a dollar in a g-string, and when they did, it was usually only one particular girl. She said it could be creepy to have the affection of a minnow.

Those men categorized as small-mouth bass tipped more and would buy drinks in exchange for some friendly under the table groping. A good small-mouth bass tried to tip all the girls on stage. A place wouldn't survive without a sizable school of small-mouth bass. Small-mouth bass were thick on payday.

Best of all were the large-mouth bass. They were guys who came in with a wallet full of cash and left with little of it. They were loud. They tipped everybody on stage, sometimes with fives or tens, often by sending another dancer to deliver the tip. The best ones had an expense account and were entertaining somebody. Hook a couple of large-mouth bass a month and you could pay the rent. A large-mouth bass usually had more than one girl at his table. That knowledge scared me because the only guy in the place with more than one girl paying attention to him was Preacher. He sat at a table to the left as I came in. There were three girls sitting and one girl standing at his table. All the girls were leaning in and talking to him. There was laughter.

As much as I wanted to go find out what was so funny, I resisted. I made my way to the far end of the bar. The bartender glanced up at me when I walked in. He was a big guy with a gray pony-tail and fading tattoos. He had to be Rich.

The bartender watched me. My shoes were polished. I was in a suit and carrying a briefcase. He had to suspect I was not there to watch the dancers. I wasn't a cop. I was an unknown visitor and might be messing up his day. He moved along the bar with me, drying his hands on a bar towel. I stood at the end of the bar. Across from me, he said, "Can I help you?"

Yep, it was Rich with his New Orleans based accent.

"I'm here to see Bobby Andrus. Is he in?"

"He ain't here."

"When do you expect him?"

"He doesn't share his schedule with me. What's this about?"

"Business."

He waited. I waited. The girl who had been entertaining the guy back in the dark corner came up and said, "Hey Rich. I need a drink."

"Get it yourself." She whined a bit and went around the other end of the bar.

To me, he said, "You wanna talk to Mr. Andrus?"

"Yes. That's what I said."

"Not Bobby. His brother, Landry."

"Well, my business is with Bobby. Is Landry the boss when Bobby's not here?"

"He's always the boss."

"Will he know where I can find Bobby?"

"You'll have to talk to him."

"Okay. I will, then."

"He's not here right now, but he'll be in. You want a drink while you wait?"

"A Coke."

He turned away, filled a glass with ice and cola and set it in front of me. I turned to look over the room. Not much had changed. The girl on stage wore only a g-string, and it had some bills pushed into it. Preacher continued as the center of a lot of attention. I couldn't wait to hear what that was about. More guys came through the door. There was a lady at the front door collecting their six dollars apiece.

Eventually, a man came out of the door next to where I was sitting. I knew it was Landry Andrus. I'd seen his picture in the paper. He must have come in a back door to the building. He, too, was in a suit, his hair combed tight against his scalp. He looked freshly shaved. I didn't look to see, but I'd have bet his shoes were shinier than mine. He looked at me, then around the room, and then back at me. He waved at Rich who nodded my way. He walked down the bar and conferred quietly with the bartender, glancing back at me.

He came back down my way. "Can I help you?"

"Hi. Samuel Locke." I extended my hand. He shook it briskly. "I came to see Bobby Andrus."

"He is unavailable. I'm his brother Landry. How can I help you?" He spoke softly, without an accent. I could just hear him over the music. His eyes were emotionless and did not stray from looking straight at me.

"I'm doing some business with him and just happened to be passing through Beaumont on other business. I thought I'd see if he was available."

"Come back to the office." He turned and led me through the door by the bar into a short hallway. To one side a door was open into what was obviously a stockroom. He opened a door across the hall and led me into an office.

There was a desk with an expensive looking leather

chair behind it and a cheap looking, scarred wooden chair in front of it. A cracked leather sofa stood opposite the desk against the wall. A bulletin board on the wall had what looked like work schedules tacked to it. Stacks of paper were all around the edge of the desk. In the cleared-off center was a legal pad with notes on it and a hand-written accounting journal. It looked to me like Landry had shoved stuff out of the way and was, perhaps, trying to make sense of his brother's bookkeeping. He sat behind the desk and turned over the legal pad and journal to prevent me from stealing trade secrets.

"What kind of business are you doing with my brother?"

"Well, I'd really rather he be involved in any discussion about that."

"He's not here. He works for me. If he's doing some kind of business with you, I'd like to know about it, please."

The please did not sound heartfelt. Having stuck a stick in the hornet's nest, I got nervous about stirring it.

"I'm sure it's okay, but I'd feel a lot better if I could call him and get his acquiescence to speak with you."

"He is unavailable. Either let me know what's going on or go."

I should have just gone.

"It's no big deal, I guess. He wasn't expecting me today. He'd asked for some information on commercial property in Houston. I'd pulled some stuff together for him."

"Commercial property?" He paused, staring at me. "Let me see what you pulled together."

I pulled out a map from my briefcase and put it on the desk. He picked it up and looked at it. Setting it down he tapped a finger on it, looking at it and then looking up at me.

"I'll get this to him. Do you have a card?"

"He knows how to get hold of me."

"I don't. Let me have a card."

I didn't want him to think something was wrong, so I gave him a card, making sure it was my lawyer card and not my Locke Smokers and Grills card. The card disclosed nothing more than a post office address and the phone number answered by my service.

He stood up. I stood up. He escorted me out of the office. I felt him watch me leave. The bar was getting crowded. Preacher was down to only two dancers at his table, both leaning in and listening intently to whatever he was saying.

Just before I reached the exit, it opened and a big guy walked in. I almost stumbled. He fit the description given by Betty Page of one of the two guys jumping the fence at Angelique's apartment complex, right down to wearing all khaki. I stepped aside to get out of his way. He expected me to do so and barreled past paying me no attention whatsoever.

The lady sitting there to collect the cover charge said, "You're late."

"Fuck you. I had car trouble."

"Explain it to Landry. He's here." She sounded a little smug.

I walked to my car. There was a mud brown pickup pulling out of the parking lot. I couldn't see the driver. It had an indistinct sticker in the center of its window. Perhaps Big D's Hispanic companion had just dropped him off at work. Adrenaline pumped and my breath shortened. I hoped I hadn't made a big mistake by walking into Fantasy King's.

I would have followed the truck, but by the time I got

in my car, I couldn't see it. I wanted to call Preacher, tell him to get out of there right then, pick him up, and drive us both away. But mindful of the security cameras at each corner of the building, I kept with the plan and drove off.

Fifteen minutes later I drove back down the street. I stopped and picked up Preacher as he walked down the sidewalk. We headed for Denny's.

Chapter Nine

On the way to meet Rocky, I looked over at Preacher. His head leaned back against the car seat and his eyes were closed. I said, "I didn't think you were going to attract attention."

"What do you mean?"

"Every girl in the bar was at your table."

"Just chatting. I wasn't giving them money or doing anything to attract attention."

"What in the world were you talking about?"

"Lots of stuff. Boyfriends, husbands, parents, kids. Interesting to look behind the stereotypes."

"You didn't tell them you were a minister, did you? Or where you live?"

"No. I'd have liked to invite a couple of them to church, but I told you I wouldn't attract attention. Maybe I'll go back someday after you're done with whatever you're doing."

"I have no clue what I'm doing."

"Yeah, sensed that. Don't worry. You're usually on the right side of things. You'll figure it out."

As I drove, I looked for the pickup I'd seen drive off. I didn't see it, but it wouldn't be hard to find again. I parked at Denny's where Rocky waited. I turned to Preacher, who still had his head leaned against the headrest and his eyes closed as if napping. Before I could say anything he smiled without opening his eyes and said, "If you don't mind, I'm going to nap here while you go visit Rocky."

"Thanks, Preacher. I'll fill you in on what's going on as much as possible as soon as I can."

"Take your time. You can pay me back by buying me something other than Denny's for dinner one of these days."

Rocky sat at a table, drinking coffee.

I sat. He said, "Learn anything?"

I told him about meeting Landry Andrus and my feeling that Landry did not even know his brother had been in Houston, at least until I'd made it clear he had. That felt like a mistake on my part. Landry had been controlled, not displaying emotion, but I had a strong sense he knew nothing.

"But," I said, "just as I was leaving, Big D the bouncer walked in. He is a big guy. He wears khaki. I'd bet he's the guy Betty Page saw. Plus, I saw a brown pickup leaving like it had dropped him off."

"Okay. That's something. I'll go back and get his picture."

"Now?"

"Sure. See this?" He tapped his shirt pocket. His cell phone stuck out the top. "I had this shirt made so that my cell phone camera lens sees all. And the cell phone is special. The little camera light doesn't come on. I'll go in, have another beer, video him if he's there and head for home."

"Good. You know what? If you can do it easily and without attracting attention, go ahead and get shots of everybody who works in the bar, including the dancers."

"You have a plan?"

"Absolutely not. I have no idea and no plan about anything, but our mess is tied to that bar somehow, might as well be thorough. Another thing. You can probably get somebody up here you trust to do this. The Andrus enterprise includes at least one salvage yard and an associated towing company. I'd like to quietly check out those places for the pickup and the other guy."

"I'll arrange that. Probably work better to get a local guy."

"Just get a good one."

"Nothing but."

We didn't have more to say and called it a night.

PREACHER AND I DROVE toward Houston. This time on the interstate. Preacher leaned his head back and began whistling something. I thought about the fact that I'd given Landry Andrus my card and wondered if I should have thought about my approach a little better.

Halfway home, I said, "Let me tell you what's going on."

He sat up alert. "If you want."

I told him about the dead Bobby Andrus, how he was found, and how he disappeared. I told him about Angelique's apartment being broken into and how we were trying to figure out what was going on.

I finished. He nodded once, and said, "That poor child. I'll be glad to help."

"Let me reiterate. You cannot tell anybody what I've told you."

"Of course not. To the grave."

"I hope not."

The glow of Houston got brighter. The city appeared on the horizon, skyscrapers magnificently lit.

My cell phone sounded. It was Jenny.

"Hey Sam, Jenny. Do you know where Rocky is? His phone is going straight to voicemail."

"I left him in a topless bar in Beaumont."

She laughed. "I cannot wait to tell Aunt Marlene about that. Is he coming home tonight?"

"Yeah. He's getting some photos. He'll be leaving soon, I'm sure."

"Ah, he must be using his stealth cell phone camera. It's a cool gadget. Guess what? Angelique and I are going to move in together. Like, for real. We found a great place this afternoon. We'd have signed a lease, but you don't want it in her name, right?"

"Right. Where is it?"

"It's in a place called Houston East Lofts. It's a really cool apartment in a converted warehouse in Houston, kind of north of the ballpark. Our windows overlook the bayou. Well, partly anyway,"

"Downtown. Can you afford that?"

"It's not that big. Two small bedrooms and a long, narrow living space. I don't need much space, and Angelique said the living room will be perfect for when she wants to practice. It has hardwood floors easy to dance on. She said she'll pay two-thirds of the rent because she will use most of the space. I think she's just being nice to me. I can afford a third even on the pissant amount of money Rocky pays me. Tell him to give me a raise." She got a lot quieter, almost whispering when she said, "Sam, she makes a lot of money. You'd be surprised."

"Security?"

"Tons better than where she was. Every apartment has access to the video feed from the front door. You can monitor the lobby, the elevator, the halls, and the parking garage, which is kind of small but there's a lot of parking on the streets down here. Don't know how safe the streets are, but there are good street lights. She said she'd like the walk to the theater. It's not far and she can warm up. If we think it's safe, that is. You have to have a key card to get into the lobby and to run the elevator. The rules are you order a pizza, you meet them downstairs. I think it's as safe as we're going to find."

"Sounds good."

"Who's name goes on the lease?"

"I'll think about it, maybe Thumperly Efforts. That's her grandfather's management company."

"Cool. Hurry and decide. We want this place."

"And have it you shall."

"Another thing. We're going to New Orleans."

"What?"

"Angelique has a gig as a guest performer with the ballet in New Orleans. I know you don't want her going alone, so I'm going with her to New Orleans. We have to fly there tomorrow. She rehearses Thursday and Friday and performs on Saturday and Sunday. The room will be in the name of the New Orleans Ballet. They're paying. We should be safe."

I could think of no reason that would be a big problem. Probably better than staying in Houston if somebody was looking for her. Her appearance in New Orleans would be publicly announced, but so were her performances in Houston. Jenny could keep her as safe in New Orleans as she could in Houston.

"Okay. Check in with me while you're gone."

"You got it, boss."

I drove, trying to think what else needed doing. I couldn't think of a thing.

The day exhausted me. If I had not had Preacher with me, I would have stayed at my uncle's place in Houston. I dropped Preacher off at his church and drove to my place.

Only the rustling night sounds of the goats next door broke the quiet when I got out of my truck. I heard nothing of my two goats. A breeze whispered through the grass flats, but I heard no night birds and no fish slapped the water. I heard nothing but the background hum of the machinery of the world.

I fell asleep quick and heavy. The night absorbed any dreams, and I woke up when I heard the sound of Joshua's truck crunch down my driveway. I heard Darla laughing about something as I made coffee.

Thumper called and agreed we should put the lease to Angelique's and Jenny's loft in the name of his company and to let Thumperly pay the bill. He told me to get it done. He asked if I thought Angelique would be safe in New Orleans and advised that he was going to his home on the river.

Rocky called and said he had video of everybody he saw working at Fantasy King's, and he'd send me images after he pulled stills from the video. He'd heard from Jenny and seemed resigned to the fact that she was moving in with Angelique on a full-time basis. He'd also heard about the upcoming trip to New Orleans.

I checked on Darla and Joshua. They were setting up a welding machine outside, Darla paying rapt attention as Joshua explained what he was doing. She wore work boots and a long-sleeved work shirt. Both wore a welder's helmet tipped back. Joshua had the work day planned. He obviously enjoyed playing boss.

A kitchen table, a couple of chairs, a bed frame, and mattress were in the back of Joshua's truck. They might just be living in their new apartment that night.

I prepared a company resolution authorizing the rental of the loft for Angelique and Jenny and, taking along the company checkbook and a briefcase full of paperwork, left to go see the loft.

The loft was as described. Two bedrooms on either end of a common living area incorporating a kitchen area. They did have a view of the bayou if you looked way to the left between two warehouses. Other than that, their view was old industrial. Lofts on the other side of the building cost more for their view of downtown.

We got it leased with possession to start the following Monday. Excited, Angelique and Jenny left to fly to New Orleans. I went to my office and did some work.

Late that afternoon I called Rocky, and we agreed to meet at a diner south of Houston. I left, headed toward Galveston. On the way, Jenny called to tell me that she and Angelique were safely in the hotel in New Orleans and ordering room service.

At the diner, Rocky gave me a file folder of photographs with five each of everybody he'd caught on his camera. He'd included a disc of the images as well. He had pictures of both bartenders, the bouncer, the lady collecting money at the door, the customers, and all the dancers. It was amazing how well his stealth cell phone did in the dim light of the bar. Some of the photographs of the dancers were interesting, taken when he'd walked up to tip the dancer on stage. He'd tried to crop the photos without featuring their breasts. He mostly succeeded.

He tapped a finger on the bouncer, the big guy I'd seen there, and said, "I'm going to show his picture to Betty Page. See if he could be our guy."

"Good idea. I'm going to show them all to Angelique, get some names if she knows any of them."

"Where are we going with all this?"

"I have no idea. It would be nice if this thing were over,

but we have no way of knowing that. I get the feeling somebody is looking for something."

"Or looking for her."

"Yeah, could be. In any event, we need to try to get ahead of whatever is going on."

"I talked to Jenny, told her to not get lackadaisical."

"Good. Last I heard they were hitting room service."

That night I put the photos on the disc into my Google drive online and sent Angelique a link, asking her to put names to the faces if she could.

ON THURSDAY I WENT to the courthouse in Galveston and finalized three no-fault, as friendly as possible, divorces. I finished by ten. I stopped back by the marina where I kept my boat. I ran the air for a bit to hold down the mildew, shined it up a bit, and checked a few of the hundreds of things a boat owner must check regularly. All was good.

Back at the house Joshua and Darla were busy working, building some of my least expensive grills. Over to the side stood a curious piece of metal sculpture, a conglomeration of scrap put together by Darla's welding practice. I met Flounder, the cat.

In an email, Angelique let me know, out of Rocky's photographs, she recognized the bartender Rich, the bouncer she knew as Big D, none of the customers, and one of the dancers, the girl she'd known as Pamela, or Stardust. Her email went on to say, "I can't believe she's still there. She looks a lot different. Older, of course, but harder. She used to have a sparkle. I can tell it's gone. That makes me sad. I am so glad I left that place."

A little more information related to Angelique's past, but, unless Rocky could confirm with Betty Page that the bouncer was the man she saw climbing over the fence three days earlier, I couldn't see that the photos were a tremendous help. I put them in the folder with all the other non-helpful information I'd collected.

I made a sandwich and ate it while I checked the tide tables. An incoming tide would be peaking mid-afternoon. It wasn't a strong tide, and it was a bit late to get started, but I put on some shorts and grabbed a fishing pole already armed with a silver spoon. Darla saw me first when I went outside.

"Hey Sam, good luck with that fishing while we work." She was dusty and sweaty and had a smile as big as I'd ever seen.

I nodded at her.

Joshua stopped what he was doing, flipped up his welding shield and said, "Sam, we're going to need some more two-inch pipe if you want us to build that big smoker the way you drew it."

I had an order for a custom competition smoker on a trailer for a new client. "Y'all find a stopping place, take the truck and see if you can find some. Take the company credit card." He nodded like he did that kind of thing all the time. It was actually the first time I'd sent him alone to buy pipe.

"Yes, sir. I'll find some good clean ones."

"Call if you have questions."

I walked down my driveway, across the highway, and into the surf to do a little fishing. It is a good thing it was called fishing instead of catching. Otherwise, I would have failed miserably at it that day.

Later, I helped Joshua unload and stack the pipe he'd bought. We don't need long sections of pipe and buy scrap from a couple of different pipe supply companies. Each of them have a Locke Smoker and Grill at their place of business and get treated once a year to a barbecue for their employees and families. It helps keep the prices fair during the year, and we get calls when they get stuff they think we can use.

I thought about letting Joshua and Darla off early to work on their apartment, but decided I didn't want to start something that might turn into trouble. We needed to build grills and get them to our retailers. I wanted them to keep their priorities straight. There was plenty of laughter and work put in moving furniture into their apartment after they went off the clock. At some point, they went and bought groceries. I knew they'd invite me to dinner if I was around when they got back. I didn't want to interfere with their first official night in their own place, so I left before they got back. I couldn't find Preacher. I ate alone in Surfside at Clara's Bar and Grill.

Early Friday morning I got a call from my lover, Cecelia. She suddenly had the afternoon free and wanted to come to my place. That was a good thing.

Late Friday morning, I got a call from Rocky. He'd taken the photo of Big D and shown it to Betty Page. He said, "She thought maybe it could be him. You know how witnesses are, the longer we talked the more sure she got. I think, given all the facts we have, we can assume it's true. Not sure where we go with that, but it's something, I guess."

We agreed to think about what we might do next. Not satisfactory, but all we could do.

I talked briefly on the phone with Thumper, updating him about what we'd learned.

Just as I hung up with Thumper, Cecelia arrived. I spent the next couple of hours with her, making love and whispering in the shadows of my bedroom. Like everybody, sometimes it was great with us and sometimes better for one or the other. That afternoon there was an undercurrent of something, but I could not decide if it was me worrying about the Angelique situation or her worrying about something secret to her. I felt an emotional distraction was preventing us from achieving the type of escape we both pursued when we were together. After her shower and just before she left, she told me that she and her husband would be taking a two-week cruise in the fall. Maybe that was it.

Later that night I sat on the porch and watched Joshua demonstrate to Darla a method of cleaning stuff out of the scrap pipe he'd bought. It involved putting a heavy cap over one end of the pipe. The cap had a port big enough to put the tip of a welding torch in. He flowed some gas in, stood to the side, and used a spark igniter at the port. It turned the pipe into a cannon and, with a whump of exploding acetylene, dirt and grass and spiders came flying out the other end. It was dangerous. Its use was absolutely forbidden at my workplace, but it sure was fun. After the first one, Flounder came running and jumped into my lap. After they'd done all the pipe, I told Darla I'd fire her on the spot if I ever caught her doing such a thing.

Joshua grinned and said, "I told her we were only doing this one time."

On Saturday morning I took it slow. A phone call a few minutes after noon shattered the complacency of the day. It was Angelique.

"Sam. Oh my God, Sam. Jenny is in the hospital. They hurt her, Sam. It's really bad. I'm scared. They didn't tell me anything, but I can tell. They think she might die."

CHAPTER TEN

ANGELIQUE TRIED TO TALK to me through huge, gulping sobs. I could barely understand her. I thought she would collapse at any moment.

"Angelique, take a big breath. Slow down. Tell me where you are. Tell me exactly what happened."

I heard her take a huge breath, start to speak, then take another breath.

"I'm at the hospital. We were going to the theater. They were in the hotel parking garage. Two of them. They came at us so fast. I didn't even see them at first. She did. One had a knife. She shoved me. I fell. I didn't understand. She went right after the guy with the knife. She saved me. She took him down. He cut her, but she took him down and kicked the knife under a car. The other one had a gun and hit her on the head. Sam, it was horrible. She had to have been hurt, but she went after him. She grabbed his gun and it went off. It was so loud. They were moving so fast. The gun went off again. She was on the ground. The first guy, the one who had the knife, kicked her two or three times while she was on the ground. Finally, they left. They got in a van and left. It was horrible. I was trying to call nine-one-one. I tried to stop the bleeding. I tried so hard. Finally, a security guard got there. He called for help. Sam, oh my God, what if she dies?"

"Are the police there?"

"Yes. One wants to talk to you."

"Is he close? Have you talked to him?"

"It's a she, and no. She hasn't been here long, and I've been kind of out of it. I'm calling you in private. I told her I had to talk to you, to let you know what happened. I've been kind of hysterical, I guess. What do I tell her?"

"Right now, you describe exactly what happened. Describe your attackers. Can you?"

"Not really. They were both in hoodies and ski masks. I couldn't see anything."

"How big were they?"

"Normal, I guess."

"Was one a bigger guy?"

"I don't think so."

"Nothing unique?"

"One of them said something in that French they speak down here."

"Okay, that's something. You tell the policewoman what happened there, but let me talk to her first. I'll tell her we're on the way and that the attack could be related to what's gone on around here. We do not tell her about what you found in your apartment, but I'm going to have to tell about you working at Fantasy Kings. I'll tell her we're looking at all possibilities, and your association with that club is the only thing in your past that is sketchy. Okay?"

"Okay. Sam, will you let Mr. Rockwell know? And Thumper? You'll keep him calm. They need to know."

"Yes. Rocky and I will get there as soon as we can. Thumper, too, probably. I'll try to convince Thumper not to come, but he will. I can tell him you're a hundred percent okay, right?"

"Yes. I have a bruised elbow from when I fell but that's all. I should have done something. It just happened so fast. I didn't know what to do."

"There was nothing, absolutely nothing, you could do. If you'd even tried, you might both be dead. What exactly have they said about Jenny?"

"Nothing, really. She's in surgery. She was so pale. She was out, Sam. I tried to stop the bleeding. I really tried."

"I know you did. The doctors have her now. We'll be there as soon as possible. Get me the cop."

"This is Detective Robichaud. Who's this?" She was undoubtedly from somewhere in Louisiana, probably New Orleans. The vowels and accents of her heritage wrapped around her voice.

"Samuel Locke. I am Angelique Cambray's attorney and Jenny Mills works for me."

"Yes. About that. What's going on here, Mr. Locke?"

"I'm hoping you can tell me. Any idea about who attacked them?"

"You tell me. Your client has not been real helpful, yet."

"She's understandably upset. I've calmed her down. She'll talk to you as soon as we hang up."

"Uh huh. You probably know how important it is that we move quickly if we expect to learn anything."

"Yes. Talk to her. I'll be out there soon."

"I have to tell you, Mr. Locke, I sense a little avoidance."

"Look, Ms. Robichaud. I do not want to get in a tangle with you. I don't know who attacked them. Do you have any ideas?"

"Ms. Cambray tells me Ms. Mills is her bodyguard. You tell me she works for you. What's that about?"

"Angelique is a dancer with ... "

"Yes. I know who Angelique Cambray is. I have tickets for tonight's performance. I'm a little pissed off that I'm probably going to miss that, so let's get down to it."

"I have to let her family know, and I have to get on an airplane and get out there. I really do not want to go round and round with you. I promise. Angelique's apartment has been broken into twice. Probably by a couple of guys. Although they took a little bit of money, the break-ins don't appear to be routine burglaries. Signs of aggression, such as property destruction, suggest that the break-ins have more to them than burglary. Something directed at her personally.

"We have an eyewitness who saw the two guys who broke in the second time, the ones who stabbed her big screen television with a knife. The description the witness gave is sketchy. She saw one very big, muscled guy and a smaller guy climb a fence and get in a pick-up. The smaller guy may be Hispanic. We've done some work, and the two may be employees of the Andrus brothers in Beaumont."

"The Andrus brothers? You think they're behind this?"

"I think a couple of their employees are. I believe the big guy is a bouncer at one of their bars. He's called Big D. I don't know the name of the other guy, yet. I'm going to tell you something that could be important, but it is something that, as her lawyer, I'm doing my best to keep private. A number of years ago, from when she was fifteen to eighteen years old, she danced at Fantasy Kings, a topless bar in Beaumont. It's owned and run by Landry and Bobby Andrus."

"Okay. How do you figure that's connected with the assault?"

"First off, her time at Fantasy Kings is the only thing in her past I've uncovered with ties to anything the least bit sordid, so I looked into it. The bouncer, Big D, matches the description given to us by our witness. From a distance, I saw him get out of a truck similar to the one described by our witness. We're working on finding that truck."

"How did you track them down?"

"Please, for the moment, just trust that I did. I'll fill you in, but I have to go let Jenny's family know and get on a plane. If I don't leave right now, I will miss the plane."

There were several seconds of silence. I was not making friends with the detective.

"Okay, you get out here. But one more question. You sent that little girl as a bodyguard?"

"Yes. Sounds to me like she did her job. Don't judge her by her size. She is seriously good at what she does. She did take on two guys, a knife, and a gun. I'm headed that way. I will meet with you and go over everything I know. Tell me how Jenny is."

"Doctors are working on her. I'm waiting to find out if I have to call in a homicide. I do hope she is lucky. I look forward to talking to you."

"I am on my way."

I gave her my cell number, and she gave me hers. I talked a bit more to Angelique, telling her to stay at the hospital until we got there. I told her to let the detective know she had no idea for sure who broke in or why and to not get pressured into talking too much. I looked at the time. There was no way I'd make the next plane to New Orleans. It would be three hours before I could catch a plane.

I called Rocky.

"Investigations."

"Rocky, Sam. Somebody attacked the girls. Jenny is in the hospital. I'm booking a flight. I assume you want me to get you a ticket. We can't leave for three hours."

"What happened? How is she?"

I told him what I'd learned from Angelique, that Jenny's condition was bad and she was in surgery.

"Dammit," he said. "We'll take my plane. It's slow but will get us there about the same time we'd get there anyway, and we won't have to check a bag."

"I wasn't planning on checking a bag, but, yeah, your plane is a good idea."

"If we don't check a bag, we can't take a gun. I don't know about you, but I'm taking mine. You know where to go, right?"

"Yes. I'll see you there."

"I'm on my way in five minutes."

Rocky keeps his airplane at Scholes International Airport, the general aviation airport on Galveston Island. Scholes is about twenty miles from my house instead of the sixty miles to Houston's Hobby Airport. I called Thumper's phone and left a message briefly explaining what had happened, assuring him that Angelique was okay and that I'd call him when I found out more.

At the airport, Rocky's wife Marlene was with him. She hugged me and said, "If y'all got her hurt bad, I'm going to kill you both."

The three of us left in Rocky's high wing Cessna and headed over the Gulf in a straight line toward New Orleans.

Rocky had called ahead to a service company at the airport and arranged for a rental car. As soon as we got close and to a point where my phone could catch a signal, it started beeping to let me know I had messages. They were all from Thumper. We landed at Lakeside Airport. Rocky quickly made arrangements about his plane. They'd started our rental car as we landed and had the air-conditioning doing its job. We headed for the University Medical Center.

I called Angelique. "Sam, I'm scared. I guess she's still

in surgery. Nobody is telling me anything."

"Hang in there. We're on the way. Is Detective Robichaud around?"

"No, but you're supposed to call her first thing. She said she'd meet you back here."

"Okay. We'll be there as fast as possible."

I called the detective. She said she'd head to the hospital.

Rocky and I didn't talk much. He concentrated on driving way too fast. Marlene sat quietly looking out the window, probably seeing nothing. I concentrated on what to tell the detective, but couldn't even plan that until I'd talked to Angelique. I tried to call Thumper, but the call went to his voice-mail. I listened to the messages he'd left. He was on the way.

At the main reception desk of the hospital, we ran into some reluctance to tell us whether Jenny was there or not, even though Rocky said he was her uncle and her guardian. Before he could lose his cool, Marlene pushed him aside and pulled a stack of papers out of her purse.

"We are her aunt and uncle and have been her legal guardians for years. Here is a certified copy of the court order making us so. Also, here is a certified copy of the Medical Power of Attorney for her we hold. I have her insurance information. Mr. Locke is her attorney, and the police want to speak with him. We are all going to where she is. Before I go, I will stop by where you want me to in order to provide the insurance information, but the three of us will be going to where she is. Thank you."

And we did. Rocky and I followed directions to the intensive-care unit on the fourth floor of the hospital. As we got on the elevator, Rocky said, "I love that woman."

The person manning the desk in intensive care looked

at her computer and told us Jenny was just out of surgery, and the surgeon would meet us in the waiting room in a moment. In that waiting room, amid the calming artwork, surprisingly comfortable looking chairs, and a variety of magazines on small tables, we found Angelique, sitting small and quiet, clutching a tissue. She wore scrubs someone had given her. She'd washed her hands and arms, but there was blood in places she'd missed and a smear of blood behind her ear. She jumped up and hugged me saying, "I'm sorry. I'm so sorry. I didn't see them. I'm sorry."

"Stop it," I said. "Nothing about this is your fault."

"She saved me, Sam. She didn't back down. She saved me from them."

She started crying.

"Is Detective Robichaud here somewhere?"

"No, not yet. I guess she's on the way."

"Yeah, she is. I may not have much time. What did you tell her?"

"That we'd reported the break-ins. That I had no stalkers I knew about. That you were trying to find anything connected to my past that might be a problem. That you think one of the two guys somebody saw is Big D. She kept coming at me all sorts of ways, but I just kept telling her I didn't know anything. She made me cry."

"We are still not going to say anything about finding somebody dead in your apartment. It should'nt come up. I will try to do all the talking from here on out."

She nodded.

"Now, are you going to dance tonight?"

"How can I?"

"Jenny is in surgery, being taken care of. There's nothing you can do here. Are you hurt? Are you mentally capable of dancing?"

"No, I'm not hurt. Mentally, I don't know. Dancing should be automatic, but do you think I should?"

"I don't see why not. As long as we can make sure you're safe."

Rocky said, "I'll go with you."

"But Jenny's here. You're going to want to be with her, aren't you?"

"My wife will sit by her bed. There's nothing I can do here. Sam will be here when she wakes up to see if she can answer any questions about who attacked you. I'd rather be with you, looking for them."

Rocky spoke with a controlled calm but vibrated with a focused, angry energy. He wanted them to come at Angelique again. He wanted to be there when they did.

"I can perform. I need to let them know. They called because I missed a rehearsal. I told them we were mugged, and my friend is in the hospital. Is that okay?"

"Perfect."

"I'll call them and tell them I'll be there."

A woman approached us. She wore jeans and a tailored jacket. Her salted black hair, almost shorter than mine, curled against her scalp. Her dark eyes focused on us, not just looking at us, but recording the scene. I knew it must be Robichaud. Angelique moved off a ways to call the theater.

"Detective?"

"Yes." She came my way and shook my hand.

"Samuel Locke. This is Wallace Rockford. He is Genevieve's uncle and another of my investigators."

She shook his hand, turned to me, and said, "PIs, lawyers, and bodyguards. Are you ready to tell me what's going on here?"

That's when a doctor entered the room. We were the only people in the waiting area, so he came straight toward us and said, "Genevieve Mill's family? I'm Dr. Smithson. I worked on her."

We made quick introductions. Speaking straight to Rocky, he said, "First, the good news. She is alive and should stay that way. I'm sorry you had to wait so long. She suffered some trauma to the head, and it took us a while to make sure she was in shape for all the surgery we had to do. She had some cuts from a knife, a couple of which did more damage than the others. One of them nicked an artery here." He pointed to the inside of his arm. He looked at Angelique. "Was it you with her?" Angelique nodded. "You saved her life. Good job." In clinical fashion, he continued, "She had a gunshot wound to the abdomen that took most of my time. Luckily, it must have been a jacketed bullet. It went straight through her, but it left behind lots of things to fix up. She's now short a kidney."

Angelique took my arm and sagged against me. Marlene arrived in time to hear that last bit, and she took Rocky's hand.

Dr. Smithson went on to say he'd been more worried about her head injuries than anything. It looked like she'd been kicked in the head a few times. A neurosurgeon evaluated her condition and continued to monitor the danger to her brain. He was hoping no surgery would be necessary. A few of her ribs were broken from the fight.

Angelique's hand tightened on my arm.

Dr. Smithson continued. "She should recover, but she did suffer some significant damage and something might pop up. We're watching her closely. She can't have visitors for a while. We're not going to let her wake up until some time tomorrow. Even then, she might be out of it. We're in that terrible wait and see stage. She's young and in great shape. Best case, unless something surprises us, she could get out of here in a week to ten days. She'll need to take it easy and have some help at home for a while. It's possible she'll be in pretty good shape in six to eight weeks if she'll exercise right. She looks to me like she knows how to work out and take care of herself."

He left. Detective Robichaud turned to me. "I guess that was as good as possible. Now, are you going to help me find them?"

"We don't know much. In fact, we might know nothing. I've told you everything that's happened and some things we've discovered." Most everything, I thought.

I told her again about the two break-ins in less than a week, one on Friday of the previous week, and the second on Monday.

She turned to Angelique. "You said no ex-boyfriend?"

"No."

"Any messages or fan mail from somebody who seemed a little creepy?"

"No. I don't get much fan mail. It comes in sometimes after a performance."

I asked, "Do you get all your fan mail? Or, is it screened by the theater?"

"It goes go to the theater. I assume they give it all to me."

I hadn't thought about looking into that. Damn. I said, "We'll find out. But, it doesn't feel like an obsessive stalker kind of deal."

Detective Robichaud said, "Why is that counselor?"

The detective and I were not yet getting along. Police are wary of lawyers and vice versa. I ignored her attitude, knowing it was something we had to get past.

"The few stalkers I've represented started with what passes for a romantic or sexual interest and they make themselves known. There's been nothing like that in her case. There have been two break-ins when she wasn't home. The highlight of the last one was a knife through the flat screen. It looks like her place got searched. It's just not the obsessive stalker kind of deal."

"I agree. Probably. But you never know about the pervs. Any underwear missing?"

Angelique said, "No. Just some cash."

To me, the detective said, "So, what do you think is going on?"

"I have no idea. We're trying to figure it out."

"Instead of letting the police handle it."

"We made a report to the police. Rocky will get you the info about who they talked to. They did as much as you would in the case of a break-in with some vandalism and nothing missing but forty dollars in cash. Maybe if you call, they'll get more interested."

She nodded. "And you're going to keep telling me she has no idea why someone is after her?"

"I told you on the phone about the two guys our witness saw going over the fence at her apartment complex. Rocky will give you the info on that witness. That was the night of that last break-in, one big and one smaller, maybe Hispanic. The bar has a bouncer called Big D. He's a big guy. Might be him. He hangs out with a Hispanic guy who we're tracking down. Angelique thinks the guy with the knife is Hispanic."

"She described the two guys who went after them this morning. Didn't say one of them was big."

"I know. Doesn't sound like it was Big D, but she also heard one who sounded local to here. Maybe he was local talent, hired for the occasion."

The detective shrugged. "Maybe."

"There's something else. Still thin. Dancing at that bar is the only sketchy thing in her past. Bobby Andrus was her boss there and the person she interacted with most. I went to Beaumont to look into Bobby Andrus and to check out the bar where she worked. I got the distinct impression Andrus has not been around for a while and nobody, not even his brother Landry, knows where he is."

"What do you think that means?"

I let a little exasperation show. "I have no idea. But I'm not willing to say that if he's gone missing it's a coincidence. Maybe I'm wrong. Maybe there is no connection to the Andrus enterprise at all." I could hear the thin ice cracking beneath me.

Angelique stood there listening. Robichaud turned to her and said, "Nothing else to add?"

"No"

"And you have no idea about why somebody from here or there or anywhere would do this?"

"No. Absolutely not. I left Beaumont years ago and have no idea why they might be looking for me now."

"Love or money, no doubt. Did you have a thing with any of them back then?"

"No. I didn't have a thing with anybody until I got out of there. Almost turned me off men forever. Bobby actually made sure I was safe. He treated me more like a daughter than a potential girlfriend, other than making money off me dancing half naked."

"Did you rip him off when you left?"

"No. When I turned eighteen, he offered to pay for a boob job. I told him I quit and walked out. He called out to me to wait, but I kept going. The club held all my tip money. I didn't even get what I was owed that night. I didn't go back and have not seen or heard from him since."

Robichaud said, "I don't know what else we're going to do. I glanced at the surveillance video at the parking garage. It caught the van leaving. One dark blue van, no plates, a driver and passenger with their faces covered. Probably stolen. We'll find it. There are people looking closer at the video, but I don't expect much." She asked Angelique, "What are you going to do now?"

"I guess go perform tonight. There's nothing I can do here. I'm not hurt and not dancing tonight would cause a lot of trouble. Plus, I don't want them to have made me stop."

"Listen, I've heard enough to think somebody is after you for some reason. I can only hope that you've been honest with me." Angelique started to say something, but the detective held up her hand and continued. "I can work with the fact that you either don't know anything or there's something you don't want to tell me. Don't say anything unless you have something new to tell me. I'm convinced enough to tell you to be very careful. From what you've said, something unusual is going on. They were in a van. That means it could have been an abduction attempt. Be careful."

I said, "If you're convinced somebody is after her, can she get some kind of police protection while she's here?"

"I'm not convinced a hundred percent. Police protection? No. I'm not even going to waste my time asking. So far, other than that poor girl who got hurt so bad, you have protected her. I should probably tell you to go home and sit behind locked doors until this is resolved, but you're not going to do that."

"Rocky's going with you," I said to Angelique. "I can't imagine that they'll come after you in the theater. I have another idea. Detective Robichaud, you have tickets for tonight's performance. Maybe we can't get any police protection, but would you like to watch the performance from backstage? Maybe escort her and Rocky back to her hotel after the show?"

"Yes," Angelique said. "I can get you backstage for sure after this."

Robichaud nodded. "I could do that. It'll screw up my date night, but it might be interesting." Turning to me, she said, "Where are you going to be staying?"

"We'll get a suite somewhere and have Angelique move in."

"I have a suite," Angelique said.

I said, "But they came after you there. We'll move."

The detective said, "I suggest the Desmond Hotel. It's kind of new, and it's nice. The head of security used to be a cop and I know him. His name is Tom Carlson. Look him up when you get there. I'll call and explain to him what's going on."

"Okay, we're going there." I turned to Angelique. "Tell whoever is paying for your room that you are uncomfortable where you are and you want to move, but don't tell them where. I'll take your key and get you moved." I checked the time. "Thumper will get here soon. I'll need to rent another car."

"Thumper?" asked Robichaud. "Who is Thumper?"

"Thumper Lee. Angelique's grandfather."

"Thumper Lee? The blues guy?

"Yes."

"This case is getting more and more interesting."

I gave Detective Robichaud a copy of all the photographs Rocky took at the bar and pointed out Big D to her. Marlene advised she would spend the night at the hospital. No one tried to dissuade her. Angelique and Rocky left to go to the theater. Angelique said she would leave a message for the detective at the will call window about getting backstage.

There was an Enterprise car rental place right across Canal Street from the hospital. As I walked that way, I called and made arrangements for a car. While signing the papers, initialing here and there, and getting the car keys, Thumper called. He'd arrived. I went to pick him up at the airport.

I filled Thumper in on details as we drove to Angelique's hotel. We checked Angelique and Jenny out of their room. I declined the opportunity to talk to management about what happened, telling them I would get in touch later. That left them a little nervous.

We drove quietly to the new hotel.

The Desmond Hotel, close to the Mississippi and east of the French Quarter offered the familiar anonymity of the typical business person's hotel. I skipped the valet and went straight to the parking garage, making sure to park in full view of a security camera. We made our way to the sleek, modern lobby in an elevator festooned with Mardi Gras posters and advertisements for the hotel's cafe and restaurant. I asked at the desk for Tom Carlson, their head of security.

Carlson arrived while I booked a suite in my name and on my credit card. Perhaps I'd get reimbursed by the ballet company. Carlson wore a nice suit and a military hair-cut. We made our introductions.

"Detective Robichaud told me you'd be here. We're happy to help out, but you have to know that my first obligation is to the hotel and its other guests. She said we shouldn't expect trouble."

"No. I don't know what she told you, but there were a couple of instances back in Houston where my client's home was broken into and some vandalism done. Then, there was an attack here that surprised us. I assume Detective Robichaud filled you in on that?"

"Yes."

"I don't even know if the stuff in Houston is connected to the attack here. It could have been a random parking lot mugging."

"Didn't sound like the detective thinks that."

"No. We think they're related. I think they picked up on my client at the theater and followed her to her hotel. So, we moved my client here and put the room in my name. There's no reason for them to know me. She'll be escorted back here, and the folks with her know what they're doing. They'll make sure they're not followed."

He nodded. "Let me know if I can help." He wrote his cell number on the back of a business card and gave it to me.

The suite was as expected, businessman nice with two separate bedrooms, one with its own bathroom and a large Jacuzzi-style tub. Floor to ceiling windows overlooked the city. The common area, large enough to entertain, had a sleeper-sofa and a full kitchen area. Thumper said he'd take the sofa, right outside Angelique's door. We settled in. He sat down in a chair with his guitar, looked out the windows at the city, and started playing sad, lonely chords.

In the smaller bedroom, I lay on the bed closest to the windows, my hands behind my head, and thought. I thought about the jumble of things happening and could find no way to make sense of them. I needed to know more. Whatever I did to get more information would increase the danger, but we had to do something. We had to get more.

I watched some television. We had a meal delivered by room service. We watched more television.

Rocky called about eleven. I gave him the room

number of the suite.

My answering service sent me a text message telling me I had a call. I called the service. Jessica, the woman who works weekend nights, said, "You had one call this evening. A Mr. Landry Andrus called. It was not an emergency. He wants to see you about some property you are selling him. I sent you an email with his number."

I'd stirred the pot.

CHAPTER ELEVEN

A KNOCK ON THE SUITE'S DOOR interrupted my thoughts before I could digest that Landry Andrus wanted to talk to me. Thumper opened the door to Rocky and Angelique just as I walked into the main room.

Angelique made a noise of delight at seeing him, and Thumper hugged her. He said, "How are you? You okay?"

"Yes. Yes. I'm okay."

"How did it go tonight?"

"Okay. Not spectacular, but I got it done." She turned to me. "How's Jenny?"

"I haven't heard anything."

"Marlene called me," Rocky said. "No change, but the doctors said she's passed some critical point in time and that's a good thing."

Angelique asked, "Can we go see her in the morning?"

I said, "We'll go to the hospital. I don't know if we'll get to see her."

That's when Detective Robichaud called.

"I just got a call. We found the van. As expected, it was stolen. They left it in a parking lot. The fact that it was stolen makes it more doubtful that this was a simple mugging for cash. Only the really stupid crooks go to the trouble of stealing a van for that. Forensics is going over it. I'm going to bed. I'll call you in the morning."

"Okay, thanks. Let's talk more tomorrow."

"You got something new to tell me?"

"No. Seriously. You know everything."

I hung up the phone, and Rocky asked, "What? Why the funny face?"

"They found the van. It was stolen."

"Yeah, I gathered that much, but why that face?"

"It's interesting that the detective called me that's all. Police don't usually share a thing they don't have to. For some reason, Detective Robichaud is invested in us. Her calling me is a peace offering. She wants some kind of an alliance."

"That's a good thing, right?"

"Yes. It's an excellent thing. Surprising, that's all."

Rocky said there was nothing he could do at the hospital right then, and he'd be better off getting rest. He went to bed. Angelique, obviously tired, said she hadn't been at her best at her performance, but she'd been good enough. She was happy Jenny had turned a corner for the better, and she'd be more relaxed during Sunday's performance. Thumper said he'd be there. We all went to bed. Rocky was already snoring in our shared room. It irritated me for the three or four minutes it took me to fall asleep.

THE NEXT MORNING, Marlene met us in the hospital's waiting room.

"She's awake. They've taken the tube out of her throat. She's getting better."

Rocky said, "Can I see her?"

"They said family only, one at a time for a very short time. So, go. It's room 403, the door right outside the nurse's station."

In a few minutes, Rocky came back with a very exasperated nurse.

Rocky said, "Sam, she wants to talk to you and me."

The very stern looking nurse said, "She's insistent and won't let me give her a sedative until she talks to you. I'm going to let you two talk to her. For about five minutes. No more. Don't get her excited. Don't piss me off."

Marlene said, "Don't worry. They won't. They know that will piss me off, and they know better than to do that. Y'all keep your priorities straight while you're in there."

Rocky and I held up our hands in surrender.

The blinds in Jenny's room darkened most of the room. A soft light over the sink and equipment with LED displays created a vortex focused on her. A soft electronic beep kept time in a quiet rush of air. Her eyes were closed. She looked too small for the bed. Butterfly bandages closed parts of her bruised face. Dark sutures etched a harsh line across her ghostly pale forehead. A few stitches extended the line of her mouth from her chapped lips to just below a dimple. Two IV's dripped stuff into her, one in her hand and one in her arm. A gauze cap covered her hair. A cup of ice chips sat on her bedside table.

The room smelled of filtered air, astringent, and injured girl.

Rocky took the hand without a needle in it. Her fingers curled over his. Bandages covered the tips of a couple of her fingers. Bruised and blackened eyes opened. I flinched. The whites of her eye weren't. They were bloody red.

She raised the fingers of her needle punctured hand to wave at me.

She started to speak and had to start again, her voice dim and raspy. I leaned in to hear. "I'm going to have some killer scars."

I said, "I'm so sorry this happened to you, but you

kicked ass."

She smiled, swallowed visibly, and said, "One of them might be local. He said something in French. He has a tattoo on his wrist. It's a couple of those masks. You know, those full face masks. One smiling. One frowning. One black, one a lighter color."

"Comedy and tragedy?"

"Don't know. Is that what they are?" She swallowed with effort. "You see them places all the time."

More information. Maybe the best yet. I asked, "Which wrist?"

She closed her eyes, thinking. "It would be his left wrist. It's going to have a big scratch right through the tattoo. I bet I made him bleed." She smiled. "Yeah, I did. I made him bleed."

I looked at her nails. She said, "Yeah, might be some DNA. I hope they didn't clean me up too much. Did the cops scrape my nails?"

"I'll find out."

Rocky took out his notepad and sketched a couple of masks, full-faced with pointy chins, one with an exaggerated frown and one with an exaggerated smile. He showed it to her.

"Yes," she said. "Their chins tilted in at each other. The frown was on the left."

Rocky revised his sketch, shading the one on the left and held it out to her.

She nodded. "Much closer."

Jenny took a deep breath, closed her eyes and tears squeezed out and tracked down her face. "I'm sorry. I don't know why I'm crying. I tried. They surprised me. They shouldn't have, but they did. Angel and I were having too much fun. It's my fault."

Rocky said, "Shut up. You fought off two guys armed with a gun and a knife. Sounds like you did your job."

"Exactly," I said. "You saved her."

Jenny whispered, "You needed to know about the tattoo."

"How about the other guy. Anything?"

"Not much," she said, her voice raspy, forced. I gave her the glass of ice chips, and she sucked on a couple. "He was small. Hard. Wiry little fucker. Dark brown eyes. Hispanic, I'm sure." She swallowed with effort, and her eyes reflected the pain. "Never blinked. Cold. I thought he'd kill me. I'll try to remember more. Later. I really want a pain pill. I made them wait, but I hurt like hell."

I patted her hand and told her I'd find the nurse. I left Rocky alone with her.

I sent the nurse in and put in a call to Detective Robichaud. I left a message for her to call me.

Rocky came out of Jenny's room, grim faced and quiet. He spoke to his wife. She patted him on the chest and went into Jenny's room. It was my fault that Jenny had been attacked and, as Rocky walked toward me, I worried about how he felt about that.

He shook his head, and said, "She made a mistake. She should have never approached their car while it was parked next to a van. She was distracted."

"I am so sorry this happened."

"Not your fault. She learned a very painful, expensive lesson. I wish she'd find other work, but she will be damn good at this. It's what she wants to do. She knows she screwed up. It's not likely she'll repeat that particular mistake."

Angelique asked, "How is she?"

Rocky turned to her and nodded. "She hurts, but she'll

be okay. I'll be going with you this afternoon unless something happens. Can I get in with you?"

"You will, or I won't dance."

He said, "Go see her. She asked about you."

"They told me family only for now."

"Screw that. Go see her. Before she goes to sleep."

My phone rang. It was Robichaud. I told her Jenny was awake and doing the best as could be expected. "And," I said, "the guy they think sounded like a local? He has a tattoo on his left wrist. It is comedy and tragedy, those happy and sad-faced theatrical masks. One white. One black. She scratched him right across the tattoo. She was trying to get a DNA sample for you."

"Tough little girl. Now that's some good stuff. If he's local and he's been arrested, we should have a record of the tattoo. We scraped her nails. Thanks to television we can't have a good trial without DNA."

"Good. There was a piece of duct tape holding Angelique's apartment door shut after the last break-in. Call Houston and tell them they should check it for DNA. I'll stay on them until they do it."

"I'll try. What are your plans?"

"Rocky is going to the ballet with Angelique. I have some calls to return. Other than that, I guess I'll be sitting around somewhere hoping you call me with some news."

Somewhere turned out to be the suite at the Desmond Hotel. It's where I spent most of that Sunday. I thought about returning the phone call from Landry Andrus. His call meant he'd entered the game. I regretted the approach I'd made that attracted his attention. Tied by needles to plastic bags and tended to by machines, Jenny brought a harsh reality to what we were doing. I'd not put enough thought into approaching Andrus. It wouldn't hurt to do some thinking before I returned his call.

I usually tried to not call Joshua on his days off but made an excuse that I needed to let him know I might not be around in the coming week. I could have waited until the next day, but, frankly, I wanted to touch base with normal. I told him my fuzzy plans. He told me he and Darla were practicing welding. He accepted the news that I might be busy elsewhere with his usual good cheer.

Trying to find something to pass the time, I called the theater to get a ticket to watch Angelique dance. The performance had sold out.

I lay on the bed thinking until Detective Robichaud called me.

"Mr. Locke, I'm at the hospital with Ms. Mills. She made me call you, and I'm doing so in order to make sure she does not get up to find a phone."

"What's up?"

"I showed her an identification photo we have of a tattoo. I showed her several, actually. She picked one without hesitation as the tattoo she saw on the arm of the person who attacked her. It was interesting watching her heart rate go up on the machine when she saw the picture."

"And a name? Do you know where to find him?"

There was a pause. Robichaud struggled with that cop reticence. "Mr. Locke, I'm telling you stuff I wouldn't ordinarily share because this case is bigger than the attack that happened here. From what you've told me it looks like this thing stretches from here to Beaumont and Houston. I'll get in touch with the police there, but I think you're better equipped at keeping them interested, a bigger fly in their ointment if you will."

"Fair enough."

"We're looking for a guy with the poetic name of

Thibaux Arceneaux, both names ending in a-u-x. He's known on the street as TeeBoy." She spelled his nickname.

"We've had him several times. Petty theft, assault, domestic violence involving a girlfriend, although it looks like she might have been the one kicking ass.

"The closest to legitimate he does is drive a tow truck. He actually earns some honest dollars with it, but he can't help himself. We got him for shaking down tourists with his tow truck, either towing or threatening to tow when he shouldn't and taking cash from them. The usual crappy little crimes for a pissant criminal like him.

"He did seven years for an armed robbery that was most likely an effort to recover an illegal gambling debt. He got in a little trouble in prison, and they sent him to the graduate school known as Angola. He's known to brag about his Angola time while drinking in bars."

"Sounds lovely."

"He ought to stay out of bars. That's how we'll find him."

"Sounds like you know him personally."

"Not really. Just reading his paper."

"Parole?"

"Nope, he's done. He can vote and everything. Not supposed to own a gun, but you know. One thing is curious. The Andrus boys are thought to be pretty smart. I don't see them hiring a swamp-trash loser like TeeBoy. He's not their type. He does work for some of our lesser skilled criminals, gamblers and enforcers, perhaps a pimp or two, but nothing approaching the professionalism of the Andrus organization. Hell, from what I hear, the Andrus enterprise is mostly legit these days."

"There's a connection somewhere. I'm sure. I'm not sure Landry is involved, but I bet Bobby is."

"And there are no more details about that?"

"No."

She made a noise. "That's the one thing where I'm not sure about you. Don't make me lose faith. Well, we'll find TeeBoy. Maybe he can enlighten me. I'm thinking his Angola stay may have disabused him of any idea that it is an honorable thing to take the fall for somebody."

"Thanks for updating me."

"No problem. I'll let the police in Houston know what's going on, but I suggest you try to convince them that the break-in at your client's apartment was something more than random. Otherwise, it's doubtful they'll get excited about what's going on."

"Will do. I will stay in touch. I'm headed back to Houston tomorrow. You have all my numbers."

I was out of things to do. I went down to the gift shop and bought a pair of shorts and a t-shirt sporting a gaudy mask and inscribed with Laisssez Les Bons Temps Rouler. I went to the hotel's health center. Working on the resistance stations and the treadmill helped me think as much as laying on the bed helped me think. I remained at a loss. Maybe TeeBoy would have something to tell us if the New Orleans Police Department found him. Robichaud seemed confident that would happen.

I decided to return the phone call from Andrus. I hoped he would be easy to divert by just telling him his brother had made inquiries about property in the Houston area suitable for a strip club. I'd tell him if his brother was no longer interested, it was no big deal to me. I hoped he'd be satisfied I knew nothing else. I'd raise more attention and suspicion if I did not return his call.

No time like the present. I used a feature provided by my answering service where I called a number on their system, entered a code, punched in the number, and it made the call. That way, my official office number showed up on caller ID instead of my cell phone number.

There was no answer. I tried to sound like a real-estate salesman and said, "This is Samuel Locke calling about the property that interests you."

Phone tag was perfectly acceptable to me.

Angelique, Thumper, and Rocky returned from the ballet.

I asked, "How did it go?"

Angelique said, "Much better than last night. I'm done, but I want to stay here with Jenny. Is that going to work?"

"If we can make sure you're safe. The bad guys are probably hiding out or back in Texas. I guess they could be watching for you at the hospital."

"Do you think ... "

"I don't know. We have learned something, though."

Rocky asked, "What's up?"

"Thibaux Arceneaux, better know as TeeBoy."

Angelique asked, "Who's that?"

"That's the name of one of the guys who attacked you. The one who said something in French. Jenny described his tattoo, and the police had a photo. He has a record for a variety of things. Detective Robichaud is confident they'll find him."

Thumper said, "I'm staying with her."

Rocky said, "Unless you need me in Houston, I'm going to stay here. I'll look out for them."

"I don't know what I'd need you for. I have no idea what's going on. Might be more for you to do here than back home. If something comes up, I'll call you."

WE DROVE TO THE hospital and, in ones and twos, visited Jenny. She looked better, still bruised and bloodied and hurting, but she was making a comeback. She seethed with anger at her attackers and wanted to know what we were doing. She wanted to go after them. In a scratchy voice, she told me, "Almost ready for round two."

I booked a late flight back to Houston Hobby Airport on Southwest Airlines. At Louis Armstrong Airport, I got in line with the weary and hungover tourists going home and the folks flying to Houston to do business. The businessmen and women all toted briefcases. The weariness in their eyes did not come from too much Bourbon Street. It was the resigned countenance of those climbing on the treadmill once again. I'd bet each of those business travelers had heard the saying: It's hard to drain the swamp when you're up to your ass in alligators. I'd also bet I was the only person on the plane working on something where somebody actually got his ass fed to alligators.

We landed on time in Houston, and Joshua met me. On the drive back to my car at the airport in Galveston, we talked about very little. I followed him back to my place. He'd installed a porch light by the door to his apartment. It was on and welcomed him home. My porch was dark.

I expected to sleep late, but woke up before dawn. I drank one cup of coffee and ran on the beach in the dark, my steps measured by the pulse of silvery edges of waves lapping the beach. The morning air, blowing cool off the Gulf and scented of the sea, created in me an undefined longing. I breathed the lonely breeze deeply and finished my run, splashing the edge of the Gulf.

I packed a bag, ready for whatever might come up over the next few days, thinking I might spend most of the week in Houston. I made two travel cups of coffee to sip while enduring commuter hell. As I started my car, Joshua came out of his place.

"Any instructions boss?"

"I'll probably be gone most of the week. Y'all work on building grills. We're going to start selling more of them. Let me know what kind of truck you think we need to get to haul them around."

"A heavy-duty pickup. Personally, I'd buy an F-350 turbo diesel or a GMC. I think we need to build a gooseneck trailer for it. That way we can haul more of them farther."

"Okay. I'm glad you've thought about it. We agree. But get to work on those grills. We'll have to sell a lot more to pay for a truck like that. Start estimating what it will cost to build a trailer. It might be better to just buy one. Call me if you need anything. Say hi to Darla"

If not careful, I'd be working for him someday.

I finished the coffee way before I parked at my office building. I lazily took the elevator up one floor. I turned toward my office and stumbled to a stop. Landry Andrus and another man stood in the hall outside my office door. Andrus was as impeccably groomed as when I'd talked to him in his bar. I'd been right, his shoes were shinier than mine. It took me a moment to realize the other man was Rich, the bartender at Fantasy Kings. He was not in a suit. A long-sleeved white shirt hid most of the tattoos on his arms. Both turned at the ping of the elevator. They waited for me.

If I'd seen them before they saw me, I'd have turned and left the building. But I could not avoid them. I put on a lawyer face and made the walk to the office. I had an innocuous smile on my face, but my mind was in turmoil. What did they want? How did they find my office?

"Mr. Andrus," I said.

"Mr. Locke," he said.

I had keys in one hand and my briefcase in another, so he got a nod from me instead of a handshake. I opened the office door and invited them in. He looked around at my sparsely furnished space.

"New office," I said, "How can I help you? Did you talk to your brother about the properties?"

"No."

We sat and looked at each other. It is fundamental. The first person who speaks in such a situation is the underdog. We began the game.

He sighed, and said, "Mr. Locke, have you heard from my brother?"

"I don't understand. He's not a really a client of mine, but I'm not sure I should be discussing his interests if you are not privy to them."

Rich stood by the door, impassive and large, his arms folded. His eyes tracked the conversation.

"Here's the deal, Mr. Locke. I'm going to be straightforward with you because we need to figure out some stuff as quickly as possible. My brother works for me. He is not an equal business partner as you seem to think."

"Okay. All the more reason to wonder why you're here. If he's doing something on his own, I should talk to him, right?"

"I would be surprised if he's trying to do any business whatsoever with you."

"I don't understand."

"I need to know if you've heard from him and what exactly you were really doing with him."

He leaned forward. He projected quiet competence, but I noticed a few things, a tightening around the eyes, a flaring of his nostrils, a slight flush on the edges of his ears. He was holding in a mounting pressure. If we were in court, and he was an adverse witness, I would do my best to light his fuse, make him explode. Truth often escaped with the loss of contained anger or fear or whatever the witness was trying to control. But courtrooms came with built-in security. Here, in my office, where I did not know what was going on and without the protection of being in a public place with armed cops nearby, I did not want to set him off.

"I want to put him on some property to buy in exchange for a commission from the seller. I have not heard from him for some time."

"I've made inquiries. Nobody knows anything about him looking to buy property for which he has no capital to purchase."

Landry Andrus talked like a businessman, but something was off. Landry Andrus might have been successful at what he did, but, to some degree, he was playing a part. I suspected he wasn't far removed from some rough and tumble roots. I distinctly felt that at any moment, upon request from his boss, Rich could roughly tumble me to whatever degree he desired.

I finally said something absolutely true. "Mr. Andrus, I have no idea what's going on, but if you're not interested in buying some property, I don't know what you want from me."

He sat back and looked at me with a cold, calculating expression. After several seconds passed, he said, "You're a lawyer, I take it?"

"Yes."

"And you build grills or some such shit?"

"Yes."

"And, God help me, if I ever want to go fishing, you'll take me?"

I shrugged. "I do lots of things."

"But the real-estate company with the listing for all that property tells me they have no idea why you're trying to sell any of those lots. They've never worked with you and seem to think it is not something you do. Evidently, you only recently got copies of the info on the property you came into my place trying to sell."

Damn.

"Mr. Andrus, as you can tell from the list of things I do to earn a living, I am open to all sorts of money-making opportunities. It doesn't look like this one is going to pan out. No big deal. I can just build a few more grills, catch a few more fish."

"No reason to be a smart ass with me. I believe you when you say you look for opportunities. I just don't, at this point, believe you about your interest in my brother. I think you came looking for him for some other reason. It would be best for you to tell me what that reason is. I don't react well to liars and cheats."

"Mr. Andrus, I tried to meet with your brother. I am not trying to cheat him out of anything. If he's not available, fine. I'll move on to the next thing. The fact that you took the trouble to look into me and drive down here suggests there's something else going on, but I have no clue what. I can only tell you I am not involved with your problems. I don't want to be. If you are interested in buying some property in Houston, I am open to helping you out with that."

"How did you and my brother get in touch with each other?"

"We got in touch because I am a lawyer. I knew of some properties for sale. I thought I could make some money."

I could see him take measured breaths. Finally he stood

up. "Neither my brother or I have plans to buy any property in Houston. I'm going to keep looking into this thing. Something's up. You call me when you decide to tell me what's going on. It will be best for me to hear from you before I learn something from somebody else."

He turned toward the door. Rich opened it. They left. I was sweating and felt hollow. It wasn't the most productive of meetings, but I'd learned more than did Andrus. He convinced me he had no clue what his brother had been up to. I learned Bobby probably did not have a lot of money of his own. Landry thought I might know where to find his brother. Neither of us had a clue about what was going on.

I tried to unravel the tangled threads of the thing. There was a connection to the attacks on Angelique and Bobby Andrus, but it must not include Landry Andrus. Bobby's death probably meant he was not in charge of whatever trouble focused on her, or, if he had been, there had been a mutiny in the ranks. I needed to look closer at the bouncer and the guy who dropped him off at work the day I was there.

I needed to look for a tie between them and TeeBoy in New Orleans. If Landry Andrus had no connection to the thing, and Bobby Andrus had not been a big part of it, I needed to look closer at Angelique's life outside of Fantasy Kings. Maybe somebody had tracked Angelique to Fantasy Kings and then signed up Bobby and Big D and his buddy as hired guns.

I got the impression Landry did not share much of the wealth with his brother. Maybe Bobby had a desire to get some money of his own behind his brother's back. I needed to try to find out where that money would come from.

My phone rang. It was Rocky.

"Sam, we're all safe here. I'm at the hospital. They've

moved Jenny to a different room. Thumper, Angelique, and Marlene are in there with her. I've called Detective Robichaud but have not heard back from her."

"How's Jenny doing?"

"Recovering. They're going to let us bring her to Houston in a few days. Marlene will rent as comfortable a car as we can find for that. Jenny is insisting that we move her stuff into the new apartment. I gave up arguing. Marlene will stay with her there for a while. Do you think I can pay Joshua to help get her stuff moved?"

"If Joshua can get into your place and you can describe what he needs to take, we can get her stuff moved today."

"Let's do it tomorrow when I'm there. I'll help him."

"Okay. By the way, I had a visit from Landry Andrus and his bartender, Rich. They were waiting for me when I got to my office this morning. I'm convinced he has no clue what's going on, but he's doing a competent job of sticking his nose into things. This thing is gathering speed."

"Guess we stirred him up."

"Yeah. Something going on is better than nothing, but I'd sure like to get ahead of it whatever it is."

"What's the plan?"

"Hope the cops find TeeBoy. If you have any ideas about finding a connection between TeeBoy and the bouncer at Fantasy Kings, you should try. TeeBoy drives a tow truck. Maybe the towing business is a connection. Have you arranged for somebody in Beaumont to take a look at their salvage and towing business?"

"Yes. I'll call him. Here's Thumper."

Thumper got on the phone and said, "Hey, Sam. I take it we're not a lot closer on who attacked the girls?"

"Nothing concrete, but we're gathering info. We need to go over things. I'll pick you up at the airport unless your truck's there."

"You can pick us up. I have plenty of room for you if you want to come up to the river. Why don't you make us plane reservations. Call me back and let me know when we need to get to the airport."

"Okay. I'm going to make them as early as possible."

"Okay. Angelique doesn't want to leave Jenny, but she'll just have to understand."

"Let her know we need to get them into their new apartment before Jenny gets out here. She needs to supervise that."

"Good idea."

Finally, a good idea.

I bought them a flight on a United flight leaving early that afternoon. Thumper objected when I called him back. He didn't think I'd book them that early.

"Thumper," I said, "I need to talk to you and Angelique about things. We still don't know enough to keep her safe."

"Yeah, you're right. We'll get there."

Rocky called and things took another turn.

CHAPTER TWELVE

R OCKY SAID, "WE FOUND THEM."

"Who?"

"The guys who stabbed her television. I don't know what we're going to do about it, but we found them."

"Tell me about it."

"I got a report from the guy I hired in Beaumont. I'm texting you a couple of photos he took. You know that pickup truck Betty Page saw? She said she could see there was something in the bed of the truck. It's a tow truck, one of those used by repo guys with the tow equipment hidden in the bed of the truck. That's what she saw. It belongs to Andrus Salvage and Towing. We have a picture of it, and we have a picture of the two guys. I'm sending some photos."

My phone chirped with a text message. It was a photo of Big D, the bouncer at Fantasy Kings, talking to a short Hispanic man, standing next to a large, brown pickup truck. I couldn't see anything in the bed of the truck because of the closed tailgate.

The phone chirped with another photo. Rocky's man in Beaumont photographed the truck picking up a vehicle in a parking lot with its towing equipment swung into place. The Hispanic man stood at its side.

I got back on the phone with Rocky. "Yeah, that's them. Got to be. Your guy did good."

"He did even better. He got their names. The little guy

is Carlos Perez. It's on his tow truck operator's permit. We'll look for official records on him. I told my guy to go ahead and find out where he lives but don't do anything to attract attention. I bet that little bastard was in New Orleans with TeeBoy last weekend."

"Could be."

"You recognize the big guy. He's the bouncer. His real name is Steve Delacourt. He doesn't have a tow truck operators license. I gave the same instruction to find out where he lives but attract no attention. We'll get any criminal records on them sometime today."

"Good. Call Detective Robichaud. Give her the names. She expects to find TeeBoy, and she expects he'll save his ass at the expense of others. Maybe she can use those names. Scare him a little. Besides, the more we help her, the more she'll be inclined to keep us in the loop."

"Will do."

I called Joshua and told him about helping move Jenny's stuff to the new place. I worked on a few things. Robichaud called me.

"Hello, Mr. Locke."

"Sam, please."

"Yeah. Anyway. I've talked to your man Mr. Rockwell. Good work getting those names. Sounds solid."

"Hope you get to spring them on TeeBoy. Have you got a line on him, yet?"

"We'll get him. I know he's out there. Our paths are going to cross."

"Good."

"But, I want to make sure you are really watching Ms. Chambray and Ms. Mills."

"We are, but what brought that up?"

"We went through the van they used. I've looked at it."

"And?"

"It was mostly empty and mostly clean. No prints were found we can use. The only clear ones belong to the owner. I'm sure he had nothing to do with this. But, your girl did some damage to somebody. They scrubbed it, but they must have been in a rush. They missed some things. There are traces of blood on an armrest. I'm thinking TeeBoy's."

"Good."

"A few things were in the van that the owner says were not his. There was a roll of duct tape. There were two heavy duty cable ties, one each underneath and on the back of the two seats up front, right down by the floor. That put the ties a couple of feet apart. They are clean and don't look like they've been there long. Looks to me like a handy place to attach another couple of cable ties to tie somebody's wrists. Somebody was ready to tie somebody to the floor, taped up and quiet. Could be somebody ready to rape is what it looks like to me."

"That doesn't make sense."

"Well, it looks like that. Why be prepared to tie her to the floor of the van? Just hog-tie her. Makes it easier to move her quickly. Maybe this is some sexually obsessed fan thing. Those guys you found would know her from her days of topless dancing. Maybe the fire has been burning in one or both of them for a while. Sometimes, the slime feed on each other and come up with grandiose schemes."

"But, two attackers? TeeBoy? He looks like hired help. The other guy there is probably Carlos the tow truck driver, and when they broke into her apartment he was probably with the bouncer, Delacourt. That makes three." Plus Bobby Andrus, I thought. "Two break-ins, vandalism of her apartment, what looks like a search of her stuff here, a stolen van, hiring TeeBoy. Something else is going on."

"I know it sounds too complicated to just be a crazed fan wanting to get close, but crazy people do crazy things. A sexual assault isn't usually the real goal of fan obsession, at least such a well-planned assault. If they happen, they tend to be more a spur of the moment groping."

"Do you really think that's what this is?"

"No. I don't. It smells like something else. Maybe somebody is looking for a side benefit. I'm not much into psychological profiling. People are just too complicated, but maybe that knife through the television is a substitute for some weird fucker's dick."

"Have you talked to the police here?"

"Yes. And if we get more info, we are to let them know. I've even got me a liaison over in the Beaumont police department, a detective Lucy Smith. She'll be calling you."

I made a note of the name. "Detective, I want to thank you for the work you're putting into this."

"It's my job."

"Well, then, I want to think you for keeping me in the loop. I'm not used to that from the police."

"I checked you out a little. You do criminal defense so we are natural enemies, but I didn't find any cop who has a problem with you down there. We don't like visitors to our city getting assaulted, and this thing is bigger than local. You're willing to use resources I don't have. Perhaps you don't feel as constrained by the legal rights of suspects. You got the line on Delacourt and Carlos Perez. Right now, I have to trust you not to screw up."

"One more thing, it looks like you were right when you said whatever is going on doesn't feel like it's related to the Andrus's business."

"Why's that?"

"I told you I'd made some inquiries at their bar in

Beaumont trying to find out what Bobby Andrus was up to. Landry didn't seem to know anything then. This morning he showed up at my office here in Houston along with his bartender Rich. He's trying to find out about my interest in his brother."

"Like maybe his little brother is involved in something all alone?"

"Not only that. I got the impression he doesn't know where to find his brother. He's looking for him."

"Interesting. And there's nothing else you have to tell me about Bobby?"

"No. Nothing."

She sighed. "Okay. So, I'll add to the long list of things we do not know the possibility that Bobby is missing. I'll let Detective Smith know. You call me if you find him."

"You bet."

She didn't believe that I knew so little about Bobby. I couldn't mention his death and digestion. I might eventually lose her trust because of that. It was good I could let the police know he was missing. That might help shake something loose.

I did a few things to pass the time until it was time to pick up Thumper and Angelique at the airport. I looked at trucks on the internet. I spent some time web-surfing. I went to the Cafe for lunch. I walked around Angelique's and Jenny's empty apartment. I'd signed the lease. That got me an access card.

I MET ANGELIQUE and Thumper curbside at George Bush Intercontinental Airport and put their bags in the back of the Range Rover. Thumper opened the front passenger door for her and got into the back seat.

Angelique said, "Rocky told me to tell you he'd be

flying back tonight. There's nothing he can do there, and his wife is staying with Jenny and driving her home. He'll leave in time to get here before he has to land in the dark."

I nodded. "Good. He's your new bodyguard. We three need to sit down and talk. Angelique, you need to get your stuff moved to your new apartment. I have somebody to help haul your stuff. He and Rocky will get that done tomorrow.

"Angelique, you need to be very careful. They found the van. There were things left inside it making it clear they intended to tie you up." I wanted to shock her and Thumper, keep them alert for danger.

"But, why, what have I done? Do they want ransom or something?"

"I have no idea. From the looks of your apartment, they may be looking for something. Whatever the reason, it's obvious you are important to somebody."

"I can't imagine why. I don't have anything worth anything."

"Yeah, we're going to look into that. And, we're now sure we know who it was at your apartment."

"Who?"

"One of the two seen leaving your apartment was likely the other attacker in New Orleans. He's a guy from Beaumont, Carlos Perez. Know him?"

She was shaking her head. "No, I have no idea who he is."

"He's a friend of Steve Delacourt, the bouncer."

"Big D?"

"Yes."

"Hold on. Big D did have a friend Carlos. I remember now. Slimy guy."

"Was he interested in you?"

"I doubt it. I didn't see him that much. Remember, I didn't work out in public."

"I'm convinced they were the two who broke into your apartment."

"But why? I mean, Delacourt wasn't a friend by any means, but we got along fine at the bar. What's going on?"

"We're going to find out. Meanwhile, we're going to keep you safe."

Thumper said, "What's your plan for doing that?"

"Rocky will be back tonight. He'll protect her." To her, I said, "We'll get you into your new apartment. It's not in your name, and it has good security. Marlene will be with you two for a while until Jenny is better."

Thumper asked, "What about tonight, what are we going to do? Go to my place?"

"No. You have to be here tomorrow anyway. We'll go rent the suite again. That will give us a place to sit and talk a bit."

He didn't argue with me. I had him scared.

I drove to the hotel we'd put Angelique and Jenny in before and rented the same suite. This time, I signed up for their reward card program. The nicely competent young woman behind the desk assured me she'd give me credit for my stay the previous week. In the room, I ordered a pizza.

Rocky called and told me when he'd get in. I told him there was no reason for him to come to the hotel. He agreed to show up in the morning to help get Angelique moved in.

I called Joshua. He and Darla were ready to work moving furniture. He already had the trailer hooked up. He and Rocky would coordinate getting together.

The pizza came. My stomach rumbled with hunger. We gathered around the table.

I looked at Angelique over a slice of pizza. "There's

nothing in your brief career at Fantasy Kings that you think could have led to all this interest in you today?"

Angelique shook her head while chewing pizza.

"But," I said, "there's some connection because of Delacourt and Carlos. Maybe it doesn't have to do with something at the club. Maybe the club is just a common denominator of some sort with something else. I want to talk to your friend from the club, Carol. Think about how we might find her."

"Okay. Maybe Ms. Canderly knows."

"I'm sorry to keep asking, but you can't think of anything in your life today that might be attracting the interest of somebody?"

"No. I've racked my brain. There's nothing."

"You said there's no boyfriend or ex-boyfriend. How about somebody who asked you out and you turned down?"

"No. I've not had a serious relationship with anybody. I'm too busy dancing. I go out every once in a while with a guy in the company, but it is super casual. We're not sleeping together and after suggesting it once, he's not brought it up again. He has other women he dates. There's just nothing like that."

"The only major thing in your life that is different from the past is your recent relationship with Thumper?"

"Yeah, I guess so."

Thumper said, "You think this is about me somehow?"

"Beats me," I said. "Maybe it's a ransom attempt. There's been some press about the amount of money settled on you. You're written up in many places. You make money. Angelique makes good money. That could be it."

"You think so? It's not widely known that I'm related to her."

"I'm grasping. It doesn't feel like a ransom thing for

many reasons. Not that I've had experience in the area, but leaving the dead guy in her apartment and stabbing her television while ransacking her apartment just doesn't feel like a kidnapping for ransom. It feels more like anger or a warning or a threat."

"About what?" he said.

"I don't know. You and she are connected. Maybe it's something in your past or her adopted family's life or the life of one of her siblings or a jealous dancer at the theater. I have no idea. But, you're here, so tell me more about you and her grandmother. The more we know the closer we can get to figuring this thing out."

I got a notepad and pen out of my briefcase.

"What do you want to know?"

"Tell me about her grandmother. What was her name?"

"Belle Anne Chandler." He paused, his eyes drifting away to the past. Angelique stretched a hand out to touch his arm. "She was a little older than me. And so sophisticated. I'd never seen anyone as beautiful as her. She was radiant. Any time she was in the audience at the club, it seemed to me that all things focused on her. She always had a smile like she knew something nobody else did, something amusing."

He laughed. "I was something back then. Young and in my prime. Paris let us be men in ways we couldn't be in the States. Belle Anne smoldered, and I could let her see she set me on fire."

I noticed tears forming in Angelique's eyes. I thought of the lyrics to one of his songs. *She smolders, like a burning coal at night, throwing sparks of fire with the heat in her eyes.*

"She first showed up with a group. It didn't take fifteen

minutes before I was watching nobody else in the place. I played to her. Between sets I just watched her. I could tell she was not with anybody in her group. Before long, I knew she was aware of me, and we were watching each other. She started showing up every night I played, always in the company of friends, but always there, always watching me. I could hear in her voice that she was from the states and from the south. France set her free like it set me free.

"One night I was onstage by myself. Just me and my guitar. She sent me a drink. After the song, I screwed up enough courage to go to her table, sit down, and thank her. She told me she had to do it because, obviously, I was not going to say hello to her unless she took drastic measures.

"Her crowd was a mixture of Europeans and Americans. They were not bothered by the idea that she might have an interest in a black man. It fit their hip world. I started hanging out with her crowd a bit. There was an after war feeling of freedom. Things were improving, and they were the young Turks. To some of them I was a pet musician, a connection to the off-beat new society they so loved. To her, I was more."

He paused again, looking off into the past. I could hear the little noises of the hotel, but I kept quiet. Waiting. Angelique never took her eyes off of him.

He shook his head, took a deep breath and continued, his voice breaking a bit. "She was something. So beautiful. We started spending all of our time together. Eventually, I moved in with her. She had a small apartment, full of light. It always smelled of her perfume and the flowers she kept on a table. She and I ... well ... "

He looked over at Angelique, obviously embarrassed, and shook his head again with a smile.

"Well, you know me as this eighty-three year old

washed up man, but ... "

Angelique moved next to him and hugged him and said, "I am glad you loved Belle. I am glad the two of you loved each other. I am glad you made love with her. Very glad. For one thing, it's why I'm here."

He nodded, hugged her, and said, "Once they found out, her family was not so happy."

He was retreating into the silence of memories. I pushed a little by asking, "How long were the two of you together?"

"Almost five years. I was doing good. Fat Leo did right by me. He was taking too much money, but what did I know back then? A French recording company got into recording jazz. I played some recording sessions for some jazz records. I was there at just the right time for them to branch out and record some blues. Things were going good.

"I had fantasies of coming back to America with Belle on my arm, but I knew that was just a fantasy. Things just hadn't changed that much over here. In fact, in some ways, they were getting worse. In the states, people were starting to peel off the scabs of the past and there was some bleeding going on.

"I was perfectly content to live over there. I started to get booked in some other countries. An American recording company took a risk on us. The fact that we played in Europe could be marketed."

I have a boxed set of Thumper's Paris recordings. Those old recordings were among those we collected unpaid royalties on in that first case I handled for him.

Thumper took a deep breath. "Yeah, things were good until Saturday night, the twenty-fourth of May." His voice turned raspy. "That's when they took Belle from me."

Angelique and I waited in a silence heavy with history

and memory.

"I was on stage at the Stallion with Cliff and Marlowe and a couple of other guys. We didn't play the Stallion as much as when we first got over there. We were playing more often at better paying places. But we felt connected to that place and played there when we could. It was coming up on midnight. She was there alone with me, not with a crowd of friends. She sat at a small table to the side, sipping a drink.

"A couple of guys went to her table. Not really unusual. She could shut down a come-on. But I could tell something was up. She stood up. One of the guys reached for her arm, and she pulled away. I stopped the music and came off the stage. Three guys I'd not noticed left the bar and confronted me. Rough guys. Locals.

"The two guys at Belle's table started dragging her toward the door. She shouted at me. The other guys in the band came down. There was a pushing and shoving match. It wasn't a big place and she was outside before I could get free. When I finally followed them outside, there was a fight going on in the bar and a car speeding away. There were three more locals outside. They took me down. The three guys inside the bar stood in the door and kept anybody from getting out.

"I was on the ground being kicked. One of them said, *Oublies la putain. Elle est partie.* Forget the whore. She is gone."

He and Angelique both had tears on their faces.

"They knocked me out with their kicks. The six street toughs took off just before the cops got there."

Thumper stood up and continued his story while looking out the window. "I guess bad cops are the same all over the world. And people. And money. A cop who smelled like garlic handcuffed and hustled me into a car. He and another cop drove off with me, ignoring everything I had to say. I ended up in a small town maybe forty miles outside of Paris.

"I spent a little over two weeks in their jail. If I yelled too loud, they put me in a small dark cell with no window and no mattress. I was crazy wondering what was going on. They pretended to understand nothing of my English or my French."

"Oh, grandpa," Angelique said.

He sat back down next to her and took her hand.

Shaking his head, he said, "There was nothing I could do. Nothing."

I didn't see how all those things happening in the fifties could result in harm directed at Angelique over half a century later, but I was the one who said we didn't know what might be important. Besides, Thumper's history fascinated me.

"I thought I might die in that jail. Finally, I was taken out, put in a car, driven a ways out of town, and let go. I wasn't sure where I was. I walked in the direction they'd driven me. They'd never taken a thing from me, so I had some cash in my pocket. I walked a couple of hours and came across a small town with a tavern. I gave them some money, and they let me call Fat Leo. He'd been thinking I was dead.

"The tavern keeper understood my French with no problem. He told me where I was and confirmed that I'd been headed toward Paris. I told Leo and started walking again. It took a while, but Leo finally showed up in a car and picked me up."

Thumper picked up a piece of the pizza, took a bite and chewed on it for a while.

Angelique quietly asked, "Did you find out what

happened to her?"

He shook his head. "The Paris cops said they'd never heard of her. They had no idea she was missing. They responded to a brawl at the bar, but they weren't involved in my arrest. Or so they said. Nobody heard from Belle. I went around to her apartment, but it was already rented out to somebody else. There was one thing, though."

He chewed on another bite of pizza.

"I talked to her landlady. She told me how Belle showed up with a couple of men, strangers to the landlady, and packed up her stuff. I think the landlady kept trying to ask Belle if everything was okay. She sensed something. Finally, Belle had a very brief moment alone with her and told her if I came around, tell me she was sorry. She had to go home, and I shouldn't try to find her. The landlady leaned over and whispered to me. She said, 'Mr. Lee, Mademoiselle Chandler, she told me to tell you they would kill you.' The landlady was obviously shocked and loving the intrigue."

He tossed a half a slice of pizza down on the table.

"I didn't know what to do. Her message made me think her family sent somebody over for her. I didn't even know where she was from. Somewhere in the South. I knew that from the way she spoke, but she never shared anything about where she came from or her family. I wanted to come back to the States and look for her, but Leo slowed me down. I'm sure he was concerned about the revenue he'd be out if I left, but, you know, in his own greedy way, Leo did look out for us. He said things I knew were true.

"This was the fifties. There were laws all across this country making mixed-race marriages illegal. There were plenty of places in the South where if a black man so much as looked at a white lady he might be killed and no jury would convict his killers. That's just the way it was. I knew it.

"I thought Belle was strong and independent. She might have been thin and dainty, but she had strength. She'd proved she didn't have a problem with me being a black man. I knew that she loved me. I thought she'd find a way back to me. I really did. A month passed, and I kept waiting to hear from her.

"One day, on a sunny day in June, Leo strolled down the street and fell over dead from a heart attack. By that time, I'd rented a new place and Marlowe stayed with me. It was two connected rooms in a boarding house. We had a sofa in what we called the living room.

"I need a drink."

He rummaged in his bag and pulled out a flask. He got a glass from the bathroom and poured himself a healthy shot of whiskey.

"Here's the part where I don't come across too good. It was a Wednesday in August. I hadn't heard from her. It still ate at me, but time passes. We'd been playing in the triangle till late and slept in as usual. I was in the bedroom. Marlowe was sacked out on the sofa. Somebody pounded on the door, calling my name. Before I could wake up enough to get out of bed, Marlowe answered the door.

"I could see from the dark of the bedroom. I was pulling on my pants and watched Marlowe open the door and start to say something. The man at the door was one of the guys who had taken Belle that night. Not one of the French guys, but one of the two who had her by the arms taking her out.

"The guy at the door said, 'Mr. Lee, this will teach you. Go to hell.' He shot Marlowe right in the face. He dropped the pistol on the floor. He turned and walked away."

Thumper swallowed the whiskey left in his glass and poured himself another one.

"I did either a really dumb or a really smart thing. I was in a panic. I thought he'd come back and kill me. I thought the cops would think I'd shot Marlowe. I'd been raised to avoid cops. I couldn't think straight. I grabbed my wallet. I grabbed Marlowe's wallet. I grabbed my guitar case. I took the box where I kept all my money, and I took Marlowe's stash of money and stuff from his guitar case. I took it all and I left. Couldn't have taken me more than a couple of minutes to get out of there.

"I figured to run. Run from the killer and run from the cops who would be after me. I thought I had less than a week before I would be arrested and put away. Nobody saw me slip out back and walk away."

He sipped his whiskey.

"I was lucky. I was lucky that the guy with the pistol had no idea what I looked liked for sure. I was lucky the landlady didn't know Marlowe was living there and confirmed the ID of my body without looking too close. I guess I was lucky Marlowe got shot in the face. I was lucky there wasn't much interest in doing an investigation.

"This was 1958. I was a black musician from another country without any family or friends to worry about. I watched the papers and saw nothing about the shooting. Marlowe had no family. Nobody would try to find him. Cliff had returned to the states to an angry wife, and he was out of touch.

"The story about me getting murdered made the rounds. It became kind of a myth among my crowd. Most of them probably thought Marlowe shot me. But that was just part of the myth. The cops never came after Marlowe. I know because I was living and playing in lots of places using his name and papers, getting paid in cash and staying out of sight."

He poured another healthy glass of whiskey.

"I barely functioned. I scraped by here and there. Luckily, my music kept me going. There are some recordings out there with Marlowe listed as a member of the band. We didn't collect for those, counselor. Guess we'll skip it now."

The whiskey started to affect his speech a bit. "You know, I used to wonder why somebody came gunning for me. I didn't figure it out until you showed up." He nodded toward Angelique.

She raised her eyebrows in a question.

"It must have been shortly before your mom was born that Marlowe got killed. Somebody couldn't handle that I'd given her a baby."

He set his glass down and said, "I'm going to bed."

He stood up. Angelique hugged him. I decided to wait until morning to talk more to Angelique about her life. A great weight burdened the night. I was weary. We all went to bed.

I fell asleep only to be awakened shortly after midnight when my cell phone rang.

I mumbled a hello.

"Mr. Locke, this is Detective Robichaud. I know it's late, but I thought you'd want to know we've got him. Thibaux Arceneaux is in the back of a squad car on his way to a cell."

CHAPTER THIRTEEN

I SAT STRAIGHT UP IN BED. The New Orleans police had TeeBoy. All sorts of possibilities had to come from that.

"Good," I said. "Tell me about it."

"Not much to tell. It's like I said we'd do. We found him in a bar. We put the word out. We got a call. A couple of officers picked him up. On my instruction, they didn't say a word about why. He's not smart enough to make them tell him. He's on his way to a lonely cell where I'm going to let him sit until morning. I'm going to sleep like a baby and get to him in the morning. I just thought I'd let you know."

"And you're going to let me know how it goes?"

"I'll let you know what I can. You haven't let me down yet. Anything new on your end?"

"No. I put everybody up in a hotel again. We're going to move Angelique and Jenny into an apartment with good security. Somebody will be staying with them for now. Probably until we get this thing figured out."

"Good. How is Ms. Mills?"

"Recovering. Her aunt will be bringing her back to Houston sometime this week."

"Excellent. You watch out for her. A lot of cops around here call her the little ninja warrior. Don't tell her that. I wouldn't want it to go to her head. I'll call you if something interesting happens that I can share. Good night."

"Good night."

That call kept me awake for a little while but not all

night. I woke up when I heard Thumper moving around. I went into the main room and told him about TeeBoy getting arrested.

"Good," he said. "I don't know how all the crap I told you about helps you any, but now you know."

"I don't know if it will help either, but it is something. It is a part of Angelique, and something that is a part of her is what we're looking for. Maybe TeeBoy will shed some light on things."

"I hope so."

Rocky called from the parking lot. I gave him our room number. He showed up at the door with coffee and kolaches. I dumped the cup of hotel room coffee I'd made and took one from him.

"They found TeeBoy," I said. "They have him."

"Did they? Great. Find out anything?"

"Detective Robichaud let him stew all night. She's talking to him this morning."

"Did they charge him?"

"Not yet. I think she's playing him for information first, probably hoping to avoid him asking for a lawyer before it's too late to do any good."

Angelique came out and said, "Did I hear you say something happened?"

"They've caught one of the guys who assaulted you, the one with the tattoo."

She took a deep breath. "What now?"

"We wait and see what they learn. Rocky is going to take you and Thumper and get your stuff moved. I'll call Joshua, see where they are with the trailer."

Rocky said, "We've already talked. He's meeting us in the parking lot of the Galleria in about half an hour. We're going now. Keep me posted if you hear from Robichaud."

"Yes. You guys be careful."

I had a while before check out time. I connected my laptop to the hotel's WiFi. I spent forty-five minutes learning about Belle Anne Chandler. I quickly found an archived newspaper article about her. A story in the Dallas Morning News from December of 1958 announced the marriage of Belle Anne Chandler of Dallas, daughter of Robert Lee and Anne Marie Chandler, to Matthew Planter of New Orleans, son of Mr. and Mrs. Raymond Planter, on December 12, 1958. Belle Anne's sister Lucille stood up as her maid of honor. The brother of the bride, Montgomery, served as the best man for the groom. It interested me that Mr. Planter had the bride's brother stand up with him. No other attendants were listed. It must have been a small, discreet wedding.

Belle's marriage came quickly after the birth of her and Thumper's baby. Texas and Louisiana in the fifties and a father named Robert Lee. A mixed-race baby. The family would have been anxious to do something with their soiled daughter, something to put a facade on their family honor. The baby must have been quickly placed somewhere with no traceable ties to the Chandlers.

In the index of articles about the Chandlers of Dallas, there were a lot of stories about the Chandlers attending social and charitable events over the years. I started through them in chronological order. The Chandlers had some money. Robert Lee was often mentioned in articles about his association with politicians in power.

On the twenty-third of July, 1960, Belle Anne gave birth to a son, Joseph Quantrill Planter.

Later that year, a tragedy struck the family. On the sixteenth of December, Robert Lee Chandler and his wife, along with their oldest son Montgomery and his wife, boarded United Airlines flight 826 in Chicago, having been there on business, to fly to New York. Later that morning, in light rain and fog, flight 826 collided with a TWA Super Constellation over New York Harbor. The United Airlines aircraft lost an engine and most of its wing, ultimately crashing into a neighborhood in Brooklyn. Every passenger on both planes and six people on the ground in Brooklyn perished.

In that 1960 article, Belle Anne was listed as a survivor of the Chandlers who died in the plane crash. There was no mention of Belle Anne in the paper after that until an article in March of 1962. On the fourteenth of March, Belle Anne Planter drowned in the Mississippi River while visiting family in Baton Rouge, Louisiana.

She walked on the water,
And the river,
The river washed her tears away.

Thumper's song. He knew.

Surviving family members included her loving husband Matthew Planter, their son Joseph, and her sister Lucille Chandler. The paper did not mention a surviving daughter conceived in Paris and born shortly before she married that loving husband.

Four years before I sat down to research her family, Belle's sister Lucille made the paper for attending a benefit wine auction. A search of her name did not turn up an obituary. She would be in her eighties.

It would have taken more digging to find out if Belle's widower Matthew still lived and what was up in his life. I put that off until later.

Thumper's tale of coercion and murder and reading about the Chandlers brought a Southern Gothic atmosphere to Angelique's troubles. Could the racist passion of the past be visiting her four generations later?

The Chandlers of old had been well to do. After scanning the news articles, I knew the family must still have money. A lot of money. Perhaps the interest in Angelique did not involve any archaic notion of family honor. A lot of money might very well make Angelique the center of somebody's attention. Somebody worried about her being an heir. I didn't see how that could be tied to her time at the Fantasy Kings and Bobby Andrus and Delacourt and Carlos Perez, and their hired henchman TeeBoy, but money at least gave me a traditional and tangible motive to explore.

To explore money as a motive, I needed to learn about any wills and trusts in the family. To explore who might be worried about Angelique being an heir. I needed to know more about the branches on the Chandler family tree. But first, I needed to check out of the hotel. I did so and headed to my office.

Once there, I called Glenn Reyes. Glenn graduated three years ahead of me from the same high school and attended the same church I did as a teenager. He graduated law school three years before I did. He is a partner in a six-person law firm in Dallas specializing in estate work.

I was put through to him, and I asked him if he would have any conflicts of interest getting me information about the Chandlers. He whistled and said, "Don't think so. I wish. They aren't the biggest money in Dallas, but they're not doing badly. Let me check and make sure."

I waited, listening to Vivaldi while on hold. With the speed of a computer, Glenn came back and said, "Nope. No conflict. What do you have going on?"

"They might or might not be related to something I'm working on regarding some property interests. I need to find out who inherited what after the death of Robert Lee

Chandler back in 1960 and if there is any kind of ongoing trust arrangement today."

"Okay. I'll bill my paralegal's straight hourly rate to do the work. And if something comes out of it and you need local counsel, you will remember me fondly."

"Yes. Yes, I will. Will you bill me or do I need to send you some money?"

"I'll bill you. No problem."

I could think of nothing else to do in the office. I thought about calling Detective Robichaud, but decided it was best to let her call me. Last we'd talked she'd trusted me. I didn't want my impatience to irritate her.

I called Rocky. He told me there hadn't been much furniture to move, and they were almost finished. Their plan was to go buy a futon for the living room so it would be ready for Marlene when she brought Jenny home. After that, Joshua and Darla would head home.

He said, "I have no real plans other than to hang out with Angelique and think about what we're going to do to keep her safe. Anything you need me to do?"

"There's one thing. Angelique's grandmother's maiden name was Belle Anne Chandler. The Chandlers were very wealthy back then, and it looks likes the money is still there. Belle Anne lived in Dallas. I think Belle Anne's sister, Lucille, is still alive. I need somebody to research the Chandler family to get as much history and gossip about them as possible over the years. It will be best to get somebody in the Dallas area. Ideas?"

"Yes. I'll call the trophy bride. I met her at a conference, and I use her when doing that kind of stuff up there."

"Trophy bride?"

"Yeah, Stephanie Blankenship. She's in her midthirtieso and a former Dallas Cowboy cheerleader with a degree in English from North Texas State. She is gorgeous. She married an older man and retired from her life as a cheerleader. Her husband is an oil guy, with all the money that implies. She freely admits to being a trophy bride but says she loves the old coot. A few years ago she admitted to herself she dislikes golf and tennis. She does not like decorating or gossiping or hanging out with the wives of her husband's friends. She went out and got her investigator's license. She specializes in records research and skip tracing. She's thorough, fast, and very good. She charges a criminally low hourly rate and donates a lot of it to charity. I understand what you want. I'll give her a call, see if she's busy. She handles only a few things at a time."

"Okay, sounds good. One more thing. Remind Angelique to think about how we find her friend Carol, the girl she used to dance with in Beaumont."

"Something up with her?"

"Not really, but she's a connection to Angelique and Beaumont and Fantasy Kings. I'd like to get in touch with her."

"Understand. How about I have my guy in Beaumont look for her, too. He can go in and ask some of the dancers if they know where she is. He can pretend he's an infatuated customer from out of town who met her once at Fantasy Kings."

"Might as well. Just tell him to be careful to not attract too much attention. Her real name is Carol Taylor. Her dancer name was Cee Cee. Might still be."

Rocky and I agreed to talk later.

I spent some time recording billing information on Angelique's matter, locked up, and headed toward the island and home. Detective Robichaud called while I was on the road.

After greeting me, she said, "Yeah, TeeBoy is a weasel. I got a little out of him when, what do you know, a lawyer showed up and shut him down. Funny thing, though, I think he was as surprised by the lawyer showing up as I was pissed off."

"TeeBoy didn't ask for a lawyer?"

"Nope, didn't call one and didn't ask for one, but one showed up. He is, evidently, working on getting TeeBoy bonded out. I think TeeBoy would like to stay in jail. He feels safer there."

"What can you tell me about what you learned?"

"Officially? Not a thing. You'll be getting a call from cops in Houston and Beaumont. We are slowly, but officially, branching out."

"Do you think somebody in Beaumont hired TeeBoy?"

"I'm not sure. TeeBoy says a local hired him. He's being cagey about who that might be. I'd have got it, but the damn lawyer showed up. TeeBoy says he was told there'd be another person coming along to help him. He says he doesn't know the guy who showed up, a guy TeeBoy calls a little Mexican motherfucker. But TeeBoy thinks the hand behind this whole thing is local. TeeBoy is torn between wanting to know nothing and wanting to look like he's part of something big. He is essentially clueless."

"What was his job?"

"According to him, the girl has something that somebody stole from somebody and that particular somebody wants it back. Lots of unknown somebodies. You have any idea what they might be after?"

"No, did he?"

"He was vague. I don't think he knows. This is where he starts to lay things off on his partner. Evidently, the

Hispanic guy knew what was going on. TeeBoy says the plan was to invite her somewhere to talk about things."

"In a stolen van."

"Yeah, there is that. Of course, TeeBoy makes the bullshit claim he didn't know the van was stolen. He claims when the crazy Mexican motherfucker pulled out a knife and then a gun he was as surprised as anybody. TeeBoy is distancing himself from the weapons. I might have let him think the girl could die. He says he only got into the altercation because that little bitch went ninja on them. Says he fought her only in self-defense. He claims he was just trying to get away when all that started happening. Too bad for him that Ms. Mills puts the gun in his hand."

"Sounds like he's talking himself in circles. Any of it do him any good?"

"No. He did have an observation to make about his partner. TeeBoy says he is crazy mean. TeeBoy's wrist is scratched where Ms. Mills got him, but he's got a cut on the right side of his face. He says he was driving the van away from what he calls the misunderstanding when the so-called crazy Mexican hit him upside the head for not giving him time to grab the girl. TeeBoy says kidnapping the girl was not part of what he agreed to do. He thought they were just going to talk to her."

"Misunderstanding, huh? So, how does he explain the duct tape and the cable ties?"

"Well, we didn't get to that part. I didn't want to tie him up in too big a knot until we talked a bit more. I told him I hoped whatever he got paid was worth the charges he is facing for attempted kidnapping and for assault with the intent to commit murder. I told him he better hope she doesn't die or he might be looking at the big one. He started stuttering about how he saved the girl's life by driving off with the crazy Mexican motherfucker when everything went south.

"For what it's worth, I did have another discussion with Ms. Mills before I called you. She's doing just fine by the way. She says she thinks maybe TeeBoy did turn and run when things went bad. She was being stomped on the ground, but one of the last things she does remember is the van starting to drive away while the guy was kicking her. She thought they were going to run her over.

"I gave Ms. Chambray a call, too. Her recollection is similar. She remembers screaming, hoping somebody would hear. She remembers the van leaving and the Hispanic guy running to get the door open and jump on board. She thinks the Hispanic guy was leaning out the window pointing the pistol at them when the van whipped around a corner and was gone. Maybe TeeBoy did save her life."

"Yeah, I'll have to thank him for that. Where did the lawyer come from?"

"I'm curious about that. TeeBoy made no calls. TeeBoy was fishing for a deal, and he's such a pissant, I'd have supported one for some good info. No way is he in charge of whatever this is. Somebody somewhere knew we had TeeBoy and called somebody."

"A cop?"

"I hope not. If so, whoever it is better hope I don't find out."

"Do you know the lawyer?"

"I asked around. He's just one of the criminal defense guys hanging out at the courthouse mucking up my life. Nobody special."

"Probably no good way to find out who hired him."

"Are you kidding? You know better than me how lawyers keep their mouths shut about important things in their pursuit to frustrate justice."

I ignored the dig.

She said, "Maybe I'll be able to find out something if somebody bails him out. We got a goodly amount of bond set. It'll have to be somebody with some scratch. That might get us somewhere."

"Anything else?"

"I'm sure there is, but I don't know what. I'm going to think on this. You got anything to share?"

"No." I didn't know enough about the Chandlers to share their connection to my clients.

She made a noise of disbelief, said something that might have been a good-bye and was gone. I felt her frustration.

Again, Detective Robichaud told me more than the police usually share with civilians. She did so because of the geographic diversity of whatever was behind the assault in her jurisdiction. The assault in New Orleans involved things in Houston and Beaumont for sure and maybe Dallas. Robichaud would not receive a lot of time or budget money to look for connections in those places for what could be, in the eyes of the budget keepers, nothing more than a mugging in a parking garage. She knew I had a personal interest. She knew I had resources she did not. She knew, without knowing all the details, I had incentives and time to keep the pot stirred until the collective, cumbersome mass of law enforcement became interested enough to work together. That was my job, keep stirring the pot.

A lawyer showing up may have been a mistake by the bad guys. Whoever hired the lawyer would most likely be connected closely to the mastermind of the thing. Perhaps we could use that to get a step ahead.

JOSHUA AND DARLA were home when I got there. I looked
over the grills they'd been working on. Darla's sculpture of
scrap had grown. I looked at the welds. She learned fast and I
told her so. She grinned. Joshua proudly put his arm around
her waist. I went inside and spent time on the internet and
went to bed.

The next morning I spent a little time writing letters
to a few clients to let them know I had not forgotten them.
I spent a lot of time doing paperwork for the welding
business and checking its cash flow and bank balance. It was
prime selling time, and the coffers were swelling nicely.
Every day I had checks to deposit.

Joshua brought me the day's mail. I told him to send
Darla to the house. I gave her all the mail addressed to
Locke Smokers and Grills and told her to handle it and ask
me any questions she might have. She took a seat in front of
the computer and went to work. As she worked, I showed
her what to do with the orders and invoices, the checks, and
correspondence.

I opened a large overnight envelope addressed to
Samuel Locke, Esq. It contained a letter from Carolyn
Donoho, Glen Reyes's paralegal, a filed copy of the Last
Will and Testament of Robert Lee Chandler. Attached to
the will was a trust document.

I settled down and read the will and trust with
considerable interest. Afterward, I took over the computer
and looked up some legal things.

Thursday morning was much the same, spending time
on routine business and other clients. The mail brought
another overnight package. I smiled because the return
address indicated it came from TBR&I, Trophy Bride
Research and Investigations. It was as interesting to read as
the family's will and trust documents. Together, the

information suggested a strong motive for the undesirable interest in Angelique.

Friday morning, Marlene rented a large, comfortable automobile and drove Jenny to her new home in Houston. The drive usually takes a little over five hours. She took it slow, leaving New Orleans about eleven in the morning and arriving in Houston in time for dinner at six-thirty that evening. Waiting for her were Angelique, Rocky, Thumper, and me. Marlene called when they were an hour out and, at Jenny's request, I went out and bought a lot of pizza. At Marlene's instruction, I bought Jenny her very own vegetarian pizza with no cheese.

Everybody greeted Jenny enthusiastically when she walked in slowly. I had not seen her since she was under sheets in a hospital bed, plugged into a variety of monitors and tubes. She'd been small then, surrounded by devices of the hospital, but as she shuffled to the couch, a hand touching her side, the sweatshirt she wore swallowed her. She looked fourteen years old. Her bruises were fading. They'd removed the stitches in her cheek. She proudly raised her sweatshirt to show off the angry red scars where the bullet ripped her open, and the doctors cut her open.

In tears, Angelique hugged her and said, "I am so glad you're home and okay. You know you saved our lives, right?"

"Yeah, all in a day's work. Wish I'd been here to help you move in. Looks great."

"Not yet, but we'll get it fixed up."

I stood behind Angelique, and Jenny looked at me over Angelique's shoulder as they hugged. She smiled at everybody and seemed lighthearted, but her eyes said something else. She looked at me with meaning. She still hurt, and she was pissed off about that.

To me, she said, "Have you found the son of a bitch

who shot me?"

"We're pretty sure we know who he is and how to find him. There are three police departments and us trying to get enough on him to get him arrested."

"Tell me about him. Give me a few days, and I'll go talk to him. Might be interesting."

"I'll keep that in mind. Right now, sit down before you fall down."

She settled into a corner of the futon, surrounding herself with pillows. "Do we know why I got shot?"

"I have an idea, and while we eat, I'll tell you all what I'm thinking."

I took a slice of sausage with extra onions.

Jenny said, "I can't believe you are all going to eat real pizza in front of me."

Each of them took pizza. Rocky handed me a beer and said, "Start talking."

"We've done some research on Angelique's birth family. I've received a lot of information from a lawyer and investigator in Dallas. Her great-grandfather was Robert Lee Chandler. The Chandlers go way back and have owned a lot of property in Louisiana and East Texas since the early eighteen-hundreds. After the Civil War, the family moved their home to Texas. They are very well to do. Some of their Louisiana property and all of their East Texas timber and farmland sit on top of a lot of oil and gas. In the early nineteen-hundreds, their fortunes skyrocketed."

Rocky said, "You think this is about money?"

"I think it's the best guess right now. It's got to be about something, and I haven't heard anything from Angelique to suggest anything else in her life capable of attracting this kind of attention."

Angelique said, "Money? I don't have any of their

money, and I don't want any of their money."

"That may be," I said. "But if I'm right, we're talking about hundreds of millions of dollars. There are people who think anybody would be interested in that much money. And those people might think you're a risk that might slice that pie into smaller pieces."

Thumper let out a soft whistle.

I continued. "Robert Chandler had three kids." I nodded toward Angelique. "Your grandmother Belle, her younger sister Lucille, and her older brother Montgomery.

"So far, we've found no record of Lucille marrying or having any children. She is still alive and lives in a home outside of Dallas. Montgomery had a son named Stuart. Stuart is alive, but I'm not yet sure where he lives. Stuart has two children, Robert and Patricia."

I looked over at Thumper wondering just how much he knew about Belle's life after him. The corners of his mouth turned up slightly and he nodded at me.

"As we all know, Belle had a child with Thumper. The baby was quickly adopted out of sight. The couple she went to live with named her Rose. I doubt if Belle ever knew her name or where she went."

Thumper said, "That family couldn't stand the thought of their daughter being with a black man. Our child must have been bigger than the apocalypse to the Chandlers."

Angelique took Thumper's hand and leaned her head into his shoulder. Nobody else moved. Nobody said a thing. I held center stage.

Thumper nodded my way again.

"Shortly after giving birth to Rose, Belle married a man named Matthew Planter. It looks like he was the son of a long-time employee or business partner of Robert

Chandler. Looking at the timing, they might have planned that marriage before anybody knew she was pregnant with Rose. In July of 1960, Belle gave birth to another child, a son, Joseph."

Angelique sat up at that, surprised. Thumper just nodded slowly. He knew. Jenny said, "Wow."

"Robert Chandler, his wife, and their son Montgomery and Montgomery's wife, died in a plane crash in New York in December of nineteen-sixty."

I took a bite of pizza and a sip of beer.

"In March of nineteen-sixty-two Belle drowned in the Mississippi." I looked at Thumper, and said, "Belle walked on water, didn't she?"

He took a deep breath and softly said, "And the water washed her tears away."

Angelique looked up at him sharply.

Jenny asked, "Did she kill herself?"

"Don't know," I said. "The newspaper tried to make it sound like an accident, in the way they used to do to protect people's reputation, but she couldn't have been very happy."

To Thumper, Angelique said, "That song. It's about her. Do you know?"

He shrugged. "Not really. Not for sure. I wasn't around. There was no way I could be. I'm sure her family told her I was dead. And, in some ways I was. Nobody knew better."

Jenny said, "This all sounds so sad."

"But," I said, "let's get down to what might be going on today. I told you earlier. The Chandler estate is worth hundreds of millions of dollars. Robert Lee Chandler's will made some bequests to his children, but he put the bulk of the family's property and assets into a trust."

"The Chandler Trust came into existence when Robert Chandler's will went to probate. That's a good thing for us because the trust documents were attached to his will and nobody ever tried to keep it secret. I have a copy.

"I'll skip the details, but what's important to us is that on the death of Robert and his wife, the bulk of estate property went into the trust to be managed for the benefit of his children and their offspring with one exception."

"Belle," said Jenny.

"Exactly. He wrote Belle out of his will."

Jenny said, "Can he do that?"

"Sure, it's possible to write one of your kids out of the will. There are some reasons you can't, but it's possible if you have the right reasons. A good lawyer will state a valid reason to do so in the will to support the validity of the disinheritance. Chandler's stated reason for not leaving Belle anything was because she abandoned the family, had disavowed any interest in inheriting, and moved away ceasing all communication. If true, that's a valid reason."

Thumper made a noise.

"Exactly," I said. "There are a couple of problems with that. Number one is that she moved back to the family home where she lived with the family. She married someone close to the family and continued to live close. Her family participated in her wedding. She had another child. It certainly looks like the prodigal daughter returned wholeheartedly to the warm embrace of the family.

"I'm not an expert on probate law, but I bet you could find more than one lawyer willing to use those facts to challenge the will and the provisions of the trust. The law really does try to do the right thing. If the stated reason for writing her out was because she'd abandoned the family, but she returned, the court should find it was obviously just a mistake that her father hadn't got around to correcting and rule in her favor. They don't like disinheriting a child.

"It is probably too late to do anything about property distributed directly to heirs in a will probated over fifty years ago, but more important than that is the property in the trust. The trust is still in effect. It does the same thing as the will, leaving Belle and her descendants out of any benefits. It doesn't really give a reason, referring only to the beneficiaries under the will. But I'm pretty sure that if Robert's real reason for disinheriting Belle was because she had a relationship with a black man, and that can be proved, the terms of the trust would be modified to put Belle and her descendants on an equal footing with the other heirs."

Thumper whistled and said, "What about her son, Joseph? Did the old man write him out, too?"

"He's not mentioned. It looks like he loses out because his mom lost out. I found that curious. Perhaps Chandler made some other kind of provision for Joseph. I'd like to know, but I'm not sure it's important to our problem."

Angelique sat up and started to speak, but Jenny beat her to it and said, "So, what you're saying is Angelique could have, like, bought this building instead of just renting?"

"No," Angelique said. "I am not a part of that family, and I don't want their money."

Thumper put his hand on her shoulder. "Now, baby..."

I held up a hand and everybody looked at me.

"It doesn't matter if you want the money or not. It doesn't matter if you're legally entitled to it or not. Plenty of people out there, when thinking about hundreds of millions of dollars, will never understand or believe that you are not interested."

"But, I'm not."

"Doesn't matter when we're talking about why somebody is a threat to you."

Rocky said, "Are you focused on somebody?"

"Keep in mind that we might not know all the players, yet." I took a copy of the chart of the Chandler family tree prepared by Stephanie Blankenship.

"The only people we know to still be alive are Belle's sister Lucille and Lucille's nephew Stuart and his children. We aren't yet sure about Belle's son Joseph. Stuart has two children, Robert and Patricia. It doesn't look like Lucille has any children. We'll find out for sure.

"Lucille is in her eighties. Under the terms of the trust, the trust will distribute its assets to the beneficiaries upon Lucille's death. Maybe Lucille is loyal to her family or maybe she's as nuts as her dad about preserving the family's honor. We can't completely dismiss her, but I just don't see her being so worried she would have someone assault Angelique.

"On the other hand, Stuart appears to really enjoy his family's money. So does his son, Robert. They've bought racehorses. They made a bid to buy a couple of professional sports teams. They both make a lot of appearances in society news.

"Robert has been arrested for DWI at least twice. One of those times he t-boned another car. Messed up his Porsche. The daughter, Patricia, isn't flamboyant. She's married to a college professor living in Florida. She hasn't made the news for her money. We need to look at everybody in the family, but I think we need to concentrate on Stuart and his son."

"Okay," Angelique said, "I have a stupid question. If they think I'm after their money, why did they break into my apartment twice when I was not there? Why did they try to grab me in New Orleans? Why didn't they just shoot me?"

"Well," I said, "if they truly know what they're doing,

there are problems with just killing you. I'll get an expert to look at it, but it looks to me like, under the terms of the trust, beneficiaries have what you might call a vested interest in the trust property. When the trustee distributes the trust assets and a beneficiary is deceased, the beneficiary's share goes to any blood relative of the beneficiary, as long as that relative is not entitled to a share of the trust property under the terms of the trust. It looks like whoever wrote the trust wanted to cover any unborn children, but they weren't thinking of Angelique's unique circumstances."

"Huh?" Jenny said.

"Assuming Angelique is entitled to a share of the trust property, if she dies, her share would go to Thumper when the trust is distributed."

Angelique gave a short laugh. "I guess that would shock the ol' family, wouldn't it?"

"Or make them want to kill me first," Thumper said.

Tears welled up in Angelique's eyes. "What have I got us into?"

"Nothing, baby," Thumper said, "This isn't your fault."

He put his arm around Angelique, who said, "Okay, then, why don't they just kill us both?"

I shrugged. "Maybe they don't think murder is necessary. If they can prove that Belle Anne is legitimately written out of the will, it might be safer for them to leave you alive. That way nobody faces the death penalty if caught. Maybe they think she has something that would prove otherwise."

"Why would they think I have something that would prove that? I don't have anything."

"If it is somebody related to the Chandler fortune,

maybe they're thinking you have something, correspondence from your great-grandfather to your grandmother for instance, that would prove the real reason Robert wrote her out of the will. That's a big danger to them."

She shook her head in frustration. "But, I don't have anything."

"Your mother got adopted out very quickly and very quietly. I doubt if her adoptive parents knew anything about her parents. I'm sure your great-grandfather would have made sure there was no connection."

"That makes sense."

"So, where did that picture of your grandparents you have come from? It did exactly what the Chandlers might fear. It allowed you to make the family connection. In fact, the photograph or something like it could be the thing they're after."

"I got it from my aunt. I just assumed my mother knew her history and had the picture, but I see what you're saying."

"We need to talk to your aunt. Let's take a trip to talk to her and to Carol if we can find her."

Angelique took a deep breath and nodded.

Rocky said, "I'll find Carol. What else? How are you going after the family?"

"Keep gathering as much information as I can find. Soon, I'll make myself known to the family, probably through Lucille. I'll get in touch with her as Angelique's lawyer."

"No," Angelique said. "I don't want their money."

"Now, baby, think about that," Thumper said. Thumper was pragmatic when it came to money.

She started to respond, but I held up my hand and said,

"Hold on. You'll get to make that decision. My goal is to make you safe from what's going on. If the attacks are coming from the family, it may be as easy as just having you disclaim any interest. But, to get their attention, they might need to think the family jewels are at risk to a claim by you."

I turned to Rocky. "We might also be increasing the danger to her. Can we keep her safe?"

He nodded. "Safer than she has been. Especially if we know more about what's going on. This apartment shouldn't be known to them. We can take steps to keep them from finding out. If they do find out, it's reasonably secure and we'll be watching over her."

Jenny grinned and said, "I have my toy bag."

I've seen her toy bag. She carries a variety of things to cause mayhem, everything from pepper spray to a pistol grip shotgun.

Marlene said, "I'll be here for a while, and I have a weapon."

Rocky said, "You know a determined person can find ways. We'll limit her exposure between here and the theater."

"Angelique," I said, "the first thing you do is help me find Carol. She's the strongest link between you and Fantasy Kings. Let's find out if somebody got her talking about you."

"I'll make some calls," she said.

"Only to folks not associated with Fantasy Kings. At least at first."

Rocky said, "So, what do we do over the weekend?"

Angelique said, "I blamed the mugging and took sick days. We're about to be on a break, but I have to get back to the company and rehearse some."

Rocky said, "I'll be going with you."

Jenny and Marlene would stay at the apartment while Jenny recuperated. Jenny planned to start exercising to get back into shape. Marlene planned to sit on her if she tried to do too much. Thumper was going to hang out with them.

"I'm headed to my place," I said. "I've got work to do and pots to stir."

I drove toward Galveston, feeling frustrated, wanting to get Angelique's problems resolved, but still not knowing enough about what was going on.

Two phone calls let me know things were heating up.

CHAPTER FOURTEEN

HOUSTON LIT UP THE SKY behind me. Just as I drove onto the causeway connecting the mainland to Galveston Island, my phone rang. The caller ID gave no clue about the caller.

"Hello."

"Mr. Locke?"

"Yes."

"This is Lucy Smith. I am a detective with the Beaumont Police Department. I believe you know Detective Robichaud in New Orleans."

"Yes. In fact, I intended to call you. You're working late."

"Yes sir, that's the truth. Thanks for taking my call."

"How can I help you?"

"Something's come up. It might be related to whatever is going on that you are involved in with the New Orleans Police and Bobby Andrus. I understand you think there's a connection between Andrus and the assault on your client."

"Yes. What's come up?"

"Bobby's brother Landry filed a missing person report on him. Landry Andrus states that he believes you have some information about his brother that you are not sharing with him. What's up with that?"

I wasn't expecting that. The gangster went to the cops about his brother being missing before I did.

"Detective Smith, please don't hold this against me,

but I have to state up front that any discussion with me about anything might get into areas of attorney-client confidentiality. I can only address a lot of things generally."

I could almost see the expression on her face in the silence. "Detective Robichaud told me she thought, for a lawyer, you are easier to get along with than she expected. Let me ask this question the best I can. Do you have any information about Bobby Landry you can share that might help us find him? Which, by the way, might help us find out who attacked your client, Ms. Chambray."

"I can tell you I agree that Bobby Andrus is missing. Did Landry say anything about why he thinks I know something?"

"Why do you think he's missing?"

"I don't know why he's missing. I'm confident he, probably with others, broke into my client's apartment. I visited the club in Beaumont where Bobby worked trying to find out information about why he might be interested in my client. I got the distinct impression from Landry he had no clue where his brother might be. I don't know what Bobby's interest is in my client. I would like to find out."

"How do you know he broke into your client's apartment?"

"Detective, I cannot let you engage me in twenty questions. I'll tell you this, my client did not identify Bobby Andrus as one of the guys in her apartment. I've made some assumptions based on history that he was involved somehow in the break-in. I can give you the name of a witness at the complex who saw two men leaving my client's apartment after a second break-in. Her description fits the bouncer, Steve Delacourt, and Carlos Perez. Carlos Perez is likely one of the two men who assaulted Angelique and my investigator in New Orleans. Those guys work for the

Andrus brothers, Delacourt as a bouncer at Fantasy Kings and Perez as a tow truck driver at their salvage yard. The fact that Bobby Andrus knew my client much better than either of those two and, evidently, went missing right at the time of the first break-in suggests he's involved. If I uncover any witness who can back up that assumption, I'll let you know."

She was quiet. Finally, I heard her sigh. "Okay," she said, "give me the information about your witness."

"I am driving and don't have her phone number. You can probably find it easy enough. Her name is Betty Page. She lives in the apartment complex where Angelique used to live, the Crester Ridge Apartments on Post Oak in Houston."

"Betty Page?"

"Yeah, I know, but that's her name."

"How can I speak to your client Ms. Cambray?"

"I'll have her call you."

"She at that apartment complex?"

"No. She moved somewhere safe."

"Where?"

"Sorry. I can't disclose that. I'll get you together if you need to see her for something."

"You seem to forget, Mr. Locke, I want to keep your client safe."

"I know and I appreciate that. I really do. It's what I'm doing."

After a moment she said, "You do that, then. You have her get in touch with me. She can call the Beaumont Police main number and they'll find me. Until then, I guess I'll go write some parking tickets."

She hung up without saying goodbye. I imagined what she said after she hung up the phone. I was not getting along with Detective Smith near as well as I was with Detective

Robichaud. Oh well, the relationship was new.

I called Rocky and told him to call Betty Page to let her know we were passing her name and number along to Detective Lucy Smith in Beaumont. I told him to call the main number of the Beaumont Police Department, tell them he was calling from my office and leave a message for the detective with Betty's information.

I turned and drove down the seawall toward my place. The phone rang again. It was Detective Robichaud with some startling news.

"Mr. Locke."

"Yes."

"Are you and all your clients and employees currently in the Houston area?"

"Yes. Why?"

"Do you have somebody following Carlos Perez?"

"Not full-time. I just asked my investigator to have someone find out where he lives."

"I'm calling to let you know that we found Thibaux Arceneaux dead up in the Basin Street Projects. He'd been stabbed a couple of times in the back."

"Stabbed?" The surprise made me inarticulate.

"Yeah. Thought that might get your attention. There's no evidence yet that it's our buddy Carlos, but we know he likes a knife. Anyway, I thought you should know."

"Any clues at all?"

"Not yet. I'm still on my way up there. I'll let you know what I can."

"Wow. Any word on who was behind bailing him out?"

"Not yet. I'm hoping this might make it easier to find out. Anything I should know about what's going on in your world?"

"Jenny's home. I'm dissecting Angelique's life looking

for anything that might be attracting this kind of attention. I just talked to Detective Smith in Beaumont. She told me about Landry reporting his brother as missing."

"Yeah, she told me about that. Looks like you were right about Bobby being missing. Did confirmation of that jog anything in your available memory about that?"

"No."

"Okay, then. I'll let you know if I have questions after checking out TeeBoy's demise."

"Thanks for letting me know."

"Take care of those girls."

Another thing added to the mystery and a trail we were following had come to an abrupt end. I wondered if that was the reason for the stabbing of TeeBoy. Was somebody covering their tracks? If it was Carlos, did he do it on his own or on behalf of some mastermind?

I regretted that his death made it more difficult to track down a link in the thing and hoped that his murder opened a new path to enlightenment.

I ARRIVED AT MY PLACE to a homey scene. Joshua, Darla, and Preacher were sitting on my screened in porch. A grill smoked and smelled like barbecue. Gretchen and a young woman I did not initially recognize sat next to Preacher. The unknown woman scratched Flounder's belly. When I got out of my vehicle, the woman looked at me and then at Preacher. Suddenly, when I saw her profile, I recognized her.

Not loud enough for him to hear, I said, "Dammit Preacher."

I knew her from the photographs Rocky made at Fantasy Kings. She looked different without make-up. Plus, she was wearing jeans and a t-shirt. In the photograph I'd seen, she wore nothing but a g-string. I'd told him to avoid trying to save any of the dancers when we'd gone to the club. I thought he'd resisted the urge to do so. He is a smart guy, capable, and I wouldn't mind him having my back in bar fight. But he cannot resist the broken ones and he pulls them in. I wondered how in the dickens he'd collected this one.

I greeted everybody and nodded at the new one. Preacher said, "This is Linda. She's a new member of my church and Gretchen's roommate."

I shook her hand. "Hi Linda."

I nodded at Preacher and said, "Hey, Preacher, come in for a second I want to show you something."

He followed me in.

"What's up, Sam?"

"You tell me. I told you to be careful in that bar. Linda out there is one of the dancers. What's going on?"

"I know, and I didn't do anything dangerous. When I was out there watching your back, I talked to a lot of the dancers. I said nothing about being from here, and I said nothing about my church. I said nothing about you and what you're doing. We just talked. I learned Linda is a single mom of two kids. Her husband was a good guy who got himself killed in a motorcycle accident. They got married at seventeen and at twenty-four she lost him. She had few options. I could tell she was looking for more, something different. I went back a couple of times after I was there with you. That's all."

"You could be putting Angelique at risk. We haven't figured out what's going on yet. For all I know she's here to spy on us for Landry Andrus."

"She's not. I promise. You're just mad at me. Sam, if two people are drowning and you can save one and I can save one, why would we let one drown?"

I shook my head.

"Besides," he said, "she's got something to tell you. I don't know if it helps, but I've heard you say many times, when you don't know what's going on, the least little bit of information might be important. So, I brought her over here tonight for dinner. Otherwise, you wouldn't have known she was here."

"What's she got? Are there others I don't know here?"

"No. No others. I'll go get her."

He brought her in and introduced her as Linda Frost. She was nervous. Who wouldn't be, leaving a bad job where she made good money and taking her kids to a strange place with no job while depending on somebody like Preacher. People meet Preacher and think one thing, but once they get to know him, Preacher is rarely what's expected. Linda had to be a little nervous about joining his rag-tag group of followers. Then, Preacher introduced her to me, a tired and grumpy lawyer not coming across as very friendly. She had to be concerned about her future.

Preacher was in a huff. He asked, "Do you want me to leave?"

"No," I said. "You're in on this. You're working for me, so confidentiality applies. Ms. Frost, what have you got to tell me?"

She was shy and nervous.

"The Preacher told me how he didn't usually go to places like Fantasy King. I could tell he was different, somehow. Even that first time he came in. We talked. He came back a couple of times. He talked me out of there and offered to let me take a break here. After I got here, he told me how you were trying to find Bobby Andrus for some reason."

"Yes."

"A lot of the girls are wondering where Bobby is. He hasn't been in for a while. When Preacher asked me if I had any idea where he was, it made me think about something. I don't know if its anything."

She paused, unsure of herself, and looked at Preacher. What was done was done. I needed to be nicer. I smiled and nodded my head to encourage her.

"It's like Preacher said, any little thing might help me in what I'm doing."

She looked at Preacher. He nodded.

"About three weeks ago I was in the office checking my schedule when Bobby and Big D came in through the back door. They were arguing about something. I heard Bobby say he was going with them. They were not going to cut him out. Big D said that was stupid and they didn't need help. Big D told Bobby it might get rough."

"Them? And, they?"

"Yeah, I don't know who else was involved, but it sounded to me like Big D and somebody were going somewhere and Bobby was telling him how he was going, too."

"But no mention of who else."

"No. I didn't even think much about the conversation until the Preacher asked me about Bobby. That's all I heard before I left the office. They saw me and quit talking. I thought about it today and realize that was the last time I saw Bobby."

"Do you know Big D's friend Carlos? Does he hang out at the club much?"

"Carlos? Yeah. We all know Carlos. He thinks he's entitled to mess with the girls because he's tight with Big D. He's mean." She shook her head, and smiled, almost laughing. "The dancers call him Tiny D behind his back. You can guess why."

"How's he mean?"

"He's not nice. He's grabby and not in a friendly way like most guys. He can hurt you when he grabs your leg or arm. Lot's of the girls won't get close to him. He never tips extra for a table dance anyway. He's not a good customer. He's one customer the managers won't make us dance for. If he wasn't Big D's friend, they'd probably ban him. He's tight with Big D, and Big D is tight with Bobby.

"I'd never do a private dance for Carlos. I've heard that in private he's even worse. Like he might enjoy hurting. One girl was kind of fighting him off, and he pulled out a clump of her hair. She said he laughed. I've never seen him laugh. I know the bartender Rich has thrown him out more than once. Rich is the only guy there who can control him. Carlos doesn't seem to get drunk. He doesn't get loud. He's just creepy, sitting in pervert's corner, staring at dancers like a snake. Probably as dangerous. If he's involved in whatever you're doing, look out for him."

"Pervert's corner?"

"Yeah, the far corner opposite the door. Not much lighting there. They think they can get away with more in the dark. I guess they can. The dancers call it pervert's corner."

That's what she had. An overheard conversation and confirmation that Carlos was mean and hung out with Delacourt. She didn't know much more about him. She did know that he drove a tow truck for the Landrys, but that was it. I wasn't sure the little she told us was worth the risk of Preacher visiting the bar and leading her away, but there was nothing I could do about it. I hoped he was careful.

Just before we headed outside, I asked her, "Do you

know the dancer Cee-Cee? Her real name is Carol."

"Yeah, redhead, right? Or at least she was last time I saw her. She's gone from Fantasy Kings now, but, you know what, you were asking about Carlos. I think she dated Carlos. She sometimes left with him after her shift."

I sat back in my chair. Preacher sat forward on the sofa. That was a startling piece of information.

I asked, "Do you know where she is now?"

"No. She was getting a little too chubby and worn out to work at Fantasy King's. I guess she could be dancing at Chuck's or some other place. Girls come and go. I don't know where she went."

Linda's information that Carol was with Carlos made it more important to find Carol. I'd tell Rocky to concentrate on her. Things were starting to tie together. It didn't make sense yet, but, for the first time, I thought we had momentum.

"Let's go eat." I nodded at Preacher to let him know he'd done a good thing bringing Linda to meet me and all was forgiven. "I'll be out in a minute. I want to call Mr. Rockwell."

I called Rocky. I told him about TeeBoy's murder and what I'd just learned from Linda about a possible connection between Carol and Carlos. He whistled and said, "Too bad about TeeBoy, but we may be getting somewhere. Not sure where, but somewhere."

Back on the porch, I asked Joshua, "What's cooking?"

"Darla's uncle is a butcher. He gave us some ribs that are almost ready."

"I had pizza earlier, but what are we having with the ribs?"

We had potato salad and beans. The salad and beans were good. The ribs were excellent.

The day wore me out, and I went in to go to bed. There were gentle noises outside, the sounds of cleaning up and quiet conversations. At some point, I heard Preacher, Gretchen, and Linda drive off. Shortly after that I fell asleep. I did not remember dreaming, but woke up early, unsettled and anxious for things I could not grasp.

CHAPTER FIFTEEN

I MAINTAINED THREE MAILBOXES at the post office, one for my personal mail and two for my businesses. Joshua or Darla, or more likely both, went to the post office and left the mail on my desk. I glanced at it quickly. Most of it I would return to when I had more time, but I did review Rocky's invoice and sent money to his PayPal account. I entered the expense in Thumper's account.

I thought again about hiring someone to handle my legal business office matters and the bookkeeping for everything. Darla was doing good and learning fast, but she was mostly interested in learning how to weld. Another employee. Deeper roots. More obligations. Stronger ties to a place. Those had not been my goals for some time. But, for the first time in a long time, I found no urgent wanderlust in my thinking.

At half past eight, the phone rang. It was Angelique.

"Hey, Sam. I called and talked to Mrs. Canderly. She's not heard from Carol for some time. Mrs. Canderly doesn't know what happened to her. I didn't try to call anybody at Fantasy King's. I'm not sure who I'd call anyway, but you told me not to call there."

"Yeah. Don't do that. I've been told she might be with Carlos. She might have told them how to find you."

"Oh, no. Seriously? Carlos. What a creep. What was she thinking? I should have dragged her to Houston with me."

"No. You know it's not your fault."

"Maybe. I've got to go to the studio. Jenny is doing good. We might have to lock her in a closet to keep her from going after those guys. We will if necessary. Rocky is picking me up and making sure I stay safe. I feel terrible all the attention people are having to pay to me. I wish I knew what was going on."

"We're getting closer to finding out. And don't worry about everybody. They're all getting paid. It's their job. You be careful. I got some more news. TeeBoy has been stabbed to death in New Orleans."

"Oh, no. Do you think it's about me?"

"I don't know. Just be careful. Go nowhere without Rocky."

Shortly after we got off the phone Rocky called.

"Sam. I'm on the way to pick up Angelique. I wanted to let you know that my guy in Beaumont got a line on Carol."

"Good. I just got off the phone with Angelique. We were talking about finding Carol."

"Yeah. She is working at Chuck's. He hung around after closing and followed her home. We have an address."

"Great. Did you tell him about her and Carlos being an item?"

"Yes. I called Beaumont right after we talked. My guy hadn't been watching for him before I called, but didn't see him after I talked to him. Do you want him to stake out her place and watch for Carlos?"

Perhaps because I'd just paid his bill, I said, "No. If he's with her, he won't be hard to find. I want to go see her, and we'll watch for him then. I want Angelique to be with me when I talk to her. She'll have a better chance of getting info from her than some stranger. We'll have to be very careful about that."

"When are you going to go talk to her? Do you want us

to try and get a phone number?"

"No. Let's do this. We'll go up there tomorrow and drop by her house. Let's have your guy ready to make sure she's there in the morning before we arrive. He can watch and follow her if necessary. That way we can find her when we get there."

"I'll put him on it and text you his phone number. Marlene will have to sit on Jenny."

"Yes. We don't need her. She needs to mend."

"Agreed."

"I'll call you later."

He hung up without ceremony.

I ran on the beach later than usual. People were staking out spots with towels and blankets spread and canopies up for shade. The folks fishing the surf had gone to more remote locations or stayed home. The sun promised a hot day. A gentle surf rolled small waves glowing green in the morning light. Sea foam marked the limit of the tide. I ran around kids building castles and forts of sand. Brightly colored bikinis made the run interesting and made me think of Jenny and Angelique, one hurt and the other under siege. Both of them deserved some carefree time.

The energy of the run settled the thought that it was time to push Angelique's problem to a conclusion, whatever it took. Back at the house, I showered quickly and called Rocky.

"Hold on," he whispered. In a moment he said, "Sorry, I'm with Angelique. I had to get somewhere to talk. What's up?"

"Let Angelique know we're going to Beaumont to talk to her friend Carol tomorrow. We'll let Carol sleep in and try to be there around noon. Have your guy sit on her starting about nine so we know where she is."

"Okay. Done. What's happened?"

"Happened? Nothing. Why?"

"You sound different."

"I'm just tired of this case. Time to push it to a conclusion."

"Okay. Are we driving up together?"

"No. I think you and Angelique should go together. We won't get them together until we're sure Carlos isn't around."

"Take Preacher. Be safe."

"Yeah. I will if I can find him and he's willing to miss preaching on Sunday."

"I've never seen him have a problem with missing church when necessary."

"Have Angelique call me when she can."

"Will do."

I called Preacher. Gretchen answered, but Preacher was nearby and she put him on. He agreed to not only go with me the next day, but to also show up that evening for dinner and spend the night at my place.

Angelique called during a break, breathing hard from the work she was doing. We talked about going to see Carol. After making plans to meet at her apartment in the morning, she asked, "When is this going to be over?"

"Soon. I'm tired of it. We're going to push and make noise until it's resolved."

"I'm sorry I'm causing everybody so much trouble, but I appreciate what you're doing. I really do. I'd have no idea what to do on my own. I guess I might be in the hospital or dead by now without all of you."

"There's no problem. Like I told you, everybody is being paid to do what they do. Besides, I think you can tell, every one of us genuinely cares about you. I apologize if I sounded upset. I'm just tired of the trouble somebody is causing you and Thumper. You should dance and make music without all this worry. I want it fixed."

"Thank you. I have to get back to work."

I spent the afternoon welding, losing thoughts of the day to the labor. Joshua and Darla had the day off, but stuck around. Darla asked if she could work with me to learn. I checked some of the welding she'd done and discovered small designs she'd worked into some of her welds, a tiny flower in one place and a tiny heart in another. I wasn't sure how she was doing it. I liked it, but told her to not let the playing around get in the way of the integrity of the weld. I suggested she wait until she'd made hundreds of good, solid welds before branching out. She blushed and apologized and said she'd never do it again. She looked so contrite.

"Look," I said, "just be careful. I like it, and we'll make it a part of our style. You'll have to teach Joshua and me how to do it, but a good weld comes first. Develop some safe, cool designs and we'll work them into our custom smokers. They can be part of our branding."

She brightened up at that. Eventually, Joshua joined us, told me they'd take off early as comp time a few days in the week ahead. We worked hard, getting several of my retail line of grills ready to sell.

At one point Darla worked up the courage to say, "You know what Sam? You ought to put some cup holders on these things. Give people a place to put a soda can or a beer."

"Good idea. Work out how we do that. Make a couple."

She grinned and said, "In fact, maybe you could get some Locke Grills koozies and cups made and sell them to fit into the drink holders. People are proud of their Locke grills, and they like to buy stuff like that."

"Another great idea. You two do some research on

getting that done and building a holder that will fit. I'll give you each ten percent of any profit we make selling that kind of stuff."

They grinned and punched each other in the shoulder. Joshua said, "How about t-shirts and caps and stuff?"

"I don't want it to get too junky, but come up with some merchandise ideas and run them by me. Anything you come up with that sells, I'll give you the same deal, ten percent each on the profits from the stuff you think up. We'll start out selling it on the website. Maybe some of our retailers will want some."

At the same time, they each said, "Cool."

"But," I said, "the grills and smokers come first."

It was one of those days when mechanical skill and effort became a meditation. If I'd been alone with nowhere to be the next day, I'd have worked until midnight, losing myself in the work. But, Preacher was on the way and the kids needed to do something else with their day. I called a halt to the work about six o'clock. A short while later Preacher came walking up the drive.

Preacher and I drove into Galveston to eat chicken fried steak at Miller's Seawall Grill. Back at the house, we talked for a while. Preacher took up his favorite place on the porch. I went to bed, slept hard, and woke up tired and restless. We were at Angelique's and Jenny's apartment by nine-thirty.

I felt like we were finally getting ahead of the curve. I was confident we had almost enough information to push Angelique's case to a conclusion. I was ready to do whatever we needed to do to get it done. I had my own opinion on how to do that. It would be Angelique's decision, but after all the fear and the assaults and the killings, I wanted to go after the money.

CHAPTER SIXTEEN

A NGELIQUE, PREACHER, AND I drove to Beaumont in my car. Rocky followed us. I was glad Thumper had gone to his place for the day. I didn't want him with us for this trip. We left Jenny whining with Maureen. Angelique mentioned that Jenny was trying to do twice the recommended rehabilitation exercises prescribed by her physical therapist.

In Beaumont, I decided to drive by Carol's house before we stopped to visit.

Beaumont routinely appeared in the top ten of the FBI's list of the most dangerous cities in Texas. Undoubtedly, folks residing in Carol's neighborhood in southeast Beaumont helped the city maintain its spot on the list. It was poor, a tired community of ramshackle apartments and small houses. It wore a look of hopelessness like a shroud. Graffiti blossomed with threat, lewdness, and nonsense. More people were on the streets than in nicer neighborhoods, but it didn't feel neighborly. Many had to walk to the nearest bus stop for their transportation needs. Others were on the prowl. People on the broken sidewalks either studiously ignored us or openly stared, trying to decide if we were predators, viable prey, or in the market for something.

Carol lived in a small, wood-framed house on a surprisingly large lot. Its green shingled roof needed repair. A rusty evaporative cooler hung from one window. Those didn't work in the humidity of the coast, but perhaps moving hot, wet air was more comfortable than the alternative. The house's white paint curled and peeled. A previous coat of yellow showed through. The patchy, overgrown front yard had a large area of dead, oil-stained dirt in its middle.

Angelique saw the old, dented Toyota in the gravel drive-way and said, "That's the same car she drove me to Houston in."

Rocky called as we drove down the block. "Hey, my guy says she should still be in there alone. He can't park and watch constantly." He laughed. "Listen to this, he was parked down the street, hunkered down trying to be inconspicuous when an old lady used her cane to tap on his window. She told him she didn't know what he was doing or who he was after, but if he didn't move she was calling the cops. So, he's been circling. He said you can see the back of the house through the vacant lot the next street over.

"There was a tow truck parked behind the house when he followed her home this morning, but it's gone now. Before it left, he risked being beat to death by little old ladies with canes and walked through the vacant lot to get close enough to check it out. He knows our case has something to do with a tow truck driver. The truck belongs to Landry Towing. I'm thinking our guy Carlos must be their on-call driver."

"Now that's something. If he's out on a call, I wonder if he could come back to surprise us."

"Are you taking Angelique with you to talk to her?"

"Only if I am one hundred percent sure we won't run into Carlos."

"I can send my guy to make sure Carlos is at the salvage yard and if he is and leaves, he can follow him. He'll give us a heads up if he comes this way. If necessary, I'll send him to the other side of town and have him call for a tow."

I started to say something and Rocky interrupted saying, "Hold on, that's him calling me."

He came back on and said, "She's leaving. I told him to follow her. Let's follow them. Get behind me." He hung up.

I pulled over. Rocky passed me and I followed, making several turns until we were on a busy four-lane street.

Rocky called me. "You see her? She's pulling into Denny's. What do you want to do? Go see her there? There's no tow truck in sight, but I guess she could be meeting Carlos for a late breakfast."

I had to make a decision. Chances were Denny's would be crowded on a Sunday morning. Carlos would be reluctant to attack us there if he did show up.

"Yes. Let's drop in on her. I want to get this thing done."

At that point, we were pulling into the parking lot of the Denny's Restaurant. We parked next to Rocky in the back, out of sight of any windows.

Standing in the parking lot, Rocky said, "I've sent my guy to see if he can confirm that Carlos is at the salvage yard. If he is, he'll follow him if he leaves. He'll call if it looks like he's coming this way."

"Good."

Preacher said, "What do you want me to do exactly? We are about to overwhelm that poor girl."

"Yeah, why don't you hang back? Come in after us. We'll see if she'll join us in a booth and you can sit at the counter. So far, you haven't been connected to this thing. I'd like to keep it that way."

He nodded. Angelique looked scared, shoulders slumping and perspiration beading her lip.

"You okay?" I asked.

"Yeah. Just nervous, you know. I haven't seen her in a while, and she's with Carlos. He scares me a lot."

"We'll be okay here. You will be surrounded by friends, and some of us are carrying guns."

She smiled grimly while shaking her head. "This is just surreal and awful. I want it over."

"That's why we're going to ask her some questions, find out if she knows why her boyfriend is attacking you."

She nodded.

"And," I said, "we need to know if she's in on it for some reason."

She looked at me, her eyes wide. "But, she ... "

"Yeah, I know, but it's been a long time. We have to ask."

She nodded again and said, "I'm ready."

We walked into the diner. Carol, alone in a booth, did not see us. I told the hostess we were meeting someone. Preacher took a seat at the counter.

Rocky and I stood next to Carol's booth as Angelique slipped into it across from Carol and said, "Hi, Carol. Long time."

Carol looked up. She looked like maybe she'd tried to remove last nights make-up by swiping at it with a towel. Heavy foundation edged the line of her jaw. She turned white with bright spots of pink on each cheek. She almost dropped her cup of coffee and rattled it to the table.

"Oh, my God ... "

She did not sound happily surprised.

"Oh, my God." she said, again. "What ... Angel? You can't ... what are you doing here?"

The hand on her cup was trembling. Carol did not look like she'd ever been in ballet dancer shape. Lines cut her face. She had a chubby roll of skin sticking out between the bottom of her sleeveless top and her jeans. Her paid for breasts were the only firm thing about her body. She looked worn and smelled of stale cigarette smoke and body odor. Her hair was redder than it should have been and needed washing. There were bruises on her arms and one on her jaw, just below her left ear. I wondered where those came from.

Angelique said, "I came to see you. I need to talk to you. This is my lawyer, Sam, and my bodyguard, Rocky."

That was smart, introducing Rocky as her bodyguard. It gave her a great opening. The waitress came over and asked if we'd like a larger booth. I said yes before Carol could say a word.

I stood back to let her out. She sat there.

"Come on, Ms. Taylor. You know we have to talk. Let's get it over with. Maybe I don't call the police. Maybe it goes no further."

She stood up and followed us to a corner booth. Doing that without asking a question meant she knew something. Rocky carried her cup of coffee. He and I ordered coffee. Angelique declined to order anything. The waitress did not look happy about having given up a big table for our meager order. I gave her a twenty and told her we wouldn't be long, but we needed a little privacy. She cheered up.

Carol said, "Angel, what's up? What are you doing here?"

"I thought we were friends. I came to see you."

"With a lawyer and a bodyguard. What's that about?"

"You know what Carol? I don't know what it's about, but I'm trying to find out."

Carol was not touching her coffee.

I said, "Ms. Taylor, you're living with Carlos Perez. Was

it you who told him and Bobby Andrus and Steve Delacourt where to find her?"

"What? No? What do you mean?"

She was rattled. I pressed. "Was it you who told them how to find her in New Orleans so they could attack her?"

"What? No. I don't know what you're talking about. Angel?"

Angelique spoke softly. "Carol. They broke into my place twice. Carlos and another guy attacked me in New Orleans. They shot and stabbed and tried to kill a very good friend of mine when she protected me. She might die. I have to find out what's going on."

Carol started to cry. "I don't know anything about that. Carlos is bad, but ... It's not fair. You don't know what it was like after you left me here."

"I tried to get you to come with me. You wouldn't."

"I couldn't. It's easy for you. I could never be what you've become. I've seen you dance in Houston. More than once. I can't do that. Especially now."

Angelique reached across the table, but Carol pulled her hands to her lap. "Angel. I didn't do anything. You're famous. You're not hard to find."

She looked at me. "Look," she said, "I can't be seen talking to you. He'll ... "

Angelique said, "He'll what? Carlos? Are you talking about Carlos? What will he do? Hurt you? Why? You have nothing to do with anything to hear you tell it."

"Carlos wouldn't see it that way. Angel, he's a bad guy. I can't get away from him, or I would. Okay. All I did was remind Bobby of your last name. He'd forgotten it and asked Carlos to ask me. He didn't know you were dancing anywhere, so I told him you were in Houston, dancing ballet. I was proud of you. Bobby just wanted to talk to you about something. That's all I know. I'm working at Chuck's. He sent Carlos there to ask me. I didn't think it was any big deal."

Angelique said, "It's a very big deal, Carol. Carlos tried to kidnap me. Why?"

"No. They just need to talk to you. I think Bobby just wants to get something from you. Something worth a lot of money to him but not to you. I made sure it wasn't anything bad before I told Carlos anything." She wiped a tear from her face. "Angel, I need some money. I want to get out of here. I want to go somewhere. I can't dance much longer. Look at me. I have to get out."

"By selling me to Bobby and Carlos?"

Carol started crying harder. "I don't know what's going on. I thought Bobby was just going to talk to you. That's all."

"Well, that wasn't all. What do they think I have? By the way, now it's Carlos and Delacourt. Have you even seen Bobby lately? No. You haven't. I think Carlos killed him."

I squeezed Angelique's leg. I didn't want her going there. She was trembling with anger.

"What? No." Carol said. "Angelique, just tell them you don't have what they're after."

I said, "What is it they're after? We don't even know what it is."

"Neither do I. All I know is Bobby was going to give Carlos a couple of thousand dollars to get something from you. Carlos said we'd take the money and move to Los Angeles. I guess Bobby made the same deal with Steve."

"So, it's all Bobby?"

She hesitated a bit before she said, "Yes."

"He hasn't been seen for over two weeks. Did he already pay them?"

"No. I don't think so or we'd just take off. Carlos has been real angry about the whole deal. He won't talk to me about it. And, I can't ask him. I just can't. He gets so angry. He can slam things around."

I said, "Things like you?"

She didn't answer. I asked, "If Bobby hasn't paid them and nobody knows where Bobby is, how does Carlos expect to get paid?"

"I don't know. I just know it's real important to Carlos. And to Steve, too, I guess. Angel, you have to know what they're after. If it's not important to you, just give it to them. Look at you, you don't need anything else. You can dance. You're famous. You're making money."

Angelique slumped back in the booth. "Carol, I really have no idea what they're after. I don't have anything. And I am afraid for my life."

"I'm sorry I don't know anything else. All I did was tell Carlos your name and that you are with the ballet in Houston. That's all. I don't know what's going on."

"No," I said, "you know something or you've heard something. There's somebody else involved. Somebody paying Bobby. Who is it?"

She looked around. "Look, I have to get out of here. If somebody tells Carlos I was talking to you, there's no telling what he'll do to me. Angel, I'm at the end of the road. I can't get away from him. I have nowhere to go. You have to leave me alone. I'm sorry I ever said anything. Real, real sorry. Okay. Let me go home." She was crying.

"You tell my lawyer what he wants to know, and we're out of here. Please, Carol. You have to help me. I have to find out what's going on. If there is any shred of friendship left between us, tell us anything you can."

The waitress hovered as close as possible, interested in

the drama to the point where she didn't mind us taking one of her largest booths.

I lowered my voice. "Who else is involved?"

Carol looked at Angelique. I saw her slump. "I have to get out of here, but there's one thing. Sometimes the three of them, Bobby, Carlos, and Big-D come over to Chuck's with another guy. You might remember him, Angelique. He used to come into Kings. He was a big tipper. You danced for him several times, so he must have been an okay guy. His name is Bobby, too. I remember it because it's the same as Bobby Andrus and he's kind of short like Bobby, only chubbier."

"I don't remember any of those guys from back then. I never paid attention to them when I danced for them. I certainly didn't try to remember their names."

"Well, he's been around for a long time. They come to Chuck's." Carol looked at me. "They all huddle in a corner and talk."

"What exactly do they talk about?"

"I don't know. If I get close, they chase me away. I asked Carlos if they were talking about whatever it is that's going to get some money. He got pissed at me. Told me nobody was talking about giving me any money. Angel, he cannot find out I'm even talking to you. I have to go. I just want to go home."

Tears rimmed Angelique's eyes. "Carol, just leave. Get out of Beaumont. Go home. Come to Houston. Something."

"I can't. You don't know what's it like. I have nowhere to go. I have one thing I can do to make money and it's almost gone. What the hell am I supposed to do?" She was hopeless and angry. It was a good thing Preacher wasn't close enough to listen in or she'd probably be riding home with us.

"Okay," I said. "Look, take my card. Hide it somewhere or memorize the number. If you have any shred of feelings about Angelique, call me if you hear anything she should know or if you hear anything about what they're after. Or if you remember something. Her life depends on it. If you're in danger call the police and ask for Detective Lucy Smith."

She took my card, stuck it in the rear pocket of her jeans, and left. We watched her car rattle out of the parking lot. Preacher joined us.

"How did it go?" he asked.

I shrugged.

"That girl looks like she needs some help."

"Don't even think about it, Preacher. She doesn't want help. She led the bad guys to Angelique, and if you somehow got her to join your flock, I'd bet a bunch of money she'd lead them right to her again. She told us some, but she didn't tell us everything she knows. And, she didn't tell us enough."

Angelique was crying silently. She brushed tears off her face and said with some anger, "What is it they want? What?"

"It has to be about your birth mom and the family fortune. That's the only thing out there big enough to warrant what's happening. But we need to know what got these guys involved."

"What do you mean?"

"Somebody else is behind this. You won't be safe until we figure out who that is. How did they find Bobby and his lapdogs? Who is the new Bobby you're supposed to know? There's a Robert in the family tree, Stuart's son, Montgomery's grandson. Maybe that's the new Bobby. We need to go visit your family. Anybody who knew you were adopted. We need to find out if they were approached at some point. We need to find out where that picture of Thumper and Belle came from." I patted her knee. "We're getting there. We're going to figure it out. We need to go see your aunt who had the adoption papers and the stuff about Thumper and your grandmother. When can we do that?"

"Now. She'll be home. She doesn't go anywhere. I want this done. I don't know what you expect to find, but I don't understand any of this. Let's go from here."

"Okay. We'll do that."

Rocky asked, "Need me?"

"No. You and Preacher can head back. We'll go to Lake Charles to see her aunt. There's a police detective here in Beaumont I can't put off seeing much longer. We'll stop back by here and see her on the way home."

THE DRIVE FROM BEAUMONT to Angelique's aunt's home in Lake Charles, Louisiana, took us an hour and a half. Angelique called on the way to let her know she was on the way for a visit. She did not tell her why, just that she was going to be close and wanted to drop in to see her.

Angelique and I talked a bit about what we wanted to ask her aunt. That didn't take us long, and we rode in silence. She looked out the window. I thought about the situation. If members of the Chandler family were causing all the trouble, how did they connect up with Landry and Delacourt and Carlos? I didn't have the answers, but at least I had some coherent questions. Things were coming together.

We crunched onto Angelique's aunt's gravel drive. She came out onto the porch. She wore tight jeans and a t-shirt.

I guessed her age at close to fifty, but her cropped hair was as white as a cloud. Her huge smile faded as soon as she saw me. She crossed her arms and stood solid at the top of her steps.

"Uh oh," I said. "I don't think she expected you to be with me."

"She'll be fine." After a moment, Angelique added, "I think." She jumped out of the car and ran up the steps to hug her aunt. I followed her to the porch but skipped the hug.

The aunt glared at me over Angelique's shoulder, stepped back, and said, "And, who might this be?"

"Aunt Stel, this is my lawyer Samuel Locke. Sam, this is my aunt, Estelle Green."

She did not look like she was interested in shaking hands. No way was I getting a hug. I smiled, nodded, and said, "Pleased to meet you Ms. Green."

She turned to Angelique. "Lawyer? You in trouble? You do something wrong?"

"No, no. He's not that kind of lawyer. He handles business stuff for me."

The aunt turned back my way, suspicion narrowing her eyes. "Well then, pleased to meet you. I guess. Y'all come on in."

We followed her into her very clean and orderly living room. She had a teapot and a plate of cookies on a tray on the coffee table.

"You two sit. I'll get another cup."

She did, and the three of us sipped tea and ate excellent oatmeal cookies while the two of them exchanged pleasantries. The cookies tasted subtly of cinnamon.

"Okay," Estelle said, "what are you really here for? Something's up. What?"

Angelique looked at me.

"Ms. Green, Angelique is having some problems. Somebody broke into her house a couple of times looking for something. Somebody tried to mug her in New Orleans. We're trying to find out what's going on."

She turned to Angelique. "Mugged? You didn't call to let me know that? Are you okay? What happened?"

"I'm fine. I was with my best friend, and she protected me. They put her in the hospital, but she's home and is going to be okay."

Several seconds passed as her aunt breathed evenly and looked at her before turning to look at me.

"Somebody explain better, please."

"Yes, ma'am. We think they're after something. Maybe something about Angelique's birth parents and her grandmother's family."

Estelle slumped back into her chair shaking her head. She said, "Dammit."

She looked at Angelique. Her eyes narrowed and her face tightened with anger. "I knew nothing good was going to come from you talking to your grandfather. No reason to do that. He had nothing to do with you, and God knows your grandmother's family is poison. They got rid of your mom as fast as she dropped out of her mom. They certainly don't want you crawling out of the woodpile."

"Aunt Stel, I love Thumper. He didn't have anything to do with me because he didn't know I existed. He's great. He is looking out for me."

Estelle shook her head and looked back my way. "What do you want from me?"

"The only thing I can think of that would create this kind of interest in Angelique is her Grandmother Belle's family fortune. You know who they are?"

"Of course. They're the worst. They would have tossed

Angelique's mom in the river when she was born if they thought they could get away with it and not lose their country club membership. You should have never searched for your family, Angelique. Your family is right here."

"I didn't search for them. I don't want to have anything to do with them, but I have to figure out what's going on."

"Ms. Green, we think somebody in the family is concerned that Angelique may come after her share of the family money."

"She don't need that money. It's bad money."

"That may be, but you know people who have that kind of money might go to extremes to protect even a dollar from somebody like Angelique."

Estelle nodded. "You got that right." She took a measured sip of tea. She reached out and took Angelique's hand, gave a small smile her direction, and turned back to me with less of a smile. "What is it you're here for?"

"We're trying to figure out who it is that broke into Angelique's apartment twice and who attacked her in New Orleans."

"Mr. Locke, right?" I nodded. "Are you keeping her safe?"

"Yes. She is surrounded by people trained to protect her. Her friend who saved her in New Orleans is a young lady working for me. It was her job to protect her, and she did. There are others on the job."

She looked at Angelique and slowly shook her head, her mouth a tight line.

"They really are keeping me safe, Aunt Stel. By the way, Thumper is paying for it all."

Her aunt made a noise at that last comment.

"What do you want from me?"

I said, "We know there are bad guys in Beaumont who somebody directed her way. We know who they are, and we've been to the police about them. One man has already been arrested in New Orleans. But, there's somebody else out there paying those guys to do what they've done. That's who we have to find."

She nodded.

"You gave her that picture of Thumper and her grandmother. We're wondering where you got it. My understanding is that her mother Rose did not know her parents."

"I never should have shown her that picture."

"No, it's been a good thing for her and Thumper to find each other. Plus, these people would have found her anyway."

"You're right about Rose never knowing who her parents were. That's the way it should be. That's the way things should have stayed."

"But, you knew?"

"Not until I got that picture, along with some other stuff in the mail."

Angelique sat forward, moving to the edge of her chair and leaning toward her aunt. "What? When? What other stuff?"

"All your recent trouble just proves me right. You should stay away from that family."

"I didn't go to them. They came to me, with guns and knives. What other stuff?"

Her aunt whispered, "Oh, Lord," and turned to look out the window.

"Ms. Green, this is not going to stop until either Angelique is dead or we stop it. We need every shred of information we can gather if we're going to stop it. We have to have enough facts to fight their money."

"Hold on. I'll get it."

She got up and disappeared into the back of the house. She returned with a large envelope. Angelique reached for it, but her aunt pulled it tight into her lap and turned to me.

"Mr. Locke, just like her mother, Angelique came into a community that looks out for their own. I'm not sure her real mom Rose was legally adopted, but it was legal enough for living where she lived. Everybody knew she was some white folks' trash baby, being half-black and all. The people who took her in were probably paid some money to take her. That don't mean they didn't take care of her as good as they could. They did.

"I guess Rose never felt like she belonged where she was. She grew up with an itch to be somewhere else. She was gone for a while and came back pregnant with Angelique. She'd took sick by then. She kept talking about how Angelique's father, some college boy from Texas, was going to come take them both away. That never was going to happen. She just got sicker and sicker and then she died."

Angelique took in a sharp breath. Her aunt reached a hand out to her and said, "You know this story. You know it has nothing to do with you. Mr. and Mrs. Cambray took you in and treated you as good as their own. Your mom worked her fingers to the bone to keep you dancing and look at you. You be thankful for that."

"I am. More than you know. Doesn't make a lot of things any less sad."

"Ms. Green, it sounds like nobody knew anything about Angelique's ancestry for some time. Obviously that changed. What do you have there?"

She sighed and opened the envelope. "Rose got a letter when she was about thirteen. Her mother obviously didn't think she needed to see it. I agree. It was mixed in with all the paperwork that my sister got when she took you in after your mother died. She and I talked about it and agreed you didn't need to see it. I don't know why either of us kept it. That picture I gave you was with it. I wouldn't have done that if I'd known your grandfather was still alive. Word was he'd been murdered. We should have burned it all. Don't matter. Here it is. I think your lawyer is going to be interested in it."

She handed me the envelope like she still did not want Angelique to have it.

"But you listen to me, girl. Those people don't want you. They're poison and their money is evil in ways you cannot imagine."

I was opening the envelope. Angelique held her hand out for it, saying, "What is it? Let me have it." I handed it to her. She shook out a postmarked envelope.

Angelique opened the envelope and pulled out several pages of what I could tell was a hand-written letter. She clasped it in two hands, held it in her lap, lowered her head, and started to read. She finished the first page, looked at her aunt, and handed the page to me. The letter wrinkled in the grip of her hand.

Rose's half-brother Joseph Quantrill Planter sent her a letter when she was thirteen years old. From the letter, it appeared eleven-year-old Joseph and his father also paid a price for Belle Anne's indiscretion. There was that letter and one more and some other stuff. Angelique said nothing while she read. She glanced at her aunt a couple of times. Her breath became more measured, deeper. She handed each page of the letters to me as she read them. She took the stack of other stuff, handed it to me without looking at it, got up, and walked to the door.

Her aunt said, "Angel ... "

Angelique held her hand up to stop any attempt at conversation and said nothing as she walked outside. The screen door chunked closed behind her.

Her aunt's hands twisted the napkin she held.

I looked through the stuff.

Bingo.

Chapter Seventeen

ANGELIQUE WAS QUIET after we left her aunt's house. The envelope her aunt gave her sat heavily between us. I asked, "You okay?"

"Yeah, I'm fine. My great-grandfather was a horrible person."

"A product of his times and heritage."

"I can understand not wanting to have anything to do with my mom or me, but why Joseph? Wow, it is weird to think that I have all this family. He's my uncle. Does he have a kid? Do I have a cousin?"

"I don't know. Now that we're focusing on the Chandler family and fortune, we need to find out. Starting right now."

I called Rocky.

"Hey, Sam. How did it go?"

"Amazingly well. If we're on the right track, we have uncovered a gun that is still warm and smoking. Let's gather at my place tonight, and we'll share it. Right now, I need you to go more in-depth on the family. We never got confirmation about whether Belle Anne's sister, Lucille, has kids. We don't know if Rose's half-brother Joseph has kids or whether Joseph is alive. We need to know those things."

"Got it. I'll call the trophy bride, and she and I will discuss the best way to proceed. What about letting them know we're after them? It might get out."

"I no longer care. Don't go out of your way to attract

attention, but I'm tired of this mess, and we're starting to rattle some cages. I have no problem if they know. We can let them think we're after the money. Just make sure everybody stays safe."

"Okay. Good. We'll get started right now. What time tonight?"

"Eight-thirty, unless I call and change it."

"Got it." He hung up.

I glanced over at Angelique. She was staring straight ahead. "You okay?"

"Yes. I'm just thinking about that poor lonely boy. He was as outcast as my mom. Maybe it was even worse because they gave him no room to create his own life. He had to live with them. And, you know, maybe if he and my mom had been able to communicate it would have helped them both. Maybe he could have given my mom a sense of herself, helped her avoid her restless problems."

She crossed her arms and rocked back and forth a couple of times. She said, "I know that wouldn't have been likely. My mom's troubles ran deep. So, what do you think about that stuff?"

"Your great-aunt Lucille sounds like a kind and compassionate woman. We'll go talk to her. The copies of all that stuff Joseph sent to your mom may be what the bad guys are after. I'd like to find out if the originals still exist. That would be the best thing. Frankly, if we legally prove the existence of that stuff, I have no doubt a court would put you in line for a share of the Chandler Trust."

"I don't want it."

"I know, but given the interest in you by somebody, the best thing might be to get it all out in the open, establish your right. It removes most of the incentive to do you harm and puts a harsh light on those who are trying.

Plus, we need to flush them out. I'd prefer to do that by going after them instead of trying to catch them coming after you."

"I don't know. I just want things back the way they were."

"I know."

I knew, but things were never going back to the way they were, not for her. She had to deal with the entanglements of the Chandler fortune. Personally, I thought with the tens of millions of dollars she stood to gain, she could find a way to deal with the hassle. She could buy a ballet company or something.

"I'm going to call a police detective in Beaumont who needs to see us. Her name is Lucy Smith."

"Do we have to do it today? I'm tired."

"Let's get it out of the way. I won't let her grill you. Right now, for some strange reason, she thinks I'm being uncooperative. It would be good to get her friendly."

"Okay. What do I tell her? How do I avoid telling her about what I found on my floor?"

"I'll do most of the talking. She won't get you alone. If she ask a tough question, defer to me. You'll be okay. We'll be ready."

I called Detective Smith in Beaumont. I left a voicemail telling her I would be in Beaumont in about an hour with my client, and we would be happy to sit down with her if she was available.

Angelique and I talked more about how to handle a talk with Detective Smith. I warned her I saw no way to avoid mentioning she used to dance at Fantasy Kings. She shrugged and said that was the least of her worries. Twenty minutes outside of Beaumont, the detective called me.

After greetings, Detective Smith said, "I thought you

were ignoring me."

"No. Today's the first time we've been in the area. I told you'd I'd call when we were here."

"Ask for me when you get to the police station."

"Okay. It will be about a half an hour."

"I look forward to hearing what you know."

"Likewise."

She made a noise. I guess it was good-bye because she hung up.

I asked Angelique, "Where's Thumper? He needs to be at my place tonight. I hope we don't have to drive up to the river to pick him up."

"No. He said he'd be back in Houston tonight. I'll call him."

She called him. In answer to something he said, she told him she'd tell him about her day later. She told him we'd call and meet him in Houston to drive to my place.

He asked her something and she said, "I don't want to talk about it right now. Sam thinks it's good. You'll find out tonight."

At the police station, I convinced myself that a car parked in the parking lot of the police station would be safe and locked the material we'd received from Angelique's aunt in one of my glove boxes.

Detective Smith had not warmed up to me near as much as Detective Robichaud. The detective was portly. She had salt and pepper hair. I got the impression she never smiled. Perhaps my lawyer speech about how we would only disclose things I wanted to let her know put her off from the start. I tried to make it sound logical and reasonable, but she wasn't buying it. I can't say I blamed her.

I told her about the break-ins and the assault. I gave her the public version of where we were. I told her the only sordid thing in Angelique's past was that she used to work at Fantasy Kings. I told her how investigating her past turned up Delacourt and Carlos and how they fit the description given by Betty Page of the men she saw going over the fence after the last break-in. I described my discussions with Detective Robichaud.

"Yes," she said, "I've talked to Detective Robichaud. I'm mostly involved because of the disappearance of Bobby Andrus. His brother thinks you know something about that."

"I think Bobby was tight with Delacourt and Carlos. I've heard he had discussions with them about something they were doing to make a lot of money. I think it had to do with my client."

"And where did you hear that? Give me some names."

"A lot of what I heard was third hand, but you know where everybody worked. Carlos lives with a dancer named Carol Taylor. She was a friend of Angelique's way back when. You'll want to talk to her. You'll need to be careful. She's afraid of Carlos, and she's likely to run. If he hears you talked to her, he's likely to take it out on her in a bad way. I learned from her that Bobby asked her about Angelique. She told him Angelique's last name and that she lived in Houston. She saw Bobby, Delacourt, and Carlos meeting with somebody at the bar where she works, but she didn't know what that was about. She never overheard anything. She thinks it's related to whatever is going on that's supposed to get some money paid to Carlos. Something that involves Angelique. Something they want from her."

"And you have no idea about what that might be?"

"I'm guessing. I think somebody thinks she has something that would prove she is entitled to a lot of money, and somebody does not want to share with her."

"What money are you talking about? She have something on the Andrus brothers?"

"No, but she is the unacknowledged great-granddaughter of Robert Lee Chandler. You've heard of the Chandlers?"

That actually got a new expression out of the detective, a look of surprise from which she quickly recovered.

"The Chandlers who own big chunks of East Texas and Louisiana, including a significant part of my town?"

"Those would be the ones."

"And does she have something like that? What's it got to do with the Andrus boys."

"No, she doesn't." She didn't have it. I did. I wasn't ready to give it up. My interests were different from Detective Smith's. I wanted the chance to study the material and put it to its best use in the interest of my clients. Depending on what I decided to do, it might be best if the information never got into the hands of the police. It was not my job to solve the murder of Bobby Andrus. It was to protect my clients.

I continued, "I think somebody thinks she does. It's the only thing in her past that might create the kind of interest she's receiving from somebody. Perhaps Bobby Andrus and his minions, Carlos and Delacourt, have been hired to recover it or make sure she's not around to inherit."

"What is it they think she has?"

"I don't know what they think. You'll have to ask them. I assume it is something somebody fears would prove she is entitled to a share of the Chandler estate."

"Is your client after the Chandler's money?"

Angelique quickly said, "No. Absolutely not. I want nothing to do with them."

The detective nodded and said, "You know it's doubtful

I can go knocking on the Chandler's front door without more, right?"

"I understand," I said.

"Are you planning to do so?"

"Absolutely."

She almost smiled. "You'll let me know how that goes, won't you?"

"Yes."

"Detective Robichaud said you might be helpful."

She poked and probed, but I didn't have anything else I was willing to share.

I told her again how dangerous it would be if Carlos thought Carol talked to somebody.

She didn't really react to that. She said, "I think you're being less than forthright, and I am not impressed with your reliance on confidentiality. Seems to me you're putting your client at risk. I might have to let our District Attorney advise me about that."

"Whatever you feel the need to do. But, your time would be better spent focusing on the case. I'm not here to get in your way, but I will protect my client. You can at least begin an investigation based on my information, just as if you got it from the same people I did."

She took several deep breaths. I thought she might be running through a list of statutes, trying to find one to put me in a cell.

We didn't talk much longer. I left her frustrated and doubtful of my complete cooperation. At least I had another cop involved. She'd talked to Betty Page but had a hard time finding somebody at the Houston Police Department with whom she could follow up. She didn't say, but I knew she would talk to Delacourt and Carlos. I hoped attention from the police might keep them from coming after Angelique.

That's what I was after. We were getting close to having enough information to act, but I still felt the tug of unseen currents as strong as a riptide.

We picked up Thumper at the Big Easy blues bar on Kirby in Houston. He respected Angelique's distance, asking no questions on the drive to my place. He sat in the back seat occasionally whistling softly. At my place, Joshua came outside to see if I needed him. I let him know we were having a business meeting and he returned to his apartment. I heard country music when he opened the door to go inside.

Rocky arrived, and we gathered around my dining room table. Rocky called Jenny and put her on speaker phone.

I gave a short recap of where we'd gone and who we'd seen. The others vibrated in silence as Angelique read the first letter from her mom's half-brother.

> *Dear Rose,*
>
> *Hi. I know you don't know me but I am your brother. Surprise. My name is Joseph Q. Planter. We have the same mom. I know she never married your daddy and I guess her dad was mad at her about that. I guess they gave you to another family. I hope it was better than this one. Most of them don't treat me very nice. Our mom is dead. I'm sorry if you didn't know that but she drowned. My dad isn't around much and isn't always nice to me either. I don't think they really like him either. I mainly live with my aunt Lucy. She is real nice but she's not a kid. I don't have many friends. My cousins are mean. My best friend is the son of my aunt's butler. His name is Thomas Wilson. He's a little older than me and he plays with me. He's a negro so we can't*

be real good friends and there's a lot of stuff we can't do, but he plays with me around here. I know your daddy was a negro and I guess that's another thing that made our grandfather mad at your mom. Thomas is mailing this letter for me so I don't get in trouble. I'm not supposed to know about you. Write me back. Mail it to him and he'll get it to me. Just don't put your name on the envelope. He said put the name of Gracie Williams. That's his cousin. One of his chores is picking up the mail from the mailbox so it will be okay.

I guess if you don't know about this stuff you may be wondering how I know about it. Grandfather died in a plane crash and a lot of his old business stuff is in the attic here. There's a desk there and I like to play business man. I use a lot of his old papers and pretend I am a business man. Nobody goes into the attic but me and sometimes Thomas. I'd get in so much trouble for messing with his stuff. I found a box with stuff in it about you. It was all locked up, but I know where the old keys are.

Write me back and maybe we can be friends. It does not bother me that your daddy was a negro. The nicest person in the world my age is Thomas. We could all be friends.

Sincerely,

Joseph Q. Planter

Angelique said, "And then he wrote down the address he wanted Rose to send a letter to and the address of Gracie to use as a fake return address."

"Holy shit," said Jenny over the phone. "Did she write back?"

"No," Angelique said, "she never knew about the

letters."

"But," I said, "he did write again. And the family had a photocopier at the house. Read the second letter."

Angelique spread the second letter out on the table smoothing its edges with the palms of her hands. She took a deep breath.

"This one was written two months after the first one." She smoothed it out one last time.

> *Dear Rose,*
>
> *This is me, your brother Joseph. I guess you never wrote back. If you did it got lost somehow. Thomas says maybe you don't believe that I'm your brother because nobody ever told you about your family. If so, you are not missing much. There's nobody I can talk to about you except Thomas. I would get in trouble for even knowing about you. If you don't write back I won't bother you again. But please do.*
>
> *I hate this family and think you're lucky you got out. Even if it wasn't your idea. There is a Xerox machine here in my aunt's office. Do you know what that is? It makes copies of papers. My aunt lets me use it to make comic books and coloring books. I draw them and make copies and staple them together just like real books. My cousins said it is a dumb thing to do. I'm going to send you one. I hope you like it. I used the Xerox to copy the stuff about you. That way you'll know this is real. Maybe then you will write me back.*
>
> *Your friend I hope,*
> *Joseph Q. Planter*

Jenny said, "Holy shit. What did he send? I should be there. Did he ... "

Rocky said, "Hush or I'll hang up on you. So, Sam,

what did he send? Our smoking gun?"

I had the stack of paper in front of me, the stuff young Joseph had copied and mailed to Rose in his desperate attempt to find a friend.

"Looks to me like Robert Lee Chandler was a stickler for records. He must have kept a file with all things pertaining to his daughter Belle Anne. Looks like young Joseph copied the whole file. Plus, it looks like somebody kept putting stuff in the Belle Anne file for a while after the airplane crash that killed Robert and the others."

Thumper said, "Anything in there about sending somebody to shoot me?"

"No. But, there's other stuff that should have been burned. Or never written down to start with."

I pulled a faded carbon copy of a letter out of the stack.

"Here's the most important thing. It's a letter from Robert Chandler to his lawyer, a Douglas Sheffield of the law firm of Sheffield and Foret, dated February, nineteen fifty-five. The letter is talking about changing his will. There's a letter from the lawyer in the file that this letter is responding to. The lawyer's letter is worded a bit more carefully about the changes Mr. Chandler asked to be made. Mr. Chandler's response is a bit more explicit.

"Chandler says, 'I guess a man ought to be free to leave his fortune in his own way. My daughter has rebelled and brought shame to her family. I'll be God damned if I'll leave her a penny. She has taken to living with a dirt-poor negro musician of all things. She knows my feelings about the dangers and sinful ways of mixing with other races. It is not only illegal here in this country, it is against God's law.'"

Nobody said anything for a moment. Everybody was looking at Angelique. She held her head high, and her chin was rock solid. Her eyes glistened with unformed tears, but

I'd been around her a bit and I knew everything about her at that moment was anger.

Thumper broke the silence, "I try to never wish bad for anybody who's died, but that man's blind hatred killed Marlowe and it killed Belle. I know he's in hell, but his hand probably reached up from the grave and killed that Andrus boy."

Angelique reached out and touched him.

Over the phone, Jenny said, "Hey, Angelique, you okay? I wish I was there."

Angelique's voice caught in her throat, but she took a breath and said, "I am perfectly fine. That man was sad. He's gone. I still don't want his money. How can we make them leave me alone?"

Rocky said, "Anything else of interest in that stuff?"

"There's correspondence from a New York based detective agency that had somebody in Paris reporting Belle's comings and goings. There are notes about where Rose ended up after she was born."

"What next?" Rocky asked.

"Run down Joseph Quantrill Planter. Let's find out what he's up to these days. Also, see if you can run down any recent photos of the family members."

"I'll do that. Give me a day, and I can get driver's license photos."

"Do it. I really want a good one of Robert Chandler, Stuart's son. That one has priority."

"Okay. Why?"

"Because Carol told us there was a meeting with Bobby Andrus, Carlos, Delacourt, and a customer named Bobby. I'm wondering if that's Robert Chandler."

Rocky sat back in his chair and whistled. "Oh, yeah. I'd forgot about that for a moment. You think it's him?"

"I don't know, but right now we don't have any connection between all the bad guys we know about and the Chandler family. There's no guarantee our speculation is accurate. We may just be conforming our hopes into facts. That's one thing we can check for a connection."

"Okay, I'll get on it." He started writing a note.

Jenny said, "I've got it. While you were all talking without me being there, I went online. I have a couple of pictures of Robert and his dad Stuart from Sports Illustrated. They tried to buy the Miami Dolphins. I'm sending them to you now."

"Good job," Rocky said.

"I know. Now, let me get back in the game in person. I'm going crazy here."

"We'll talk about it."

"I think we're going to go visit Lucille Chandler soon," I said. "I want you to go if you're truly okay. I might want to show off your scars."

"I am. I promise. And the scars look real good, right now. Much longer and they will start to fade."

My phone chirped to signal Jenny's incoming email.

"Let's open it on the computer, so it's big enough to see," I said.

We gathered around my computer. I opened the first attachment to Jenny's email. It was a well-photographed image of Stuart and Robert Chandler. Angelique made a noise and took a step back and then two steps forward. She pushed Rocky aside to get closer to the monitor.

"I know him," she said. Her finger touched the screen over Robert's face. "Oh, my God."

Over the speakerphone Jenny said, "What? Did you say you know one of them? What?"

Angelique said, "He was a customer. I danced for him.

More than once. Oh, my God."

Chapter Eighteen

Angelique had danced for Robert Chandler. She remembered him as Bob. A Bobby had been seen by Carol with Bobby Andrus, Delacourt, and Carlos gathered around a table at Chuck's. More things were tying together.

Angelique stood back from the computer, looking at the photograph of Robert Chandler. She said, "That could not have been a coincidence. He had to know who I am. We're what? Some kind of cousins?"

"Second cousins," I said.

"He found me and came in there and had me dance. He looked at me. More than once. Probably tried to touch me." She turned and walked out the front door.

Everybody was quiet, except for Jenny. She said, "What's going on? Somebody tell me what's happening. Dammit. I am not sitting at home anymore. Somebody talk to me." Rocky finally took the phone off speaker mode and walked into the kitchen to talk to her.

I looked out the window. Angelique sat on the porch, her arms wrapped around her knees.

I poked my head out the door. "Hey, you okay?"

"I want to go home. I'm tired."

"Do you want to talk about what we're going to do next?"

"Do you know what we're going to do?"

"Not yet. We need to decide."

"You decide. I'll do whatever you say. Just let me know.

But, unless we're doing something tonight, I want to go home."

From behind me, Rocky said, "I'll take her. It's late. I assume you need to think on what you want to do. I'll take her and sleep there tonight."

Angelique stood up, walked to me, and gave me a hug. "Thanks," she said. "I know you're getting things done. Please tell me we're going to get this resolved."

"Yes. I'm sure we know enough now to get this thing ended, one way or another."

"Okay. Whatever it takes. The ballet season is over, so I have some time, but I do not want to miss dancing in The Nutcracker. There are things I need to do. I am easily replaced. Can Thumper stay here tonight?"

"Sure. We're going to have to go back up to Dallas again. I think it would be good if you were there. I'm going to press that family about your interest in your great-grandfather's estate ... " She started to interrupt, but I held a hand up to stop her. "I don't know if we'll be able to prove who in the family is behind the attacks on you. Even if there is enough evidence to arrest Delacourt and Carlos, we might not be able to get back to the family.

"I suspect Bobby was the go-between and knew what was going on. Delacourt and Carlos may not even know enough to get us to the family. The best way to remove the dangerous attention from somebody in the family is by making it irrelevant. We do that by legally establishing the right. You can then formally let go of your interest if that's what you want to do, but we can't just ignore it.

"I want you there when I drop in on the family, probably Lucille by herself at first. After that, I'll hire another lawyer in the area to represent you regarding your interest in the estate. He can do what's necessary without you being there."

"Can't you do that?"

"I know somebody with more expertise. Besides, the more folks on your team, the harder it will be for somebody to just kill us all."

"Okay. Whatever."

Angelique was listless. The events of the day had affected her deeply. Time at home and the support of Jenny would be good for her.

Thumper, sensitive enough not to argue with her, agreed to spend the night with me. She hugged Thumper and me, telling him she loved him and thanking me. She left with Rocky. Everybody agreed to meet back at my place the next night. I bet myself that no force on earth could prevent Jenny from joining us in person.

I went to bed and stared at the ceiling for the longest trying to think my way through things. I came to no grand insight. I finally went to sleep with jumbled thoughts, worried I was missing too much.

IN THE MORNING, I heard Thumper rustling around before I got out of bed. It took me a while to get up and out. There was coffee, but no sign of Thumper in the house. I took a cup outside. I could see him sitting on the edge of the dock at the end of the boardwalk. He turned around when the boardwalk creaked under my feet. He had a line dangling from a fishing pole over the edge.

The pass was at a peak high tide, and the water was still. There would be no good tidal flow until mid-afternoon. There would be no good fishing off the dock until then. But fishing is all about hope.

"I borrowed some fishing stuff."

"You won't catch much like that," I said. "Do you want

me to set you up for fishing out a little deeper? Might be something hanging around out there."

"Nah. I ain't really fishing. I'm just thinking."

"I understand that." I sat down next to him and looked out over the flats. The sun was coming up over our shoulders. Things were still. Even the egret that hangs out at my place wasn't trying to fish. Way out toward the pass were a few gulls. They'd probably spent the night out there. A couple of boats were headed out for a day on the Gulf. I envied them.

"So, Mr. Lawyer man, what are we going to do next?"

"I'm not completely sure. But we're going to start pushing back. I'm going to email that picture of Robert to the detective in Beaumont with the suggestion she talk to Carol about his meeting with the others. I'm going to call Lucille and ask if she'll meet with us."

Thumper snorted and said, "Don't you think that'll just cause that entire family to put up some major walls?"

"Probably. Then I'll do it more formally with a certified letter."

"Well, whatever you think is best is fine with me."

He looked out over the flats. A cool breeze ruffled grass and water. The sun brightened the day, casting our shadows over the water.

"You know what Sam? I know she keeps saying she doesn't want that money."

"Yeah."

"I'm thinking that is foolish on her part. Don't let her turn it down too fast."

"I agree. She eventually can if she wants to, but I'm certainly going to try to convince her otherwise."

"Good."

I went back up to the house. I sent the picture of

Robert Chandler to Smith's email, copying Detective Robichaud. My cover message explained who he was, how he was related to Angelique, and that I'd heard from Carol that somebody named Bob met with Andrus, Delacourt, and Carlos.

After calling information and being advised Lucille Chandler had an unlisted phone number and being unable to find it online, I called and woke Rocky up, ignored his cranky demeanor and asked him to find me a phone number for Lucille Chandler. I knew he had access to a magic database that, somehow, often turned up unlisted phone numbers. I know how much it costs because it is a common item of expense on Rocky's invoices.

I sat at my desk making notes on a legal pad while drinking my second, third, and fourth cup of coffee. At some point, Thumper returned to the house, told me he was going to walk to the beach and left. I heard Joshua and Darla open the doors to the shop. I went out to check on them. They were positioning the portable fencing so Briggs and Stratton would trim the grass behind the house. They planned a day of welding. I returned to my note taking and contemplation.

I thought about how to formally introduce Angelique to her biological family. If asserting Angelique's right to a share of the family trust, I probably should find the lawyer doing their trust business and correspond with him or her. But my client insisted she had no interest in the family fortune. Primarily, I wanted to find out if there were connections between the family and those attacking Angelique. The longer I could stir that pot without the interference of a lawyer, the more options I had. I decided on what we would try first.

I didn't wait long before Rocky called. "Sam, I've got

some phone numbers for you."

"Let me have them."

"There are several numbers related to Chandler businesses, but I've got two that might get you where you want to be. The first is the unlisted number for the household. There were two, but one is out of service. Somebody answered this number. I pretended I was selling a carpet cleaning service. The man who answered told me to erase the phone from my call list."

He gave me the number.

"The other number is listed for the Chandler Trust and was answered by an answering machine at the law office of Douglas Sheffield."

I wrote that number down even though I hadn't wanted to know it existed.

"Okay. I'm going to call the household and see if I can talk my way into a visit as soon as possible. What are you up to?"

"I'm going to get Angelique to the ballet studio for some kind of workout or practice. She wants to walk to warm up so we're walking. Jenny is going with us on her first foray out of the house. It'll do her good."

No more note taking would help. I made the call. A man with a soft, southern accent answered.

"Chandler residence, Thomas speaking." Wow. Thomas. I wondered if it could be the same Thomas mentioned in the letters sent by Joseph so many years ago. Perhaps the butler's son grew up to be the butler.

"May I speak to Lucille Chandler, please?"

"May I inquire as to the purpose of your call?"

"My name is Samuel Locke. My business is personal and if possible, I'd prefer to tell her directly."

"I understand. Unfortunately, I am instructed to put no

call through without a bit more information. Your option is to write her a letter. A real letter. She won't respond to email."

"I understand." We were being so polite to each other. I had the trust lawyer's phone number if I had to pursue things that way. I decided to go for broke. "Tell her I am representing her great-niece. She'd like to meet Ms. Chandler."

There was silence for several seconds.

"Her great-niece?"

"Yes. Belle's granddaughter."

"I see." I heard him take a deep breath. "Hold on, please. I will relay your message." The phone clicked to on-hold silence.

"This is Lucille Chandler. To whom do I have the pleasure of speaking?"

She spoke with an accent, but not exactly deep south and certainly not of Texas. It was Louisiana gentry, the accent I've heard in the private clubs and in exclusive restaurants on the Gulf Coast of Louisiana. Her gentle voice, calm and assured, bespoke that special, unyielding politeness of a southern woman, resistant to the strongest of forces. It pushed me into a formal politeness.

"Ms. Chandler, thank you for taking my call. My name is Samuel Locke. I represent Angelique Chambray. She's the granddaughter of your sister Belle Anne. She would like to meet you."

"I assume you are her lawyer."

"I am her lawyer. She does not desire to make any sort of claim against your family, but there are reasons she wants to meet you."

She was quiet for several seconds.

"I was told decades ago that my sister's daughter died

during childbirth."

"You were misinformed."

"I see. I've often wondered. Hold on for a moment."

The phone clicked into silence once again.

She came back on the phone. "Well," she said, "Thomas informs me that I might very well have been misled. When do you wish to meet?"

"Tomorrow. We are in Houston and will fly up to Dallas in the morning."

"Very well. But if you think you're going to come up and scam an old woman out of anything whatsoever, don't waste your time. I have not lost a single marble, and I have dozens of lawyers who live for the opportunity of getting more of my money."

"I assure you. This is not about money on our part."

"Very well. Do you need directions?"

"I should be able to find my way. If not, I'll call when we're there. And Ms. Chandler, may I make a request that I hope does not offend you?"

"You can even make an offensive request if you desire. I'll decide whether or not to acquiesce."

"There are some issues we think may be related to your family. I'd like to ask that you not yet let any other members of your family know that we have reached out to you."

"Ah, intrigue at last. I won't bother asking because I'm sure you must tell me in person. Very well. Come tomorrow. Just remember what I said about trying to scam me. I'll leave word at the gate to expect you."

"Thank you."

That conversation went about ten thousand times better than I expected. I called Rocky's phone and left a voicemail telling him that we'd be catching an early flight to Dallas in the morning.

I HAD A GOOD FEELING about the way things were moving. Feeling good lasted all the way through lunch, right up to the moment I got an excited phone call from Rocky.

"We might have just encountered Carlos."

"What?"

"We all walked to the ballet studio this morning. It took a while because Jenny took it slow. I checked outside before we left and I'm confident nobody watched us leave. I didn't see anybody following us. Angelique went in and did her workout. Jenny stayed with her. I went and got some coffee and did some phone work. She finished about one, and I walked back over to meet them. We were going to get lunch.

"We were walking down Louisiana toward the bayou, headed for the Spaghetti Warehouse. There's a parking garage right there. Maybe he'd been keeping watch from there. Jenny noticed first. The sound of a motorcycle coming down Louisiana behind us. Fast. It's one way and if he'd been in that parking garage he'd had to go around a couple of blocks because of the way the streets run.

"Jenny said 'Rocky' and turned back the direction the bike was coming from. The bike was coming fast, weaving. Couldn't see the driver's face. He wore a helmet. I knew there might have been a motorcycle up at Thumper's place. I reacted mostly because of Jenny's alert and kind of pushed Angelique behind me. There wasn't any place to take cover. Jenny had her gun out. She moved into the middle of the street between two lanes of traffic and started running toward the motorcycle. He'd just crossed the intersection. Drivers started to notice the crazy girl with a gun and cars were jumbling as they tried to get out of the way. I'm glad she didn't get blown away by somebody driving along and excited about finally getting to use the gun they've been carrying."

I'd never heard Rocky talking so fast.

He continued, "Maybe it was just some guy on a bike who saw a crazy lady coming at him. Whatever. He skidded and almost laid his bike down turning around and taking off down Preston."

"But what do you think?"

Rocky took a breath or two and slowed down. "I've got a picture in my head of the guy coming at us. It's hard to pull a gun and shoot on a motorcycle if you're right-handed. You have to let go of the throttle. But in my mind and I think in reality, he already had a gun in his hand. Awkward, but possible. Plus, I think he had binoculars around his neck."

"Where are you now?"

"We went back into the ballet studio. Marlene is on the way to pick us up."

"How are the girls?"

"Fine. It happened so fast. I think Angelique is kind of fatalistic at this point. Jenny regrets, and I quote, not having a chance to shoot the mother-fucker."

"Yeah. Try to calm her down. Cops?"

"I heard sirens, but I haven't gone back out. I don't know what the cops might do. I doubt if any of the witnesses stuck around. I didn't know what you want to do."

"I'll call Detective Smith in Beaumont and let her relay word about what happened. Maybe she can get better attention than we've received so far from HPD. Why don't you or your Beaumont guy call Andrus Towing. See if you can get some idea whether Carlos is at work today."

"Will do."

"Other than that, get some take-out and go back to the apartment."

There was a pause. He said, "Sam. This could have been bad."

"Yes. But it wasn't. Get them settled down and rested. We catch a six o'clock plane to Dallas out of Hobby in the morning. We're going to go meet Lucille."

"Okay, then. Things are starting to move, aren't they?"

"Yes. That they are. Talk to you later."

I called Detective Smith in Beaumont and told her what happened. She said I should call the police in Houston. I told her it would take me longer to get somewhere there than it would her. They'd yet to take much interest when I talked to them. She reluctantly agreed to call, mainly because I made it clear I would not. She did say she'd go try to talk to Carlos and Delacourt right after she called Houston. She said if Carlos wasn't around, she would talk to Carol. I reminded her, again, to be careful talking to Carol.

In a bit, Rocky called and told me they were safe at home. He'd called, and the dispatcher at Andrus Towing told him Carlos was off and not working.

I could think of nothing more to do other than go to Dallas in the morning and see Lucille Chandler. In anticipation of official interest, I typed up a statement describing the encounter they'd just had in downtown Houston, giving enough information about the break-ins and the attack in New Orleans to justify Jenny's reaction.

I received a phone call from an Officer Willet with the Houston Police Department following up with me after Detective Smith had called him. I gave him the case number for the break-ins at Angelique's apartment. I gave him Detective Robichaud's number in New Orleans. I sent him the statement I'd typed up by email. I agreed to have my clients available for an interview, if necessary after he'd reviewed things.

I paid as much attention as I could to a couple of other legal matters, wrote some letters, and put them in the outbox for Darla to mail. I did some customer relation calls to my best grill customers. Three out of five upped their inventory number. I made copies of stuff out of Angelique's papers to take to Dallas and locked the originals in my fire safe.

Finally, I provided the fixings, and Joshua and Darla grilled burgers and some potatoes. We had a nice dinner. I let them know I'd be leaving early to fly to Dallas, and I went to bed.

For some reason, I fell asleep with no problem.

WE WERE IN DALLAS a little after seven and in a rental car by eight. Rocky, Angelique, Jenny, and Thumper were with me. Jenny wore a short sleeve top that showed off the still healing scars on her arms and collarbone. Jenny and Rocky had retrieved their handguns from baggage claim while I got the car. I hoped there would be no reason to shoot the elderly Lucille Chandler.

We headed north and east toward the Chandler residence in a community called Chandler Ranch Estates. There, we were checked off a list by a guard at the gate. He said, "Just take the road you're on as far as it goes. It terminates at the drive to the Chandler residence."

We could see a few houses at first, large and set back from the street on meticulously landscaped lots. As I drove a bit farther, the houses disappeared behind landscaping and stone fences, their locations marked only by entrances to their drives. I saw one woman out for a run, toned and in a brightly colored outfit with matching running shoes and headband. The only other traffic we encountered were trucks belonging to two different landscape companies.

The street we were on ended in a cul-de-sac at a tall steel gate between two massive stone pillars. A stone fence extended both directions from the gate. I drove through the open gate onto a drive made of brick. I assumed the Chandlers had developed the subdivision. They'd kept a sizable chunk of property for their home. I drove for a couple of minutes before the house came into view.

The house commandeered a slight rise, standing over the rest of the property. Built in the style of an antebellum plantation home, substantial columns supported the roof two stories above the porch. The house gleamed white. Evenly spaced across both floors were windows framed with black shutters. The doors were also black, the front door off the porch and the door to a balcony on the second floor. The only whimsical features were bright red flowers in pots cascading over the balcony wall, dropping almost to the porch below.

I'd half expected a Confederate flag to be flying out front. In the middle of the circular drive, crystal clear water splashed in the bowl of a fountain held aloft on the hands of sculpted, nude women. Perfectly groomed flowers surrounded the fountain.

As we parked, Jenny said, "Wow."

Rocky said, "Old times here they aren't forgotten."

"Here we go," I said.

Angelique's hand shook as she opened the car door, her mouth a thin line. Thumper was not saying a word.

Three steps led up to the porch where I let a heavy brass knocker fall with three measured clunks on the door. An African-American man opened the door. He had short, gray hair, black trousers, and a crisp white shirt, with cuffs rolled back and held in place by garters. A formal waistcoat and tailed jacket would have completed his butler image.

"Good morning," I said, "I'm Samuel Locke. Ms. Chandler is expecting us."

"Yes," he said. "Please come in." I noticed he looked closely at Angelique.

We entered the bright entryway. It wasn't what I expected. I thought there would be dark, heavy furniture and portraits of old dead people. Instead, an abstract painting hung on the wall, an organized canvas of color, curves, and angles of the type I recognized as being very good without understanding why.

"Ms. Chandler is this way."

We followed him down a short hallway, made a left turn into a magnificent room centered around a polished, ebony grand piano. Double glass doors in that room opened to a room at the back of the house. That room had floor to ceiling windows looking out over a perfectly coiffed backyard. In that room was Lucille Chandler. She was the next surprise.

I expected the eighty-something-year-old Lucille Chandler to look more like a dowager of the old south. Thin, dressed in jeans, a white tank top, and white tennis shoes, she had the suntanned look of a Dallas socialite who played a lot of tennis. She did not look to be in her mid-eighties. Silver hair framed an angular face featuring clear, greenish eyes.

Our escort introduced me by tilting his head my direction and saying, "Ms. Chandler, Samuel Locke. Mr. Locke, Lucille Chandler."

I expected to find her wary and stand-offish, but she smiled and nodded at me.

He turned to go and she said, "Oh, Thomas, get back

in here. You're not going anywhere." Turning to us, she said, "Thomas likes to pretend he is just my butler, but he is also my oldest, and perhaps my only, friend. Plus, I suspect he might know things he can add to our conversation."

She shook my hand firmly saying, "Mr. Locke."

I introduced the others, referring to Rocky and Jenny as my associates, and Thumper and Angelique as my clients. She nodded at each of them. I saw her look at the surgical cuts and stitches on Jenny, but she said nothing. Her lips did something as she looked and nodded at Thumper. Her gaze stayed the longest on Angelique, who stood tall with her chin up under the scrutiny. Ms. Chandler took a deep breath.

"Well," she said, "have a seat." After we were all seated so civilly and comfortable, she looked at Angelique again, then back at me and said, "Now, what have we here?"

"Angelique is your sister Belle's granddaughter. Thumper here is her grandfather."

Lucille nodded once while she looked at Angelique and Thumper. "As I said on the phone, this is news to me, even though I've had some suspicions over the years. And you said it wasn't about a share of the estate. I continue to process what you've told me, but I need to know, why are you here?"

Initially, I didn't expect to get in the door. Then, I expected to be met with a solid wall of resistance, perhaps by Chandler family lawyers. I needed to adjust quickly to the apparently gracious Lucille Chandler. When in doubt, either don't say a thing or stick to the truth. I remained wary of an ambush but decided to mostly go with the truth.

"Ms. Chandler, Thumper has been a client of mine for a long time, but I only recently met Angelique. She became my client because of a couple of break-ins at her apartment and some threats, culminating in a physical attack." I nodded toward Jenny. "Ms. Mills was with her to protect her. Those wounds you see are the result of her getting stabbed and shot while doing her job."

Lucille Chandler's lips compressed. She shook her head. "You poor dear."

I continued, "We are working diligently to find out what's going on and why. There is nothing in Angelique's background to suggest that anybody has a reason to harm her unless somebody is concerned about her being entitled to a share of your property. Her relation to you is the only thing I've been able to uncover that might stir the kind of attacks she's experienced. We've developed information that some thugs were hired to try and get something from her that somebody thinks is worth a lot of money."

Despite Lucille's civil and genteel acceptance of us so far, I still expected to be thrown out right there. She had to know I was accusing her family.

"What do you think they're after?"

"Something that would invalidate your father's attempt to write your sister out of the will and prevent her from benefiting from the family trust. If there is something like that, Belle's interest will flow to Angelique. That might bother somebody."

"I see," she said. She closed her eyes, drew a deep breath, and let it out slowly. "My father did burn hot enough to destroy his own family over certain things." To Thumper she said, "Where did you meet Belle?"

"In Paris, ma'am."

Angelique opened her purse, and said, "I have a picture here. This is how I found out."

She pulled out a copy of the old photograph of Thumper and Belle from her mother's things.

Lucille handled it for a moment. I watched her closely.

There may have been tears in her eyes. She opened a drawer in the end table beside her. "When they got Belle home, they kept us apart as much as they could, but we were living in the same house. We had some secrets."

She took an old black leather document case out of the drawer. "She smuggled this all the way home in her underwear. She hid it in a place in an old tree that was one of our secret places all our lives." Out of the folder, she pulled the original page of a magazine with the photograph. To Thumper she said, "She loved you. I know that."

His voice caught as he said, "Yes, ma'am. We loved each other."

"After she got back, she was so eternally sad," Lucille said as she traced a finger over the face of her sister. "They told her you'd been killed in a robbery attempt." Turning to Angelique, she said, "They told us all your mother died at birth, and we should never ever speak of the pregnancy to anybody. They made Belle marry Matthew Planter. Even with everything, I don't know why they made her marry him. I guess he was convenient. I'm sure he and his daddy saw it as an opportunity. Perhaps Mr. Wilson can shed some light on what went on back then. Thomas?"

Her butler cleared his throat and said, "All I know for sure is that Belle's baby was born alive. We had a maid back then we called Candy. She tended to Miss Belle. Candy was my friend. She knew the baby had been born alive and immediately taken away. Someone in the community where Candy lived adopted her. I know that, but couldn't tell you who did the adopting. I don't know anything about why they had her marry Planter. He did go to Paris with Montgomery to bring Belle home."

Thumper drew a sharp breath, loud enough it caused Lucille to turn and look at him. He stared off into the backyard and said, "There were two men come and took Belle." He looked at Lucille. "I kept thinking she'd find a way to come back. A couple of months after they took her, in August, one of them came back and shot my friend Marlowe when he answered our door. The shooter called him by my name and shot him dead. I disappeared for a long time after that."

Lucille slumped back in her chair, shaking her head. "Thomas, what do you know about that?"

"Nothing ma'am. I know nothing about that. All I know is Montgomery and Matthew Planter left and came back with Belle."

"Get me a whiskey," she said. "Anybody else?"

We all declined. Thomas went to get her drink.

"I have a lot to think about. Are you all staying in the area tonight?"

"We can," I said.

"I want to stop this for now. Can you come back in the morning? You needn't bring the bodyguards, but your friends are welcome. I promise you're safe here." She looked at me. "And we won't share the fact that you came to see me with anybody." She looked at Jenny. "You need to get that little thing back to bed. It doesn't look like she should be up and about. But I would like to talk to you about this tomorrow. I hate to think that the attacks are coming from somebody in my family, but I also hate to think about what happened to you in the past at the hands of my family. Thomas and I need to talk more. How about nine in the morning? We will feed you breakfast."

I agreed. If I decided it was a bad idea for some reason, we'd just call with regrets. If she was fortifying her defenses, there was nothing I could do about it.

Lucille shook our hands formally, maintaining her

southern lady strength. Until she took Angelique's hand. She didn't let go of Angelique. Tears glistened in Angelique's eyes.

Lucille said, "You are so very beautiful." And she cracked, taking Angelique in her arms and hugging her. Angelique sobbed. "I am so sorry."

To me, she said, "I will help you find out if it is coming from my family. Trust me, I'm not close to what little is left. I pray that it is not. I am just so damn tired of the utter destruction caused by the prejudices of the past." She still held both of Angelique's hands. She turned to speak to her and to Thumper. "In any event, I want to get to know both of you better."

I said, "I think we can come back tomorrow. Angelique?"

"Yes."

"Thomas will show you out." She looked at him.

"Yes, ma'am. This way folks."

Rocky spoke to me quietly, as we walked to our cars. "That was not what I expected."

"Yeah, me either. Did you get the feeling she thinks her butler and friend Thomas knows more things about her family history than she does?"

"Absolutely. Actually, I think she's smart enough to have had some idea about things that happened to her sister for a long time now. She's just been too genteel to make inquiries. I think she and Thomas are going to have a long talk this afternoon. I wasn't sure we'd surprised her at all, the way she was so well composed."

"Oh, I think we did. That's why she got the whiskey."

"What now boss?"

I looked at my watch. "If anybody is hungry, let's get something quick on the way back downtown. We'll drop in on a lawyer friend of mine, Glen Reyes. I'm adding him to the team. I don't know if he'll have much to do, but I want him prepped just in case."

"More lawyers to pay," Thumper said.

"He won't charge us for this afternoon. I'm going to tell him not to do any billable work until I tell him to. But, he's smart. He'll be doing a lot of research on our behalf before I give him the word to start."

"About what?" Angelique asked me.

"About trusts and estates is what about."

"I told you I don't want any money. I don't think we even need to make the threat. I like her. She seemed nice."

"Yes, she did. And she apparently doesn't like her family much. She may want to cut you in without being asked."

"That's not what I want."

"Now, baby," Thumper said. "Sam just wants to be prepared."

"Thumper's right," I said. "We still don't know where this is going to end."

I called Glen while we drove toward downtown, and he agreed to meet. I stopped at a Whataburger. We had time, so we ate inside. It seemed to me there was a lessening of tension. There had been no fireworks at Lucille Chandler's house, but I wasn't sure it was time to lessen my concern. I'd met a couple of women from the south, grandmotherly types, with slow gentle speech and the melodious accents of their heritage. They never raised their voice. They seemed to accept or agree with everything anybody said to them. And, they always got their way. They are three times tougher than any other negotiator I've ever met. I could not accept the Lucille Chandler we'd met. Not yet.

Glen welcomed us and ushered us into a conference room. I explained to him everything that was going on, leaving out the dead Bobby Andrus. He and I signed an agreement about representation, including a clause that he would not undertake any action without my authorization and that any investigative work, other than that done by an attorney subject to our agreement, would be coordinated and supervised by Rockwell Investigations. He took some information from Thumper and Angelique and we concluded the meeting. He asked to speak to me privately.

In his office, he said, "Man oh, man. Please tell me that Ms. Cambray is not going to continue to insist that she wants nothing from the Chandler estate."

"Patience," I said. "Thumper is extraordinarily pragmatic about dollars. He will have a lot of influence over her. Let's see where it goes."

"If this thing goes forward, and I get to play, I will love you forever. You just let me know what my role is. Even if it is a small role. A small piece of a Chandler matter would not be a bad thing for me."

"Don't get excited or greedy. My first job is to keep Angelique safe. After that, we'll see what happens."

"Mi oficina es tu oficina."

We shook hands. I left him drooling. I knew I would get a bunch of free legal work out of him. He would not resist starting to research and planning a legal strategy without getting the authorization entitling him to bill me for his services.

Glen's secretary booked us a two bedroom suite at a hotel off the loop in north Dallas. I just wanted to rest and think. Rocky got on the phone in one room and tended to his business. The girls were restless and decided to go see the sights at the Galleria. Rocky told Jenny to not overdo it.

Thumper told Angelique to be careful. Eventually, Thumper went to sleep on the sofa in the main room with the television on.

I sat at the desk in one bedroom reviewing notes, thinking, and coming up with nothing. I wondered if there was a trigger of some sort. A thing that caused somebody to go after Angelique. At a loss about what to do, I called Joshua and talked for a few minutes. I returned some phone calls collected by my answering service. Angelique and Jenny returned with shopping bags. We ordered room service. I watched some television. I went to bed.

The next morning I brushed my teeth with a toothbrush with what felt like steel bristles. I'd bought it from a vending machine in the hotel along with a disposable razor. I painfully scraped my face. We left for Lucille Chandler's house right on time. Jenny and Angelique were in fresh clothes, products of their visit to the Galleria. The rest of us weren't so fresh.

On the way I asked Thumper, "We've been keeping you from your house, and I think we need to continue doing that for a while. Is that okay?"

"Yeah, no problem. Grant Cole is keeping an eye on my place."

"Good idea."

Angelique did not say much. She mostly stared out the window as we drove. She visibly took a deep breath as we turned up the drive to the house.

Thomas answered the door as sartorially composed as he'd been the day before. He led us to an office where Lucille waited for us, sitting behind a table she used as a desk. There were comfortable chairs for us all. Behind the desk were shelves with books and framed photographs.

"Welcome," she said.

We each greeted her and waited.

Hands on her desk, she took a deep breath, and said, "Thank you so much for coming back this morning. We'll have breakfast in a moment. Thank you for giving me the night to think about things."

Angelique sat in a very calm repose. I couldn't guess what she was thinking. She looked serene, with a small, relaxed smile. Thumper had a hand cradling his chin and a foot moving to a silent beat. I couldn't tell if his heart held a sad or happy song. Rocky and Jenny were behind me, silent observers. Thomas sat to the side, legs crossed, hands on his knee, obviously more than a butler at this meeting. He, too, looked at Lucille.

Lucille wore jeans and a pale yellow silk blouse. She'd pulled her hair into a short ponytail. She maintained the soft look of a rock hard southern woman.

"Well," she said. "Thomas and I had a long talk over a lot of brandy last night. He confirmed a lot of things I've thought might be true, but which I lacked the courage to pursue. I am a little angry that he never felt right telling me what he knew." She looked at him. He smiled and dipped his head. "But, I'm more angry at myself for lacking the courage to look at things back then."

She tried to continue. "I think ... I wish ... I ... " She stopped. She took one huge breath. She turned to Angelique and said, "My dear, welcome to this godawful family."

Angelique's mouth parted, and tears welled up in her eyes. They both stood up. Lucille came around the desk to embrace Angelique. "And you," she said to Thumper. "My sister loved you. I know that. And I am so sorry for what happened to the both of you."

Thumper stood up and got a hug all his own.

I looked behind me. Jenny was grinning. Rocky raised

his eyebrows. The corners of his mouth went up and he gave a little shrug. He and I were, perhaps, too cynical. It looked like things were working out, at least with Lucille.

Somebody was still out there, though. Somebody who had aimed a couple of thugs at Angelique. Somebody who'd almost killed Jenny. Had we focused on the Chandler fortune too easily? Was there an unknown motive for the assaults? If the Chandler situation was the problem, would Lucille's acceptance of Angelique into her "godawful family" take away the danger, or would there still be a deadly focus on Angelique?

I was missing a few things, my fears more justified than my hope.

CHAPTER NINETEEN

FROM A DRAWER OF HER DESK, Lucille pulled a few loose photographs of Belle. She spread them on her desk. Thumper and Angelique huddled over them. Jenny got up and stood to look over Angelique's shoulder. Thumper reached out and touched each one, letting his finger linger. Angelique rested her hand on his shoulder. Lucille and Thumper talked softly.

I looked around the office, trying to learn more about Lucille. When I first called her, I did not expect to get past the gate at the end of her drive. I thought I'd be writing certified letters and making threats in order to get some lawyer to get back to me. After I met her, I feared the encounter with her was going too easy.

The books on the shelves behind the desk included recent best sellers and older books with covers so pressed with age I couldn't read the titles. There were a dictionary, a thesaurus, and a book on word usage. There was a Bible. There were what looked like a collection of biographies and history books.

Interspersed among the books were knickknacks of the type people accumulate, an old wind up clock, keeping accurate time, a plaster bust of some famous person I did not recognize. A brightly colored ceramic butterfly had wings of many colors spread wide. There were photographs of groups of people, some in color, but more in black and white, stretching back over time. Lucille took one of the photos off the shelf and put it in front of Thumper and Angelique.

"This is the family the year before Belle ran off to Paris."

I leaned in for a better look. The parents sat in two chairs in the family home living room, the children standing around them. Robert Chandler would have been in his mid-sixties. With thinning gray hair and a hard-lined, gaunt face, he could be mistaken for Anne Marie's father instead of her husband. Anne Marie had delicate features. Even in the black and white photograph, I could tell her hair was blonde. It fanned out behind her neck, held in place by a silver band that was not quite a tiara. Approaching fifty at the time of the photo, she looked much younger.

Montgomery, the oldest child, looked stocky strong, his seriousness allowing only a slight smile. His sisters, Belle and Lucille smiled as if somebody had just said something funny. They were beautiful.

Lucille glanced at me and said, "Do we not look like the happiest of families?"

"Very nice," I said. "Looks like you and your sister are about to bust out laughing."

"Oh, we were. Father was so insistent that we get the photograph done. I don't think mother cared. Belle had just said the most scandalous thing. Father said something about having the family finally get together for a photograph, and Belle suggested we should, perhaps, wait for Montgomery's wife. That was not going to happen and mentioning it was out-of-order. When father got mad at any one of us, he would loudly proclaim we were out-of-order. He was all about order." She traced a finger over the face of Belle. "Belle was my salvation from all that order."

She moved on to other photos. I looked at the ones on her shelves. In one, a group of disheveled women dressed in matching skirts and sweaters held hockey sticks in front of a banner hung haphazardly on a fence. The banner read "Wellesley College Field Hockey." The young women were laughing, hugging, and not paying much attention to the camera.

I recognized the teenager Lucille in the photo. She had her head thrown back laughing without restraint. She held a hockey stick in her left hand. Her right arm intertwined with the arm of a team-mate. The girl to her right was in profile to the camera looking at Lucille and laughing. The photograph captured a moment of spontaneous group joy.

I noticed Lucille looking at me as I looked at the photo. I said, "You went to Wellesley."

"Yes, for a while. Part of my father's plans to expand his business interest by having me refined by northern sensibilities in order to catch a husband with connections. I was to be his introduction into the aristocracy of the northeast. I think he'd finally realized the Civil War was not going to be won."

"He didn't want you to find a nice southern boy?"

"My father had curious pretensions. My brother Montgomery was doing his job of continuing the family name. It was up to us girls to expand the influence of the family by marrying into the right kind of people. Belle scared him. She refused to adequately represent the family in society. He saw me as the last chance and decided a school up north was the proper place to insulate me from the things that influenced Belle. He wanted me to marry a man, any man, from Harvard.

"Much to his chagrin, Wellesley turned out to be way too liberal. It actually sought to teach things other than marital responsibilities." She paused and looked into the past. Her eyes focused on the wall behind us. "My father ... my father was a frightened man. Belle left and I failed him. Eventually, he jerked me home. He thought he'd lose us both to a world he refused to admit existed."

She swallowed, eyes glistening, breathing deeply.

I said, "He jerked her home, too, I guess."

She looked at Thumper and Angelique. "Yes. And that's too bad. I was pliable and not nearly as courageous as Belle. I wasn't here when she got home. I was still in school at that point, but I hear she did not submit happily to leaving Paris." She looked at Thomas who nodded once in her direction.

"When I got back home, I was unhappy and self-centered. I didn't fully appreciate the change in Belle. She was withdrawn and so very sad. I wasn't as good a sister as I should have been. Then she married Matthew Planter. That kind of shook me up. The possibility of that happening never crossed my mind. It shocked me that dad would even let her marry him. His dad worked for my dad. That should have made him unworthy of marrying into the family. Then, she was pregnant. Then she wasn't. Then there was that horrible plane crash." Lucille's shoulders shook and she closed her eyes. "I'm sorry. Give me a moment."

Thomas stood. She held a hand up and said, "No, I'm okay."

She recovered after a moment. She and Angelique sat shoulder to shoulder looking at photographs. Jenny sat next to Angelique, their shoulders touching. Thumper stood looking over their backs. I wanted to dig into members of her family that might be trying to kill Angelique, but the emotional experience needed its space. Rocky sat quietly. Every time I looked at him he'd raise his eyebrows. I'd shrug.

Finally, Lucille sat back, turned to me, and said, "But, you have some concerns, and we must address them. What do you know about my family? Do you really think one of them is behind the attacks on Angelique?"

"I have no idea. It could be a totally unrelated stalker. We're doing our best to look into that, but your family's estate is the only thing I've been able to find that might incite the problem she is having."

Angelique spoke up, "But I had no idea about Belle's family, and I seriously have no interest in whatever it is you have."

Lucille smiled and said, "Well, dear, what we have is several hundred million dollars of property, cash, and income. That kind of money subverts reason and judgment. It makes people do stupid, stupid things. No member of my family with an interest in the trust has to worry about working. It spins off enough money for all of us to live nicely. But there are those who have not done smart things and who seem to have a bottomless appetite for money. I understand Mr. Locke's feeling that it is a big deal and must be looked into. What have you learned about my family, Mr. Locke?"

"I know your father was a significant landowner in Louisiana and East Texas. The family fortune got its start from agriculture. He was a big cotton producer and was smart enough to buy land and hang on to it. Lots of that land sits on oil and gas. I suspect that's where most of your estate's income comes from now."

She nodded. "That, and a lot of real estate and other things."

"You are one of three children. There were Belle and a brother, Montgomery. Belle had Thumper's child, Rose, and a son, Joseph, from her marriage to Matthew Planter."

She nodded, and said, "You've looked into the family, haven't you? I guess you know that I never married or had a child."

I nodded. "Your brother Montgomery died in the plane crash with your folks."

"Yes. He had one child, Stuart. Stuart's wife died in 1974 in a car crash. Stuart had two children, Robert and Patricia. Both of them are alive. They were pretty much raised by nannies and they spent a lot of time here with me. Patricia is married but has no children. Robert is not married. Although it would not surprise me to learn he has children, I know of none."

"I don't know much about Patricia."

"Patricia is the nicest of us all. She and her husband live in Florida where he is a history professor at Florida State University. They have as little as possible to do with the family. She calls every once in a while just to check on me. They come to mandatory family gatherings like Thanksgiving and Christmas. She's as sweet as can be. She enjoys but doesn't hunger for the money. She pretty much votes with the prevailing view when it comes to making decisions about the trust assets. The trust gives her husband freedom in his profession. They travel a lot."

"How about Belle's son with Matthew Planter?"

Lucille shook her head. "Another sad consequence of Belle's indiscretion and my father's stunted views. My father laid Belle's sins on her husband and their issue. I don't know what Matthew expected to gain from his marriage to Belle, but he didn't get it. He became a lapdog.

"After the plane crash, I really thought maybe our family could become something. I floated the idea of bringing in Belle for a full share. The lawyer advised it wasn't possible and would trigger provisions that would drastically change our circumstances. I was voted down.

"Matthew passed away in the seventies. Colon cancer. I did my best for Belle and Matthew's son, Joseph, but he grew up angry. He got married his first year in college. She was a bartender somewhere. He got her pregnant and they married. He dropped out of school. She left him shortly after Joe Jr. was born. She dropped their baby off with me and disappeared. He divorced her in her absence. I have no idea where she is. Joseph never went back to school. He has a job at one of our oil companies. He drinks and does not have a stellar attendance record, but we take care of him financially through the job."

"Where's Joe Jr. these days?"

She shook her head. "Dead. Stabbed in the parking lot of some bar in Beaumont twelve years ago."

I looked at Rocky. That startled him as much as it did me. It had to be a coincidence, but wow, a bar in Beaumont and a stabbing. It got our attention. He tapped his cell phone in his shirt pocket to let me know he was taking notes on his stealth recorder.

"Excuse me," Jenny said, "I need to use the restroom."

Lucille directed her, took a deep breath and said, "My father passed down a sense of entitlement to some in this family. We need to talk more about Robert and his dad, Stuart."

And talk she did. Stuart lived in Dallas, but spent a lot of time hunting, traveling all over the world in pursuit of trophy killings. She did not know exactly where he was at that moment. Stuart's son Robert accompanied his dad occasionally on hunts but preferred a more public, glamorous life. He hadn't missed a Superbowl in years. He liked fast cars and beautiful women.

Lucille said, "Stuart and Robert are able to spend every dime the trust throws off to them. And, they always want more. In fact, we've had a bit of a problem. The trust takes good care of me. I want for nothing and, for the most part, I don't care much how it's managed. We have some good people looking out for it. I won't outlive the money. But occasionally I pay attention.

"Some time ago I discovered the trust often made loans to Robert. The loans were huge. He was slow paying them back. I think he was waiting for me to die. That's when the trust is distributed, and he can cash in a lot of stuff he can't right now. He'll do that, and he'll be broke some day. It upset him when I told the lawyer to stop allowing loans like that. It upset him more when I personally took over those loans, paid the money back into the trust, and made him assign seventy percent of his voting interests to me as security."

Jenny returned. She had a look on her face.

I'd forgotten we'd been invited for breakfast. I wanted her to keep talking about the family, but the phone on Lucille's desk chimed softly and she said, "Let's have some breakfast. It's ready. We'll continue afterward, but during breakfast, I want to hear about your dancing, dear."

In the shuffle to breakfast Jenny tugged my sleeve and whispered to me, "Look at the message I just sent you."

Once again Jenny was on top of the research. She'd sent Rocky and me a text message that said: "OMG!!!! Joe Jr. killed in parking lot of CHUCK'S!!!!"

Rocky was reading the text on his phone.

We looked at each. Silently, he said, "Wow."

I mouthed back, "OMG."

Breakfast was good, but I was too distracted to casually enjoy it. Angelique talked about dancing, telling Lucille about growing up in Lake Charles and trying out for the Houston Ballet. Lucille told her she would attend her next performance. Angelique was reticent about talking much, and Lucille graciously turned to Thumper. He told her stories about her sister in Paris and the crowd she hung out with there.

Finally, Lucille turned to me and said, "If this has to do with the trust, what do you think is going on?"

I remained wary. Lucille seemed too good to be true. I wondered if she was trapping me into letting her in on what I'd learned. But we had the letter from Joseph to Rose. I believed it would clinch a court's decision giving Angelique a share of the family fortune. I felt like we were getting ahead. I couldn't think of any reason not to speed ahead. I told her.

"When he was just a boy, living here I assume, Joe Senior sent Angelique's mom a couple of letters. He'd evidently learned about her by playing with some old business files of your father. In his letters, he sounded lonely. He was reaching out to her as a fellow family outcast."

She looked sharply at Thomas. He nodded.

"Go on."

"Rose never got the letters. Her family intercepted them and thought it best to shield her from their contents. Some of the things Joe sent her, trying to prove they were related, were papers regarding her birth and adoption. Those papers included a carbon copy of a letter from your father to his lawyer making it clear that Belle Anne was written out of his will and the trust for consorting with a black man. That letter and the surrounding circumstances would cause a court to rule that she was entitled to a share equal with you all."

Angelique spoke up. "I don't want any of your money. I really don't."

Lucille waved her hand at Angelique and said, "I understand Mr. Locke's concern. The type of money we're talking about is brought to life by the people who have it and the people who want it. It can become good or evil or powerful and threatening."

To me, Lucille said, "Do you think that's all they're after, that letter?"

"I certainly think it started out that way. They searched her house a couple of times. We have witnesses who know the bad guys expected to be paid by somebody for something tangible. Something like that letter. But now, it looks to me like they're getting desperate."

"Perhaps they think I'm going to die soon, and they want to tie up loose ends. I had a mild heart problem a little while ago."

I shrugged. "I don't know, but their violence has escalated. You see what they did to Jenny when she kept them from grabbing Angelique. There might have been another run at Angelique on a street in Houston day before yesterday. Luckily, she wasn't alone."

I briefly described the encounter with the anonymous motorcycle operator.

"Well, then," Lucille said, "we need to put a stop to this. What's your plan?"

I wanted to believe she was real, but I guess I hesitated too long.

She said, "You're not sure you can trust me yet, are you?"

"I have to admit that your response has been a big surprise. I'm just trying to think of the best thing to do."

She said, "In some ways, I am as big an outcast as was

Joseph. I am practically a recluse now. Other than Patricia, Belle was the last good person in this family. She loved greatly, and that was taken from her. I sit here alone. I fell in love once, too. In college. But, it wasn't a Harvard man, and it was not a person acceptable to my father. Just like Belle, I paid the price for that, and here I sit. Maybe I'm desperate to find a decent person in this family."

She turned to Angelique and said, "I know you say you don't want any benefit from the family's wealth, and I admire that."

Angelique nodded.

"But I'm not long for this world and maybe, finally, some good could come from it. Maybe you and Patricia can do some good. Lord knows what Robert and Stuart will do with it once they get what they have coming. I'm going to try to convince you otherwise. Besides, I get the feeling that your lawyer might think that is not a bad way to keep you safe. Once it's a done deal, the interest in you should go away. Right, Mr. Locke?"

"Yes." I thought it might go away if Angelique formally disavowed an interest, but if one was as sure as another, she might as well take the money. She would be set for life, and I'd have another very wealthy client. Those are not bad things.

Lucille said, "I've always had the benefits of the money. I've seen plenty of the bad side of it, but I'm proud to say that other than to take advantage of what some might consider tainted money, I have not done bad with it. I have a firm belief that as long as you have a good head on your shoulders, having it is much better than not having it."

Thumper nodded at that.

"Besides," Lucille said, "you don't have to decide today. Let's give your lawyer a chance to get things done and protect you from whatever harm is aimed at you. And to protect you from me if I'm being tricky somehow." She smiled at me when she said that. She'd almost won me over. "You can decide about the money later. Do you have a plan, Mr. Locke?"

"Yes. I don't know how good it is, but it's a way to get started."

CHAPTER TWENTY

EVERYBODY LOOKED AT ME EXPECTANTLY, waiting to hear my plan.

I said, "First, any chance you still have the originals of your father's file on your sister and her indiscretions? I'd really like to have the original copy of the letter from your dad to his lawyer about writing Belle out of the will."

Lucille said, "I doubt if it exists. I trust the lawyer to keep all the documents that need to be kept, and I had the attic cleaned out some time ago."

Thomas cleared his throat.

"What?" she asked him. "Is there something more you haven't shared with me?"

"When we were cleaning out the attic, I thought it might be a good idea to save the file on Belle. You know, for family history reasons."

"You have it?"

"Yes, ma'am, I do."

"Go get it, then."

He left. I said a silent prayer to Saint Thomas More that Lucille was the person she appeared to be and that I was not being led down a path to calamity.

I shared my simple plan. To start, I wanted to get the entire family in a room, let them know about Angelique and see what they had to say and how they reacted. To do that, I needed Lucille's cooperation. I proposed to get the entire family in one room for a meeting of the family along with Sheffield, the lawyer, as beneficiaries and trustees of the trust.

"I'll get them here," said Lucille. "I have to give them a two-week notice." She looked at her desk calendar. "I assume you want to move quickly, so let's plan on noticing them for Tuesday, the twenty-first. Let's write the letters right now."

I drafted a letter addressed to Lucille as a trustee of the Chandler Family Trust. In the letter, I advised that I represented Angelique Chambray and, based on an investigation, she was asserting her right to an interest in the estate. I always carry stationary in my briefcase. I printed a copy of the letter on Lucille's machine and hand delivered it to her.

She drafted letters to her relatives and to Sheffield, referencing my letter, copy enclosed, and calling a meeting to discuss the matter. Her letter advised each of them she expected them to appear in person.

In the midst of all that letter preparation, Thomas returned with the box of material he'd been holding. Lucille gave him the letters she'd written and a credit card to use for postage. He left to go to the nearest post office to mail them by overnight mail, proof of delivery requested.

"Are you ready?" she asked. And she hit a key to email a copy of the letter to Sheffield's office. It took less than five minutes for him to call her. He was not calm.

"Mr. Sheffield," she said, "I don't know why you haven't heard of this young lady before. I just received the letter from this Mr. Locke today. ... I don't know why he didn't send it to you. Perhaps he did not know about you. ... I assume, if you think it necessary, we can have her do a DNA test. ... We will discuss it here at my house on the twenty-first."

She kept up her polite gentle-woman demeanor. Because I'd been talking to her for some time, I picked up on the fact that, the more she talked to Sheffield, the more lyrical her voice became as her accent deepened. They talked for some time. Eventually, she said, "Mr. Sheffield, some time ago I addressed this matter with your father before you took over. I am somewhat concerned that some of what he told me was not true. ... Let me finish please. ... What I want you to do is bring copies of all the originals of correspondence you have between my father and yours regarding establishing the Trust. ... Please, I must insist on you just listening. ... It shouldn't take that long. Right now, I'm only interested in correspondence from when they first created the Trust. I want to make sure we each have the same records. I have copies of the correspondence, and I will know if your firm has misplaced or failed to keep all the correspondence. ... Mr. Sheffield, if I must, I will have one of my attorneys at your office within thirty minutes with a written instruction from me to pick up all your files. In fact, now that you sound somewhat reluctant to do as I ask, I will expect you to bring those copies to me today. I will double check certain items, and if they are not in your files, I will know they are incomplete, and I will do what I think is necessary. ... No, I have not discussed it with the others. I am instructing you not to until the meeting I just called. As you so very well know, I don't really have to explain anything to them right now. Get those copies here. Today. Bring them and leave them with Thomas. ... No. I do not have time to meet with you. I have other things to attend to. I will expect them as quickly as possible. ... I really don't have time for more discussion. Good day, sir."

She smiled and said, "He sounds nervous."

"Ms. Chandler," I said, "I am glad I am not the one

tangling with you."

Thomas's box did contain the original carbon copy of the letter we'd taken from her aunt. And other good stuff.

She said, "You need to take those things and keep them safe. Who knows when somebody from the family will show up looking for them."

"I would like copies, but I think it's important, for chain of evidence reasons, that you keep them under your control. Maybe with one of your personal lawyers. One you really trust."

"Good idea. I'll do that."

"I'm worried. Your family does not sound close-knit. Is there a chance someone will seek to cause you harm to get their hands on this correspondence?"

"I do not plan to be available for the next two weeks. Thomas will be here. As far as they know, I will be gone, and he won't know where. They'll know he's lying of course, but oh, well. The security service will be instructed to not let anyone in without my express say so. I will have security keep a close watch on the house. We can stay safe.

"I would appreciate it if you stayed until after Mr. Sheffield comes and goes. You can make copies of what he brings to me."

I worried her desire for us to stick around was a set-up. I didn't want us all to be stuck in one place. I told everybody, other than Rocky, to go back to the hotel. Jenny started to speak, but I gave her a look and she stayed quiet. The three of them took the rental car and left.

Lucille Chandler smiled. She knew why I'd sent them away.

A COUPLE OF HOURS LATER, the main gate called to announce the arrival of Sheffield. Thomas told the gate to let him in.

Lucille said, "I changed my mind. I'll meet with him in the dining room. Thomas, show Mr. Locke and Mr. Rockwell into the butler's pantry. I think you'll be comfortable there. It's close to the dining room, so be quiet."

I thought the choice of a pantry as a hideout was a bit much, until we'd settled in the room. It shared a wall with the dining room. Just above head height was a metal grill. In the old days, it was a way for the kitchen staff to monitor a dinner party to know when to serve the next course. We could hear every word said between Lucille and Sheffield. Rocky held his recording cell phone up to the grate. I needed to do a little research on the wiretapping laws before I'd know if Rocky was violating the law. Maybe I would do that later.

Not much was said in the dining room. Lucille told Sheffield she wanted to make sure their records were complete before the meeting she'd scheduled.

He said, "Keep in mind, there may be things in the file that could be taken out of context and, perhaps, should not be shared outside the family."

"Thank you for the warning. I'm sure you'll give us your best legal advice. In fact, if there are such things, send me a letter with which things you think we should be careful about. I'm sure the others would like to know when we have the meeting."

"Do you really want a letter like that?"

"Do we have something to hide? Is there something flawed about the trust?"

"No. Of course not, but somebody on the outside attacking its terms might be able to take things out of context."

"Let's skip the lawyer doublespeak, shall we? If the claim by this girl is accurate, that she's Belle's granddaughter, does she have a valid claim?"

"Anybody can file a lawsuit and make a claim. Do you want the family to be dragged into the court? Perhaps, we can all discuss a reasonable way to settle her claims."

"Perhaps. I will look over these things. Thank you. I'll see you in a couple of weeks."

"Shouldn't we discuss ... "

"Not yet. We'll all get together. Thank you for going to the trouble of coming out here."

We heard the scrape of a chair as she said that and, with the utmost politeness, Lucille ushered him out of the room and handed him off to Thomas. Thomas led him to the door.

Lucille came into the kitchen.

"Well," Lucille said, "could you hear?"

"Yes. That was excellent."

"Belle and I used to sneak down and listen to the grown-ups and their dinner parties. It was usually boring but felt deliciously scandalous at the time."

The copies of things he'd brought were complete. In an old folder, pressed by the weight of the Trust's history, was the original of the letter sent by Robert Planter. It had his clear, bold signature. We made copies of everything in the correspondence folder.

I flipped through the trust document looking for something I'd seen before. I found it and called Lucille to my side.

"You know," I said, turning the trust to her and tapping a paragraph with my finger. "You have the right under the terms of the trust to record any meetings of the trustees. It's right here in the document. Perhaps Rocky could set up some recording equipment for you in the pantry and you could meet in the dining room."

"I think that would be an excellent idea. Then, I could leave the room for one excuse or another and let them all talk about me without restraint. We might just hear more truth that way."

"My thoughts exactly. Do that Rocky." He nodded.

We agreed to discuss the meeting more in the next two weeks to develop a strategy about how she would conduct the meeting. Although she wanted to find time to spend with Thumper and Angelique, we agreed it would be best to not run the chance of them being together until after decisions were made at the meeting of the trustees.

She had Thomas drive Rocky and me back to the hotel. We didn't talk much, but just before we got out of the car, Thomas said, "Mr. Locke, this is a good thing you're doing. You can't tell, but Lucille has been sad all her life. You have brought her joy. Thank you."

Hearing that, I decided I could, perhaps, trust her after all.

THE CONVERSATION IN OUR CAR the next morning was animated. Angelique and Thumper were happy to have made a connection with Lucille.

At one point, Angelique said, "She seems so sad for some reason. I wonder why she never married."

Jenny said, "Yeah, her terrible father ruined her love life, too. Maybe that's why she is so sympathetic to you, Thumper. She knows what it's like for her old man to screw up your life."

"Could be, could be," Thumper said.

I said, "I think it might go a little deeper than just having her dad pull her out of college and away from her love. I think her situation might be closer to yours."

Jenny said, "What do you mean?"

"I mean maybe her love was as forbidden as the one between Thumper and Belle."

Angelique said, "You mean because her man wasn't a Harvard man."

"She said she fell in love in college. She went to Wellesley."

Jenny said, "Yeah?"

"At the time, Wellesley was an all girl school."

There was silence for a minute. Jenny said, "You mean ... oh ... you think maybe ... wow."

I shrugged. "Might explain her sympathy."

We discussed what everybody would do over the next two weeks. Glen and I would be talking about what to do next. Jenny and Rocky would stay close to Angelique and Thumper. Given the chances already taken by our foes, it seemed likely that things could get really hot after the family received their mail.

I noticed one thing as we made our plans, Angelique never reiterated that she did not want the money. For her sake, I hoped meeting Lucille Chandler had taken some of the ugly edge off the family fortune.

As we approached the airport, I said, "We have to be really careful to remember, there is an outside chance this whole thing has nothing to do with the Chandlers. Stay aware and ready for the unknown."

We flew to Houston and split up there. Everybody but me went in Rocky's Suburban to the apartment downtown. I picked up my phone messages as I drove alone toward Galveston. One was from Detective Smith in Beaumont asking that I call her on her cell phone as quickly as possible. It was not good news.

CHAPTER TWENTY-ONE

DETECTIVE SMITH ANSWERED immediately. "Mr. Locke. Thanks for returning my call."

"What's up?"

"I talked to your client's friend Carol Taylor last night after she got off work. I talked to the bouncer Steve Delacourt this morning and Carlos Perez this afternoon. I didn't have enough to arrest anybody, but they know we're interested."

"Okay." I could tell there was something else.

"Mr. Locke, the real reason I wanted you to call was to let you know that Ms. Taylor was murdered. Somebody called us this evening. We found her body on the street some distance from her house. She'd been beat to death. I'm looking for Carlos Perez now."

"Do you know it was him?"

"No. But I'm looking for him anyway."

"I guess you heard about Thibaux Arceneaux being killed in New Orleans?"

"Yes."

"Looks like somebody may be tying up all the loose ends they can find."

"Could be. Did you talk again to Ms. Taylor? By phone maybe?"

"No. Only the one time I told you about."

"She had your card in her pocket."

"She hadn't called. I gave her the card when we met."

We said a few more things, but, in the end, there wasn't a lot to say. The detective and I didn't express it, but we each feared we'd got her killed.

I pulled off the highway and stopped in a parking lot to called Angelique's phone. She answered sounding more light-hearted than she had for several days. I hated having to tell her about Carol. She reacted badly. I heard Jenny trying to comfort her and asking what was wrong. Rocky got on the phone and I told him the news. I could hear Angelique crying that it was her fault.

I told Rocky, "They're looking for Carlos. If it was him, he may be on a rampage that could suck us in."

"No kidding. We're at their place right now. We're not going anywhere for a while. Let me know if we need to do something. Do you think it's Carlos or Delacourt?"

"If not, we've got an extraordinary string of coincidences going on. I'm going to assume it is. I'm going to assume that TeeBoy got caught up in the same shit storm. That means it's easy for somebody to kill. If one of the Chandler clan is pulling the strings, it could get massively worse after they get the meeting notice in the mail tomorrow. Or I guess, it could stop. Doesn't feel like something that will just go away, though."

"I agree."

"How is she?"

"Jenny has her arms wrapped around her. We'll be okay. This thing is about over. Part of me wishes he'd show up. I'd end it quickly. Are you going to feel comfortable at home?"

"I'll take precautions."

I got off the phone with Rocky, called Joshua, and told him I was involved in a case with a dangerous person. I told him to take Darla somewhere else for a while and that he could use our company credit card if he needed to get a room somewhere.

He asked a few questions. He volunteered to stay and sit on the porch with a shotgun. I told him if it came to that, I'd let him know, but, at that moment, he needed to get Darla and himself to somewhere safe.

When I got to my place, I had to punch in a couple of extra codes because Joshua had turned on the security system. The lights on the alarm keypad indicated there had been no intrusion, friendly or otherwise, since the system was turned on. Another button pushed and the gate opened. I sat in my vehicle just inside the gate until the gate slid back into place, locking itself and re-arming the alarm system.

I thought I'd be safe, but before I went into the house, I called my next-door neighbors. Maude answered the phone.

After pleasantries, I asked, "Maude, could I let a few of your goats into my yard? I could use the extra security for a few days."

"What have you got yourself into this time? Never mind. It's none of my business. Sure. Hang on and I'll come down and pick out some real talkers for you."

I met Maude at the gate between our properties. Her goats gathered around her. She handed out a few pieces of carrot to the crowd. She picked out a half-dozen goats that were already demonstrating their greater than average vocal abilities. She helped get them through the gate, along with a couple of others that pushed through without being chosen. Brigs and Stratton started making noise in their pen.

I thanked her. A few minutes after she went back up to her house, her goats settled in for the night, munching on my grass. I let Brigs and Stratton out to join the crowd. If anyone got on the property without setting off a real alarm, I knew the goats would let me know. The only thing better would be if I had two or three geese.

I went to bed, feeling secure, with my handgun and a shotgun within reach.

NO ELECTRONIC OR ANIMAL ALARM went off during the night. Halfway through the morning, I had a short telephone conversation with Douglas Sheffield, the attorney for the Chandler Trust. We jousted in the typical way of attorneys starting a battle. I knew things he did not and that shortened the conversation.

Politely put out, he said, "I'd appreciate it if you got in touch with me as the attorney for the Trust from now on."

"Do you have something to communicate to me about the claims of my client?"

"Not at this moment."

"I won't sit on them much longer."

"The trustees are meeting regarding your client's claims in a couple of weeks."

"Okay. So, I'll hear from you in a couple of weeks?"

"Yes. Can I ask you why your client is coming forward now?"

"She just learned of how her great-grandfather was unable to revise his will before he was killed in the plane crash and how no one saw fit to correct the issue after his death."

"I'm not sure you're characterizing the situation appropriately."

"Okay. I'll look forward to hearing from you in two weeks."

"If it is proved that your client is the grand-daughter of Belle Chandler, I'm sure the family will see fit to reach a settlement with her."

"Where shall we go to get DNA sample? I assume that Lucille Chandler would be the best source. We can have that done before your meeting. Then, you can call me after the trustees decide whether to give her a full share or go to trial."

"Frankly, Mr. Locke, I'd hoped for a more productive conversation with you."

"I think we've efficiently cut to the chase. Is there anything more productive you can add?"

He was silent for several seconds.

"I'll get in touch with you. Remember, all communication must go through me."

"Even if a trustee gets in touch with me directly?"

"I trust you'll tell them you cannot talk to them, but only to their attorney."

"You represent the individual trustees? I thought you represented the trust, as do they."

"Mr. Locke, you talk to me."

"Have a nice day."

He hung up without a goodbye before I could tell him I enjoyed breakfast with Lucille the previous day. The telephone conversation invigorated me. I made a note of what was said. I'd have to do some research to see what I was ethically required to do if any of the trustees called me directly. I thought he might have been overstating his status.

I worked on several things that day. I had to turn down a request to guide a fishing trip the coming weekend. I reviewed outstanding orders for grills. I wrote letters to some clients. I returned some calls. In the afternoon, I joined Joshua and Darla in building grills. Joshua convinced me they would be safe at home. He said if the alarms went off, he and Darla would wade into the flats and hide in the grass.

In the evening I picked up Preacher, and we went to eat at Clara's diner. Before I went to bed, I organized fishing stuff and loaded it into my pick-up truck. I planned to spend the next day fishing. I needed a fishing day. I went to bed.

THE NEXT MORNING I left the house in the dark, my pickup adorned with rods in the rod holders, ice chests packed with food, drink, and bait. I drove to Clara's for breakfast and coffee. Clara filled my thermos with coffee. I left the diner just as a sliver of light on the horizon began to focus into the sun.

I had no plans other than to fish the coast, hitting the surf and the bays from Surfside to Bolivar, not thinking about any case, especially Angelique's. I trusted the rhythms of the surf and mechanics of fishing. My mind would work on problems in the background. Perhaps I would gain an insight into something else we should do. Perhaps not. If nothing else, the meditation that is fishing would be enough to call it a good day.

The people watching me were patient and discrete. I never saw them.

CHAPTER TWENTY-TWO

THE FISHING OFF THE QUINTANA JETTY on Surfside was good. I boxed some fish and drank coffee. I left before I caught my limit. Otherwise, the day would have ended too soon.

I drove back toward Galveston on the beach. I waved at a few of the guys I knew who were still fishing the surf, their long rods bent gently to the tug of the sea. They would be gone soon, giving way to those coming to enjoy a day on the beach. There were early risers staking out places in the sand, but not many.

While I drove the beach, oblivious to me, the people following me went on over the toll bridge to wait for me on the beach on Galveston. Not only were they patient, I'd been watched and smartly analyzed. They picked a spot to find me and got it exactly right.

I crossed the bridge to Galveston Island and turned off the highway to drive down the beach, windows open, enjoying the fresh breeze off the water. On a stretch of the beach where there were no other people, a woman leaned over the open hood of her car. As I approached, steam billowed from her engine compartment, and she jumped back, her shoulders slumping in exasperation. She looked to be in her early to mid-twenties and in need of a new radiator hose.

She glanced my way. I stopped in her tracks, got out of my truck and asked, "Problem?"

"I guess so. I don't know. Looks like it. Can you tell what's wrong?"

I walked up and bent over to look under her hood. He'd hidden in the dunes. He came up on me from behind. I saw nothing and don't remember hearing a thing. Perhaps I stood up before I got hit. I don't know. It didn't even hurt until I started to regain consciousness. Then, it hurt like holy hell.

My head hurt so bad I thought I might vomit. That would not have been a good idea because my mouth was firmly sealed with duct tape. The rubber smell of the tape was the first thing I noticed other than the pain filling every cubic centimeter of my head.

My shoulders added their minor pain to the list of things that were wrong. My arms twisted behind my back, wrists crossed and firmly bound by more tape. Tape secured my ankles as well. I was sitting half on the seat on the passenger side of my truck, bent and twisted so that my head was in the driver's seat. I knew that because I bumped my head on the steering wheel when I moved. I couldn't see thanks to more duct tape wrapped around my head. I knew it was my truck because I knew the texture of my seat cover and the smell of my truck. For a split second, I had the incongruent thought that it was good to have a bench seat to lay across.

For another split second, I worried about whether I'd lose my eyelashes when the duct tape got pulled off. Then, I had the overriding worry that the tape would only be removed by the coroner if they found my body. That seemed a likely possibility.

The sound in my ears wasn't a ringing noise. It was a roar of static, pulsing with the painful beat of my heart. The windows of the truck were still down. The sound of the sea slowly overcame the sound in my head. I could hear seagulls. And a conversation just outside my truck. I recognized the melodious voice of the man. It was Rich, the bartender at Fantasy Kings.

He said, "Okay, all done. You take this car up and get yours. Just leave the keys in this one. Keep those gloves on until you're in your car ready to leave. You hit the highway and head for home. Don't ever come back to Texas."

"Not a problem. I hate this place. You'll never see or hear from me again." It was the voice of a woman, undoubtedly the woman I'd stopped to help with car trouble.

"Good." There was a pause. Perhaps they hugged. He continued, "Listen, find you something else to do. A new job. Waiting tables or something. Don't waste that money."

"Don't worry." She laughed, a short, choked off, emotional laugh. "I'll be smart about the money. It will get me there."

"It's not that much. You're smart. Get a real job. Go now."

From farther away I heard her for the last time. She said, "Is he going to be okay? Are you going to kill him?"

"I have no idea. You don't worry about it. Just remember, you don't breathe a word of this to anybody. You got me? Nobody. I don't want to have to come looking for you."

She said something. All I understood was the last thing she said. "Good-bye."

The driver side door next to my head opened.

"You awake?"

I nodded through the pain.

"Rest as easy as you can. It'll be a while before I can make you comfortable. We're going to take a drive. I'll put you in the back seat. I want you laying down and covered up. You cause me the least little bit of grief and I'll tap you again. Understand?"

Tap me? Pain centered at the back of my head like I'd been hit with a baseball bat. I most definitely did not want to be tapped again. I nodded.

"Hey," he said. "This doesn't have to end bad."

I didn't believe him, but pain and helplessness tend to make a person grasp at straws. I decided to be compliant. The only part of my months of martial arts training I could apply were the instructions about patience and waiting for opportunity.

He raised the narrow back seat of my truck and shuffled me onto the floor. I moved to get as comfortable as possible.

He said, "I've been sapped. Hurts like a son of a bitch, but you'll be okay. I was careful. Might help to have a pillow. Good thing you have blankets in here." He rolled up one of my truck blankets, lifted my head gently, and put the roll under my neck. "Better?"

I nodded. It still hurt like hell, but it did help.

He tossed another blanket over the top of me. He drove off the beach, bumped onto the highway and turned right. I thought I'd try to remember turns and track where we were, but it was just to give myself something to do. I reckoned our destination was Beaumont and that I was in for a long uncomfortable ride. All I could do was hope for a traffic stop.

We drove until we were clear of Houston. I could tell when we were on the interstate. Eventually, the truck slowed and exited and, after a short while, bounced over a cattle guard. I had no idea where we were. My sense of time failed me. The drive so far seemed long enough to get to

Louisiana, but, at the same time, I knew we'd not driven far enough to get to Beaumont. I was lost.

The car stopped. I heard Rich get out. He did not shut the door, and it was quiet. I heard crickets chirping over the soft rush of highway noise in the distance. I thought the chances good that Rich had kept me calm long enough to get me somewhere he could kill me and leave me.

The sound of him peeing was calming. That was as valid as a reason to stop as killing me. In fact, if he was going to kill me there, he wouldn't be peeing. If he wasn't going to kill me, I needed to pee. I hoped he didn't expect me to do that bound in the floorboard of my truck.

We were on the same wavelength. He said, "Need to pee?"

I nodded.

"I'm going to take the tape off your mouth. We're nowhere anybody can hear you scream. And if you misbehave, I'll tap you out and you can piss your pants. Deal?"

I nodded. His casual calm terrified me.

He leaned over the seat and pulled the tape off my face. My eyes teared up. He was a blurry hulk leaning over my seat. I blinked to clear the tears, wondering if my eyelashes came off with the tape. He pulled the tape off my mouth. I'd been worried about my eyelashes when I should have worried about my lips. I tasted blood.

"Okay?" he asked.

"Yes" I tried to say. I cleared my throat and said it again.

"Remember." He tapped his sap against the top of the front seat. It was dark brown leather shaped like a huge spoon and undoubtedly filled with lead shot. It had a loop that wrapped around his wrist.

I'd heard about saps and seen them in movies, but I'd never actually seen one in person. The throbbing in my head had lessened to a dull ache radiating down my neck. Unless I moved my head, then it insinuated itself with a swelling pain. I did not want to get hit again.

Thankfully, Rich pulled me gently out of the backseat. He pulled a knife out of his pocket. The sap bounced against my butt as he cut the tape off my wrists.

He asked, "Do you need to shit?"

"No."

"Then I'm leaving your ankles taped. Probably hurt to hop."

He wrapped his arms behind me from behind and carried me a few feet from the truck.

"There, unzip and do your business. Any unusual move and I'll put you back to sleep. I hope I didn't scramble your brain so much that you think you can get away with something. I have permission to shoot you if necessary."

I unzipped and did my business. He went back to the truck and searched under my seat. He found some random fishing gear and tools and tossed it all into the back of the truck. I zipped up. There was no way I was going to ask him to carry me back to the truck. He grinned at my bravado as I hopped back to the side of the truck. My head throbbed with every move.

"Tough guy," he said. "Good. Just be smart, and you'll probably be okay."

"What are we doing exactly?"

"You know where we're headed. You're going to have a talk with Landry. I guess he's curious about some things. Don't ask me what because I just work for the man. Hey, you don't have any traffic warrants outstanding or anything, do you? It would be bad to get stopped."

"No."

"Good. Just so you know if we do get stopped it would be best if you keep your mouth shut. I will, and if you try to blame anything on Landry, you'll learn that he's in Memphis tonight and knows absolutely nothing about what's going on."

"Surely we're not driving all the way to Memphis. It will raise some attention if I'm gone that long."

He grinned. "Don't worry. The last thing we want, you and me, is attention." He looked at me for several seconds. "I think you're smart enough to bide your time. I'll let you do that up front if you want. Best not be trying to talk about anything, but it'll be more comfortable for you."

"I agree."

"Promise to be good."

"Yes."

He picked me up, set me a few feet from the hood of my truck and tipped me toward it until I held myself up. With my ankles taped, I teetered. He bent down and sliced through the tape. He stepped back to let me remove the tape and stand back upright.

"You stand right there until I get in the truck. Remember. Be smart."

He got in behind the wheel, and I climbed in the passenger side, doing my best not to move my head. He shifted the sap to his left wrist. He was as confident of his ability to control me as was I. Maybe I could reach over and turn the steering wheel hard to the right. At highway speed that might mess up his control, but I wasn't ready to roll the dice on me surviving. Something about his demeanor and the things he'd said made me hopeful I would survive. I wouldn't fight a futile fight until it became clear I was about to die. Hope is a strong thing in us humans. It springs eternal.

It was, in some ways, an eerie ride. Neither of us spoke. I sat with my head back, mostly with my eyes closed. He just drove, both hands on the wheel with the sap dangling from his wrist. He did not shift in the seat. He made no noise. He drove a little faster than the speed limit, but not so fast as to attract attention. We passed a couple of Highway Patrol cars parked on the side of the highway. He did not even glance their direction. We were on the road for over an hour before I realized he wore thin, flesh-colored gloves.

Close to Beaumont he exited the highway and drove again to a small, lonely road with no traffic.

"Turn around," he said. "Hands behind you."

"What's going on?"

"Nothing to worry about. We'll be in Beaumont soon. There may be video cameras somewhere. I don't want a recording of your truck with two people in it. That's all. You're gonna need to ride in the back until we get there."

I sat there, contemplating whether it was time to fight or run.

"Look," he said. "If I was going to kill you, I'd have done it a long time ago. Probably in your own bed. Now, turn around."

I did. I made the rest of the trip bound hand and foot on the floor of my truck covered by the blanket. At least he didn't put tape over my eyes or mouth.

Wearing my fishing hat and his sunglasses, he drove us into Beaumont, exiting and driving through traffic on city streets. Every so often he stopped at a traffic light. I'd tracked our turns and counted our stops. I had no idea where we were.

He finally made a right turn and stopped. There was a rattling of a gate opening and we were there.

There turned out to be a salvage yard. He pulled me out of the truck in front of a low, cinder block building with dust-caked windows and a solid metal door. Over the door, a grimy sign identified the place as Andrus Towing and Salvage.

Rich removed the tape from my wrists and ankles and led me into the office saying, "Mr. Andrus would like to talk to you."

"He could have called."

Rich actually laughed. "Ah, now, more fun this way."

He led me into what was a reception room with a counter down one wall. In the back wall was a service window with what looked like thick, bulletproof glass and a drawer to slide paper and money in and out. We went through a heavy steel door propped open next to that fortified window. The walls of the reception area were freshly painted, and the scent of new paint permeated the air.

The office to which he led me was partially painted. A plastic drop cloth covered the floor. Two metal chairs were in front of an old desk. He indicated I should sit in the chair farthest from the door. He stood close as I sat down and quickly put handcuffs around my left wrist and the arm of the chair.

He picked up the phone on the desk and dialed a number. He said, "The lawyer's here ... no, not yet ... yeah, he's on the way ... no, not a word ... okay." He hung up and said to me, "Make yourself at home. It won't be long. Don't try to make a call, or I'll notice." He left the room.

His comment about the phone made me realize my cell phone was missing from my pocket. I thought I should have grabbed the steering wheel on the highway after all. I had a bad feeling about my situation, like I'd walked willingly to my own execution.

Landry Andrus entered the office and sat down behind the desk, his whole bearing as manicured as his nails. His shoes still held a glossy shine. I still thought he tried too hard to look like a civilized businessman.

He said, "You okay?"

"No. What are we doing?"

"We're waiting on Delacourt. I want to find out what happened to my brother. I suspect I'll know more before the day is over. Just be patient and do not lie to me and you might just make it home tonight."

I was not comforted. He left the room before I could think of something to say, closing the heavy door.

The room was so soundproof, I did not hear anyone approaching. But, eventually, the door opened and Delacourt walked in, large and blustery, looking over his shoulder at Rich and saying, in a tough guy voice, "What are we supposed to talk about?"

Before Rich could answer, Delacourt noticed me and said, "Who is this?"

Rich said, "Sit down and shut up."

"You don't have to talk that way to me."

Rich sighed. "Sit down."

"Where's Landry?"

"Sit down Delacourt. He'll be along."

Rich did not sound threatening, but he stood close to Delacourt. Delacourt was sweating. I could smell him. He looked to me like he wanted to resist, but like me, knew he wouldn't win the fight.

He put his hands on the arms of the chair, and Rich quickly had his right wrist handcuffed to the chair.

"What the hell are you doing? Take those off."

"Shut up. Landry's on the way."

"What's going on? Take the damn cuffs off me now."

"No."

Rich picked up the phone, dialed four numbers and said, "All ready." He sat down in a chair against the wall.

Delacourt looked at me and asked me, "What the hell is going on?"

I shrugged. He noticed the handcuffs on me. He lost some bluster.

Landry entered the office and sat behind the desk, his hands folded together and resting in front of him.

He looked at us. We looked at him. Delacourt spoke first. "What's up Mr. Andrus? Why did he cuff me? What's wrong?"

Landry said, "My brother has been missing for so long I think he's dead. I want to find out what happened. There is a rumor in certain quarters that you and your Guatemalan friend Carlos might know something about that. I know the police talked to you. Just like there's a rumor that Mr. Locke here may know something."

I remained quiet, breathing deep and thinking. I needed to assess the situation and do it fast. Delacourt was not so patient.

"I don't know what you're talking about. I don't know nothing. Hell, right now I don't even know where Carlos is."

Landry stared at him with cold, unblinking eyes for several seconds. He visibly took a breath and turned to me.

"How about you Mr. Locke, do you know more than you've seen fit to share with me to this point?"

The people I've met with the strictest sense of ethics are some of my professional criminal clients. Not the ones who just get caught doing something stupid, but the smart ones who engage in criminal activity as a well thought out and planned profession. I've learned to trust some of my criminal clients to a much greater degree than I would ever trust a business person exercising hard-nosed business ethics. The trick is knowing the time and place.

Landry Andrus impressed me as wanting to be a legitimate businessman. Of course, he had just had me kidnapped and chained in an office with plastic on the floor. It might prevent paint from getting on the ugly floor of his office, but it served just as good to keep blood splatter evidence at a minimum. I wondered if Delacourt realized that when he decided to act like he knew nothing. I had a greater chance of getting killed than I did staying alive. I decided to take a chance and trust Landry's criminal ethics.

I said, "I'm sorry. I don't know why, but your brother's body was found on my client's apartment floor."

Andrus closed his eyes briefly. Delacourt said, "I don't know nothing about that Mr. Andrus. Nothing."

I gave Delacourt a look of disbelief.

Landry turned his way. In a colder, more precise voice, he said, "Mr. Locke seems to think you may not be telling the truth."

Delacourt started speaking too fast and a little too loud. He was afraid. "I don't even know this guy. He doesn't know me. Who is he? What's going on? I don't know nothing."

Andrus visibly took a breath and nodded at me to continue.

"My client came to me. By the time we got back to the apartment, the body was gone. I have no idea where it ended up. But it looks like your brother was killed there. I have good reason to believe that Delacourt and his buddy Carlos were there when it happened." I was lying just enough to protect my clients, but still impart what Andrus needed to know if I was to have any chance to survive. I sounded confident. My gut churned with fear.

Delacourt took a breath to say something. Andrus held up his hand. "Be quiet. Go on Mr. Locke."

"A few days later there was another break-in at my client's apartment. A witness described two men leaving in a pickup outfitted with tow equipment. The description of the men matches Delacourt and Carlos. The description of the truck matches your repo tow truck. My client's place had been trashed. I have no idea what they're looking for."

I turned toward Delacourt as if I expected an answer. He looked at me. Sweat beaded his forehead. His jaw clenched as if he wanted to say something.

Andrus spoke. "Steve, did you and Carlos Perez break into somebody's place?"

Delacourt looked back at Andrus, opening and closing his mouth, as if he had trouble coming up with something to say. I goaded him some more.

"They attacked my client and one of my employees in New Orleans. They took a shot at my client and put my employee in the hospital with knife wounds and a bullet in her side. That's why the New Orleans police are as interested in talking to them as the Houston police."

Delacourt turned to me, red-faced. "I don't know what the hell you're talking about. I haven't been to New Orleans in years."

"That's not what TeeBoy says. He says y'all hired him to drive the car when you tried to kidnap my client."

Landry watched us like a tennis match, his head swiveling between us.

"I don't know no TeeBoy."

"Well, all I know is he told the cops in New Orleans that you and Carlos hired him to drive the van when you tried to kidnap my client. We can't ask him, of course, because y'all killed him the other day."

Delacourt's brain was on overload. Without a lot of thought, he said, "I didn't have nothing to do with that. Mr. Andrus, I didn't even go to New Orleans."

"Maybe you didn't, but the people paying you to break-in to my client's place are the same ones who paid for the kidnapping attempt in New Orleans. You're a part of all that."

He turned to Andrus. "I didn't have nothing to do with that stuff in New Orleans. I swear."

"You think I care anything at all about what might have happened in New Orleans? I'm here for one reason. I want to know who killed my brother."

Andrus stared at Delacourt whose mouth continued to open and close.

"Mr. Locke, why didn't you mention any of this to me when I came to your office like a gentleman?"

"Because I didn't know you. I didn't know if this whole mess involved you. You do have a reputation that gave me concern."

He nodded. "I have a past, but it is my past. How did my brother know this client of yours? The one you are doing such a good job of keeping confidential."

I knew it was coming. I'd originally planned to take the information to my grave. But, I was starting to think there might be a way for me to avoid the grave. Besides, it wouldn't take him long to find out my client's identity even if I was dead.

I said, "She's a young woman who danced in your club when she was fifteen."

Andrus closed his eyes and breathed deep. I'd lit a fuse.

"Underage dancers are not allowed in my clubs. I

acknowledge to you that it has happened in the past. My brother did not always appreciate the ins and outs and needs of running a business." He looked at Rich, sitting stoic next to the wall with the slightest of smiles. "Others were complicit because they did not understand my firm desires. It does not happen anymore."

Rich nodded.

"Mr. Delacourt, why were you in this titty dancer's place with my brother?"

"Why do you believe this guy over me? I've worked for you for years. I wouldn't do nothing to hurt you or your brother. You believe him over me?"

"Yes."

The handcuff holding Delacourt in his chair rattled. I sat quietly, feeling like an actor in improvisational theater, hoping Delacourt didn't get us both killed, but still expecting to die in that shabby junkyard office, wishing I'd spent more time fishing.

Andrus said, "Please tell us what you and Carlos and my brother were doing in her place. Tell me how my brother ended up dead. I don't believe some dancer fought you off and killed him. Tell me now."

Delacourt realized he was in trouble and started to dance. "I didn't know exactly what was going on. Mr. Andrus, I'm sorry I lied, but it wasn't my fault."

Andrus closed his eyes. I counted three deep breaths before he looked back at Delacourt. "Stop the bullshit and tell me what happened."

"All I know is Bobby paid me and Carlos to go to her place and try to find some kind of paperwork. We didn't know what exactly. We planned to just take everything we could find. Make it look like somebody broke in and stole stuff. I don't even know why Bobby was there. He paid us to do it. I didn't even know he'd be there."

I made a face at that and Andrus noticed.

"What Mr. Locke?"

"I don't know what they were doing there exactly or what they were after, but Bobby was overheard arguing with Delacourt. Bobby wanted to go. Delacourt told him he didn't need to."

Delacourt stared at me and said, "You need to shut the fuck up. You don't know what was said by nobody."

Andrus said, "Mr. Locke seems to have been very resourceful. I suspect somebody does know. But, I tell you what, I am getting real tired of you pussy-footing around. Why is my brother dead?"

Delacourt had sweat running down his neck. I could see a twitching knot in his neck.

"Okay, okay. What happened was we didn't find whatever it is we were supposed to find. Carlos said we'd stay and talk to the girl and do what had to be done. Him and Bobby got into an argument. It got violent. Carlos killed your brother, Landry. I'm not sure he meant to. I mean, he hit him with something. It wasn't me. That's the God honest truth."

I could hear Andrus breathing long, deep, controlled breaths. He turned his head my way. "What do you think Mr. Locke?"

I shrugged. The air in the room seemed heavy.

Andrus turned to Rich. "How about you, Rich. Any thoughts?"

"I don't think Steve's ever met Mr. Locke. I think Carlos and Steve are joined at the hip. I think if Carlos meant to kill Bobby he'd use that knife he's in love with."

Rich put his hand over his ears. I wondered about that for a split second. Before it really registered with me, Andrus pulled a pistol from his desk. He shot Delacourt. Pop. Pop. Pop. Three shots. Delacourt slumped dead in the chair. Perhaps he made a noise, but my ears were ringing from the sound of the gun, and I heard nothing. The pistol had a small barrel. I realized it was a twenty-two as I closed my eyes, expecting to die.

When it didn't happen, I opened my eyes. Andrus was standing and handing the pistol to Rich who started wiping it with a handkerchief.

Andrus spoke to me. "Can you hear me?" I nodded. "I want you to listen carefully. I don't know why that ass-wipe and his buddy killed my brother. I don't even really care. I don't think you had anything to do with it, and I understand why you were reluctant to tell me about it. Doesn't matter. What happens now is that Rich is going to give you some instructions. You do exactly as you're told, and you walk out of here alive. You cause him any problems whatsoever and you die. I don't kill needlessly. Understand?

"Before we get to all that, tell me right now if you know anything about what's going on that I should know. I don't really care about anything other than finding Carlos, but if there's something you think I should know, you tell me. I don't want to have to kill you later. Understand?"

"Yes. I don't know what's going on. I've just been trying to protect my client, the dancer."

He said, "Fine. But if something comes up, you let me know."

I nodded.

He continued. "First, you need to understand that Rich and I are not here. We are in Memphis. If you try to tell anybody any different, trust me, we will be alibied by several people including a respected member or two of the government. Do you believe me?"

"Yes."

"Good. Do as he tells you. Rich, I will see you at breakfast." And he left.

Rich took the handcuff off Delacourt's wrist. He picked up the three casings ejected from the gun and put them in his pocket. He took the magazine out of the pistol and all the cartridges out of the magazine. He wiped down the magazine and handed it to me.

"Here, hold this."

Using his handkerchief, he put three new cartridges on the edge of the desk with the ones he'd taken from the gun.

He pushed my chair close to the desk and, standing behind me said, "I want you to reload the magazine, put the magazine into the gun, and put the gun on the desk. Do not move that gun in a way that I don't like or I will shoot you."

I did as he said. He picked up the gun using his handkerchief. He took one of the plastic, five-gallon paint buckets sitting around and put it on the desk in front of me. He put some ear muffs on the edge of the desk.

"Shoot the bucket three times. Don't worry about making a mess. It's full of sand. I like you. Don't make me shoot you by making the wrong move. I'd put on the ear protectors if I was you."

I did, and I shot the bucket three times. I carefully placed the gun back on the desk.

"Good job."

I took off the ear protectors. He handcuffed me to the chair using both sets of handcuffs. He picked up the expelled brass casings and the gun and put them in a paper bag. He used duct tape to cover the leaking hole beneath Delacourt's eye and the two holes in his chest. He pulled the body to the floor and took the chair he'd been in out into the hall. He put tape over the three holes in the bucket leaking sand, brushed the sand on to the drop cloth on the floor and took the bucket somewhere outside.

Back inside, he pulled the plastic drop cloth from beneath the desk, bunching it at my feet. With a small sound of effort, he picked me up, chair and all, and moved me off the plastic to the floor beside the desk. He rolled up Delacourt's body in the drop cloth and used tape to secure it. He picked up the body, slung it over his shoulder and said, "I'll be right back."

I heard a couple of bumps against the wall. I heard the lobby door open. I had a bad feeling about what he was doing with the body.

He came back in carrying the chair from the hall and sat down in front of me.

"Okay," he said. "You are a lucky man. Mr. Andrus mostly believed you. You're lucky he is a respectable businessman."

I was able to keep from laughing.

He smiled a bit. "Here's what's going to happen. We're going to leave here in your truck and drive out of town to where you will drop me off. You'll drive with no funny business. After I get out, you can go wherever you want to go and do whatever you want to do. But remember, we have the gun with your fingerprints. Mr. Andrus and I are in Memphis along with some very respectable people who will swear they partied with us.

"Delacourt is in the back of your truck. You need to take him somewhere and do something with him. I'm thinking it would be harder on you than on me if you take him to the cops. All trails will lead back to you. There's a little Mexican gal waiting to scrub down this office just like she does every day. I don't think the cops will find much here.

"When you get back to your part of the world, if you go to that spot on the beach where we met this morning, there's a trash can. Your cell phone is buried in a baggie about a foot and a half straight down beneath the can. I used it to make one call. I called Delacourt to tell him he needed to come into the office today to meet with Mr. Andrus.

"You know Mr. Andrus has spoken to the police here about your interest in his brother. He's also mentioned your interest in the guys who work for him. You might be able to get out of things, being a lawyer and all, but they'll eventually find the gun that killed Delacourt with your fingerprints. Could go really bad. I suggest you accept the fact that Delacourt was a piece of trash, and you should just dump the trash somewhere far away from here. Too close and the cops will find the gun.

"By the way, the sand wrapped up with him is from your beach."

I put my odds at survival a little higher than they'd been an hour before. I didn't see how I could improve them by driving the body to the police station. I believed Rich and Andrus when they said they'd have no problem proving they were in Memphis.

Too many random and unlikely things needed to happen to get me out of trouble. Bobby's body was missing. I was about to have another body. The detectives on the case already thought I kept secrets. I had not bonded well with Detective Smith in Beaumont. Things were a mess.

We left with me driving and Rich in the passenger seat with the pistol in his lap. He wore a windbreaker with the hood pulled up over his head. He also wore a handcuff around his right wrist. I got it. If I attracted the attention of law enforcement, he'd toss me the gun and handcuff himself to my door. It would not look good for me.

He directed me to drive south out of Beaumont on Highway Ninety-Six. The drive was quiet. Neither of my passengers had anything to say. We did not go far. Twenty miles down the road he had me stop on the edge of the highway next to a shopping mall in Port Arthur. He got out of the truck, slipping his pistol into his pocket.

Through the passenger side window, he said, "Bye, now. Have a nice day and don't be stupid. Don't sit here long, or you'll attract attention. If you happen to get a line on Carlos, get in touch."

He turned and walked toward the parking lot, hunkered into his hooded jacket, head down, hands in pockets. I looked through the back window of my truck at the plastic wrapped load I carried. I entered traffic and started to drive.

Undoubtedly, I thought, there were things I should do, things I needed to do, and things I shouldn't consider doing. I just couldn't tell them apart. But I had to make some decision. I picked one. I got off the highway, made a U-turn, and drove back toward Beaumont.

CHAPTER TWENTY-THREE

I LOOPED AROUND BEAUMONT, trying not to think about the cargo in the back of my truck. I exited to go west on the state highway toward Houston. That's where I finally got the shakes. I needed to pull off. I had to buy gas and weighed the choices of a large, anonymous service station where I would be lost in the crowd or a smaller one where I was less likely to appear on a security video. I went small. I gassed up at the island farthest from the store, paid cash, and left. I wanted coffee but didn't want to leave my truck sitting alone. The shakes subsided, but I remained burdened by gut-churning fear.

A pay phone on the wall of the service station made me think about calling someone. But I didn't want to attract attention or leave any kind of record. Besides, I remained unsure of exactly what I was going to do and had no idea who I would call. I kept driving and, finally, decided what to do.

Less than two hours after I dropped off Rich, I pulled into the drive at Grant Cole's house. Grant and another man were moving boxes of frozen fish from the warehouse to a truck. I did not want to park close and pulled around to the back of his house, past the warehouse. Cole paused and watched me drive past.

He walked to where I parked, glanced in the back of my truck and did not look away from the bundle wrapped in plastic until he got to where I stood.

"Hello, counselor. I hope like hell that's not what it looks like."

"Yeah, well."

"God damn. Get the hell out of here."

"Let me explain."

"Let me get rid of my driver."

I leaned against my truck in the heat watching the dark, still water behind the bulkhead on the edge of Cole's property. There were currents and bubbling movement. I thought about the creatures there, out of sight at the moment, but present, silent and still. The truck drove off. Cole returned riddled with anger. I explained everything. I held nothing back. I had to trust somebody.

I finished the story. Cole looked toward the river, his eyes dark. He ran a hand over his suntanned face, wiping away the sweat of the day.

He jerked sharply. He said something under his breath. Then, "Okay. I understand you're in a hard place. I'm the only person who knows, right?"

"Other than Andrus and Rich."

"This is it, counselor. Don't be expecting this as a regular service. Help me get him into the cooler. We can't do anything till tonight. How much gore are we going to find when we unwrap him."

"Not much. As I said, it was a twenty-two. There were no exit wounds. He taped over the holes."

Cole snorted. "Smart guy."

We carried the dead Delacourt and put him on the floor of Cole's cold storage. We moved boxes of fish as far away from the body as we could get them. He poured bleach over the plastic wrapped body. We filled fifteen heavy cardboard boxes with ice and stacked them on top of the body to hide it. I drove my truck into the truck washing bay at the side of the warehouse and scrubbed and bleached the back of my truck with his power wash equipment.

"Go," he said, "come back after dark. Do you think it's safe to bring my family back?"

"Maybe. One guy is still out there, though."

"Are you hunting for him?"

"The police are."

"Too bad you didn't bag them both at the same time."

I started to respond before I realized he was joking. Sort of.

I drove to a place on the river where I've gone before and spent the rest of the afternoon fishing. Anything I caught I released. At sunset, I drove back to Grant Cole's place.

GRANT HAD AN OLD PIECE OF PLYWOOD atop some sawhorses on top of a blanket of newspapers at the edge of the slough on his property. My penance was to hold the feet while he hacked off the legs and the hands as he took off the arms. It did not take long. I was glad he left the head on the torso. There was much less blood than I expected.

There were swirls in the dark water after the first piece was thrown in. Before we were done, the water churned in a reptilian violence.

We burned the plywood in his fire pit.

Hours later, back on Galveston Island, I dug up my cellphone. I'd missed fifteen calls. I decided to look at them later.

I went home and got to bed as the sun started to lighten the sky. I slept, but not well.

AFTER MY VISIT to Beaumont and the river, I took a couple of days off. I stayed close to the house but got in some fishing. We did some welding, but I left most of that to Joshua and Darla. In the ten days following my experience with Andrus, I'd not heard from Sheffield. I'd not heard from Andrus. I checked in with Detective Smith. They had not had luck finding either Carlos or Delacourt.

Lucille Chandler called and told me she'd quit answering phone calls from family. It looked like the entire family would be at the meeting she'd scheduled. She gave me some good news. It sounded like Patricia was open to Angelique being a welcomed member of the family. I told her that her lawyer Sheffield told me not to speak directly to her. She laughed and said, "I hereby countermand that order."

On Friday morning, the week before the scheduled meeting, Jenny and Angelique drove down to my place to stay while Rocky went to Dallas to install recording equipment. We wanted him to get it in before the family started arriving. He would be there the day of the meeting to operate and monitor the equipment. We planned for Lucille to leave the room at some point so he could listen to what the family had to say in her absence. She would give them a few minutes and then call the lawyer out on some pretense in order to give the family a chance to talk without him. At some point, she would call Patricia out to give Stuart and Robert a chance to talk alone. I thought it shaky, but hoped it would get us some information.

Joshua and I worked on a custom grill ordered by one of the downtown Houston hotels while Angelique and Jenny visited with Darla and Flounder in Darla's apartment.

Preacher, Gretchen, and Linda, the dancer Preacher had taken under his wing, were coming by at some point to spend the day. I'd left the gate open for them. I was not too worried about security. Carlos Perez and Steve Delacourt were being looked for by Texas and Louisiana law enforcement. There was a growing opinion they'd both skipped the country and were together on the way to Guatemala.

A car crunched to a stop outside, and I went to see who it was. I recognized her with some surprise from photographs I'd seen over the past few weeks. Getting out of the car was Patricia Chandler. She was demure, dark hair cut short. She wore jeans and what looked like a man's white dress shirt, tucked in and fitting her trimly. She had a shy smile and a purse over her shoulder.

"Hi," I said, "can I help you?"

"Mr. Locke?"

"Yes."

"We've never met, but I am Patricia Chandler. I'm sure you've heard of me."

"Yes." I was confused and wondering what in the world she was doing at my place.

"I hope this isn't awkward. I thought it was time I meet the newest member of our family."

"You mean Angelique Cambray?"

"Yes. I've heard so much about her, of course, and I am just so ashamed that my family might have caused her some trouble. I'm here to assure her we don't all feel that way and to welcome her to the family. I found your address, but not hers. Is she here?"

"No." I was not comfortable with her surprise visit.

She looked past me. "Oh, hello."

I turned to see Joshua standing in the doorway to the shop wiping his hands on a rag. The expression on his face changed. He threw his hands in the air and said, loudly, "Don't shoot."

Confused, I turned back toward her.

Patricia said, "Come out here and join us please."

That's when I saw the revolver she'd removed from the bag over her shoulder. It was large and silver, and she handled it with an easy familiarity. Joshua stood frozen with his hands high in the air. The expression on his face was horrible. He was trying to warn the girls who could see him through the window between the apartment and the shop.

She said, "Get out here and help me, please."

I thought she was talking to Joshua. She wasn't.

Carlos Perez came off the floorboard and out the back door of the car she'd driven. He held a sawed-off shotgun pointed at Joshua. Patricia pointed the revolver my way.

She was still smiling. "Yes," she said, "this is not a good day for you. Please do exactly what I tell you to do or you're going to watch that young man lose his intestines. I am angry with you, and it won't take much." To Joshua she said, "Get out here now."

Joshua walked out to stand by me. Carlos had a tight smile. He was not exercising any of the good trigger discipline I'd learned in my weapons classes. His finger was on the trigger of the shotgun. It was quiet. I could smell the acrid scent of welding. There was no sound. Until Flounder meowed. He walked from around the side of the shop and went to lay in the shade of my porch. I hoped that meant the girls were all out of the apartment, hiding somewhere and calling the police.

"Now, quickly, is there anybody else here?"

"No."

"Mr. Perez, you go search that garage and his house. If you find anybody, kill them."

Joshua looked at me, his eyes wide. I subtly nodded trying to assure him I knew what I was doing. I prayed I was right about the appearance of the cat.

He said, "Sam ..."

I said, "It'll be okay. Trust me." I nodded again.

He started to say something again when we heard the sound of Carlos kicking in the door between his apartment and the shop. I held my breath waiting to hear the blast of the shotgun.

Carlos appeared around the side of the shop and headed for the front door to my house. The girls had escaped somewhere behind the shop.

Patricia said, "While we wait, I need the two of you to sit by the car, legs straight out in front of you and your hands on your head." She directed us with her gun. "Each of you sit by a tire."

Joshua and I followed directions.

It took Carlos a few minutes to go through my house. He came out and stood next to Patricia and said to me, "Not so smart now, are you? I was hoping that puta was here. I want to finish with her. Slow." His eyes glittered.

"I'm sure she looks forward to it."

He stepped toward me, but Patricia barked, "Stop. Don't let him get under your skin. We have things to discuss."

Carlos spat at me and raised his chin sharply.

"Now, Mr. Locke. You have some correspondence and paperwork from my great-grandfather that is causing all sorts of problems. I want all of that stuff. You need to tell me where it is."

"There are copies of that stuff everywhere. It wouldn't help to get it from me, even if I had it here."

High points of red appeared on her cheeks. Her eyes and lips narrowed. Her features sharpened into ugliness.

"One goddamn thing at a time. If it's not here, where is it? I know it's not in your office downtown, I looked there this morning. I'm sorry about the broken glass in your door. We're here right now. We're going to solve the immediate situation. Then we'll work on the next. We're all going somewhere and talk about it and, believe me, before we're done, you'll tell me or you'll hear this young man scream until he dies.

"Just so you know. If you give me nothing or you can't convince me that whatever you give me is everything you have, I'm going to leave you conscious on the floor while I burn this whole goddamn place to the ground. I can't think of a way that you survive today, but it can be quick or it can be very, very bad."

"Look," I said, "I don't want anybody else to die. Let's figure out how to work this out. Angelique has said several times she does not want your money. We were just trying to stop y'all from attacking her. Leave her alone and all this goes away."

She laughed. "Sure. That bastard half-breed doesn't want my money. You expect me to believe that? She came out of nowhere. She wants the money. I've waited too goddamn long for precious Aunt Lucille to die. I want all of what's mine."

Carlos said, "I don't want to stick around here. Let's kill them and burn this place."

"Shut up. You're getting paid a lot of money to do what I tell you. You all failed before. We're not failing today. There are things I have to get. Try to understand that."

Behind her, there was movement in the grass flats behind the shop. The ground behind the shop slopes gently down to the edge of the grass. Out in the bay, where the water sits still, Darla and Jenny appeared, covered in mud, slowly moving through the grass to get closer. I hoped Jenny had her gun and would shoot both Carlos and Patricia in the back, starting with the shotgun-toting Carlos.

"Obviously," I said, "I don't want to die. Let's figure out how to make you happy and stay alive. You think I give a crap about Angelique. She'll be here in a little while. Let's do something for her to sign, so she can disavow an interest in your property. That's all you need. Besides, I don't have what you're looking for here. Was it you behind all this? I'd decided it was Robert."

I knew she had to be strung tight as a drum. She was not used to being a murdering madwoman. The difference between her and somebody like Landry Andrus is she would find it hard to contain the emotion of the moment. I knew there was no way she intended to leave us alive. I wanted to buy time and get her talking. Carlos enjoyed the experience too much to be in a rush to really push her. The whole thing excited him. He would want to stretch it out. At least that was my hope.

Darla and Jenny crept closer and closer, moving as slowly as Marine snipers. They were at the edge of the grass and started to pick up handfuls of rocks and the oyster shells that cover the yard. I wondered what they were up to. Throwing rocks at our captors was not my idea of what was needed.

"Robert." Patricia laughed. "Robert is an idiot. He found out about the girl years ago from Joe Senior and kept track of her, but that's all. He did what I told him. I'm the one who came up with all the money to pay to get stuff from that girl. Maybe I wasn't too smart to trust Robert's criminal contacts. So far, they've flubbed just about everything."

"I have a question." The girls crept closer and closer. I finally realized what they were up to.

"What? I guess it doesn't matter now, does it? You and

your friend are not going to live much longer."

I kept my voice steady, not wanting her to know just how scared she had me.

"Did you have Carlos here stab and kill Joseph Junior?" I heard Joshua move, pulling his feet closer to his body. He, too, knew what was about to happen.

"That should have been the end of it. He was making noise about how maybe his family would finally get their share of the money. His daddy filled his head with that nonsense. Robert started hanging out with him, pretending to be friends to keep track of him. God knows Robert wants all the money he can get. Just like me, he's waited all his life for his money."

I took that as a yes. Meanwhile, Jenny, moving excruciatingly slow, pushed rocks and oyster shells into a two-inch pipe on the pipe rack behind Patricia and Carlos. Darla opened the valve to a cutting torch's tank and was carefully unwinding the hose. She had the end-cap that fit over the end of the pipe in her hand and the sparker in her back pocket.

I spoke a little louder than normal, hoping to cover any sound the girls might make. "How many people are you planning to kill? Do you know how many people now know about Angelique's claim? Are you going to kill Lucille? She controls your brother's voting shares you know." Patricia made a face at that. I didn't stop talking. Darla was flowing gas into the end of the pipe. "You can't believe you're going to get away with this. You know you're committing a death penalty crime, right? They will put a needle in both of you."

"Shut up," she shouted. "Lucille is going to die soon, anyway. It is my money. It will be okay. If anything, they'll blame Carlos, and he's getting enough money to get out of the country."

Carlos grinned at that.

Jenny was leaning on the end cap. Darla held up the sparker. Joshua and I put our heads down, pulled our knees tight together and folded our arms over our head.

Patricia started to say something. There was an explosive whump. Heat and bits of oyster shells peppered me, slicing into my arms in a couple of places. Joshua and I leapt to our feet.

Carlos was in front of me. He'd screamed when hit with the debris and turned to see where it came from. He swung back toward me just as I got to him. He'd not dropped the shotgun. I grabbed it. There was blood on him.

When Patricia screamed, she'd dropped the revolver. Joshua scrambled and grabbed the handgun. He held it pointed at her. She was bent over holding her neck. Her hands were bloody.

I heard sirens in the distance. Angelique's role must have been to call the cops.

Carlos recovered quickly. He fought me for the shotgun. I tried to keep the barrel pointed anywhere but at Joshua or me. He had the grip in his hand. He had the discipline not to pull the trigger without a good target, but he was winning the battle, grunting with the effort of trying to wrench it from my hand. I had the barrel and mainly wanted to keep it pointing somewhere behind me. Joshua swung the pistol back and forth trying to get a clear shot at Carlos while holding Patricia at bay.

Just as I was about to lose my grip, there was the sound of a blow. Carlos seemed to rise two inches into the air. His eyes grew large. His mouth gaped. Jenny had kicked him between the legs like she was kicking a soccer ball. She quickly kicked him again before he could get his legs together. I wrenched the gun from his hand. Jenny was all over him from behind, her fingers going for his eyes.

I stood up just in time to see Patricia, her face etched with the edges of her skull. Her eyes were wide in fury and her mouth open in a silent scream. She was coming at me with a furious, crazed anger. I hit her hard on the chin with the grip of the shotgun. She went down.

"Angelique called nine-one-one," Jenny said. Angelique rose and walked out of the flats.

Carlos was curled on the ground. I stood to his side and placed the barrel of the shotgun against his neck.

"Move," I said, "and you will die."

He was saying things I used to hear from the Hispanic kids in junior high gym class.

To Darla I said, "Go get the cable ties."

She ran into the shop and returned with a handful. We wrapped three of the large ones around the wrists of Patricia and Carlos and three around their ankles. Carlos was cussing in Spanish. Jenny kicked him in the side and said "No me jodas. Pinche pendejo."

She came at him again, but I held a hand up to stop her and said. "Okay, we've got him. I didn't know you spoke Spanish."

"I looked it up and learned it. I was hoping this moment would come."

He said, "Puta."

I lowered my hand and said, "Okay, maybe one more time."

She kicked him again. She grinned big time, her face streaked with the mud.

I didn't know what Angelique said when she called nine-eleven, but a State Highway Patrol and three Galveston County Sheriff cars came skidding down my driveway. More sirens were in the distance. Joshua and I put the weapons on the trunk of the car and held our hands up high.

To the girls, I said, "Get your hands up. You look like dangerous creatures from the swamp. They might shoot you. By the way that was smart to let the cat out. Joshua was about to do something brave and foolish."

Darla said, "That was my idea."

"It worked."

Joshua went to her and kissed her.

"Get your hands back up," I said.

Angelique walked muddy from the flats. She saw us and the cops and put her hands up.

A brief explanation put Patricia and Carlos into the back of separate patrol cars despite her ranting about how she'd just come to see me to talk, and I'd tried to kill her.

When they frisked Carlos, they found his knife in his boot.

"Be careful with that," I said, "I know a couple of people he killed with it. It's his favorite."

Carlos said something unfriendly to me in Spanish. The knife went into an evidence bag.

IT TOOK A WHILE, as such things do. The four of us sat on the porch for a while attended by a couple of the many deputy sheriffs who showed up. I made sure everybody knew they should talk only about what happened that morning and let me handle the background. Joshua and Darla knew nothing about what was going on anyway. Jenny worked for me, and Angelique was my client. They deferred a lot of questions to me.

I spent a long time with a couple of detectives and the Sheriff himself telling them just who Carlos and Patricia were and why things happened the way they did. I gave them the names of Detectives Robichaud and Smith. I told them that Carlos was wanted in Beaumont for the murder of Carol Taylor and that Detective Robichaud wanted to talk to him about the murder of Thibaux Arceneaux in New Orleans. I gave them copies of surveillance videos with that morning's confrontation recorded. Darla had flipped the switch to start the surveillance system as she left her apartment for the flats.

The last thing said to me by the Sheriff before he and his detective left us alone so they could go make a lot of phone calls was, "You have quite the shit storm going on here, don't you?"

Personally, I was thinking the shit storm was finally over.

I called Rocky and Lucille and told them what had happened and that I'd see them as soon as possible.

Rocky said, "So, Jenny got her licks in. Good."

Lucille said, "Patricia? Oh, no. Not her. Oh, my God. I told her I'd spoken with you and that Angelique seemed to be a very classy woman. She agreed with me that it was time to set right the sins of the past."

"Her idea about how to do that differed significantly from yours."

It must have made Patricia crazy to hear that her fears were being realized with Lucille's blessing.

I took calls from Robichaud and Smith. The Galveston County Sheriff asked me to come in with my clients to make a more detailed statement and answer more questions. I declined. We compromised and sat for a couple of hours at my kitchen table with the Sheriff, a detective, and a digital recorder.

CHAPTER TWENTY-FOUR

MONTHS LATER, I sat on my porch with Rocky and Preacher. Court proceedings regarding the Chandler Trust had concluded earlier that day. Joshua and Darla were off somewhere. Rocky and I each had a whiskey. Preacher had a Dr Pepper. Rocky had been doing some surveillance for one of the refineries, and we'd not had a chance to talk earlier.

"So, tell me how it went in court today," Rocky said.

"Angelique and Joseph each got a full share of the trust."

"That makes her your richest client."

"Yep. Richer than her grandfather."

Preacher said, "She told me she wanted to make a large contribution to my church's building fund. I told her we didn't have such a thing She said we were about to get one. You tell her that's not necessary."

"I'll tell her, but you might as well start planning on how to spend it."

Rocky said, "Having money is not a bad thing. Patricia and Bobby get to keep their share even though they're in prison? That hardly seems fair."

"Well, that's the way it works. The trust will make sure their commissary account stays fully funded."

"How's that work when it's time to make decisions about business stuff?"

"They get to vote, but Lucille and Angelique can

always out vote them. Joe Jr. assigned his voting rights to Lucille. Plus, she still gets to vote seventy percent of Bobby's interest."

"That's good."

"The interesting thing about the way that seventy percent security interest is structured, when Lucille dies, her share of the trust is distributed to them all, but that seventy percent is different. Unless redeemed by him paying off the debt, it converts to seventy percent of all his stock that carries a voting interest. If he's alive when she dies, her estate retains ownership of that security interest."

"What's that mean?"

"That means she will hand down a controlling voting interest in his shares to her heirs. And she changed her will. Her only heir will be Angelique."

"Will Angelique stay entangled with them?"

"I doubt it. I've set her up with an investment adviser, and Glen is advising her on the estate stuff. I expect her to slowly liquidate anything still tied to the Chandlers and put all that money somewhere else once she inherits and the trust property is distributed.

"Good."

I didn't tell them, but Glen and I sat down and did some rough calculations with Angelique. Depending on the price of oil on any given day, she was now worth somewhere between fifty and seventy million dollars.

I said, "There will still be plenty for Robert and Patricia when they get out. It's not like they can spend much."

"When exactly will that be?"

"Robert caved first. Thanks to his very expensive lawyers being able to control the dialogue about who did what, he got a deal in exchange for his testimony against his sister and the Beaumont gang. He's doing fifteen years for criminal conspiracy to commit kidnapping. If he behaves, he can get paroled after he does half that. Patricia took a plea of fifty years and will have to do half that before she's eligible for parole."

Rocky whistled. Preacher shook his head and said, "So sad that folks with so much could not be happy with what they had."

I said, "The prosecutor let her lawyers know that if they tried it, he'd ask for life with no parole. He was sure he'd win. I guess her lawyers were, too. She took the deal."

"Good riddance. Still luckier than Carlos."

"That's true."

Carlos took a plea, but it was one to avoid the death penalty. His plea got him life with no parole. A part of his deal was to testify against Robert and Patricia, and Delacourt once they caught him. He testified he was first hired by Bobby Andrus to steal any paper files he could find at Angelique's place. He denied knowing anything about what happened to Bobby. After Bobby went missing, Carlos made his own deal. For a hundred thousand dollars, he was to take care of Angelique and anybody else involved however Patricia decided was necessary. He made it clear Patricia was in charge. She didn't trust her brother enough to delegate.

Carlos admitted only to the murder of Carol and Joe Junior. The prosecutors laughed at his claim that each was a case of self-defense. He refused to budge off his claim that he had no idea what happened to Bobby Andrus. The long reach of Landry Andrus scared him more than the prosecutors. The prosecution finally decided to let that go. They didn't have a body, and that made it tough. Personally, I think Andrus will someday exact his revenge behind the walls of the prison.

Louisiana talked to Carlos about TeeBoy. He denied knowing anything about that. Detective Robichaud told me they'd keep the file open, but it wouldn't be worked on much. They were happy to let Texas pay for his living expenses for the rest of his life.

Nothing could be tied to Stuart, the father of Patricia and Robert. Maybe he really had nothing to do with the thing. Watching the way things turned out, I'm sure either of his kids would have shifted blame to him if they could.

Rocky asked, "What next?"

"Angelique and Lucille are flying off to New York to go see a ballet. Thumper's making music tonight at the Big Easy."

Preacher said, "Things are good."

We sipped our drinks.

Rocky asked, "How's Samson?"

He scared me. I thought maybe he knew something, but he was just making a joke.

"Last time I saw Samson he was fat and happy and doing just fine."

Bonus Material

Continue reading to enjoy a sample from the next
Samuel Locke novel, *Peak Performance.*

Available in 2019

CHAPTER ONE

C YNTHIA FULLER LOST HER VIRGINITY to Ricky Smith the night they graduated from Kenwick High School. It happened on the beach among the pilings supporting an abandoned nightclub on Follett's Island. The morning after their tryst, a man fishing the surf found Ricky's body hanged from the deck of the old club. The investigation into his death resulted in a ruling of death by suicide.

Cynthia did not learn of Ricky's death until she returned to Kenwick for her twentieth high school reunion. She disagreed with the ruling of suicide.

THE MORNING I MET CYNTHIA FULLER, the phone rang in the shop while I was welding stainless steel bullhorns to the lid of a grill we were making for the Miller Ranch out in West Texas. Darla, one of my welders and my office assistant, flipped up her flamboyant welding helmet and yelled, "Got it."

Her helmet, a gift from my other welder, her boyfriend Joshua, had a bright pink lightning bolt graphic slashing over a cartoon drawing of a voluptuous woman holding a flaming cutting torch. Fiery purple letters spelled out *Girl Handling Fire and Steel*.

She wiped sweat and grime off her face with the tail of her work shirt before she picked up the phone. In a most professional voice, she said, "Law Offices of Samuel Locke, how may I help you?"

She listened for a moment. "May I have your name

please?" She made a note on the pad by the phone. "Hold please, I'll see if Mr. Locke is available."

To me, she said, "A Cynthia Fuller would like to come see you today if it is convenient."

"Take a break. I'll talk to her up at the house."

A look passed between Darla and Joshua. They were young, in love and lived in an apartment attached to the shop. On my way out the door, I told them, "I'll be back in a minute. Keep your clothes on."

I expected Cynthia Fuller to have a routine problem. In my law business, the most often received calls were for divorces or other family matters, issues of custody or child support. Coming in second were arrests for driving under the influence or other mundane criminal matters. I took on few cases. They limited my fishing time. I made a bet with myself that Cynthia Fuller's husband had done something bad and it was time to divorce him. I planned to tell her I wasn't taking on new cases at the moment and refer her to Harry Faulks.

I picked up the phone on the desk in my office, hit the button and said, "Hi. This is Sam. How can I help you?"

"Mr. Locke, my name is Cynthia Fuller. I'd like to come see you and get some advice."

"Can you tell me a little about what's up? I might not be the right person."

"It's kind of unusual." She paused for several seconds. Long enough for me to think it probably wasn't as unusual as she thought. I was wrong.

"I just found out somebody I knew in high school died twenty years ago. They called it suicide. I don't believe that."

Okay. That was different. She'd caught my attention, enough so that I didn't say anything while I thought.

"I'd like some advice. I'll pay you. Money is not a

problem."

That, too, caught my attention.

"I wasn't worried about that. It doesn't cost you anything to talk to me a bit. I was just processing what you said."

"So, can we meet?"

"Yes. I have offices in Houston and Galveston. Which would be convenient?"

"Galveston. I'm calling you from my room at the Gulf Grand Hotel."

"Okay. When do you want to meet?"

"As soon as possible. I have some things coming up in the evenings, and I plan to fly home to California on Monday. Will you have time?"

"Yes. How about in an hour?"

"That would be great."

I gave her directions to the small office suite I shared with Rockwell Investigations in a building close to the courthouse. After a quick shower and a change into some jeans and a golf shirt, I left for downtown Galveston. As I drove from my place on the westernmost tip of the island, I called the private investigator with whom I shared the office. Wallace Rockwell did my investigation work when needed. I doubted much would come from my visit with Cynthia Fuller, but if it did, I'd need him.

"Investigations."

That's how Rocky always answered his phone, but this time his niece Genevieve Mills answered. She worked for Rocky. He wished she would do something else but lost that battle. In fact, Jenny had recently received her license as a private investigator.

"Hi, Jenny."

"Hey, Sam, what's up?"

"Rocky around?"

"He's at the courthouse for some case. He expected to be done about now."

"Which courthouse?"

"Galveston."

"I'm headed for the Galveston office. Leave him a message to drop by if he gets done before eleven."

"Sure. Need me?"

"Are you in Houston, or down here?"

"I'm with Marlene at their house. Rocky still doesn't like me living in Houston, so he passively aggressively makes me come down here to answer the phones when he's out. I can come to the office now, no problem."

"Sure. If she retains me and I need you guys, I'll introduce you to the client. This may be our only chance to talk to the client in person for a while because she's headed home to California."

"I'll be there. I'll let Rocky know."

Rocky and his wife Marlene took Jenny in as a teenager when her parents were killed in a car wreck. Jenny lived in an apartment with a roommate in downtown Houston. She was in her twenties, but being on her own bothered Rocky in a cute, fatherly way.

The weather promised a great beach day, the temperature slowly climbing but not expected to break ninety degrees. There were a few clouds, mostly far out on the horizon over the Gulf. I rolled down the windows and breathed deeply to enjoy the sea-scented air. On a Wednesday in October with school in session, the traffic wasn't bad. I made good time driving down Seawall Boulevard toward town.

I got to the building fifteen minutes before I expected Cynthia Fuller. I nodded to the woman behind the security desk in the quiet, sterile lobby and took an elevator to the third floor. Our office suite consisted of four rooms—a small reception area, a conference room and an office each for Rocky and me. The main door has both our names on it.

I sat at the desk in the reception area to wait.

Right on time, she pushed the door open. We introduced ourselves to each other and shook hands. Cynthia appeared to be in her mid to late thirties, slender and wearing a long sleeve white men's dress shirt, starched and tucked into sharply creased blue jeans. A leather messenger bag slung over her shoulder served as her purse. Her dark brown hair, trimmed serviceable short, had touches of gray. She wore functional, black-framed glasses, not likely to be carrying any fashion designer's name. Her eyes focused on mine and betrayed no nervousness. Everything about her looked confident and smart. She might have been wearing make-up, but if so, it was minimal.

We sat on either side of the conference table, my hands rested on a blank legal pad, hers on her leather bag.

Before I could ask her how I could help her, she said, "Thank you for seeing me on such a short notice. I'm only out here for a few days. I read an article about you and that ballet dancer in the *LA Times*. When I decided to seek assistance out here, I looked you up online. I'd like to find out if there's anything you think can be done."

The case involving my ballet dancer client made a big media splash. The dancer was Jenny's roommate.

"I'm glad you found me. What's up?"

"I'll expand on what I told you. First, as I said when we talked, a boy I went to high school with died the night we graduated twenty years ago. I'm out here for our twentieth reunion. The ruling was suicide. I don't believe that."

"Why?"

She took a deep breath and looked out the window over my shoulder. She returned her total focus to me.

"You need some background. Twenty years ago I graduated from Kendrick High School. My parents were deceased. I did not really enjoy living in Kendrick. High school wasn't fun for me. I had a scholarship to MIT and a lab internship I could start immediately. I was seventeen but legally emancipated. I left Kendrick the night we graduated and never looked back. I never came back for any reason until this year.

"The boy's name was Ricky Smith. They say he hanged himself the night of graduation. I don't believe it and I'd like to know the truth. How do we do that?"

"I don't know yet. Tell me why you think that."

"Because of what I know about Ricky. It was high school. He had some issues he believed were bigger than they were. But he had plans. He knew what he wanted to do. He was as excited about his plans as I was about mine and not in a place where he wanted to die."

Suicides often surprised those left behind. The things she said were what people say. Chances were he killed himself. But Cynthia Fuller was obviously smart. MIT smart. And survivor smart. She spoke with the precision of those who are super smart. I noticed she'd never actually called him a friend or a neighbor or anything like that. She'd left him behind like she did her high school experience and the entire town of Kendrick. There would be more to her story.

"How well did you know him? Was he a friend? A boyfriend?"

She smiled for the first time. "I had no real friends back then. Certainly no boyfriends. I didn't really talk to him much until that night after graduation." Another long pause. Finally, a deep breath, and she said, "I need to get something out of the way so we can get past it. Ricky and I had sex on the beach that night. It was my idea and my first time."

That was unexpected.

She continued. "That's merely a fact. It has nothing to do with my belief about something happening other than suicide. You need some context."

I didn't believe her. Ricky Smith being her first lover had to color her thinking about his death. I nodded to keep her talking. I needed thinking time before I shared that thought.

"First, my life. My dad was a chemical engineer. He got a job at Deshinell Chemical the year I entered junior high. We moved to Kendrick. My elementary school had recommended I skip the fifth grade but my parents said no, hoping I'd socialize. By the time it was time to go to junior high, I'd made some plans. I took the SAT as part of a talent search program. The school system suggested I go straight to high school and get in a gifted children's program. Instead, I agreed to skip one grade and go into eighth grade."

"Your choice?"

"Yes." She smiled. "I hoped to make some friends before I had to endure high school." She shrugged.

With most clients, I wanted to hear the interesting stuff first—the dead boy and more about why she didn't believe he'd killed himself. Only after I heard that story would I refine the problem by understanding more about the client. But Cynthia Fuller knew what she was doing. She wasn't bragging by telling me her history. She knew I needed to know her to trust her opinion about the boy's death. She'd already convinced me to trust her enough to not interfere with questions.

"I should have just gone on to high school. I didn't fit in at the junior high anyway. Just like I didn't fit in at the high school. I didn't understand much about the social aspects of those years. I am still confounded by what most people consider important in life.

"It did not help my high school experience when my dad died in an accident at the plant my sophomore year. Then, that summer my mom got her cancer diagnoses. She spent a year fighting cancer and putting things in place for me. She died just before Christmas my senior year."

"I'm sorry. That must have been miserably hard."

There were tears in her eyes but she never lost the look of being in absolute control of herself.

"Yes. They left me plenty of money—lots of insurance, a settlement from the company. The cars and house were already free and clear."

"Did you go into foster care?"

"No. My mom understood what I am. She knew I would be able to take care of myself. She even had a lawyer ready. Olivia Greenbaugh?"

"I've heard of her. Never met her."

"She does wills and trusts and stuff like that. I called her yesterday to ask about you. She said you had an interesting but excellent reputation."

"Interesting?"

"She asked me if I needed a lawyer or a barbecue grill. Your excellent reputation covers both."

I laughed. "Good to know."

She smiled, something I would come to learn was the closest she came to laughing.

"Anyway, Ms. Greenbaugh was appointed my guardian ad litem and the trustee of my assets until I went to court and became emancipated. Evidently, my mom had things arranged so well that it got done in record time.

Ms. Greenbaugh also took care of getting my house sold shortly before I graduated. By the time I left, everything I owned was in my car. Everything else I sold, donated, or threw away."

"You really were ready to leave."

"Yes."

So far, the only notes I'd made were Cynthia's name, Ricky Smith's name, Olivia Greenbaugh's name, and the phrase "sex on the beach."

"I sense you viewed life after high school as a new beginning. Was it what you hoped for?"

She shrugged. "Mostly. Obviously, I had a lot to learn about the real world, but I finally had a purpose and a comfortable place. At MIT there were others like me. Being able to have conversations with people close to my age was a new experience. I liked it."

"What did you study?"

"Computer science. I won an award at a science fair my junior year of high school that caught the attention of Dr. Concannon at MIT. He became my faculty advisor and mentor at MIT. He was instrumental in getting me scholarships and grants at MIT. He made it possible for me to work at the school the summer after high school. I worked in his lab during college and for my postdoc. I went with him when he moved to UCLA. That's where I am now, on the faculty at UCLA."

She convinced me of her extraordinary intelligence. I wanted to hear why she came to see me.

"Tell me about Ricky Smith."

"Ricky was a big deal in high school. The top of the social pyramid. He ticked all the benchmarks. Quarterback, dated a cheerleader, class president, a member of all the right organizations. He and his girlfriend were homecoming king and queen. He was even in the honor society. His future was bright. Everybody thought he'd play football at Texas Gulf Coast University."

"You knew him well?"

"Not really. Not until the night of graduation."

I heard either Rocky or Jenny enter their office. I doubted I would bother them. I'd buy them lunch for the inconvenience of showing up.

My already weak confidence in what she wanted me to do waned. She obviously got to know him somewhat the night before he died but, despite having sex with him, could not have known him very well. But she was willing to pay me to investigate his death twenty years after whatever happened. It had to be the sex. Even superintelligent people can be not so bright when sex enters the equation. She noticed my confusion.

"I know," she said. "I'm not making sense, yet. I'll jump to that night."

"Please."

"I was on the cusp of my life finally beginning. I was getting out of Kendrick and leaving all the silliness of high school culture behind. My car was packed with the few things I was taking to Massachusetts. Sitting in the crowd at graduation, waiting for my name to be called, there were girls on either side of me talking about the big party at the beach after graduation. It amused me that the thing marking graduation in their lives would be another high school beer bash. It was so alien to what was happening in my life.

"My group, the smart kids, had nothing planned. I guess a lot of them were going to dinner or whatever with family. I didn't have that. I was alone. A few of my teachers tried to make the whole thing special for me. I got some graduation gifts from them. I turned down their dinner invitations. They really were kind. But I had nowhere special to go. I'd sold the house and been out of it for a week. My plan was to go to the hotel where I'd been staying, go to bed, get up and leave early the next morning."

"I'm curious. Were you the valedictorian?"

"Yes. Initially, I wasn't going to go to graduation, so I declined to give a speech. They got the president of the Honor Society to give that one.

"I didn't go back to the hotel immediately. I stopped and got a Whataburger. I sat in the parking lot eating it and felt . . . melancholy. I was sad my parents didn't see me graduate. Before she died, my mom knew about MIT, but my dad never did. He would have been proud. I didn't want to be so alone, but I was. I drove around a bit. I decided to go to the beach. Not because I expected to suddenly be a part of the crowd, but . . . I don't know . . . I guess as kind of a final farewell to the high school part of my life even if I didn't really know the people there.

"I didn't stay long. I stood around watching things for maybe half an hour. I spoke to a few people. It was typical and what you'd expect. Noise and beer mostly. I left. I'd parked down the beach, so I could get close without being noticed if I decided I didn't want to be seen."

"Nothing happened there that is important to your doubts about Ricky's death?"

"Not at the party. I'm telling you about it just so you'll know why I was on the beach."

I nodded.

"Down the beach, away from the noise and people, there was an abandoned building. It was a nightclub at one time. I stopped there, underneath that building. I guess I was still antsy."

She paused, pursed her lips and nodded.

"To be honest," she said, "I guess I was a little nervous—scared really—of heading off on my own. It was peaceful on the beach. I could think. I enjoyed the waves. I could hear the music and laughter from the party. There were lights out on the Gulf."

"I think I know the building you're talking about. It's still there."

"Really? I thought about driving down there but haven't"

"Yes. Over on Surfside, right?"

"Yes."

"I take it something happened there."

"I'll try to make this quicker."

"Take your time."

I made another note. I wrote down "Surfside old nightclub."

"I don't know how long I sat there before Ricky came walking down the beach. The moon was bright enough to recognize him. He was alone. He entered the darkness under the building. I said hi to him. Scared him, I think."

"I bet."

"He recovered quickly. He said hi and came up and sat down next to me. He was just as nice as always. I've known him since junior high and he's always been nice. Never a snob like most of them in his social strata. I'll skip a lot of what we talked about. I was shocked and curious about how interested he was in what my plans were. He knew I was going off to MIT.

"I congratulated him on going to Texas Gulf Coast to play football. That's when things got deep. He opened up to me. He did not want to go to TGC. Unknown to anybody, he'd applied to Rice University because he wanted to study political science. He'd not told anyone. He'd done it all on his own. I take it he couldn't get a football scholarship. He applied too late or something. But they wanted him. He had good grades. You have to involve your parents' to get financial aid. Somebody at the school wanted him enough to work with him. They put together some scholarship money for him and promised an athletic scholarship as soon as possible. His plan was to just present it to his parents and try to convince them it was the best thing."

"Wow, choosing Rice over TGC was probably a big deal for a football player. TGC was the champion around then, weren't they?"

She smiled. "Like I would know. He said his dad might disown him. He was worried about what everybody would think. But he had plans. He knew the chance of him going to the NFL was slim. He didn't really want to even try. He told me he didn't want to be one of those good athletes who didn't plan for the future. He did not want to look back when he got older and realize he peaked at his greatest talent in college or high school.

"He surprised me when he started talking about wanting to do good in the world, something important. He'd found one of the best political science and government programs in Texas. He had some big ideas. He wanted to go to graduate school at the University of Texas School of Public Affairs."

Tears in her eyes were a surprise. She'd been so matter of fact in the telling of everything. So far, we'd ignored how all that intellectual conversation led to sex.

She took a deep breath and said, "He told me I'd inspired him the way I'd finished high school on my own and how I was going to MIT. He said I was a big reason he'd had the courage to do what he'd done to get into Rice. I had no idea anybody else at school had a clue about all that."

There it was. Her emotional interest in Ricky. He was the first classmate to acknowledge her in such a way. I feared, in reality, Ricky Smith realized he was stuck, that Cynthia was following a path in ways he could not, and he made a tragic decision. She was smart. She had to have thought of that. She wanted to buy herself out of guilt by hiring me to prove it wasn't her fault he died. I did not want that job. I hoped she'd be able to process the likelihood that he'd killed himself. I hoped she'd accept that it wasn't her fault. She needed to go home to California and leave the dark mysteries of the past behind.

"I've condensed our conversation and left a lot out. Mr. Locke, he was happy with his decision. He understood there would be some rough moments. But he was ready to deal with them. He was ready to move on. He did not even want to play football at Rice unless he had to for the scholarship. He intended to focus more on studying for a degree than football. It sounds silly, but he wanted to make changes in the world. He wanted to help people. He was eighteen and the possibilities of the future were still boundless. Just like me, he was about to come to life.

"I am sad that he's dead, yes. On the last possible day, I made one friend back then. I am not immune to being sad. But it's more than that. I believe I have filtered out the fact that I had sex with him. I listened to him. We talked. He had plans as firm as my plans. We both had difficulties in our lives, but he'd charted a course to resolve his issues just as carefully as had I. I have few close friends, even now. I want to know what really happened to my friend."

She had yet to say it, but what she wanted was to know who murdered her friend. "I just . . . "

"Obviously, I am the only one pursuing the question at this point. I want to hire you, and I will pay you to look at it. If you assure me you can do that and not be hindered by your doubts about my reasoning, I'll still hire you. Anybody else will have the same doubts, but this is something I do not have the knowledge of how to do.

"If you can do your best, I will understand you may not be able to find out anything one way or another. You may discover there was a reason for him to kill himself. If you promise me you'll work hard despite your doubts, I'll accept that."

She was not the least bit emotional. She approached the issue like a scientist, applying the best tools she could to analyze the unknown. I could live with that. She was offering to pay. I've taken plenty of criminal cases on for money when I didn't believe a word of what my client said. I've won some of those.

"Okay. I'll get a retainer from you, and I'll look into things. I'm going to use an investigator or two. I'll pay them out of the retainer. I'll report to you, and we'll decide if you want to go further."

"Okay."

She pulled a bank card out of her purse. I mentioned a number large enough to test her desire, told her my hourly rate, assured her that the investigator's hourly rate would be less than mine, and I'd reimburse her any funds we did not use. I printed an agreement providing for her retaining me to look into the circumstances of the death of Ricky Smith. She read it, signed it, and paid the retainer with a bank card. I wrote down all of her phone numbers and her home and office addresses in California.

"I think my investigators are in their office. I'll get them and introduce you."

She said, "Wait a moment. I know you think I'm being emotional and making an irrational decision but I assure you, one thing I never am is irrational. You're thinking about the sex, so I'll tell you how that happened. Maybe then you can start to ignore it. Having sex with him was not irrational. At least not on my part."

"Okay."

"Ricky broke up with his girlfriend a couple of weeks before school was out. It was talked about so much at school even I heard the story. That night on the beach we talked about that. She'd been planning to follow him to TGC.

"She planned for them to live together. He tried to talk her out of it, explaining that he would be living in the athlete's dorm. He told me he knew that if he was not the big football star she would quickly lose interest in him. They would not have the same interests going forward. He was nice and all, but I could tell he knew there was not enough substance in their relationship for what he had planned."

"Okay. It sounds like you're right. He was making some definite plans for his future."

Or, I thought, dumping his girlfriend before he killed himself.

"It's not just that. We sat there and talked for four hours, Mr. Locke. It amazed me the things we talked about. He even told me how he wished he'd been smart enough to get to know me better, to ask me out. I almost laughed when he said that and told him it would have shocked the school. He agreed."

She looked at me. Took a deep breath and continued. "Mr. Locke, yes, I have a high IQ and I didn't particularly understand all the social rituals of normal high school students, but I was seventeen and not immune to nature. It is in our DNA to be attracted to others. At that age, biology is driving us to seek suitable mates."

"Yes. I remember."

"He kissed me. I told him it was my first kiss ever and he asked if it was okay to kiss me again. I said yes."

"I'm glad you got a chance to make out on the beach. Every teenager should."

"It went further. At my suggestion. I knew the science, the chemical attraction and urges. I made a reasoned decision. I wanted to get empirical. I moved his hand to my breast. He pulled away and asked me if I was sure. I told him how clueless I was about flirting, that I knew it was just biology, but that I wanted to experience some things I never had. Like the kiss. And more. So, we did. We kissed and touched. A lot. Eventually, I asked him if he would have sex with me. I wanted to experience that.

"At first he didn't want to. He said my first time should be with somebody I loved. I asked him if he was in love with the first person he ever had sex with and he had to admit the answer was no. I explained how I was just as curious as the next teenager and asked him if he had a condom. He did."

"Wow."

"Yes. The valedictorian got lucky with the captain of the football team that night. He was perfectly gentle and caring and took care of me and made sure I was comfortable every step of the way. It was as good as anybody's first time should be but, from what I hear, usually isn't. And that concluded my high school experience. I was ready for college.

"Eventually, I had to leave the beach. It was after midnight, and I wanted to leave early in the morning. I made it clear he would not hear from me again. Our plans would not sustain a relationship and trying to do so would be detrimental to what we each wanted to do. I thanked him and he thanked me. It is probably bad of me, but I put our experience on the beach behind me as a part of my high school years.

"We kissed one last time, and I left him there sitting on the beach. Somebody found him dead the next day about the time I passed through Beaumont."